WATERFIRE

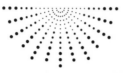

To Elizabeth —

WATERFIRE

BOOK THREE OF THE RIDNIGHT MYSTERIES

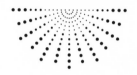

STUART JAFFE

Charlotte, NC

FALSTAFF
BOOKS

WWW.FALSTAFFBOOKS.COM

For Gabe
You guessed it. Your fault.

PART I

CHAPTER ONE

Axon

Standing in the back of the Asterling Theatre, Axon thought she would never be more uncomfortable for the rest of her life. Traveling east over several months with Zev by her side and consistently being mistaken for his wife did not bother her. Watching as his father recovered from illness and realizing Zev intended to fold back into the city life he had tried to escape did not bother her. Even knowing that his actions left her as a foreigner in Balica City did not bother her. She managed to handle the situations with strength and pride.

Yet it did not stop there.

Over the course of the next year, nothing could halt the war that had begun. The events that had occurred at Ridnight Castle surrounding the Shield of Taladoro—the same events which a group of actors portrayed in melodramatic fashion upon the stage in front of her—these did not stop the war. Postponed it, yes. Even managed to weaken all fronts from large-scale engagements. But in the end, a year of heavy skirmishes littered the border between the East and the Frontier with blood and bodies.

During it all, Axon wanted to mount her horse and race off to aid in the fight. But King Robion no longer trusted her, and she had made a vow to protect Zev.

As it turned out, she and her great Water Blade would never be needed. King Robion had arrived in Balica City two days earlier to negotiate a peace treaty with the company heads of the East. It wasn't overwhelming forces or heroic battles that brought this day so quickly, but of all things, it was their third enemy—the Dacci.

That's what this play should really be about, she thought. Rather than squeeze the Frontier by fighting along the Western front, the Dacci chose a subversive method to war. They moved in small groups and never met on the fields of battle. They jumped in from the shadows, slaughtered all they could, and disappeared long before help arrived. Axon had no doubt they employed their witches to cast spells that would enhance their secretive attacks. Especially the attacks that plunged deep across the land—far into the East. But it felt like they were stalling. Biding time for a big strike.

That's what brought the Frontier and the East to a peace table. They both knew they were doomed if they did not join forces. Whether doomed to lose against the Dacci or doomed to expand the skirmishes into the full slaughter of war, nobody knew. Those with an ounce of intelligence did not want to find out.

And during it all, never once did King Robion reach out to Axon. She had been at his side, his trusted warrior, and now—nothing. Her face had become a mask every bit as fake and stylized as those worn by the actress portraying her on stage. She was empty inside and had to summon the facade of feeling in order for others to believe her. Not that she had many to talk with here.

What would these people surrounding her think, if they knew that the story they watched riveted in their chairs had been experienced for real by the woman standing behind them?

Why do I torture myself? I knew I shouldn't have come.

Axon could not bear to continue watching the play. The actor portraying Zev spent half the time on hands and knees inspecting the floorboards for clues while those representing the Dacci flung mud at each other as if toying with feces. The audience appeared gripped by the experience, but Axon squirmed as if they all looked at her on a stage.

Her eyes roved upward, taking in the hundred arches that braced the wide ceiling. Asterling Theatre had been constructed over a century ago by Zev's distant ancestors and was a testament to Eastern achievement. They had autocarts and flameless candles and all manner of wonders throughout the city, none of which required casting spells, yet Axon would have preferred to be back on the Frontier, mounted on a horse, and taking in the fresh morning air of the forest or a farm or even the stench of a roadside tavern airing out from the previous night.

She glanced towards the archway exit. On stage, the actors representing Zev, Mr. Duke, and her all sat at a long table as they interrogated another actor portraying Philune. She looked back at the exit.

That's when she saw the Vashon.

He wore a tan cloak and black boots. A simple shirt covered his broad chest. Like all Vashon, he wore a wooden mask painted red with white designs. Each design was unique, and this particular one had painted cracked lines as if his face might chip away.

Axon had read about the Vashon—an insular, religious group that stayed out of view most of the time. They believed in "the thousand-faced god" who left the world ashamed of what he had created. Waiting for his return, they devoted their lives to reshaping the world in expectation of a great reward when the day arrived. But all of their work tended to be done quietly and in the shadows. Odd that one would show up at such a public gathering. Odder still—the Vashon appeared to be staring back at her.

The pretend world on stage and the real world surrounding her both disappeared as her old instincts fired off. Something about the way this man stood like a cat ready to dash off, the way he inclined his head as if trying to communicate with her, the way he appeared calm yet out of place—it alerted Axon to potential trouble. Violent trouble.

She weaved her way toward the exit—not easy when wearing the ridiculous fashions of the East. Constricting dresses with flower petal shoulders and immodest low-cut fronts seemingly designed for the sole purpose of preventing women from moving like human beings. In the past, Axon had often mocked the ostentatious dress of the Frontier court, but she found the fashion tastes of the Eastern rich no less ridiculous. However, she would have stood out in this crowd had she worn her normal work clothes—leather slacks, comfortable shirt and vest, and always her scabbard with the Water Blade.

Offering apologies as she bumped into one person after another, she finally reached the hallway leading to the lobby. The Vashon had vanished. She hurried down the hall, her heeled shoes clicking on the century-old tile floor—a mosaic with a kaleidoscopic pattern designed to draw the eye away from the less impressive chipping walls.

When she entered the lobby, she spotted a young constable standing near the entranceway. He wore the black cloak with white piping of a new recruit. No surprise there—none of the seasoned constables wanted to miss out on the show.

"Excuse me, sir," she said.

Tipping his round cap, eager to deal with anything beyond standing at the entrance, he hurried toward her. "Yes, ma'am? What can I do for you?"

"Did you see a Vashon man come through here?"

"A Vashon? No, ma'am. And don't you worry, I would never let those sorts into this fine establishment."

"But he *was* in here. I saw him. He came this way."

"No, ma'am. Nobody came this way except for you. Perhaps you need some fresh air or a cool drink. I hear it can get awfully hot inside. Makes the mind see all sorts of things."

Axon's hand headed down for her Blade, but of course, it was not there. She thought about grabbing this idiot by the lapels and shoving him against the wall, but no good would come of that. While the constable could not be certain that she was a foreigner, he could make an educated guess. Her accent, her coarse hands—these alone betrayed that she was no wellborn, Eastern lady.

I wonder what he would say if he found out that I could've been a princess.

"Ma'am? Are you okay?"

Her thoughts must have risen to her face. She saw the confusion in his eyes—confusion and a touch of trepidation.

With a healthy laugh, a voice from behind said, "If you kill him, it won't bode well for our peace negotiations."

Axon whirled around, her face brightening. "Pilot! By Qareck, I never thought I'd get to see you here."

She knew Pilot and Bellemont would have come with King Robion—after all, Pilot was Captain of the Guard now and Bellemont had become one of the King's trusted advisors—but Axon had not entertained the idea that she might actually get to spend time with either of them. She wrapped her arms around him and kissed his cheek. Pulling back, she gazed upon his dark features with the first genuine smile she had felt in nearly a year.

"I've missed you," she said, a bit shocked that she would be so blunt.

He chuckled. "Believe me, I miss you more than you know. Your old job for the King is hard."

"Not mine anymore. It all belongs to you."

"That's the problem. Looking back on it, I think I've always done much better under your direct leadership."

"I'm sure you're doing fine. Where's Bellemont?"

"Right next to the King. That's pretty much where she is all the time. Especially with the war going on, he relies on her knowledge of the Dacci more than anything."

Axon glanced out the doorway. The late-night crowd bustled along the streets, and she wondered if she might spot the Vashon. To Pilot, she said, "Something's happened. Something that might be nothing, but it might be important. I should really see the King to let him know."

Pilot's dark face turned a shade darker. "You know that's not a good idea."

"He's still angry with me?"

"The anger went away fast. But I think it will take a lot for him to ever trust you again." Pilot placed his hands on her shoulders and turned her toward the street exit. "Listen, you shouldn't be here, and I really don't want to be here, either. Watching absurd imitations of us on stage is unsettling. Isn't there someplace we can go and have a drink? Forget about our past mistakes and toast to our future ones?"

Axon tapped her chin like one of the actors pretending to think. "I do know a place or two. But first we need to go back to my apartment. I cannot wear this dress a moment longer."

Arm in arm, the two friends left the theater behind.

CHAPTER TWO

As Axon and Pilot walked toward the transit stop, she noticed his mesmerized gaze. He had been in Eastern cities before, but not in many years. So much had changed. Back then, autocarts were in their infancy and flameless candles were only for the wealthy. Now, autocarts ruled the streets—one rarely saw a horse anymore—and flameless candles lit up every home as well as the sidewalks throughout the city.

At the transit stop, as they waited for the public autocart to arrive, Axon said, "Is King Robion prepared for the duplicity of the Eastern leaders? Don't answer that. It was a foolish question. King Robion must have put together contingencies, back-ups, and alternates for every possibility he could conceive."

"All of Ridnight has been made insane by his overly-detailed approach. But I simply remind myself that when the goal is peace, when his success or failure will result in lives lived or lost, well, I find it in my heart to give the man whatever he needs."

As the large autocart pulled alongside the road, Axon could feel Pilot watching her step into the vehicle, pay the driver, and find a seat. He wanted to follow the correct procedure but didn't want to ask her directly. As he settled in next to her, she considered teasing him, but then it struck her—she had adapted so easily to this life which she did not enjoy.

Balica City slipped by as the autocart lurched into motion. Building after building passed her view, each one with as much personality as a block of stone. The older buildings like the theatre had great individual character. But the city grew too fast of late, and those responsible for keeping the city running had no time for artistic expression. They needed buildings to rise as if Dacci witches had conjured them.

They traveled many blocks, and Axon could see on Pilot's face that he noticed the change in the area. The newer buildings disappeared but the rich architecture of the old, cherished buildings could not be found. They had entered the poor sections of the city. Here the buildings were old and uncared for. They lacked beauty and barely had functionality.

In the distance, lit bright enough to be seen from any corner of the city, the Thalmew Building shined. Axon pointed it out. "That's where you'll be spending most of your time. The negotiations and, hopefully, the treaty will be signed there."

"Thalmew runs the largest company, right? And that gives him all the power here?"

"Partially. The country still allows its citizens to vote on various measures—that's what they call decisions around here, *measures*—but after all the trouble we caused at Ridnight, after the war broke out in earnest, it wasn't difficult to manipulate people with their fears. The whole idea of the citizens running their own government, each person getting a vote on all matters—it just went away. The companies took over and formed the Government Council—really, it's the owners of the largest companies making all the decisions. No single person holds all the power."

"Thalmew is at the head of it, though, right?"

"Yes, but the title of Head Council is actually second-in-command. That's Janu Dermont. Thalmew's title is Leader of the Council. He's kind of like a king of kings. They still call it a democracy, but it's really something else. I find the whole thing ridiculous."

Pilot's eyes widened. "Is that why all the fashion changed? I mean, last year all the Easterners who came to Ridnight had those huge hairstyles and big dresses and absurd things like that."

"I know. I don't understand these people, either. Thalmew took over, and suddenly, they all rejected the previous styles. Now, it's all tight dresses and dots on the nose."

"I can't say I'm upset about the dresses, but I don't grasp the dots."

"Zev told me that even before the democracy thing failed, people followed the leadership for fashion trends. That much I understand—plenty of Frontier women would dress like the Queen, if King Robion would finally pick a queen. Apparently, though, one morning, while Mrs. Thalmew painted her face for the day, she accidentally left a dark dot on the side of her nose. It became a hit."

At the next stop, they hopped off the autocart and walked another block. Axon led the way into one of a row of faceless old buildings and up four flights of stairs. The inside looked as decrepit as the outside, and she gave Bieck a quick prayer of thanks that Pilot kept his adolescent comments to himself. When she opened the door to her apartment, she had to put her shoulder into it.

"The door sticks sometimes," she said.

While the single room was functional, it was no bigger than her private quarters in Ridnight Castle. Enough room for a bed, a small dresser, a chair, and little more. Though indoor pipework had yet to reach her part of the city, it was becoming more common throughout. Someday, she would be able to enjoy it here. At least, they had flameless. That extraordinary invention spread fast and wide—mostly because it was cheap to install and saved the landlords the risk of candles starting fires.

Pilot sat on the only chair as Axon stepped into a narrow closet to change. "The world is so different today," he said.

She couldn't tell if he had commented upon her living conditions or upon the war, but she decided they would have a better evening if she confronted things head-on. "I know this place looks bad, but I don't require much. Remember, you're talking to a woman who would much rather be sleeping around a campfire and using a rock for a pillow."

"Oh, I know. But I'm surprised Zev let it come to this. What happened between you two? I mean, he's Zev Asterling—they named the theatre after his family. I should think he could afford to give you a better living situation. Of course, you come from a wealthy family, too. You could do better if you wanted it."

"That should tell you all you need to know."

"Come on. You're talking to good ol' Pilot."

Stepping out of the closet, wearing her everyday clothes and feeling far more comfortable, she sat on the edge of her bed. "Well, good ol' Pilot, you know there is no way I'm going to ask my family for money. Never. As for Zev—I chose to work for him as a bodyguard because I believed his intelligence was going to be paramount to the survival of the Frontier during this war. The plan was for him to visit his ailing father, make whatever amends needed amending, regroup, and move forward. Figure out what he wanted, so that he could forge ahead with his life. I was simply going to protect him until the King called upon us once more."

"But the King never called."

"No, he didn't." She walked over to the small window looking upon the street. "Within a week of being here, Zev had settled in quite well. He had been popular when he was young, and many of his friends were thrilled to see him again. I suspect they saw dollar signs in their eyes or political positions for their futures. The politics around here are insane. These people ingratiated themselves around Zev, inviting him to meals and parties, and they made him feel very welcome. His time on the Frontier was treated like youthful folly, and the women seemed to really appreciate his heroic adventures."

Pilot snickered. "I'll bet."

Raising an eyebrow, Axon glanced back. "If he learned any of that, he learned it from you."

"I take it after being treated so warmly, Zev decided he didn't want to leave this life again."

She nodded. "I can't blame him. This place must feel safe. No monsters were jumping out of the woods trying to kill him. No Dacci witches were ripping out their teeth to cast spells that would split him in two or mutate him into a beast or any other horrors. He has enemies here, but they are rival companies and the violence they commit is through business dealings, rumors, and innuendo. It was a big part of what changed. Not just the lack of danger that our lives had followed, but nobody called upon Zev, nobody sought him out the way they did in Ridnight. His brilliance, his ability to solve these seemingly unsolvable crimes—they had no call for that here. The constable service keeps the criminal element at bay, and the wealthier people would never want to entrust their problems to a rival family. Even the families that are friendly with his wouldn't want to risk giving the Asterlings any leverage by sharing their troubles."

"I think I see how this goes." Pilot sat back and the chair creaked. "Zev's all comfortable in this city, and he doesn't need a bodyguard anymore. There's no place for you."

"I'm a warrior. That's all I've ever wanted to be. Yet now—I've been put out to pasture. I thought about returning to the Frontier, I suppose I might still, but it would be hard to live in the land I love so much when I know the King would not want me there."

11

"Hey, just because he doesn't want you in the castle, doesn't mean you can't live in the country."

"Don't. I've had all the arguments with myself. I know all the angles. For now, living here is the best for me." She turned away, looking out the window once more. She did not know if her face would betray the lie, but she suspected Pilot knew she had lied anyway. "At least, Zev and I still see each other regularly. We'll have a lunch or dinner every so many days. And thank Qareck because he's the only person in the East who can comprehend anything I've been through."

With caution in his voice, Pilot said, "If you would like, I could try talking to King Robion. Perhaps I could change his mind on how he thinks of you."

"Maybe." She barely heard him. Her attention had locked upon a man standing on the street near one of the flameless. Unlike the Vashon at the theatre, this one tried not to be seen. He hovered around the edge of where the light and dark met. His cloak helped keep him in shadow, but his red mask—this one with the row of white Xs stitched across the forehead—could not be mistaken. Especially since this Vashon repeatedly glanced up in her direction.

Easing away from the window, she looked to Pilot. "Another Vashon."

Pilot jumped from the chair. He headed toward the window, but she stopped him. "You've seen two of these guys in one day," he said. "Is that normal?"

"I haven't seen two of them in one week since I got here."

"Then we should talk to him. Don't you think?"

Slowly curling her fingers around the hilt of the Water Blade, she said, "Definitely."

CHAPTER THREE

Axon flew down the stairs, skipping more than she placed a foot on. She heard Pilot struggling to keep up—he still wore his formal Guard dress, which hindered his progress. When she reached the bottom, she bolted out the front door and surveyed the area. A light drizzle had begun to fall causing the dirt roads to become sticky and the paved brick to become slippery. It also made the deep footprints of somebody running away quite easy to see.

"This way," Axon said as Pilot joined her.

The footprints on the street soon became mud splotches on the sidewalk. The further they went, the less she saw of the prints. The mud had been flaking off.

Pointing to the corner, Pilot said, "Over there."

They crossed and hastened up the street. The drizzle turned into fat droplets of rain. Those out to enjoy the night scurried away to avoid getting covered with grime and soaked through. No matter. Even with a few dozen people crouched and rushing through the rain, there was no mistaking the Vashon.

Axon counted three of them.

Two rushed off while the third attempted to meld into the crowd further down. Pointing to the third Vashon, Axon indicated she wanted Pilot to go after that one. She would take care of the others.

Pilot tapped her shoulder twice in acknowledgment before heading off. Axon kept her eye on the two. They hovered near the entrance of a building that had been rotting for months after a fire left it in ruin. Checking up and down the street, the two slipped inside.

Axon hurried across, garnering some angry words from autocart drivers that nearly hit her. Pausing at the entrance, she listened for the Vashon—didn't want to be ambushed as she walked in. Rain showered down creating a symphony of noise as drops banged against the congestion of buildings and walkways. She couldn't hear anything else.

Glancing around, she saw the street had emptied. No pedestrians at all. A few autocarts whisked by, but driving in these conditions required great concentration. Nobody would notice her. She pulled out the Water Blade, its shimmering blue glowed against the damaged doorway, and she entered the building.

Even months later, the smell of burnt wood permeated the air. Rain found its way through the holes in the roof, down the destroyed floors, and plinked in puddles on the warped wood floor. With the surfaces mostly charred black and the storm blocking the moonlight, Axon had to rely on the limited light bleeding in from the street and her own awareness.

She held still, perking her ears at every sound. No running steps. No heavy breaths. No murmured voices.

These Vashon were good. But considering that they spent much of their lives trying to go unnoticed in the world, she would expect nothing less. They had become statues, and she would not succeed by trying to wait them out.

She inhaled deeply, hoping to catch the unique smell of sweat, but the charred aroma had overwhelmed any other scents. Waving the Blade from side to side, letting its blue glow light her way, Axon moved forward with ginger steps and cold eyes. She stopped. If she could see her surroundings in the Blade's light, then the Vashon could see her as well.

Before she could sheath the weapon, she heard the shot. Handgun or rifle, she didn't know—she had yet to train with these weapons enough to learn such distinctions—but it didn't matter. The bullet cut through several walls, never coming close to her. She did see the flash of fire, though.

With a strong stride, she bounded toward the position, raising her Blade to strike. The Vashon dashed off before she reached him. She paused to listen, but a thought popped in her mind—*why take a random shot and give yourself away? Unless you weren't aiming at all and simply wanted to set up your target.*

The click of the second Vashon cocking his rifle betrayed him. Axon whirled around and lunged. Despite wearing a mask, the Vashon's surprise registered clearly. He fumbled the rifle as she swung her Blade across the muzzle. The metal barrel sheared off and thumped into the dull wood.

The Vashon—the same cracked mask design—put out his hand, shaking it vigorously. But Axon swung fast, and the hand joined the barrel. Cradling his bleeding stump as he muffled his cries, the Vashon rushed off into the dark.

"I think he was trying to give up," Pilot said from the entrance.

Axon eased back, letting out a tense breath. "Not a smart way to go about it. Did you catch yours?"

"No. Chased him down an alleyway, but he disappeared."

"From a spell?"

"From the fact that he knows this city well and I don't. Whatever door or window he slipped through, I missed it. If anybody saw, they weren't going to tell me."

Using the light of the Blade, she crouched over the Vashon's hand and weapon. The rifle looked rather new, which may have been the cause of the man's failure. She would have never let a soldier go off to fight with unfamiliar weapons.

"What's that?" Pilot had moved in close and pointed at the bloody hand.

Axon held the Water Blade over and saw a metal bracelet. She snatched it up and walked outside. Under the nearest flameless, she inspected the details but she already knew what she would find—a snaking line down the middle of the bracelet with nine unique markings along the rim, each one a reference to nine gods and goddesses of the Cassun.

The rain let up, and a sweet smell of wet brick took its place. Axon pocketed the bracelet.

Pilot said, "I didn't know the Vashon were religious."

"They're not. At least, they're not supposed to be, anymore. Just waiting on their god to return." She bit her bottom lip before patting Pilot on the shoulder. "You should probably go."

"I don't know if that's a good idea. I mean you certainly brought me an entertaining evening, but if these Vashon come back..."

"You know I can handle myself. I promise that if I find out anything, I'll let you know."

"That may sound good in your head, but you taught me that we shouldn't go alone into dangerous situations."

"It's worse for us if you stay. If we get into any trouble that becomes public, then you'll be caught causing problems in the most important Eastern city during peace negotiations with the Frontier."

"Okay, okay, so it'll look bad."

"It might sabotage the whole process."

With a despondent huff, Pilot nodded. "I'll go back and inform the King."

"Be careful what you say. We don't know anything substantive yet. Only that these Vashon are not behaving like they have in the past."

"Don't worry. I've certainly learned how to talk with King Robion. Besides, you know him—he doesn't panic or go running off on supposition. Now, the big question I have is what are *you* going to do?"

Axon felt the bracelet pressing against her leg. "The Vashon aren't religious, but I am. I know the perfect Shul to ask about this."

CHAPTER FOUR

E ntering the Balison Temple of the Cassun Nine, Axon kissed the
palm of her hand and wiped it across her forehead in respect.
Named for Jero Balison, a wealthy man who liked adventure and
discovered the Cassun religion while exploring the sparser regions of the
Frontier, the Temple bore both the marks of the Frontier religion and the
Eastern city it stood within. All six of the Life Cycle deities were given
honor through beautiful tapestries hung on the high walls. The three
greater deities were each given an enormous statue, their heads brushing
the ceiling three stories up. Each floor looked over this central point in
the temple allowing numerous visitors to enjoy the sculpture, the
artwork, the skill and creative craftmanship involved in building such
marvelous symbols of appreciation.

At such a late hour, Axon knew the place would be empty. She also
knew the doors would be open. There were always variations to a religion
depending on location. Just as each town, each city, each country had
their own dialects, their own traditions, so it was true for religion, too.
Perhaps moreso. But despite these variations, Axon knew that any Cassun
temple would never lock its doors to the public.

Of course, most of the temples she had ever visited were open air,
situated atop a hill, overlooking a small town. No doors to lock. The Shul
lived in a small shack nearby, ready to offer prayer and guidance at any
moment. Whatever money the Shul brought in for the temple went to the

construction and maintenance of the statues or to the well-being of those living in the town.

But here, with so many people crammed together, the temple had to be in a building or it would have been swallowed by the other city buildings long ago. Likewise, there was no place for a small shack, so the Shul lived within the temple. The large number of people also meant a lot more money flowed in, and that meant better statues and better conditions for the Shul. Yet somehow those living in the neighborhood did not benefit much from the added revenue.

With her head bowed, she approached the statue of Tortu, god of woman. To the side of the statue, a small box contained prayer cloths. Axon plucked one free—blue with a yellow border—and rested it atop her head. She then settled on her knees, bowed once more, touching her forehead to the cold stone base of the statue, and prayed.

At length, she rose to her feet and approached the statue of Pralma, goddess of man. Again, she lowered to her knees, bowed her head, touched the base of the statue, and prayed. She had rested her eyes a bit too long—not helpful to finding out about the Vashon and the bracelet, but restorative. Though she craved several hours sleep, this short rest gave her enough energy to pursue her answers.

"Hello?" Shul Ranon called, his voice echoing from down a hallway.

Axon kept her head bowed. She heard the Shul's shuffling steps and the wooden taps of his cane. As the sounds grew louder, her muscles eased more. Even this late at night, she could trust that a Cassun Shul would answer the call of his flock.

"Ah," he said with a warmth that dried her rain-soaked skin. "I should've known you would be the one to get this old man out of bed."

Axon grinned. The Shul stepped between her and the statue, grunted as he lowered down and placed his hands upon her head. She listened as he murmured rapidly through the basic prayers. When he finished, he lifted the prayer cloth and returned it to one of the small boxes next to the statues.

"Well, my dear," he said, his voice scratchy with sleep, "what troubles you tonight?"

Axon lifted her head. Shul Ranon's stubby body and thick-lipped face reminded her of the woman who had taught her to ride a horse. His gray curls that sprang out the sides of his balding head and the way he slouched on his cane echoed the man who tutored her in math and history. Even the gentle rhythms of his speech called back that of her Shul from growing up in Ridnight. Perhaps that was why she found this temple so appealing—it connected her to the Frontier.

"Come on, now." He rubbed his eyes. "You didn't wake up an old man like me for nothing."

"I'm sorry to have disturbed you."

"I should think after a year of you visiting this holy place every week, sometimes more, that I've come to know you a bit. I hope you've come to know me as well. For example, I know that you would never have entered this building so late in the night unless something serious had occurred. And you know that I would never be upset at a late-night visit from one of my favorite people. Now, are you going to talk with me or must I pull out another prayer cloth so you can face Qareck's statue and go through the cycle of prayers again?"

Axon uttered a soft laugh as she rose to her feet. But when her hand dug into her pocket and touched the bracelet, all humor left her. "What do you know of the Vashon?"

Shul Ranon's eyebrows lifted. "Of all the things you could have said that was not one I anticipated. The Vashon, huh? Well, they're more like a cult than anything else. At least, those Vashon I've seen behave that way. Nobody outside of the group knows who leads it. Some of my fellow Shuls think that they are a leaderless group, that they have no central organization making any decisions. Maybe they did at one point, they must have because they still have their temples—they call them *komo*—but now it appears they are lawless within. They just bought a building a short while ago and converted it into a new komo. You've probably seen it—the one a few blocks from the constable headquarters. See? If they had any real authority within their group, they'd never pick that building. An isolationist group setting up a komo near the constables? Ridiculous."

"Do you think it's possible that one of them, an individual, or perhaps a few of them, might believe in the Cassun Nine?"

"Hard enough for them to believe in one god let alone nine. Why are you asking about this?"

"Several Vashon have been following me lately."

"Oh? That's odd."

"At least, I think that's what was going on. I confronted them, and in the resulting fight, I cut off one of their hands."

"Are you okay?"

"I'm fine. I've faced far worse than a bunch of zealots. But with the hand, I found this." She held out the bracelet. "Maybe we have a new follower."

"No. They only follow their lost god."

"Then I worry about where this came from."

The Shul reached for the bracelet, his fingers trembling as his eyes narrowed. He licked his lips.

Axon said, "You recognize this, don't you?"

Pocketing it, he let out a halting breath before clearing his throat. Gazing up at the statues, he mouthed a prayer. At length, he faced Axon once more. "I do recognize the bracelet. It belongs to a man named Byn Forsean. He is my assistant, and one day, he'll be Shul of this temple."

"Your assistant? How come I've never met him? Never even heard of him."

"That is a bit of a tale, but I think you are meant to hear it. I've often wondered what plans the Nine have had for you that they should bring you to the East, to this city, to my temple. The day you walked in, I knew that a divine hand had intervened in our lives, and I believe our dear Sazieck, god of adulthood, has brought you here for this moment because I can think of no other than you who holds all the skill and bravery necessary to help out this temple." Gesturing toward a door behind the statues, the door to the Shul's private residence, Shul Ranon said, "Come. I will explain everything."

Axon followed into a narrow corridor. The Shul's feet brushed the floor with a soft scratching while his cane kept steady time. Ahead, she saw a kitchen with a washtub on the wall and a door that appeared to lead into the Shul's study. But he did not head in that direction. A few steps down the corridor, he slid aside a door on the left and entered a steep stairwell.

"Where are we going?" she asked.

He simply raised one hand and waved her onward. At the bottom, the temperature dropped a little, and she smelled dampness. Mold and rot.

The Shul turned the switch that ignited two flameless mounted into the beams on the ceiling. They stood in a dirt cellar. Numerous paintings had been stacked against one wall and countless articles of clothing had been piled against another.

"Here," he said, bringing her to a small desk that had been set up at the far end. Plain wood, small chair, just enough space to take notes—a school desk. The Shul pressed his hand on the wood as if it might crack open.

"This was where Byn did all he could for our people. This was where I made a grave mistake."

"Is he dead? You weren't talking that way before."

"He might be. I hope not. But that bracelet being in the possession of the Vashon does not suggest a good outcome for my sweet friend."

Axon lifted the Shul's hand and gave a comforting squeeze. "You can trust me. Tell me what's happened. How can I help?"

With a sigh, he plopped down into the chair. "Are you familiar with the Cistern of Qareck?"

Frowning, she said, "I have a vague memory of a story my father would tell me when I was little—about an orphan girl who was beaten every night by—"

"Yes, yes, that old tale is just a way to reinforce that you should always listen to your elders. There's also the one about the boy who finds the Cistern under his house and creates a lot of problems for himself. Other stories are out there, too. But those are all nothing more than stories. I'm asking if you know about the real Cistern?"

"I suppose I don't."

From a small shelf under the desk, the Shul produced a thin book. "This contains the oldest story I ever found on the Cistern. It's not a parable of any kind. It's simply a bit of history describing the first people to have discovered the Cistern."

Axon reached for the book, but the Shul snatched it back. "What's wrong?"

"I need you to listen—not be distracted by old books." He returned the book under the desk. "I wanted you to see a little of what Byn had found. That's what he did for me. He found things. Paintings, books—anything I needed to further the hunt."

"The hunt?"

"For the Cistern—the fountain with the source of waters far more powerful than even those that made the Water Blade. It's not a fable. I've been searching for many years, and when I discovered the possibility that it was located here in Balica City, I transferred to this temple and got to work. That's when I first met Byn."

"He worked here before you?"

"Yes. When the previous Shul left, the boy remained. But, unfortunately, our congregation dwindles. I had no real need of an assistant to handle the temple's operation. However, when I showed him all I knew about the Cistern, he became fascinated. I could tell that he was like me. A searcher. A hunter. And so, for several years, Byn became my young, brave researcher. When a lead required travel throughout the country or into the Frontier, I could send Byn and remain here to serve the community's religious needs."

"But why did you hide him? Surely, I would have seen him at some point."

"Perhaps you did and did not realize his importance. Perhaps not. I did not so much hide him as keep him from discovery. Because if people knew that there really was a Cistern of Qareck, blood would flow. Companies and governments would finance searches, and I promise you that nobody would have a holy thought about it. They would dream of using its power to destroy each other."

Axon stepped back, her eyes widening. "I'm a fool. You're sitting here telling me all of this because he found it, didn't he?"

Placing the bracelet on the table between his hands, the Shul said, "Perhaps. Several days ago, he said he thought he had uncovered something important and wished to investigate the matter. He never returned. I worried, but he has been gone for lengthy times before. Not until you brought his bracelet did I truly fear." When he looked at Axon, his eyes glistened and his voice cracked. "I need somebody I can trust to look into this."

"I know the perfect man. My friend, Zev, is brilliant, and this is exactly the kind of thing he's brilliant at solving."

"No. Not an outsider. I need you."

"But I'm not a solver like this."

"Perhaps not, but you are a warrior. From what you've told me about the Vashon, I suspect I need a warrior more than anything. Please. Byn deserves the best the Nine can bring him, and they have brought you here. You know the Nine don't gamble. How else can you explain that you, a warrior retired, finds herself with a Shul in need of a warrior?"

Axon pictured Byn sitting at this desk in this cellar. She had no clue what he looked like, but she imagined a young man with a brave face and a determined brow. He hunched over his books, searching and searching for any nugget of information that would point him to a great artifact. Then she imagined him cowering under the cloaked and masked figures of the Vashon.

"Okay," she said. "If you think I can do this, then I will."

"It's not up to me. The gods and goddesses have made it so."

"I don't know what help I bring, but I'll see what I can find."

"Thank you," he said, sniffling as he lifted the desk open. "Remember all the Nine teaches us. Life is best lived in balance. Always seeking balance is the truest way. As a warrior, you understand that a balanced sword is best. That holds true for all aspects of life." He pulled out a leather folder containing several loose pages. "These are Byn's notes. His form of balance was through knowledge and seeking the Cistern. These papers might help you. Perhaps."

Though only a handful of pages, when Axon picked them up, she felt as if she lifted several hundred. She hoped her apprehensions did not show.

CHAPTER FIVE

Zev

The morning sun prodded Zev's face with golden hues, and he pulled the thick covers over for a few more moments of peace. The soft pillow covered in authentic Gollit silk encouraged him to dig deeper into the welcoming mattress, and he could feel sleep lingering nearby, happy to return. Living in the Frontier had given him a great appreciation for the luxuries of the East—especially a large, warm bed.

"Good morning, my dearest," Lady Jos purred with a gentle nudge on his shoulder. She pulled the covers back and kissed his cheek. "We have to get up and get ready. We've already slept in far too late."

He set his hand on the soft skin of her waist and pulled her close. Feeling the heat of her naked body brought life back into him. In a craggy voice, he said, "We could be a little later."

She giggled and pushed him away. Getting out of bed, she said, "We did enough of that last night." She picked up a handset off the wall. "Wesso, dear, we're awake now. Please send up some breakfast and make sure the autocart is ready for later. We've an awfully busy day today. An important one."

Though Zev could not hear the butler answer, he knew old Wesso spoke with an exacting and annoying tone. *Yes, ma'am. I shall see to it right away.* Zev could not imagine Wesso talking to him like that. Even now, when the butler threw out his common phrases—*Yes, Mr. Asterling. Of course, Mr. Asterling. No, Mr. Asterling*—Zev wanted to bludgeon the man. In every tone and glance, Wesso made it clear that he did not approve of Zev sleeping with Lady Jos. None of the staff did.

When Zev had first returned, they all acted appreciative to the fact that he had saved Lady Jos's life during the craziness at Ridnight Castle. But as he and Lady Jos began an intimate relationship, their attitude changed. He could hear them snickering, catch them tutting, and most of all, he could feel their disapproving eyes. Yet when he asked them for anything, he received polite bows and proper curtsies. Living in luxury held many allures, but Zev could do without all the false respect given by the staff.

Not that he deserved their respect. Or anybody's. Still, he had not treated Lady Jos poorly. He used her to comfort himself, true, but he understood that she used him as well. It looked like it would play out as it had for countless wealthy families before him, and that would be fine. Everything else he had tried turned to the crud a Dacci witch could cast a spell with. After a year in the city, after accepting the world as it was, he saw the sense in—as his father would put it—joining the civilized world.

"Stop thinking and get dressed," Lady Jos said.

Zev lifted his head. She wore a robe with flecks of silver glitter and brushed her hair at a vanity of hand-carved dark woods. Through the mirror she smiled at him. He had to admit it—she was astonishingly beautiful.

Groaning, he swung his feet onto the cold floor. She had a suit hanging on a stand near the dresser. He knew it would fit him perfectly.

"Don't get grumpy this morning," she said. "You need to relax and be sharp. Everything is going to work out fine. In the time we've been together, everybody has forgiven your past behavior and you're pretty much accepted among those who matter."

"My past behavior?"

"Don't start. You know what I'm talking about. But now that you're back where you belong, and now that you're with me, I'd say our prospects are looking quite grand. After you are tapped to be the representative of the Asterling family for the peace negotiations, your political future will begin in earnest. From there, you'll have no trouble getting one of several strong seats with prominent organizations which can only lead to a truly powerful seat in a few years. By that point, we'll have married and as long as we have at least two children, preferably a boy and a girl, then you will be in the exact position necessary to make a run for the Government Council. Give that a few years and you'll be primed for Head Council. Then, if we want it, you take Leader of the Council which pretty much gives you control of the entire country. Not bad for us, if you ask me."

"Sure," he said, scratching his side. "Whatever you want."

Slamming her hairbrush down, she scowled at him. "What is wrong? You have the world at your fingertips and you act like I'm planning a boring day cleaning trash off the sidewalks. What's happened to you? Where's that bold man who saved my life a year ago?"

"You sound like that play."

"Oh? You mean the play that honored you which you refused to see? *That* play?"

"What's there to honor? I happened to be at the castle that night when things went horribly wrong. I tried to help, but I failed. I failed at the castle, and before that, I failed in the West. We tried to prevent the war, but it happened anyway. Nothing brave or honorable about it."

"You're talking nonsense. I was there at Ridnight. I saw those vile Dacci and their disgusting spells, and I saw you help people. Me, especially. I'd be dead if not for you."

"I doubt that."

With her tight lips forming a dot, she closed her eyes and calmed. "I know today feels stressful for you. It is for me, too. But your father—"

"No, no. Don't bring Father into this."

"He's in everything when it comes to you. He's the reason you came back here in the first place. He was dying, and you imagined you'd have some deathbed confession or perhaps a reconciliation or something. But he refused to die. He got stronger—well, strong enough to keep going, at least. Yet you never got any closer, never got your confession or your reconciliation, you never got anything."

Zev picked up the suit and walked toward the bathroom door. Mounted on the wall in a glass case, the Jos family pin—braided gold ropes forming a circle with a red gem in the center. They had lost a lot of power over the years. Marrying into the Asterling family would do much to restore the value of that pin.

But that didn't change the fact that Lady Jos had spoken the truth. She simply refused to see the rest of it—the fact that he had floated along since then, that he didn't deserve the praise she wanted to mine for political gain, that all her plans for their future required him to succeed. But he never really did succeed. Part of him felt like a liar—she wanted an Asterling to help her family, but he would probably only increase her family's losses.

Returning to her hair, she said, "You're going to be fine. I'll be with you, right by your side, and together we'll take those first big steps toward our bright, bright future. You'll see."

Zev paused, forced some levity into his tone, and said, "You sure you don't want to jump back in bed? Nothing relieves stress better."

She giggled again. It almost sounded genuine. "Do a good job today, and we'll have plenty of celebrating to do tonight. But get dressed already. We're going to be late, and your father hates when people are late."

CHAPTER SIX

Each time Zev stepped foot inside the Asterling house he experienced a wealth of conflicting emotions. Mostly, nostalgia and pain—the marble foyer where he and his brother, Marcel, would slide across in their sleeping gowns until he fell one time and broke his arm; the living room to the left where he would spend summer mornings reading books as the sun rose but also received punishments whenever Father deemed it necessary; the living room to the right where he would introduce his girlfriends to Father only to have them rejected for one minor infraction or another. He did not want to think about the other rooms in the house. There were too many.

Nestled in the heart of the wealthiest district, the house was really two dwellings with the shared wall torn down. Four stories high and in the middle of a long row of such homes. Across the tree-lined street, the Fullings, the Teratios, and the Wyncos all lived. Those three families alone owned close to a quarter of the city.

Watching Lady Jos enter the foyer, watching the awe in her eyes, reminded Zev that even among the wealthy there were degrees of success. Or perhaps he saw more hunger than awe. It didn't matter. In the realm of *Women of Whom Father Approved*, Lady Jos was one of the few potential wives that Zev thought could also lead to a life of happiness.

Avett, the butler, took their coats and gestured toward the curved staircase. "You are expected in your father's study."

Zev held Lady Jos's gloved hand as they ascended to the second floor. She moved well despite her form-fitting black-and-white stripped dress, and Zev noticed the three dots along her nose matched the color scheme. No matter what else, he presented a stylish and capable woman to the family.

Though the wood in the stairs was old, it did not creak. It never had. Carpet runners and regular oiling covered such blemishes. Zev could smell that oil—or perhaps he simply remembered the smell. Awful stuff.

"They're here," Marcel's wife, Mercy, said from down the dim hallway.

When they entered the office, Zev felt Lady Jos tighten her grip, so he plastered on a smile. "I apologize for being a little tardy. I'm still not used to getting all dressed up like this. Took me forever to remember how these double-wraps work."

His family stared back at him with stoic impatience as if sitting for a portrait far beyond the allotted time. And what a portrait they made—the high-ceiling study constructed in the jagged, dark stylings of five decades ago, all sharp-edged wood and angular details. Even the bookshelves threatened to cause harm if one failed to remove a book with care. A wide-mouthed, marble fireplace covered much of the left side and in front of it, Father's enormous desk weighed down the room. Two heavy brown couches angled toward the desk. Marcel and Mercy sat on one side of one couch.

Between the couch and the desk, Father sat in a wheelchair. Gone were the dagger eyes and hefty bulk of a man who could destroy a person with a single word. He looked exactly like he was—an old man, near death, hanging on to what little life remained. Gaunt, bone thin. He still wore his sleeping gown and had a blanket covering him. Nobody had bothered to even comb his hair.

"Sit down," Father said, his tone making it clear that his mind was still sharp.

Zev and Lady Jos settled on the opposite couch. Mercy sat straighter. Her pert nose, recently given four blue dots down the side, wrinkled even as she mustered a pleasant grin. She placed a hand on her husband's knee as she inclined toward Lady Jos and said, "I'm so happy you and Zev are together. He needs someone like you to set him on the right path in this world. It's so good of you to lower your standards for our benefit."

Lady Jos said nothing. Merely nodded as if she had received a true compliment. That action—or lack of action—hit Zev hard. For the first time, he saw how scared Lady Jos felt and how important this appointment must be. For her to hold back a biting remark, or even a gentle quip, churned his stomach.

Marcel stood. He looked like an older, paunchier, balding version of Zev. With a slight limp, he walked over to a small table in the corner that held three clear bottles. Pouring a drink, he glanced at Zev, lifted the bottle as if to offer it but then decided his brother shouldn't drink anything, and returned to his seat with a glass for himself and for Mercy.

"Are we waiting for anybody else?" Zev asked.

"Like who?" Marcel said.

"I don't know. Usually when Father has an important meeting, the family banker is here."

Zev's father lifted his chin. "No. Rholune will not be joining us today. This matter is not an immediately financial one."

A tense silence filled the room. Zev rolled his fingers along his knees as Father, Marcel, and Mercy stared at him. But when Father peeked at Marcel, Zev finally understood—the old patriarch had yet to decide who would represent the family at the peace negotiations. Like so many other interactions with his father, this one was a test.

As far as Zev could tell, both Lady Jos and Mercy had no clue that they were watched, too. Marcel had to know. One did not survive growing up in the Asterling household without a keen perception of Father and the games he played. Likewise, when Father made a fist and pounded the side of his desk twice, Zev knew a decision had been made at last.

"Over the next several days," Father said, his voice forcing a sternness he had not held for years—especially not since his body began to fail, "the country will be in a precarious position. As one of the important families, we have a duty to those who work for us and those below us to represent the Asterling interests as well as those of the country. It is a delicate and narrow path to walk. It requires bravery, intelligence, and fearlessness."

Lady Jos inched to the edge of the couch, her face as bright as the future she pictured.

Father continued, "Zev, you have shown a lot of strength over the years. It was not easy for you, I'm sure, to go out on your own, to start your own business."

"One that failed," Mercy said with a snicker.

"You also have gained some fame with the work you've done for this King Robion. That bit of success as well as your connection to the King and your knowledge of the Frontier give you great value toward these negotiations." He lifted a bony hand and pointed at Marcel. "You, son, have been a steadfast worker for the Asterling Company. More than any other except me, you understand how we operate, what pressures we face, and why specific decision have been made—even when they have been unpopular. You've helped grow the company and have managed to create a few new revenue lines on your own. You should be proud."

"Thank you, Father." Marcel stared straight ahead, dead-eyed, like a gambler afraid to give away a tell.

"Both of you boys bring much to the job, and you have not made my decision easy. A year ago, I wouldn't have hesitated to give Marcel all of the responsibility. But Zev, you've shown great promise since your return. Don't think your efforts go unnoticed."

Zev managed a nod and a smile.

"In the end, though, there is only one logical choice. Marcel, you will be the Asterling representative."

Mercy clapped her hands and kissed her husband on the cheek. "I'm so proud of you, my dear. Thank you, Father. We won't let you down."

Zev expected Lady Jos to break into tears or perhaps clench his hand tight with anger until they returned home where she would release her frustrations. Instead, she stood tall like a warrior glaring down upon her enemy.

In a fierce voice, she said, "Marcel? For this important event, you choose a spineless, narrow-minded, risk averse boy who can only claim to have been a good servant to you? I thought you were smart. I thought the success of the Asterling Company or the Asterling family was due to your firm and well-thought leadership. Now, I must assume it's all been luck."

"You ought to be careful with what you say." Marcel gripped his jacket tight as if this held his hands from striking out at her. "You are not an Asterling, yet."

Lady Jos opened her mouth but said nothing. She snapped her attention to Zev. When he did nothing, she nudged him with her leg.

Father snorted a laugh. "That is the reason I have picked Marcel."

"Because Zev and I haven't married yet?"

"Because Zev sits there and accepts it all. The fight is gone from him. But to represent the family and our business means to fight for us. I guess we should mark it down as yet another failure."

"But what about everything you said—that Zev shows great promise, that he's shown strength and bravery, that he has the connections with the King and the Frontier—what about all of that?"

With a gentle touch, Zev pulled Lady Jos back to sitting on the couch.

"You don't understand," he said. "I was never going to get picked. My father treats everything in life like a fight. All those nice things he said were nothing more than setting up for the biggest punch he could achieve." Zev looked over at Father. "But he failed. I already knew the outcome."

"You could have told me," Lady Jos said.

Mercy put on a sympathetic face. "I think he expected you to know already. That's a big part of marrying into this family. Don't worry, though, I anticipated all of this. I suggest that Zev can do his part for us by using his relationship with the King."

"Oh?" Marcel said, a snide grin on his lips. "How so?"

"Somebody must inform the King who will be our official representative. I can't think of a better person."

Zev brushed his pants as he stood. He bowed slightly to Mercy. "I couldn't agree more."

Mercy kept her smile though her lips quivered. "I'm glad to hear it."

Offering his arm to Lady Jos, Zev said, "Dear, come along. I have to go see my old friend, the King."

CHAPTER SEVEN

Of all the facts proving Lady Jos was livid, none hit harder than that she refused to join Zev in visiting the King. Until that moment, Zev thought this fight would recede like an ocean tide. But as he walked the city blocks alone, he wondered what dance he would have to perform, what nonsense he would have to say, to calm her and return to a neutral life.

None of it was fair to her, of course. He knew that. But he also knew that there was no perfect world waiting for them, no perfect life that brought happiness each day. He had travelled into the real world and he had seen what it had to offer. Such things as she wanted didn't exist.

Up ahead, he spotted The Bending Branch—a high-end lodging in a seven-story building that often served visitors of political importance. The bidding war to house King Robion and his entourage had been intense and slanderous. In the end, The Bending Branch won out of tradition and sizeable donations to the three families responsible for making the decision.

At the entrance, two Frontier Royal Guards stood at attention. One recognized Zev—Pilot had probably given his men orders to watch for Zev's arrival—and provided a pass to the top floor. Despite the heavy odor of old ale and older cooking, Zev found the glorified tavern to be rather comforting. It reminded him of the Frontier taverns, only much larger.

On the seventh floor, after nudging by guards posted on every landing, Zev flashed his pass and approached the main door. He knocked. King Robion opened the door, and no other action could have brought such a smile to Zev's lips.

The King had always been a plain man in the best of ways. He did not bask in the privileges of being royalty. No roster of servants, no wake of mistresses, no overindulgence in food or drink. Rather he approached his life as a solemn duty, a sworn oath to protect and preserve his people, and nothing would undermine that goal.

"Zev," the King said, brandishing a smile of his own. "I had hoped to see you after the play last night, but I was told later that you didn't go."

"I didn't really want to watch a re-creation of that night. Did you?"

The King laughed. "Not at all. I'm glad you came by today, though. Come in, come in."

Zev stepped into a beautiful room filled with fine rugs, impressive paintings, and furniture designed to show off wealth and power. None of it suited the King. The long, functional table to the side where he had papers strewn about and an advisor with her head buried in more papers came closest to the King's aesthetic, but Zev suspected that if he removed all the papers, underneath would be a gold-lined artwork embedded in the plain wood.

Two people caught Zev's attention as he crossed the room. In the back corner, he spotted a godwalker—one of a group of former Shuls who sought to use the power of their nine gods and goddesses. In practice, they were the King's personal spellcasters. Zev also noticed the woman sitting in a reading chair, and his heart doubled-over with joy.

"Bellemont!" He rushed over with a hug. Though born a Dacci, Bellemont had been taken away and raised in the East. She ended up joining with Axon and eventually, she worked with Zev at his failed problem-solving agency. "It's wonderful to see you. I wasn't sure if you'd be here."

Though she still wore the Dacci veil that covered the mouth to hide how many teeth a witch had left for casting, the rest of Bellemont's clothing were all Frontier—a simple dress with a modest lace neck and clean but rugged boots.

"I work for the King, now," she said. "You would know that if you ever bothered to write."

Zev reddened. "I'm sorry. Truly. It's been a difficult year."

"Then when you're finished with the King, you can treat me to some lunch and tell me all that has happened."

Zev glanced over at King Robion. The man had already settled next to his advisor and murmured thoughts over a handful of papers. "He seems a bit busy right now."

"Trying to run the Frontier while in the East while also preparing for peace negotiations isn't easy."

"He didn't leave somebody in charge while he was gone?"

"No need. The godwalkers can communicate across great distances. The King is in regular contact with his staff back at Ridnight. Of course, Mr. Duke handles the implementation of the King's orders, but King Robion is still in charge."

The godwalker in the corner did look exhausted. Perhaps the King should have brought a few to spare. Zev said, "I could come back another time."

"He'll be like this until we return to the Frontier. He hates it, but he would never stop blaming himself if things fell apart at home because he wasn't doing his job. Did you come simply to visit or is there an official reason you need to see him?"

Zev paused. Until that moment, he had assumed Mercy suggested this errand as a way to humiliate him. But hearing Bellemont speak brought the truth to the surface of his mind. Mercy needed Zev to deliver the news so that King Robion would accept it as *official*. Nobody else would be giving such announcements. The other family representatives would simply present themselves at the first meeting and that would suffice. But not so for Marcel.

When King Robion walked into the Thalmew Building and met Marcel, he would be expecting Zev. Marcel would then have to explain that he was the Asterling representative. And finally, there was the risk that King Robion would reject Marcel and insist on Zev taking the position.

Mercy wanted to avoid any possible embarrassment and all possible loss of status. *She's smarter than I thought.* If Zev spoke to King Robion before the meeting, he would be in the position of not only preparing the King for Marcel as the representative, but should King Robion object, Zev would be required to defend the family decision.

Zev stood and offered his arm to Bellemont. "I came only as a friend. If the King is so busy that I never get to see him while he's here, please remind him that I did stop by. And, if you wish, I'd be thrilled to take you to lunch."

Bellemont's eyes crinkled—Zev knew a smile grew under that veil—

and they headed out. Since she couldn't be away for too long, they opted to dine at a corner tavern called Pickled Breath. Neither of them could understand why the owner had chosen that name, though the stale odor of the room suggested one reason, and they opted to enjoy the tables set up outside.

"I don't like cities," Bellemont said after giving her order, "but I must admit that it's far more pleasant than I expected. The autocarts are quieter than horses, and of course, there isn't manure everywhere. Much easier on the bottom of a dress."

Zev basked in the warmth of sitting with a true friend. "Tell me about you and Pilot. You're still together, right?"

She blushed. "Things are very well between us. I worried that his family would object to me—after all, what mother wants to hear that her son has fallen for one of the Stolen?—but he doesn't have much family. Those he has are not willing to let my parentage ruin his happiness."

"The King seems to approve, too. Otherwise, I doubt you'd be welcome as his aide."

"Oh, yes. King Robion has championed our relationship. In fact—well, I shouldn't say."

Zev leaned forward on the table. "Do you really think that will work? Save us both the trouble of forcing me to pull it out with questions and simply tell me what you were going to say."

"I think the King is going to have a talk with Pilot. One in which he will strongly urge Pilot to propose marriage with me. I try not to think about it, especially if I'm wrong, but the King keeps dropping little hints and winks and such. He once even said that he's starting to see me like a daughter and how happy he'd be to officiate my wedding." She lowered her head and covered her eyes. "I feel so foolish even thinking about it. I have no reason to believe it will happen, and it certainly won't happen now. Not while these important talks are occurring. Perhaps when we get back, but not before. That's why I hesitate to say anything."

The waiter set down two foamy mugs and walked off. Zev picked up one and said, "Here's to peace for our countries and happiness for you."

"Stop that. It is exactly why I didn't want to tell you. If Pilot proposes, that's wonderful. But I don't require it for my happiness. I don't even seek happiness."

"Everybody seeks happiness. Isn't that the whole point?"

"Being happy is a momentary state. One cannot be happy non-stop. To me, it seems a foolish goal when it, by definition, cannot last. What I seek is contentment. You can be content and happy, but you can also be content and sad. It is a far more level emotion, and one that I have achieved with Pilot as we are. If he desires more from our relationship, I'll be happy, of course. But when that passes, I know the two of us can continue a life of contentment." She placed her hand on Zev's arm. "What about you? Are you content? Or happy?"

Zev gulped down half his ale. "I don't know what I am. There's a life ahead of me—a good life—and it might even be a content life." He stared at his ale, and the sloshing liquid suggested the only true answer rested at the bottom of the mug. "I don't think that's enough. Happiness might be fleeting, but it's the purpose of everything. Animals and humans all avoid pain and seek out pleasure. Why? Because pleasure brings happiness. I'm glad for you and Pilot, and if contentment gives you the same sense of purpose, then that's wonderful. Not for me, though."

"I hear you're with a woman."

"Yes. Lady Jos."

"Does she give you this happiness that you want?"

"I think so. Maybe. I'm not really sure." Finishing his ale, he set the mug down and pointed at her. "That's the trick, isn't it? Because happiness is a passing emotion, then it's difficult to know when you've truly achieved it."

Bellemont chuckled. "You overthink things. A good trait when seeking out murderers and finding stolen treasures, but not so good for relationships."

Zev barked out laughter, drawing a few annoyed stares from other diners. "I can think of a few women who would heartily agree with you on that."

They spent much of the afternoon sitting outside, drinking ale, and reminiscing about various cases they solved together. It wasn't until the daylight dimmed that Bellemont realized how much time had gone by. She apologized for rushing away (which made Zev laugh yet again) and hastened off to the King. It had been a lovely way to end a day that began with such unpleasantness.

Before his mind could spin around replaying the darker morning, Zev paid the bill and went for a stroll through the city blocks. He thought about Bellemont and Pilot. If nothing else good ever came from his adventures in the Frontier, at least he helped in a small way to get those two together.

Thinking of the happy couple—the content couple—brought to mind

37

Lady Jos and her dreams of the future. She had a map toward their happiness, and he had done nothing to help her. That wasn't fair to her. In fact, it was wrong. He needed to make a choice—join her with the same goals or break up and let her find somebody worthy of her.

That's the real problem, he thought. Like the actors with their aggrandizing play, Lady Jos gave Zev virtues he knew he did not possess. Bravery? Man of action? Master solver? These terms had been applied to him, but he knew better. He did not rush into battle—he cowered while others fought around him. He did not take charge—he followed orders. And Master Solver? That was a label given by a king desperate to keep a room full of important people calm during a crisis.

Of course, he did have moments to be proud of, but they did not add up to a man worthy of great praise. Father knew it, too. Zev saw it in the man's eyes. That's why Marcel represented the family.

Zev stopped mid-step. He had been a fool for too long. Day after day since his return Lady Jos showed him the path forward and he had ignored her because it didn't suit his idea of himself. She understood the world around them, and she alone had welcomed him with a way to return to the people he grew up with, the life he knew. It wouldn't be the life he wanted but it would be better than any other options in front of him. And it might bring him a few moments of genuine happiness.

With his chest puffing out and his pace quickening, Zev strode all the way back to Lady Jos's home. By the time he rang her door, dusk had arrived. He waited.

Twice more he pressed the button. Ringing doors had been around for several years, but Zev still preferred the more natural knocking. So, he did that, too.

At length, the door opened and Wesso, the butler, blocked the way. His heavy jowls and plump nose overpowered his face, but Zev could not miss the man's disdain. With a thick, wet voice, Wesso said, "My apologies, sir, but you are no longer welcome in this home."

"What?"

"In her wisdom, Lady Jos is cutting you off."

"You don't need to sound so pleased."

"I'm never pleased to see Lady Jos upset. But she has come to the inevitable conclusion that you are not of value. I agree."

"I'm starting to think you fit in with her just fine," Zev said and turned away.

As he closed the door, Wesso said, "Your belongings have been transferred to the Asterling house. There's no need for you to return here ever again."

Zev stood with his back to the door and watched the city pass him by. Part of him wanted to pound on that door, break it down, and demand for Lady Jos to see him. Part of him laughed at the situation. Most of him, though, felt as if he had been walloped across the head and did not know how to react.

Flameless flickered on. Night approached. He refused to go back to home. Enduring Mercy, Marcus, and Father's smugness would be too much for one day. Plus, he had no desire to visit a jail cell because he murdered Mercy.

Instead, he hopped on a public autocart and rode far to the south. It was a long trip, but he trusted nobody else to take him without question.

Axon answered her door on the second knock. She looked him over and stepped back to let him in. "It's just the floor," she said, "but you're welcome to sleep there as long as you need."

CHAPTER EIGHT

Axon

Zev's gentle but steady snoring woke Axon long before dawn. Moonlight cut through the window framing the man on her floor in a pale blue rectangle. She watched him sleeping and tried to find a path through the misery he hefted upon his own shoulders.

After showing up at her door, they had spent several hours discussing Lady Jos, his father, and all of Zev's problems. She listened and urged him to remember the version of Zev from the Frontier. But he held onto the ridiculous notion that he had failed. True, he had proven beyond all doubt that he was no farmer nor was he a mastermind of business, but his brilliance could not be denied.

She even said, "Sazieck watches you now and must be laughing. When the King of the Frontier relies on you not once but twice, you can rest assured that you have some great talents to offer."

But his losses blotted out any encouragement she could impart. She tried some logic. "Do you really think I would have come all this way, to the East of all places, if I thought so low of you?"

He dismissed her point by citing her loyalty and friendship. "Besides," he said, "you are the real hero and deserve so much better than you're getting."

They continued this back and forth until both had nothing new to contribute. Exhausted and frustrated, they silently agreed to sleep it off. All the ale Zev had drunk earlier knocked him out fast, but Axon spent a long time replaying their talk in her head. When her mind left that subject, it focused on the Shul and the Vashon—not any better for inducing sleep.

She had spent part of that time debating how she would approach the Shul's request. Most of the night, however, she tried to find a plausible excuse with which to turn the Shul down. The word *plausible* proved the sticking point. Nothing she could think to say sounded like anything more than what it was—a pathetic, weaseling pretext.

She looked upon sleeping Zev once more. They both needed a break from the constant pressures of living in this city. Family pressures, political pressures, religious pressures. All of it so unnecessarily complicated. The Frontier proved life could be simple, rich, and fulfilling.

Axon grinned. Her thoughts were not true, and she knew it. The Frontier overflowed with all the same pressures and complexities. Whether one had to deal with the difficult relationships of a small-town community or navigate the treacherous terrain of the King's court, it was every bit as unnecessarily complicated as this city life.

Rolling onto her back, she sighed. Sleep. She needed sleep and a fresh morning. Her only thought that she could agree with—they needed a break from the Shul and Lady Jos. Simple as that.

She heard rustling clothes and the clink of a plate. Squinting, she discovered the morning sun showering the room and Zev sitting in her chair. He had two steaming cups of Cassun secret tea—it looked like hot water but could be one of nine flavors. Difficult to make, expensive to buy, and rare to find in the East or the Frontier.

Axon bolted upright. "Where did you get this?" She accepted her cup, closed her eyes, inhaled the sweet aroma, and sipped—berra sapling in honor of Tiq, goddess of birth. "Delicious."

"I figured this was better than simply saying *Thank you*. Besides, after listening to me complain all night, you deserve it."

"What flavor is yours?"

"Not sure. It's got a strong, smoky taste. Almost like meat on an open fire."

"That's posco—well, an attempt at posco. The actual plant is extinct."

"Is that why this one honors your goddess of the elderly, Orlar?"

She choked on some tea, coughing and sputtering. When she could talk again, she said, "It was named long before it went extinct."

"I know. I'm sorry. I wasn't trying to kill you with a joke, I promise."

Propping her pillow against the wall, she leaned back. A flutter in her gut preceded the question that flashed in her mind. She had no idea why she should feel nervous, and like a strong warrior, she pushed on ahead anyway. "I thought I might watch some of the opening ceremonies today. The parade and then there's some speeches and I'm sure other things, too. Mostly, I want to see the parade—Pilot is going to look hysterical acting all proper. Why don't you join me?"

Zev sipped more of his tea. He shrugged. Then nodded.

CHAPTER NINE

efore they could head to the north end of the city, Zev needed
clothes. He refused to fetch his belongings from the Asterling
home. Eventually, he would do so, but not yet. Not for a while.

Axon knew of a store that sold clothes purporting to be authentic
Frontier styles, and while that boast turned out to be far from the truth,
they did have items that were both rugged and comfortable. It didn't take
long to outfit Zev in a pair of pants, shirt, and vest that served him well
enough. With a bashful turn, he had to admit that most of his cash would
be with his things at the Asterling home and that he used all he had to
purchase the tea, but Axon didn't mind paying. She rarely spent money
and lived such a frugal life that she had plenty to spare.

They took a public autocart close to the parade. As they hiked up the
final handful of blocks, the crowds grew thicker and the noise grew
louder. After a year of war, most people wanted to celebrate even the
possibility of peace.

By the time Zev found a spot near enough to see the street, the drum-
beats could be heard coming closer. Horns blared the Eastern anthem,
and the crowds closed in, pushing Axon against Zev. As the front of the
parade approached, soldiers of the Eastern army marched along led by
the Captain of the East astride a magnificent horse. He kept his face stern
and his eyes locked forward. Zev thought of Philune, the old Captain who

had sacrificed himself to stop this war. Hopefully, the man would be proud of this day.

Autocarts outfitted with weapons rolled by next as well as an older model with the city mayor sitting in the back and waving. A troop of girls representing several of the area schools danced in flowing cloaks and bright smiles. Another group of autocarts drove by with the family representatives.

At the head, a tall man stood wearing the finest of new suits. Balding and gray, he had a sharp nose and sharper eyes. He did not wave or even smile.

"Is that?" Axon asked.

Zev said, "Hiko Thalmew. Yeah. This whole new government revolves around him."

Standing at Thalmew's side, Mrs. Thalmew smiled and waved. She wore a stunning and bold red outfit, but what caused gasps throughout the crowd—instead of red dots painted on her nose, Mrs. Thalmew had a line of seven red gems.

"They certainly act like royalty," Axon said.

"For now. All of the changes in Eastern government are a reaction to the fears surrounding the war. The old guard—people like Lord Radugo and Lord Etz—they lost everything to Thalmew and his followers. One day they had power, the next it was gone. Radugo took his own life because of it. Odd thing is, if this peace treaty happens, the wartime government might lose its power. Thalmew might be putting himself out of a job."

Axon felt Zev tense and thought he reacted to this troubling idea, but then she saw the next autocart driving by—Marcel stood with a plastered grin and a stiff wave. His wife, Mercy, had a more controlled smile and a happier wave. Forcing a merry tone, Axon poked Zev in the side, "Remember when we had a parade thrown for us?"

"That was all for you. We were entering Ridnight after you saved the entire city from a siege. And it was more of an earnest thank you than the false praise he's getting up there."

"You really think they're not going to succeed in making a treaty? Because of Thalmew?"

"I think the parade is premature. Shouldn't we wait until the treaty is done?"

"We can have a parade then, too. Nothing wrong with extra celebrations. Plus, this lets the governments of both countries know that the people really want this badly. Maybe they'll work a little harder at it because of this. Not so easy to hold onto power when everybody is angry with you."

The crowds cheered as another section of the parade marched along. Many of the people waved flags for the East and even for the Frontier. Banners hung out the windows of the surrounding buildings—mostly displaying company logos and colors.

A short while later, they watched Pilot lead the Royal Guard on horseback. He attempted to look dignified, but Axon and Zev giggled at his proud, stern face. He wore his favorite flat-brimmed hat and a tight-fitting shirt that showed of his muscular chest. Several women in the crowd squealed as he trotted by.

Zev shook his head. "Even when he's no longer trying, he gets women to go crazy for him."

"Bellemont's got nothing to worry about. Pilot has always enjoyed women, but he's fiercely loyal."

"Oh, I wasn't suggesting that. Besides, he'd be insane to cheat on a woman who could cast a spell that would turn him into a eunuch—if he's lucky."

Four horses pulled a long, flatbed trailer. King Robion stood at the front, waving at the crowds, while several members of the court did the same from the sides. Everyone wore their finest clothing and most spectacular jewels—a display of riches Axon could not recall seeing since the King's coronation.

But next to the King stood a woman wearing an exquisite, sleek gown that glistened in the light. Simple, elegant, it highlighted her slender shoulders, smooth neck, and the sparkle in her eyes. But not her mouth—she wore a veil.

Axon stopped from a further comment because she had to point ahead. "That's her, right?"

"I don't see any other Dacci on that trailer. Wow. I can't believe she's wearing that. I mean, she gave up the drab, dark cloth strips of the Dacci when we worked together. But even then, she wore very conservative dresses. This is…"

"Stunning."

"Absolutely."

Glancing around at the crowds, Axon noted that everybody appeared awed by the sight as well. "Maybe we really will get a peace treaty out of all this. If people can see Bellemont—a woman wearing a Dacci veil—if they can see her in a good light, there's hope."

"I think they accept her because she stands next to the King. If he ever were to lose confidence in her, you'd discover how quickly the public's acceptance would disappear."

"I see you're feeling as optimistic as ever."

Zev snickered as they watched a large group of Frontier musicians walk by playing a rowdy tune that the crowd clearly enjoyed. Seeing him smile and relax, even after watching Marcel roll by, Axon thought this had been the right plan. A day removed from the pace and problems of their lives. For a breath, they could meld into the crowd, be nothing but one of the masses, and that could feel good.

Until she saw the two masked figures standing not too far away. Vashon.

One had a black teardrop painted on the cheek. The other had a realistic drawing of flesh pulled back to reveal bits of skull underneath. Like the others she had encountered, these two attempted to blend into the crowd while also keeping a close watch on her.

"I've never seen this many Vashon in two days. Something is going on," she said, after pointing them out to Zev.

"Possibly. But there's also been a lot happening because of King Robion's visit. These Vashon are people, and they're probably every bit as interested in a big theater production and an even bigger parade like the rest of us."

"What about the one standing outside my apartment the other night?"

"You mean the one you chased down and cut off his hand? Isn't it possible that he was waiting to meet somebody that had nothing to do with you? He's just passing the time until his friend or date arrives when suddenly this woman bursts out of her apartment building with a glowing sword and a lot of anger. He ran for his life."

Axon glanced back and saw that the Vashon had not moved. "Possible? Sure. Isn't it equally possible that this group of zealots, a group that keeps out of sight almost all the time, decides that now is the best moment to act? By using all of these public events, they can hide some nefarious activities with ease."

"Hide? They're wearing those crazy masks?"

"To most people around here, the Vashon masks are just part of a silly religion. If anything, people see those masks and steer clear. Nobody wants to be preached to by those fools. And the constables aren't paying attention—they're working hard simply keeping the mass of people from overwhelming everything."

"I suppose. What is it you think they're up to, then?"

"I have no idea. But my instincts are on edge."

Turning around, Zev said, "Well, we're supposed to be forgetting about our problems today, and that won't happen if you keep worrying about a couple of Vashon. Stay here. I'll see what they want."

Too stunned to stop him, Axon watched as Zev approached the masked men. As he maneuvered forward, they tried to back away, but they could not get through the thick crowd. Axon's heart raced. Part of her wanted to rush ahead and divert Zev from the Vashon, but part of her wanted answers, too.

She heard him say in a loud voice, "Excuse me."

She missed the next exchange, but one Vashon shoved him. Axon pushed her way toward them when the teardrop one kicked Zev's shin. He bent over and the other punched Zev on the back of the head.

Axon shoved those in front of her away. When she reached Zev, the two Vashon had taken off. But Zev waved her on.

"You were right. You were right," he said. "Go get them!"

CHAPTER TEN

Moving through a throng of parade watchers proved more difficult than Axon thought possible. Each time she weaved by a handful of people, others pressed in, jostling her back some of the distance she had already traveled. But she saw up ahead that the Vashon had similar troubles and kept her eye on them most of the time.

She angled toward the storefronts, hoping to reach a point where the crowd thinned. The Vashon checked back on her, but even when they looked right in her direction, they seemed unable to find her. Perfect. She took a chance and broke directly for the back of the crowd.

As expected, there were less people here. Moving fast to make up the lost distance, she hustled along the sidewalk, bumping a few parade gawkers, but mostly moving smoothly. The Vashon stood out—not many cloaked and masked figures shoving a path away from the parade.

Keeping pace with them, she paralleled their movements. At one point, they stopped, stared back and searched for her. When they couldn't find her, they appeared to relax and headed straight toward the back area she had been using. Straight toward her, in fact.

The first one through was Teardrop. Axon dashed forward, locked Teardrop's arm behind his back, and yanked the man over against the nearest building. As people backed away, forming a half-circle of fear around her, she spotted the other Vashon darting deeper into the crowds.

"Help me," the Vashon said in a whispery voice. "She's crazy."

Zev caught up, pushing through the wall of people watching both the parade and the conflict. "It's okay," he said, as if he had the authority to disperse the crowd. "Enjoy the rest of the parade. We've caught the criminal."

"Criminal?" an elderly lady with three green dots on her nose said. "You're no constable."

Most people didn't care and turned their attention back to the marching horses, but a few took interest in what the old lady had said. "Is that right?" a heavyset man asked. "If you're not a constable, you can't arrest this man."

"Well, I'm not *not* a constable," Zev said. "What I mean is that, well, you see—"

"Are you or ain't you?" the man stepped closer into the half-circle.

"He's lying," the Vashon said. "They're trying to rob me."

Axon cinched the Vashon's arm tighter. "You better stop talking or you'll end up losing more than a hand like your friend with the cracked mask." To the man asking questions, she said, "Hey, big guy, take a look around you. The constable service is overworked managing all of you people today. We're here to help them out, and this Vashon is being charged with assault. If you want to be charged with interference, keep getting in our way."

The man blanched as he scooted off. "Sorry," he mumbled. "I didn't know."

When Zev approached her, Axon lowered her voice. "What should we really do with him?"

"Exactly what you said. Let's take him to the local constable office. Charge him with assaulting me."

"We can do that? I mean, don't we have to be in the constable service to arrest people?"

"I'm an Asterling. I think I can make it happen."

49

CHAPTER ELEVEN

Zev

The nearest constable office was two blocks over and one block down. Teardrop kept quiet and did not struggle against Axon's tight grip. Smart man. Zev knew she would break her captive's arm rather than let him loose.

A thick, metal pole stood on one corner with the constable emblem atop—two rifles crossed and their distinct round cap above. Nine curved stairs led into the building. Though no longer a religious people, remnants of the East's older, more fervent views appeared throughout the city—even in the architecture. Strange to imagine the main policing force had once been an offshoot of the Cassun Shuls. Zev wondered if Axon knew that part of her religion's history—thoughts for another time.

The constable office consisted of two wooden benches stretching the length of the walls ending at a wide counter. A door off to the side led deeper into the building, but it could not be opened from the lobby side. The high ceilings had been painted in great detail, displaying the story of *Fretch and the Fengel*—an old tale about a man who fights a creature with hundreds of heads that it carries at its side, switching out different heads depending on its emotions. The Fengel does what it pleases, causing great troubles, and Fretch eventually tames the monster by teaching it to accept the consequences of its actions. Perfect for a constable office.

The benches were empty and only a few constables meandered in the back. Zev guessed that everyone was either working the parade or enjoying it.

"What's this now?" a man behind the counter said. He had a pinched face and white piping on his uniform. Of course, they stick a new recruit with desk duty during the parade.

Zev stepped forward. "This Vashon assaulted me."

Muttering, the recruit reached behind at one of several stacks of papers. Taking the top sheet off, he hunched over the form. "Assault, huh? Where did this incident occur?"

"A few blocks over at the parade route."

"Okay, okay," he said, reading over his form. Evidently, he had never filled out this particular one before. "Let's see now."

Axon said, "We need to speak with the Chief Constable."

"Oh, really?" the recruit said, but Zev shared the same thought. "You think that on one of the busiest days of the last few years, you can simply walk in here and demand to see Chief Constable Drick? Who do you think you people are?"

"I'm nobody," Axon said. Then she inclined her head. "But my friend here is Zev Asterling."

"Asterling?" the man said, fumbling as he jumped to his feet. "I-I'm sorry, sir. I didn't know you were part of the Asterling family." He snapped his fingers at two others also with new recruit piping. "Riner, lock this Vashon in Holding. Tulon, run up to the Ardenson Street office and get Chief Constable Drick down here. And I mean *run*." Before Tulon could complain, the man added, "Tell him that one of the Asterlings has been assaulted."

That got Tulon moving. Zev rarely took pleasure in throwing his name around, but in this case, he had to hide his widening grin. Especially because Axon appeared to be enjoying it, too.

Despite the desk constable's assurances, Tulon's urgency must have left him the moment he cleared sight of the constable office. Or perhaps they ended up waiting so long because the parade caused traffic problems —even for the pedestrians. Zev only knew that they had wasted too much of the day sitting on those hardwood benches.

When he finally arrived, Chief Constable Drick entered through the back. Zev spotted the man as the other constables approached him, battering him with hushed discussions, gestures toward the lobby, and befuddled questions. The Chief Constable shook his head as he glanced at Zev and then headed through an archway deeper into the building.

Axon said, "That didn't look too promising."

"Based on how long he's kept us waiting, I think he's only stopping by here because it's on his way home."

"And the Asterling name."

"That works with lesser-positioned people. But there are a lot of families on the Council. It's very possible Chief Constable Drick has loyalties that don't align with my family."

Before Axon could respond, the lobby side door opened and Chief Constable Drick entered along with the desk constable. Despite nearing an age when most men had slowed down, Drick stood straight and tall. His salt-and-pepper mustache covered his mouth while his wide nose and thick neck created an imposing figure. He crossed his arms in a manner that threatened yet also appeared stylish—barely caused a wrinkle in his uniform.

"As I understand this," he said in a thick, wet voice, "you are claiming that the Vashon in our custody assaulted you. Is that correct?"

"That's right," Zev said. "My friend here and I were watching the parade when two Vashon kept staring at us. I walked up to ask them if there was a problem, and they immediately attacked me."

"You went up to them?"

Axon said, "These Vashon have been harassing me for two days now."

Chief Constable Drick raised an eyebrow as he cocked his head towards her. "This will proceed a lot better if you keep quiet until I ask you a question. Understand, Miss—?"

"Axon Coponiv."

"Of course. The one who caused so much trouble a few years back. The big famous warrior of the Frontier."

"I just did my job. Same as you."

Zev wanted to step between the two. He wanted to shush Axon and pull Drick's focus, but he had dealt with constables like this before. Anything he said or did would be perverted into the opposite of his intent. If he tried to calm things, he'd be accused of inciting violence.

"I don't think you understand the first thing about what I do," Drick said. "Maintaining law and order throughout a city this size is a monumental task. While you had the freedom to gallivant across the Frontier, to pick and choose your fights so that you only had to deal with the ones you could win, I have to handle whatever criminals come into the city. I don't get to choose."

Axon popped to her feet, startling Drick, but Zev managed to wave her back. He offered a sympathetic bow and said, "Please, Chief Constable, we're sorry if bringing our problem to you is causing more trouble. With the parade going on, I'm sure you've had your hands quite full."

Drick sneered. "What would you know about hard work? You abandoned your family and only came back when the government changed so that you could try and get your brother's rightful position on the Council."

"That's not what happened."

"Of course not. You love your family and missed them so much after running away that you had to come back. The convenient timing means nothing."

"That's wrong. My brother—"

To the desk constable, Drick said, "You can go let the Vashon go. We won't be holding him any longer."

"What?" Axon said. "He assaulted Zev."

"If he did, you're the only two witnesses. I had my men ask around before I came here—the only thing anybody recalls was you, Ms. Coponiv, shoving the Vashon against the wall and nearly breaking his arm."

"They were attacking us."

Zev said, "Look, you've made it clear that you don't like me, but that's no reason—"

"I don't like the Vashon, either. Not at all. They're a crazy sect of the Cassun which are a crazy group to begin with."

The fiery rage radiating off Axon heated another ten degrees, but she held still.

Drick continued, "I'd love to see the whole lot kicked out of the city or tossed in jail. But that ain't the law. I can't lock them up based on just your word. From everything I can tell, from what witnesses are telling me, it's you two that are the real cause of the problem, not these Vashon. I know that you had some successes in the Frontier. Became real stars in the King's eyes. But this ain't the Frontier. We don't have a king. You have no authority here. My job is hard enough without vigilantes mucking things up, so do me a favor—go home, and stop playing hero."

As Chief Constable Drick turned away, Zev blocked Axon's path forward. He knew that determined scowl. She teetered on the edge of taking action—action that would result with her in a jail cell for the night. Gripping her arm, Zev escorted her outside.

"This is absurd," she said, turning back toward the entrance.

Zev pulled her further away. "Of course it is. Which is why you and I are going to head over to the nearest tavern and start drinking. I give you permission to scream and yell and spew every foul word you want about Chief Constable Drick while we drink. Because anything else is only going to cause us a mess of trouble."

He watched her weigh the possibilities, and for a moment he had no clue which way the evening would fall. Luckily, good sense prevailed. Rather than spend the rest of the night dealing with constables, lawyers, and hefty bribes in order to free her from the grip of the law, they headed down the street, searching out the nearest tavern.

CHAPTER TWELVE

After the third tavern had kicked them out, they had worked their way to the Dead Mule—a pit of drunken despair only two blocks from Axon's apartment. Zev had vomited twice on this final leg of their alcoholic journey, and he had started to sober up. As best he could tell, Axon never needed to stop drinking. The woman could drink a table under the table.

Sitting at only one of two such tables not cobbled together from pieces shattered over years of intoxicated brawling, Axon ordered another South Tar—a thick brew from the southern cities strong enough to get most people drunk from its fumes alone. Zev, however, had switched to water.

"You know what the real problem with everything is?" Axon said.

They had spent their time at the first tavern complaining about Chief Constable Drick, the constable system, and the government in general. The second tavern covered topics such as Lady Jos, the Vashon, the joy they felt for Pilot and Bellemont, and their mixed feelings towards King Robion. At the third tavern, they rehashed and reminisced over their exploits together. They laughed at their strange beginnings, recounted some of their narrow escapes, and took time to languish in the memories of their triumphs. They even found room to discuss the difficulties of being at odds with each other during the events at Ridnight Castle with the supposed theft of the Shield of Taladoro.

But now, Zev had no clue where Axon planned to take this conversation. With less of a slur to his words than he had at the last tavern, he said, "Enlighten me, o beautiful warrior."

Axon's eyes lit up as her head wobbled. Then she belched. A short bout of laughter followed before she said, "The problem—the real problem—is war. No, no, I'm not talking about the horrors of war. I mean the opposite. See, before in the Frontier, we lived under this threat of war, and life kept everything clear and simple. Stop the war. That's what we were trying to do."

"We didn't do such a good job with that one."

"But we tried. And that's not the point." Axon tipped back her mug and when she set it on the table again, she stared off. Zev nudged her. With a shake, her brow furrowed and she rubbed the side of her head.

"You were about to tell me the point."

"Yes. The point. You see, now that we're here in the East, there's nothing but confusions and complications. Everything here is not about the war. But it should be. All these families—and I don't just mean the rich ones, I mean everybody in the city—by Wiq, everybody in the entire Eastern country has family affected by the war. People that've died. But they don't seem to care. As long as the money keeps rolling in."

"You think it's any different back in the Frontier?"

"I think for a woman like me, it's only clear when you're doing what you're supposed to be doing. Give me soldiers to command or a group of willing warriors, and I can ignore the rest. Give me a weapon and an enemy. But this place—I don't belong here."

Zev knew she spoke inebriated honesty, and while he did not want to take advantage of it, his own alcoholic intake had weakened his moral fiber. Besides, the thoughts he had rang true. "Why don't we pack up what little we have and leave? Go back."

"To the Frontier?"

"Absolutely. We could pool our talents together and start a business. Not that I've had any success in business, but it would be better than rotting away here."

"What kind of business?"

"I'm not sure. When somebody needs a fighter or a master solver, they come to us."

"Like a mercenary and a constable?"

"Maybe. Though I don't think the constables are that good at solving issues. It doesn't matter. We can figure it all out when we get there. I just know that being here isn't healthy for either of us."

Slapping her hand on the table, she said, "It's a wonderful, well-reasoned plan. But what about Lady Jos?"

"Did you forget the reason I'm sleeping on your floor?"

"She'll forgive you."

"I doubt it."

The door to the tavern opened, letting in two constables. Sudden quiet overtook the place. Even the drunkard half-asleep in the back corner stopped singing to himself.

The lead constable, a gruff man with deep-set eyes, searched across the patrons. When his focus reached Zev, the constable stopped. "There you are."

Zev held still. He knew Axon's hand lowered to her Blade, but he didn't think she would be foolish enough to wield it. Not here.

As the two constables approached, the one in the back fumbled with a piece of paper. The gruff one said, "You're Zev Asterling, eh?"

"That's me."

"You're being summoned to appear before Master Hiko Thalmew, Leader of the Council and owner of—"

"Everybody knows who he is. Why does he want to see me?"

"That's not really my business, is it? Now, come on. Get up and let's go."

Axon stood instead. Swaying a bit, she said, "I see how it is. We came to you bastards needing help and you threw us out. But now Thalmew wants our help, and you come groveling, expecting us to obey you?"

"You best sit down, ma'am. I don't know what problems you've got with the constable service, but I guarantee you'll make it a lot worse the way you're talking. And nobody here is groveling. I'm ordering your friend to come with us now. Whether he does so peacefully or with a lot of bruises is entirely up to him."

With a placating spread of his hands, Zev said, "Please, everyone, there's no need for threats. There's talk of peace going on around us. Let's have some here, too."

Axon's ale-tinged breath warmed Zev's ear as she leaned close. "I don't trust these men. You shouldn't go with them."

"I've got nothing to worry about."

"Why do you say that?"

"Because you're coming with me. You're still my bodyguard, right?"

Axon straightened. She raised one finger, turned her back to everyone, and stuck the finger down her throat. After heaving her ale onto the floor, she returned with a clear-eyed nod. "I'm Mr. Asterling's protection. You two constables can lead the way, but if you try anything, you should know that I've fought the Beast of the West. You won't be a problem."

Though the men scoffed as they headed out the door, Zev caught a visible shudder cross the gruff man's shoulders. Zev and Axon followed.

CHAPTER THIRTEEN

The back of a constable's autocart had not been designed for comfort. Nobody cared if a criminal had enough room for their legs or if the seat provided a decent cushion. By the time Constable Gruff had driven across the city and parked in front of the Thalmew Building, Zev had sobered considerably. He doubted Axon had as well, he detected a slight wobble when they walked toward the front entrance, but she maintained a stern concentration—her eyes in constant search for threat. Few but those who knew her well would see beyond the surface. As long as she didn't start talking, Zev thought none of Thalmew's people would realize how drunk they had been.

Two constables stood at attention on either side of the building's entrance. Odd. Zev wanted to ask but thought better of it.

Gruff and his partner drove away, leaving Zev and Axon in the hands of the building's doorman who hurried up to them with an eagerness that betrayed his youth. "My name's Tip," the doorman said. "Anything I can do for you, all you have to do is ask."

Zev shook his head. Typical Eastern business strategy. Act rough up front and then offer loads of comfort. Anything to keep the opponent off-balance.

Tip escorted them through an elegant lobby designed more to impress than to be comfortable. Axon nudged Zev, indicating two more constables at attention—one by a small fountain, the other guarding the stairs.

Before they turned toward this last guard, Tip ushered them in the direction of a metal box with a slatted door. When he held the door open, Zev and Axon stared at him but did not move.

Shifting in his stiff uniform, he said, "It's rather new. We call it a *lifter*. You won't need to take the stairs. It's perfectly safe. And I'll be in there with you. I'm the driver."

Zev glanced at Axon. She shrugged and pushed by him. After a short peek inside, she entered. Zev followed and Tip brought up the rear.

The lifter was a narrow cage surrounded by a sturdy railing. Tip closed and locked the door, squeezed to the side, and grabbed a lever while pushing several buttons. With a lurch and a metallic whine, the entire thing rose into the air.

Zev's stomach shifted at first but settled fast.

"Only takes a moment," Tip said, keeping his eyes on his work.

Zev stayed quiet—half-amazed at the ingenuity of the East, half-nervous that he relied on that ingenuity not to plummet to their deaths. More of the same strategy. Anything to keep him off-balance, not thinking clearly. He snatched a peek at Axon. She kept her eyes locked forward and her mouth locked tight. *Great. Stuck in a tiny cage with a tough, hard-drinking warrior who might vomit at any moment.*

Another strong lurch and the lifter ceased moving. "Seventh floor," Tip said as he opened the door.

Axon stepped out first. She stomped on the floor, making sure it was solid, and appeared to relax. Zev strolled forward and followed Tip down the immaculate yet simple hall—spotless tan carpeting, gold-trimmed mirror, several portraits of family—until they reached the heavy double-doors at the end.

"Have a good evening, sir," Tip said with a bow.

CHAPTER FOURTEEN

G rowing up in the city, Zev had spent plenty of time in the wealthy and notable homes of Eastern families. He had never seen such opulence as the Thalmew's home—not even inside the King's castle.

A white marble floor—which could only have been imported from the Posbrey quarries near the border with the Frontier—rimmed a sunken, carpeted study. A modern and expensive conference table dominated this carpeted section which paralleled a massive work desk. Busts of former family leaders lined one wall while a single painting dominated the opposite wall—an abstract depiction of the Balica skyline. Zev had not embraced this new art style, but he had to admit that within the context of this room, it impressed.

Three people sat at the far end of the long table—Thalmew, his wife, and Chief Constable Drick. A clear decanter of liquor sat between them—near empty. Mrs. Thalmew clutched her husband's forearm. Tears glistened against his dark skin while hers vanished beneath her pale visage. Only the sliding gemmed dots along her nose gave evidence that she had been crying.

Upon seeing their arrival, Chief Constable Drick twisted in his chair. "You two? When I said you had no authority around here, I meant it."

He motioned and a constable standing off to the side stomped forward. Before the man could pull out a weapon, Axon pivoted her back against his chest while latching his arm and flipping the man over. Hitting the hard marble made a damaging sound and the constable did not move for a moment.

"How dare you attack a constable," Drick said.

Axon backed off with her arms out and hands open. "He threatened Mr. Asterling, and I'm Mr. Asterling's protection."

"It's okay, Chief Constable," a familiar voice said from an unseen hallway. A moment later, Marcel entered under an archway in the back. He carried a fresh decanter and set it on the table. "While you were securing the building, Mr. Thalmew and I thought it best to call my brother in. We had some of your men find him and escort him here."

"It's true," Thalmew said, his voice crackling as he spoke. "I'm sorry I forgot to mention it."

"Not at all," Drick said, readjusting his coat as he turned away from the embarrassment. "Quite understandable. You have far more important things on your mind. I'm glad my men were able to help."

With an eye on Zev, Marcel gestured toward the table. "Don't stand there gawking at us. Come, sit down, this is important."

As Zev approached, he noticed Axon remained back by the doorway. When he looked at her, she stood at attention with her eyes focused ahead. Of course—saying she had come to be his bodyguard was not an excuse for beating up a constable. She meant it. Plus, Zev suspected she enjoyed standing firm and strong while the man she had flipped crawled away.

Taking the first available seat, Zev folded his hands on the table. "Clearly something is wrong. How can I help you?"

Marcel stepped behind the Thalmews and placed a hand on the shoulder of each one. "Earlier this evening, as the parade dwindled down, Mr. and Mrs. Thalmew's daughter, Mosol, went missing."

Mrs. Thalmew shuddered before breaking down into a deep cry. Her husband pulled her near. Dabbing at her eyes and nose with a handkerchief, she buried her head against his chest.

Zev said, "Are you sure she's missing? There's a lot of celebration going on tonight. Is it possible she left with some friends and has lost track of time?"

Crossing his arms, Chief Constable Drick pointed a thick finger at Marcel. "If you're going to bring your imbecile brother into the matter, at least be honest with him. She hasn't gone missing. She's been kidnapped."

Marcel strolled to the opposite end of the table. Standing next to Zev, he said, "Yes, you're right. I was being too polite, and there's nothing polite about this."

Zev could not be sure how Marcel ended up in this room, but a lot of other questions had become clear. For one, Marcel intended for the Asterling family to benefit from this tragic circumstance. For another, Zev had no intention of helping out. Nothing good would come from getting involved in such a powerful family's problems.

With a sharp breath, Mr. Thalmew sat straighter and attempted to regain his usual dignified look. "No ransom has been demanded, but I do not expect one."

"Why not?" Zev asked, gritting his teeth—he shouldn't have asked any questions. He didn't want to know the details. If he knew nothing, he would have nothing to think about. Nothing to spark his curiosity into jumping up and down like a birthday boy about to open his presents.

"Because if all the kidnappers wanted was money, there are far better targets than me."

Interesting. "I should think you're the best target. The biggest, at least."

"That's why I'm no good. Yes, you could demand huge sums of money from me, but I have power—the reason Chief Constable Drick is sitting right here is because it's my daughter. Do you think he sits down with every parent missing a child in the city? All resources are being utilized to find our Mosol, including you. With the brains necessary to pull off the kidnapping in the first place, I should think these criminals have enough intelligence to realize that a less connected target would have a higher percentage chance of fulfilling the ransom."

Thoughts of Marcel and Drick drifted away from Zev as he focused on Mr. Thalmew. "I think you're absolutely right. You obviously have had more time to consider the matter. What do you think they're going to demand, if not money?"

"Considering the timing, I see only one possibility."

"The peace treaty."

Thalmew lowered his head with grave concern. "Either they want me to make sure the treaty does not happen, or they have specific requirements of what the treaty will say."

Zev pinched his bottom lip. "This is a delicate and dangerous matter. But, as you pointed out, you have the entire constable service at your disposal. I don't think there's much more I could do."

"You see?" Drick said. "Even the imbecile agrees. We can handle this."

Marcel hurried up the length of the table. "Please, forgive my brother.

It has been a long time since he's been called upon as a master solver. He does not realize that our father has requested his assistance in this matter. The Asterling family has always been a friend of the Thalmews, and we always will be. With such a brilliant mind in our family, we would be remiss not to offer our help."

"Enough," Mr. Thalmew said, the force in his voice making it clear that he had spent a lifetime commanding people. "Mr. Asterling, our daughter has been kidnapped. While I fully expect the constable service to use much of their resources in getting her back, I can't actually call upon all of the resources available. We can't let the city fall apart. King Robion of the Frontier is here along with many of his people. If the entire constable service was out looking for my daughter, not only would criminals have free reign, but these valued guests would be vulnerable. Perhaps that's what my enemies want. However, if I have a man like you, a true master solver, then my wife and I feel the chances of a positive outcome are far greater."

Zev noticed Drick's fingers white knuckled around his elbow. That man hated the idea of Zev anywhere near this matter. But more than vindictive joy, more than Marcel's not-too-subtle explanation of Father's expectations, Zev felt swayed by Mrs. Thalmew.

Rather than storming around her enormous home throwing a fit, rather than demanding action and punishing those who did not move fast enough, her true self showed in her behavior. She was not spoiled. She did not seek to be the center of attention in her sorrow. By staying quiet, crying, and seeking comfort in her husband's embrace, Zev saw a distraught mother who only wanted her child back.

"Mrs. Thalmew," Zev said and waited until she looked his way. "I will do everything I can to bring your daughter home."

CHAPTER FIFTEEN

Stiff-backed and mumbling furious words to himself, Chief Constable Drick led Zev and Axon through a hall toward the staircase leading up. The Thalmews stayed behind along with Marcel. Zev had no doubt that Marcel felt torn—he wanted to keep an eye on Zev, make sure he knew every detail of Zev's findings, but he also had to remain by the Thalmews' side, assure them that the Asterlings were loyal friends.

Zev shook his head. How could Lady Jos have ever thought he wanted that kind of a life?

The floor above contained four bedrooms, two bathrooms with running water, and an extra study. A constable had been posted in front of one door about halfway down. After receiving a proper salute, Drick admitted Zev into the bedroom. Axon halted in the doorway as Zev got to work.

A storm had ripped through the room—much too large to be called a bedroom, Zev thought of it as a second apartment—with clothes scattered on the floor, paintings askew, drawers haphazardly opened, a chair knocked over. On the bed, he noticed a jaur-skin blanket. As he ran his hand along the predator's smooth fur, Drick dumped a few books off a chair and sat.

"She was an odd sort," he said.

"Please, don't move anything else. Where I find things could be important."

Spreading his legs wide, Drick snorted as his mustache curled up on one side. "Don't you worry about what I do and don't do. I earned my rank and know how to conduct a search."

"Is that what happened here? Your men *searched* this room by tossing everything about?"

"This is how we found it."

Zev let his attention pan from one side to the other. "Is this normal for her? To be this messy? Is that why you called her *odd?*"

Picking his teeth with his pinky, Drick said, "The only reason I brought you up here is because Thalmew wants you up here. I have no intention of helping you get in the way of my legitimate search for this girl."

As if giving these words thoughtful consideration, Zev sat on the edge of the bed. "I see. I suppose I have to accept that. After all, you are the Chief Constable. Of course, I still have a job to do. You know better than anyone that if Mr. Thalmew wants something, he gets it. He wants me to find his daughter, and as difficult as that's going to be, my family name is at stake. Although I suspect you'll solve this soon enough, and the Asterling family will suffer for it."

"Don't worry. I'll shed a tear for you before I go to sleep."

Slapping his knees, Zev stood. "Well, I should go back and inform Thalmew that I can't help. He'll wonder why, naturally, and I'll explain that without basic information, there's no point in going forth. However, I'm sure that the Chief Constable—"

"Okay, okay. You don't have to be a Dacci about it."

"Oh? You'll answer my questions then?"

Leaning forward in the chair, Drick stabbed a finger at Zev. "I'll answer your stupid questions. But you listen to me right now and right clear—you are not to get in my way. If that poor girl is harmed or killed because of you mucking up this case, you'll wish you never came back to Balica City. And if you ever threaten to go tattling to Thalmew again, you may find yourself on the wrong side of an accident."

Axon took one step into the room, but Zev put out his hand to stop her. "Thank you, Chief Constable," he said with a proper bow. "Your assistance is greatly appreciated. Now, I believe I wanted to know if this mess was normal for Mosol Thalmew."

"Of course not. Do you really think her parents would allow such untidiness? That girl was raised better. And I guarantee that anything she failed to clean herself would be handled by the staff. This mess is obviously the result of the kidnapping."

"Did you find any blood? I'm not seeing any."

"Blood? No. They didn't try to kill her, if that's what you're thinking."

"Not at all. But if all of this was a result of her fighting back, then there should have been blood—intentionally caused or not. Which suggests that these criminals were searching for something. Perhaps the kidnapping was not the original purpose of their crime. Perhaps they entered here trying to find an item while Mosol was expected to be in the parade with her parents. Mosol enters her room and discovers the criminals."

"And they kidnap her to keep her quiet? That's a bit much to believe. We're on the eighth floor of the most famous building in the city. Not the kind of place for an impromptu abduction."

Zev inwardly cringed—Drick was right. "Then they intended both crimes." Zev paused before glancing over the jaur-skin blanket. His eyes drifted to the books Drick had tossed on the floor—*Merat Groun's Anthropological Primer* and *Living off the Land*. On top of a vanity, next to the vials of perfume and small containers of makeup, he noticed a well-worn pocketknife. "You said that she was *odd*. Did her parents know that she had an interest in a more rugged lifestyle?"

"I don't know for sure, and we're not going to ask them. The type of girl she is ain't relevant."

"Everything is relevant. If she likes rougher sports or hanging out with a crowd of dangerous types, we need to know that. It'll help narrow down where she could possibly be."

Drick leaned so far over, he barely touched the chair. "Now you listen here, you privileged prick, we are not going downstairs to put that poor woman through facing up to the fact that her daughter might not be the pristine, virginal innocent she thinks. And we are absolutely not going downstairs to put Mr. Thalmew through that as well. You just remember that the same powers which brought you here and have you sifting this room can turn on you quick."

"I should think you'd relish that idea. Send me down there and have me executed by Thalmew's rage."

"You make it tempting, but getting you screwed over don't bring Mosol back. Right now, that's what matters. You? You don't matter."

Holding back further comment, Zev refocused on the room. He hated to admit it, but Drick was right again—he didn't matter. None of their petty problems mattered. Not at that moment.

He walked across to the window. It provided a stunning view of the city. It also remained intact. Zev slid it open and stuck his head out. Looking above, to the sides, and below, he didn't see any logical way for a kidnapper to climb up. Especially when the window faced the main street which rarely didn't have traffic—as proven by the numerous pedestrians walking below him right then.

Closing the window, he scanned the room again. "Is there any other way in here besides the main door?"

Drick shook his head.

"Even with the parade going on as the greatest distraction a kidnapper could hope for, how could he possibly have entered this building, climbed to the seventh floor, entered the apartment, climbed up to the eighth floor, took control of Mosol Thalmew, brought her down to the bottom while she thrashed about, and escaped without anybody noticing? It doesn't make any sense."

"If you're going to stand there and spout the obvious—"

From the doorway, Axon said, "He's trying to tell you that the kidnapper had to have help from somebody with access to this building and this apartment."

Drick frowned. "One of the staff?"

"Or the doorman. Or any number of people. I assume with a man as politically important as Thalmew that there are a lot of people with access." Zev snapped his fingers at Drick. "You need to send a bunch of constables to ask Thalmew's connections where they were tonight."

Bursting to his feet, Drick said, "I'm done with you. I don't take your orders. Even if I did, what you're suggesting is moronic. These are not people you question like a criminal. They'd have me fired before the sun came up. Not to mention that diverting all my constables on a ridiculous errand like that means that all my constables are not searching the streets for this girl."

Zev returned to sifting through the bedroom. No point in pushing back when he knew the Chief Constable would not help. "Oh," Zev said, when he opened one of the few closed dresser drawers. Inside, he found a copy of *Govon's Guide to Love*. "I guess Mosol's no longer a girl."

Flooding red in the face, Drick said, "Put that back and don't you dare even think of telling her parents."

"How old is Mosol?"

"Seventeen, I think."

"Old enough then to be a woman."

"I'm warning you."

Axon said, "Again, you're missing the point. Zev is trying to say that it's possible this is not an abduction but something more of a romantic nature."

"You think she eloped with some guy?"

"Think a little more practically and more embarrassingly."

Drick's eyes widened. "She's pregnant?"

"It's possible," Zev said. "If her parents found out, they could have sent her away to hide the incident. All that we see in this room would make a lot more sense because she never was kidnapped. This would just be a show for us to be unwitting actors in."

Slowly looking about the room, Drick shook his head. "Poor girl." He flopped back into the chair. "We're going to have to play along. We can't confront them with this. We must act like this is all real."

"I'm afraid so."

As Zev moved back through the room, his foot banged against something light that made an unusual noise. Brushing aside a shirt, Zev's heart froze. He shivered.

"What's wrong?" Axon said.

Zev snapped his focus to her and then to Chief Constable Drick. "We're wrong. Mosol has been kidnapped." He lifted the object—a Vashon mask painted with dark cracks.

Axon bolted over and snatched the mask. "This is the man I fought the other night. I cut off his hand."

"You what?" Drick said, staring at the mask.

Zev said, "We have to assume that these Vashon have been planning for a while now. They kept an eye on Axon, watching her movements, perhaps trying to make sure she did not get involved or at least was kept away long enough for the kidnapping to occur."

"But she doesn't even know the Thalmews. Why would they care about her?"

Axon's hand went toward her Blade. "Because I have a reputation for stopping big things like this."

Turning to Drick, Zev said, "I'm going to give an order now, and you will obey it. Before you argue, you should know that doing so will only slow this process and endanger Mosol more. Besides, I'm going to report this to Thalmew, and he'll simply order you to do the same anyway."

"Then shut up already and tell me what you want."

Zev could see how painful those words hit Drick. "There are two Vashon we need to talk with. The one this mask belongs to—he should be easy to find, he only has one hand—and the Vashon we brought to you earlier today. The one with the teardrop painted on his mask."

Drick swallowed hard as the implications raced through him. Standing with military precision, he marched out of the room. "Give me a few hours. I'll take care of it."

CHAPTER SIXTEEN

Axon

A t Axon's insistence, Zev drank a full glass of hot kerew. Though childishly sweet, the juice of the kerew fruit jolted the body, keeping it awake and aware far longer than natural. With dawn closing in, she knew Zev would be tired. But he had to be focused—more than just a girl's life rested on him. If Mosol Thalmew could not be found or turned up dead, the entire peace negotiation would crumble under the weight of Mr. Thalmew's despair. Worse, he might turn his loss into a rage that lashed out against the Frontier, expanding the war beyond border skirmishes.

But more than the political ramifications, Axon's gut turned under the thought that the Vashon had been involved in this while also connected to the Shul's assistant, Byn Forsean. Several times during the drive to Constable Services Headquarters, Axon considered explaining all of what had happened. Zev needed to know. Except, even with the kerew brightening his face with energy, she didn't want to burden him with greater stresses. After the interrogation, she promised herself. Once they were clear of all the constables and Thalmews and everyone else, then she would tell him what she knew.

"I'm a little surprised Drick managed to find the one-handed Vashon so fast," she said as they exited the autocart provided by the Thalmews. "I was expecting you and I would have to find the man ourselves."

Zev walked a sturdy pace, heading toward the huge main building for all the constable services in the city. "The Vashon have always been a private, secretive group. But a few facts are widely known about them. Most important for us—a Vashon's mask is everything to them. Drick knows this, too. Without his mask, your Vashon cannot rejoin the group. And without the group, a Vashon acts like a lost farmboy in a big city. He'll stick out worse than a famous warrior from the Frontier living in the slums." Zev stopped at the base of the stairs leading into the building. "Why have you always turned me down when I offered you help? There's no reason for you to live in such a place."

"There's no reason for Thalmew to live is such a place as he does, either. Twenty homeless families could live in that same space. Why doesn't he help his people?"

"Perhaps I need more kerew. I don't understand your point."

"We are where we are because of the lives we've been born into and the choices we've made since. Few of us are ever permanently moored. It can feel that way at times, but the truth is that we only have to embrace change to make a change. Unfortunately, most people are afraid to accept any kind of change." She saw the confusion crossing Zev's brow. "Don't worry about me. When I'm done with my situation, I'll change it. When I'm ready to leave this city, I'll leave it. But tonight, we have a young woman in a lot of danger to find. Let's focus on that."

Zev's face tightened in an expression Axon knew meant that he accepted her final words though he did not like them. They climbed the stairs and entered a building that had to have been designed by the same people who created Thalmew's ostentatious home. The obnoxious lavishness of the main lobby overwhelmed the senses.

Brown speckled stone had been used on the floors and walls and massive pillars holding up a ceiling three stories high. An enormous statue of Syruit hung like a chandelier, her wings spread open and her Sword of Justice held overhead as if ready to strike. Axon did not know the full story of Syruit, but she knew that it was an artifact from the religion of Dahvism. They had three deities, and Syruit represented truth and punishment. Or maybe justice and mercy. She couldn't remember. Dahvism had died out centuries ago. Yet many of the images remained.

A constable who looked as if she couldn't wait for the night shift to be over called to them. "This way," she said. "We're just waiting for the Leader of the Council and we'll begin."

When Axon and Zev left for headquarters, Mr. Thalmew had been caught up in a small argument with his wife. She wanted to be present at this interrogation, but he refused. Though Axon had not heard the outcome, she expected Thalmew to appear without his wife. If for no other reason, they needed Mrs. Thalmew to stay at home in case the kidnappers tried making contact there—or that would be the excuse given to keep her away from the constable office.

With their footsteps echoing in the cavernous lobby, Axon and Zev followed the constable down several flights of stairs, through a hall of barred cells, and into a plain interrogation room. Chief Constable Drick stood against the back wall along with two other officers in their full uniforms. Drick bristled at the sight of Zev, and Axon tried to control her pleasure. No matter how difficult that proved to be.

Black-green grime streaked the walls and filled the room with a stale, moldy odor. The stone floor looked wet and the only light came off a single flameless hanging from the middle of the ceiling. Two armless, wooden chairs faced each other in the center.

Drick pointed to the chair with its back to him. "You sit here." He jabbed his little finger at her. "You stand with us back here."

Before Axon could argue the orders, Zev took the indicated seat. He gave Axon a slight nod, then stared straight ahead. Tamping down the sliver of anger threatening to take control of her, she stepped behind Zev, making sure to keep some distance between her and the constables. She resisted the urge to grab Zev and run out of this place. Never a good idea to go into the dungeons of an enemy—and though it could be argued that Drick and the constables were not the enemy, they weren't allies, either.

But she would not make that move because she saw the glint in Zev's eye. A spark of joy she had not seen in nearly a year. He belonged here. Not in the dungeon, of course, but in the chair, questioning people, seeking out the solutions.

The door to the interrogation room opened and Drick snapped to attention. The other constables did the same when they saw Mr. Thalmew enter. Behind Thalmew came a large man wearing a suit that strained against his muscular form. The way he stood behind Thalmew, the way his eyes checked the room, the way he kept his weight balanced and ready—Axon recognized it all. She kept loose with her hands at her sides, she bent her legs slightly for balanced weight, she studied the room with awareness sharp and clear—minus the alcohol. The point was to be a warrior ready to defend her charge. She knew that role well, and clearly, this new man did, too.

Thalmew managed a weary nod toward Zev before Drick guided the Leader to join the group. The bodyguard stayed close, always hanging back enough to let Thalmew have an illusion of privacy while also being able to jump in and protect his charge, if necessary. Drick whispered to one of his men, "Get the prisoner. We're ready."

Axon's skin prickled as her awareness doubled. Watching Zev sit while surrounded by those who distrusted him and those who placed all their trust in him, she wondered if they had any safe path through the night. At least, she still had the Blade. The constable service should never have allowed her into the room with it—they needed better training.

Zev rolled back his shoulders and turned around. "When this interview begins, you must trust me even if I say things that sound wrong or the opposite of our goal. The techniques I've been working on require me to pay attention to the subject and adjust my attitude accordingly. I seek whatever information I can get from this man, but it will only work if he believes whatever fiction I create. You all must keep quiet. Do not engage with the subject even if he tries to engage with you." Axon noticed how Zev never looked away from Thalmew. Finally, he inched closer to Thalmew and said, "I know this is difficult for you, but please trust me. I only want to see your daughter returned safely."

When the door opened again, a constable with a short beard brought in the Vashon and thrust the prisoner into the empty chair. The clatter of chains chimed as the constable secured the locks in place—the Vashon's hand was cuffed to a chain that fastened around a ring bolted into the floor. The second chain was wrapped around the prisoner's waist. The constable then saluted the group before exiting the room to stand guard in the hall.

Without looking back, Zev snapped his fingers at one of the constables and pointed to the door. The observing group had been situated far enough in the shadows that the Vashon would not see them or the constable's startled expression. He certainly did not see the way the man looked to Chief Constable Drick for an answer.

For his part, Drick did not resist. He silently motioned for the constable to do as told. Thank Qareck that Drick held that much sense. Axon understood right away—and apparently, so did Drick—Zev orchestrated this entire scene to intimidate the Vashon. Old One-Hand would see Zev commanding these men and would have to wonder how the circumstances had become so dangerous—calling in a man who could command the constables.

In the silence that followed, Zev kept still and stared at One-Hand. The Vashon's veins pulsed against his pasty skin. Fresh bruises and abrasions dotted his arms and cheeks. Older wounds scarred his face like the cracked pattern painted on his mask. Even without the mask, Axon noticed how he moved as if he wore it, as if he could only see by turning his entire head in a direction. And the lines—deep red lines carved the outline of a mask against his jaw and forehead. *Do they ever take the things off?*

"Didn't do wrong," One-hand said, rubbing his stump against his thigh.

Though Axon could only see Zev's back, she knew he suppressed a look of triumph. She had been through this with him before. He would have sat in silence all night, if needed—as long as the Vashon broke the silence first.

Once, during their long trek leaving the Frontier, Zev explained that questioning a criminal involved knowing the facts, having the evidence, a bit of intuition, but mostly, it was a mental game. While he admitted he was still developing his method, he tried to make sure that every aspect of the interrogation was controlled and presented to push a slew of answers —all from a man who had no intention of answering anything. Thus, making him speak first meant breaking down the man's first defense —silence.

"What is your name?" Zev asked.

"Not telling nothing."

Axon smirked. *You'll be telling Zev everything before the sun rises.*

"Okay. But I need to call you something. How about Stumpy?" Titters rippled through the observers.

The Vashon's nostrils flared. "Call me Wiquron—brethren of the god of Death."

"If that's what you want. Now, Wiquron, let me save us both a lot of time. I could ask you the basic questions and you could pretend you don't know what I'm talking about, but I really have no interest in that game. Instead, I'm going to tell you exactly what you did and exactly what's going to happen to you should you choose not to co-operate." Zev put up his hand to stop Wiquron from talking. "You'll get your chance, but right now, we both know anything out of your mouth is worthless."

Behind her, Axon heard Drick mutter, "This whole thing is worthless, you ask me. That man doesn't know anything about the real work of a constable."

Zev went on, "Obviously, we know the Vashon have kidnapped Ms. Mosol Thalmew, and we also know you were one of those responsible. Your mask was found in Miss Thalmew's bedroom. Of course, it's possible that your fellow Vashon placed that mask for us to find, that they wanted to implicate you, which doesn't look good for you, either. However, I find that unlikely. Too much preparation had to go into this brazen attack on the Thalmews. The Vashon wouldn't want to add another layer of complexity to their mission. Yes, I feel confident you were there."

"Not tell nothing. Never find her," Wiquron said, spitting the words as much as speaking them.

"Please, sir. I asked you to hold your tongue until I finish. The Vashon are an ancient branch off of the Cassun religion, and I know those people are exceedingly polite. Should I think less of the Vashon, or will you do a better job of representing them?"

Zev crossed his legs and waited as Wiquron struggled to process what had been said. At length, when the Vashon had been steadily silent, Zev continued.

"I also know that you and several of your fellow Vashon have been watching my assistant, Axon. One of you wears a teardrop mask, and well, look at your hand. That's all the proof we really need. I'll skip over the details, but clearly, I know what you've done. You'd be a fool to think Mr. Thalmew would let it go. In fact, I'm certain you have some ransom in mind. Not you, really, but whoever is in charge. You can wipe that protest off your face. I'm not going to ask you to betray that information."

"He's not?" Drick whispered. "What's the point of all this then?"

Axon fought down the urge to spin back and quiet the man—possibly with her fists. When she heard a harsh shushing sound followed by Drick apologizing, she knew Thalmew had done the job for her. If they still had a democracy, she would have voted for the man based on that action alone.

"You'll want to listen carefully to this next part," Zev said, edging closer in his chair. "Remember? This is the part where I tell you what's going to happen to you."

Wiquron rattled his chains with mock fear. "Scary threats."

"Not threats at all. Promises."

"Can't beat out the answers."

"Oh, I see. You think I'm threatening you with torture. No. That's the method of these lugs. But not me. I'm not with the constable service." Zev lowered his voice. "I don't follow their rules."

The menace that filled the air chilled more than the Vashon—Axon saw Thalmew and one of the constables shiver.

As if thinking up new horrors as he spoke, Zev knocked the side of his chair in a steady rhythm. "At first, I wanted to get you banished from the Vashon you love so much, but I suspect you've already done that for yourself. Isn't that right? You can't return without your mask. Once they learn you don't possess your mask anymore, that you even failed there, it's probably over for you. And once they learn that you spent the night locked in here, chatting with the constables, it's *definitely* over for you. But I can do worse than that. Right this moment, Chief Constable Drick—the bushy-faced man behind me—right this moment, he has his men digging up all they can find out about you. It shouldn't take long to locate where you live. They'll confiscate or destroy everything you own. During that process, they will find something—a painting, a letter, a locket—something that points them to a person you care about. Maybe your mother? Or a sister? Maybe an ally or a close friend? Maybe a lover. Doesn't matter to me. Whoever it is will be brought in here. I'll have that person chained to a chair right next to you. That's when the beatings will begin. You'll sit and watch Chief Constable Drick's most sadistic officer gleefully wreck the face of the one you love. Do I need to promise you more or can we finally talk?"

Axon felt a twinge of hesitation in her thoughts. Part of her knew Zev bluffed all of it. Drick had not assigned anybody to seek out the Vashon's home or loved ones, and even if he did, Zev would never agree to torturing people. But she reminded herself that they both had gone through a lot of changes alongside the world. Perhaps he—*No.* She refused to think him capable of that.

She hoped.

"Can't talk," Wiquron said, slouching his shoulders. "No answers to give."

"You have plenty of answers. For example, how many of you were involved in the kidnapping?"

"All. Each has a part. Each contributes to the whole."

"Then what was your specific part?"

The Vashon lifted his gaze toward the shadowed men in the back.

Axon saw the concern dancing in his eyes. She guessed what he would say and prepared to move fast.

Wiquron turned aside—as much as his chains allowed. "Stop the girl from fighting."

"When you and your friends broke into the bedroom, your job was to control her? Stop her struggling? How?"

"Punch. Kick. Get close and make her sleep."

"With a drug?"

He shook his head and whispered, "Punch. Kick."

"Bastard!" Thalmew lurched forward, spitting curses, his body taut, furious. "Where's my daughter?"

The constables around him had been so engrossed in Zev's interrogation, they failed to stop the man. Or perhaps they didn't want to. But before Thalmew moved beyond Zev's chair, Axon leapt forward, blocking the way.

She didn't have to do anything more. The constables woke to the situation and pulled Thalmew back into the shadowed area. But even before she heard the Vashon's snickering, she saw on Zev's face—the damage to the interrogation had been done.

Until that moment, Zev had convinced Wiquron of his failure. The Vashon's plans had been foiled and terrible retribution waited on the horizon. But Axon knew Zev saw the same thing as she did—Wiquron's posture strengthened, his eyes narrowed, and he had a damn grin on his face.

"Little girl sits with little boy," Wiquron said. "Never to return."

Screaming his throat raw, Thalmew said, "You harm her and I'll see every last Vashon in this city destroyed."

Returning to her space as the constables quieted Thalmew down, Axon tried not to betray anything—not her disappointment at the damaging outburst and not her anger being stuck under the whim of this horrible criminal. But mostly, she feared she might betray the way her heart jumped at the Vashon mentioning another. Could the *little boy* be the Shul's assistant, Byn? Is that how this Vashon got hold of the young man's pendant?

Wiquron laughed as if an audience of admirers watched him. "You too weak. All of you. That's why we took two. Little boy too weak. Little girl too weak. Maybe together they be strong enough."

Using a calm, deferential tone, Zev said, "You've seen through us. We're not like the Vashon. You all have such power. To stay out of the public eye, to live such devoted lives, and yet you never try to claim credit for your accomplishments."

"Vashon smarter."

"I'm afraid so. I had hoped to help Mr. Thalmew get his daughter back, but you've made it clear that will never happen."

Wiquron crossed his arms and puffed his chest like a conqueror. "Vashon too strong for constables."

"True, true. Even if we could find the girl, we are no match for your wits and muscle. I can only hope that you will grant me a small mercy. Would you please tell us why you want these little ones?"

"The end of East, the end of Frontier, the end of West—it all closes soon. Bones, blood, and bile. Bones, blood, and bile. The new god will rise and lay waste to the old."

With every word spoken, the Vashon shifted more and more. The clinking chains grew louder. He squinted at the group in shadow, his head lolling from side to side. Though she dismissed the thought, she could not stop it from rushing back into her head—that Vashon kept his eyes on her.

Wiquron's breathing turned shallow and fast. With an ecstatic moan, he jumped to his feet. Thalmew, Drick, and the constables flinched back. Axon held firm. If that Vashon wanted to stare at her, she could stare right back.

Zev remained seated, though his voice did not sound as calm as he tried to convey. "I didn't know the Vashon sought the end of everything. Tell me this—"

"No more." Wiquron said, wrapping himself in a hug, chains bumping against his body. He took one step closer, his gaze over Zev's head, his eyes blazing at Axon.

She clamped down the urge to storm forward and yell.

Wiquron jerked his body as if breaking his own rib. Axon swore she heard a snap. But then the sour odor of excrement wafted through the room. She glanced at the floor. Had the Vashon shat himself?

Knocking back his chair, Zev bolted to his feet and pressed back to the group. He shook his finger forward, but before he could speak, white foam spewed out of the Vashon's mouth.

"Stop him!" Drick ordered.

"Stand back!" Zev said.

Axon pulled Zev a few steps further away from the Vashon.

The blood drained from Wiquron's face leaving behind a vein-marbled alabaster as if he had been carved of fine stone. His shoulder twitched, spoiling the effect, as his head rolled back. With a nauseating crack like the opening of a yara melon dried out in the fields too long, the Vashon's head split down the middle.

Thalmew gasped and Drick spat out a curse. Nobody moved.

Except for Axon. She lurched to the left side of the room and pulled out the Blade. Its shimmering light overpowered the dim flameless and cast the room in blue.

One final cry and Wiquron's entire body split apart. Black, oily tendrils emerged from within the carcass. With a wet, hissing sound, the tendrils wriggled like newborn snakes.

CHAPTER SEVENTEEN

Though Axon's heart hammered, she kept her warrior's calm. The creature attacked. Several of its tendrils spiraled around each other and shot forward like a battering ram bent on destroying the wall of men in front of it. Another burst out of the stub at Wiquron's wrist, aiming for Axon. The first blasted one constable in the head, knocking him unconscious. The second caught Axon in the chest, thrusting her against the stone wall.

She slashed with the Blade, severing the tendril with ease. It flopped to the floor in a splash of dark liquid that smelled of rotting meat. Pushing off the wall, Axon looked up in time for a new braided tendril to bash her right back.

"I'll kill ya, bastard," Drick said, his voice strained, but Axon did not dare look over. This creature would take advantage of any lapse.

With another slash, she cut apart this new tendril but did not make the same mistake. Side-stepping, she avoided any potential direct attack as she raised her weapon and pressed forward. Another javelin of oily flesh stabbed out of the Vashon's shredded body. Axon cleaved it into pieces, never stopping her progress. Another tendril. Another slash. The closer she moved in, the less time she had to react. But still she took another step.

Uttering a rancid belch, a dozen tendrils whipped across the room at her. Axon swept the Water Blade in a wide arc as she spun and lowered

81

her body. She finished the move with the tip of the Blade pooling water on the stone floor and her back to the creature. But the sound of all the tendrils slapping the ground like week-old fish told her she had won.

Straightening, she turned to face the others. All but Zev stared at her like new recruits after their first battlefield experience. Zev, however, beamed.

The moment did not last, of course. Drick called in the hallway guards to take the injured constable off for medical treatment. Doing his best to avoid stepping in greasy dead tendril, Zev looked over the body—what remained of it.

As Axon approached, she saw Zev bend down and retrieve something. He looked at it closely before showing it to the rest. When Axon finally saw it, she understood—a metal tube small enough to fit in the palm of a hand. It had been cracked in the middle and brown liquid could be seen on the edges.

Zev said, "I didn't know the Vashon could cast spells like the Dacci."

"They can't," Drick said.

"This little vial suggests otherwise. As does this mass of human waste that just tried to kill us."

Thalmew displayed a surprising amount of control, and Axon wondered if he had some combat experience in his past. He said, "The Chief Constable is right. The Vashon have been a useless little cult for the lost and confused. None of what we've seen makes any sense. They aren't gutsy enough to orchestrate such a bold kidnapping, and they aren't smart enough to perform magic."

"Again," Zev said, gesturing to the disgusting heap around them.

But Axon saw something else. "They're right," she said, garnering Zev's raised eyebrow. "I agree that this Vashon broke open that vial—we all smelled it—but I never saw him pull out a tooth. Did anybody?"

Zev set the vial aside and crouched near the remains of Wiquron's head. "Not enough mouth left here to tell. But I think you're right. Which means that someone else cast the spell. Perhaps it was cast much earlier, set up like a tower of kindling, and he simply had to break open the vial to ignite the whole thing."

Axon lifted her Blade. "Or perhaps the spellcaster is nearby." Using all the authority years of commanding had given her voice, she said, "Chief Constable Drick, get your men searching the building as well as a three-block radius outward."

He clearly wanted to argue. A peek at Thalmew stopped him. Instead, he stomped out of the room. From down the hall, they could hear him barking orders that matched Axon's wishes.

Curling his nose as he approached, Thalmew stared at the mess that had been Wiquron. "I want to say that I'm glad he's dead, but without him, how can we possibly save my daughter?"

"I won't give up," Zev said, placing a reassuring hand on Thalmew's shoulder. "I promise you, I'll do everything I can to bring her back to you."

"I hope it's enough."

Axon said, "With Zev leading this, it'll be more than enough. He knows how to turn a setback into an advantage."

"Oh? What advantage did we gain by losing our only lead?"

Zev said, "Plenty. The biggest being that we now know the Vashon have found a method of creating spells. That is not something which happens in isolation. They will have made a larger impact on the city around them than they usually do, and that means we can find somebody who knows more about them. We can and will find a path to your daughter."

Several constables rushed by the door. Axon heard one say, "Three Vashon assaulting a constable." Another several steps behind said, "Cassett Street exit."

Axon hastened to the door, and she felt a surge when Zev moved as well. But before she could speak, he halted and turned back. "Mr. Thalmew," he said, "I urge you to go home. Be with your wife. She needs you and we need to concentrate."

"You can't do your job with me around?"

"I can. But others—especially the constables who you can fire with ease—they are probably a bit intimidated having you watch over everything."

Sticking his hands in his pockets, Thalmew shook his head. "I find my presence often sets people under pressure to perform their best. That's what I need from these constables tonight."

"That pressure can also cause mistakes to be made. I won't risk that with Mosol's life at stake. I'm sure you don't want that, either. I promise we'll let you know anything that happens as soon as it happens, but I can't have you in the way."

Thalmew appeared to weigh out the situation, so Zev added, "Good night, sir."

Without waiting to see Thalmew's reaction, Zev gestured for Axon to lead onward. They climbed the stairs to the main lobby and dashed to a door with the words *Cassett St.* above in small tiles that sparkled like gems. Already several constables stood guard at this door as others banged through.

Off to the side, a man sat on the floor soaked in sweat. Blood streaked down his face like tears. Two others tended to him—one standing behind, holding a needle and thread while forcing the man's head back. As Axon neared the door, she saw a large splotch of crimson on the walkway outside. More than should have come from the wounded constable.

When they stepped through the door, Zev squatted next to the blood. Axon gazed up and down the road. Numerous constables had lined up like soldiers guarding their barracks—facing outward, tall and straight, five paces between each, faces grim. She suspected they encircled the entire building.

From further up the road, Chief Constable Drick tramped toward them, ten men behind him—each armed with a rifle and deadly determination. Zev stood, but before he could ask, Drick slashed an arm through the air. "Out of my way."

"What are you going to do?" Zev asked. "The Vashon's already dead."

Clamping his mouth hard enough that Axon could hear his teeth slam together despite the man's overgrown mustache, Drick said, "I've got one constable inside with a head wound, and you're standing next to all that's left of Constable Worthum. They took him away."

"This doesn't make sense. Why did they attack?"

"To get their man back, obviously."

Zev looked at the blood, then the building. "They shouldn't want him back. Wiquron lost his mask. He failed them."

"Well, you've failed us and we haven't thrown you out. Admit the truth —you were wrong about them, and now they've got one of my men. I want to believe they'll seek to trade him for their man, but they haven't even bothered with demands for the Thalmew girl. What hope could we possibly have for Worthum."

Axon listened but kept her eyes roving the streets. No strange masks peeking out of alleyway shadows. Just curious and concerned pedestrians quickening their pace as they recognized something bad had happened and they didn't want to be caught up in it.

"You can't be serious," Zev said, and Axon realized she had missed part of the conversation.

Drick pointed to the door. "Go back inside. Do whatever you want. I don't care. But we're going to get our man back and see justice done."

Zev tried to say more. Drick shoved him aside, and while Axon would fight, if necessary, she did not relish the idea of taking on the entire constable service. Fortunately, Drick had no immediate plan to harm Zev. He just wanted a clear path. Marching onward, Drick and his posse of armed men headed further down the street.

Facing Axon with a frustrated grimace, Zev said, "They're going to hurt a lot of people trying to find where the Vashon took their man."

But Axon's stomach twisted at the truth. "They already know."

"How could they? Wait, do *you* know?"

"The Vashon have a few komo in the city. They're just buildings but the Vashon treat them like holy temples." She pointed in the direction of Drick and his men. "Several blocks that way is one of the newest komos."

"Then we go after them."

She clutched a handful of Zev's shirt and yanked him back. "Don't be an idiot. You get in their way and you'll be lucky if they only arrest you. Probably you'll end up needing a healer of some kind. Or a gravedigger."

"We can't sit back. They show up at that komo with their rifles and their bloodlust—all chances we've got to find Mosol Thalmew will be gone."

Axon jutted her chin toward the constable office. "That's why you are going to go back in there and search through what's left of Wiquron. If Orlar is looking over us today, she'll see to it that you find another way."

Relaxing his shoulders and rubbing his neck, Zev nodded. "Fine. I'll see what I can find. What about you?"

"Oh, I'm going to the komo. You can't take on all those men, but I certainly can."

CHAPTER EIGHTEEN

For all the tough talk she threw out, Axon had no intention of fighting ten well-trained constables. Especially after one of their own had died. But she needed Zev out of the way. And she had told the truth—though capable, he was better using his brain.

She moved fast, skirting around the block toward the Vashon komo while paralleling the posse. As long as the pedestrian traffic remained near empty—and at this late hour, she did not expect a sudden wall of people—she would easily be able to head off Drick and his men.

"Slow down, you lovely thing," a buxom prostitute said while leaning against a building decorated with garish colors. Moans blending with music rolled out of the upper-floor windows. "You in that much of a hurry for it, I'll give you a discount. Half off if you're a constable."

The prostitute yammered on, but Axon had already crossed half a block. By the time she heard the woman cursing her out for not giving her any attention (or money), Axon cut the corner and sprinted the rest of the way.

When she entered the center of the road, Drick and his men were approaching. They still had a quarter of the block to go. Axon wanted to pull out her Blade for intimidation, but she knew better. A weapon should never be drawn unless it was to be used.

"You don't want to do this," she said with a firm tone she hoped held the strength of a sword.

"Out of the way," Drick said.

"If you go in there, you're as good as killing Thalmew's daughter."

That stopped him. Raising his hand, he halted the group. "Every step we've taken tonight—every step that you and that Asterling bastard pushed us into—has led to one of my men dying, another one seriously hurt, and we're no closer to saving Thalmew's daughter. But you want me to believe that having *me* take charge here is the dangerous move?"

"You've got to trust Zev. He got more information out of that interview than you or I could have ever figured out. He's brilliant."

With a mocking snort, Drick spoke over his shoulder toward his men. "Oh, do you hear that? The Asterling bastard is brilliant. He's got it all figured out. Looks like we can just quit our jobs, men. Zev Asterling has the whole thing under control."

"At least he's not about to go destroy the best leads we'll have tonight."

"Those Vashon attached us."

"And your big plan is to go shooting up their komo. That won't accomplish anything."

"Go back to the Frontier. You don't understand the way things are in the East." With one arm, Drick forcefully pushed Axon aside and continued marching.

She wanted to resist—by Qareck, she wanted to latch onto the Chief Constable's arm, drop to the ground, use her weight to throw Drick off balance, post her foot in his gut and flip him over. Instead, as the men marched by, she said, "Doesn't matter if it's the Frontier or the East, I understand tactics. Your bit of revenge amounts to a squabble in something far bigger."

Without looking back, Drick said, "Of course. But I understand the streets. If we allow this to go unanswered, every criminal in the city will think it's okay to kill a constable."

"But Thalmew's daughter—"

"Good night, Miss Coponiv."

Axon watched the constables trudge off, and she considered running ahead. If she reached the Vashon first, she could attack them with the Blade. The sudden violence might cause them to scatter, leaving fewer victims for Drick's men. But that would be falling into the same mental trap as Drick. She needed to focus on the larger matter—Mosol Thalmew.

She headed back to the constable office headquarters and Zev.

CHAPTER NINETEEN

Zev, Pilot, and Bellemont stood on the corner when Axon arrived. Zev glanced at her and his face dropped. "That bad?"

"I couldn't stop them unless I killed them, and I don't think that would help our situation," she said. She then smiled at Bellemont and gave her old friend a hug. "It's good to see you. Even under such circumstances."

The corners of Bellemont's veil lifted from her smile. "Isn't it always under such circumstances?"

"Probably so. Still, it's good that you're here. Hold up a moment—how did you to find out about all this?"

Pilot tipped back his hat. "Why, yes indeed, for me, it is a pleasure to see you again, too."

"Ignore him," Bellemont said. "Leader Thalmew sent a message to King Robion not too long ago. I think he wanted the King to know that the negotiations might be postponed."

"And when King Robion found out that you and Zev were heading up the search for Thalmew's daughter, he sent us to give assistance."

Zev said, "They arrived shortly after you left."

"Good," Axon said. "Working with the constables is ridiculous. I think we'll do far better on our own." She noticed one empty face after the next. "I take it you didn't find anything else useful with the Vashon's body."

"Not really. Our best bet is to wait until Chief Constable Drick finishes with the Vashon in the komo. Then we can see if they'll talk with us."

In the distance, the dark street filled with the orange glow of the sun. But dawn would not arrive for a while yet.

Peering down the street, Pilot said, "Is that a fire?"

"Indeed," Axon said. "I don't think there's going to be much left of the Vashon to question."

PART II

CHAPTER ONE

Zev

They could do nothing more than wait. The fire blazed for hours, and while the brigade worked hard to control it, Drick's men had done a thorough job. By the time the fire had been extinguished and the brigade left the area, hardly anything remained of the Vashon komo.

Zev, Axon, Pilot, and Bellemont stood before the ashy ruin. The morning sun added unnecessary warmth to the street which would radiate the heat of the fire for the rest of the day. Zev tried to hide his anger and disappointment. Drick's undisciplined behavior had pushed them back several steps, and should Mosol Thalmew die because of it, Zev wondered if he might encourage a harsh reprisal. He glanced at Axon. Very harsh.

With careful steps to avoid hotspots, the group poked through the smoldering wreckage. It appeared that the brigade or another emergency group had disposed of the Vashon corpses. Or perhaps the fire had burned hot enough that even the bones had turned to ash.

Zev's stomach soured. The pleasant campfire aroma no longer smelled pleasant.

"Look here," Pilot called out. With a grunt, he heaved a charred beam aside.

Zev stepped over a pile of rubble and found Pilot with his face close to four caskets that had been stacked together. Three were barely more than blackened outlines, but the fourth retained half of its walls and a partial covering. Stranger still—there were no bodies inside. Each casket had been filled with dirt that had bluish streaks running through like dead veins.

"Is this some kind of Eastern burial thing?" Pilot asked.

"No," Zev said. "At least, nothing I've ever known about. But it might be unique to the Vashon."

"You don't sound too convinced."

"If you were running a group built on isolationism and insular behavior, then you would rely on ceremonies to keep the group together, to make them closer."

"Like a funeral."

"Exactly. How we treat our dead is vital in a society, and unless the Vashon have some way to turn their dead into blue-streaked dirt, I don't know why they would do this."

Standing back with his hands on his hips, Pilot said, "The one you fought used a spell. Maybe they've used other spells. Maybe they can transform their dead."

Shortly after, Axon came across a pile of books, papers, and scrolls. Fire had destroyed the bottom half, and the top half had been turned into a smoky mess.

"Not a smart way to store these things," she said.

Zev scanned the area for other piles—nothing. "This wasn't storage. If it were, there would be more. This—I think they wanted to destroy these particular works. Someone had the smart idea of using the fire to their advantage."

Bellemont joined, inspecting one of the scrolls least darkened with soot. "This is Dacci writing."

"What does it say?"

"I don't know. It's too old for me. There are three, arguably four, different eras of the Dacci language. I only ever learned Modern. This is mostly gibberish to me."

Scratching the stubble on his face, Zev realized how tired his body felt. His brain was even worse. Especially with each new piece of information he learned.

"This makes no sense," he said. "Why would the Vashon want anything to do with the Dacci? More than the Frontier, the Dacci want to obliterate the East. That includes the Vashon."

Axon peeked over Bellemont's shoulder. "That one in custody that used a spell similar to a Dacci spell—maybe this is how he did it."

"You think the Vashon stole Dacci papers on how to cast spells?"

"Figuring these things out is your specialty. I'm only saying that it's rather suspicious to have two incidents of Vashon being connected to the Dacci in one night."

Zev agreed with that. But as he moved closer to see where this line of thought might take them, the steady drumming of boots on stone turned all attention up the road. Chief Constable Drick marched in with seven men behind him.

Facing Axon, Zev said, "What did you do to the other three?"

"Nothing. I swear on Tiq's honor."

When they reached the property line of the komo, Drick continued straight toward Zev while his men spread out to tie a bright orange rope around the perimeter. Well before he stopped marching, Drick said, "By order of the Balica City Constable Office, this premises has been declared a criminal activity investigation. Only constables and official investigative personnel are permitted in this area." With a smarmy curl of his lips, he pointed to each one of them. "To put it in words you might understand— You. Must. Leave. Now."

CHAPTER TWO

Wait, wait, wait," Zev said, as he strode to meet Drick on a small hill of rubble.

Drick rubbed his nose with one finger before pointing that same finger at Zev. "Get your little group out. We'll be the ones to look into what happened here."

"You happened here," Axon said, stepping in front of Bellemont. "This is all your doing, and you know it. You want to hide this in a bunch of paperwork and false arrests. Anything to protect your ass."

Drick stood firm as he bared his teeth—not an easy feat for a man with such a thick mustache. "I'm done with you lot. You're not in charge here, and you have no authority."

Zev glared up at the man. His fingers trembled and a shiver rushed through his chest. "This is exactly why I never wanted to do this work again. We're trying to save a young woman's life, and it's a bunch of self-centered pricks like you that weigh your decisions based on the advantages to your own pathetic life. This isn't about your life."

"You best watch what you say. Give me enough of an excuse, and I'll have you all locked up immediately."

"You're still doing it. You're so worried about your own position in all of this that you threaten to put us behind bars, to slow down all of our progress, cause us one bureaucratic mess after another, for what? To show us you're in charge? That won't matter. Because if you do anything to block our progress, Thalmew's daughter is dead. That is if burning down the Vashon's komo didn't get her killed already."

"That's it." With trained movements, Drick took control of Zev, spinning him around, wrenching the arm behind the back, and kicking out Zev's legs.

As Zev dropped to the charred surface, he saw Axon rushing forward, the Water Blade half out. Bellemont already had a small dagger unsheathed, and her other hand gripped the small pouch at her side. There would not be time to cast a spell, but her instincts guided the action. And Pilot removed a short rifle from his coat—the barrel no longer than his forearm—and rested it on his shoulder.

Zev also heard the constables raising their rifles and getting in sturdy firing positions. He could feel Drick's fingers digging in, gripping tighter, but not entirely steady and sure.

"Call your people off," Drick said. "Call them off, and I'll only arrest you. These three can go and continue their search for Mosol Thalmew."

Axon pulled the Water Blade further out, enough that its shimmering blue light could be seen. "You call off your men, let Zev go now, and I'll allow all of you to live."

Pilot gestured toward the row of constables behind Zev. "You boys look smart to me. You should do the smart thing. This woman with the glowing sword—why, she's a living legend. She is so good with that weapon that I don't have to aim my gun. You'll all be dead before I can even take it off my shoulder."

Zev wished he could see those constables' faces. Their nervous silence told him enough. But he also knew that the distance to get to those men was too far. They would pull off several shots before Axon could cleave her Water Blade through their weapons or their necks. More importantly, battling the constables would only hinder their search. Worse than getting arrested.

But he could not accept that outcome, either.

Drick bent over, talking directly into Zev's ear. "This is going to get messy. You better convince your people to back down. No matter how this happens now, none of your people have any standing in the law. I'm well within my authority to arrest them all."

Zev perked up. "Authority? That's right. You keep saying that we don't have authority. But we do."

"Just because Thalmew asked you to look into this doesn't mean—"

"It absolutely does. If you ever thought that wasn't true, you would never have allowed me into that interrogation room. But like everything else, you're looking out for yourself. You hoped I actually would succeed in there so you could claim credit, say that you were the one who brought me in."

"Maybe we should just kill you all, and I'll put together any story I want."

"Then you really would be responsible for the death of Thalmew's daughter. There wouldn't be anybody left to blame. But if you're thinking that doesn't matter, that you're smart enough to bluff your way through it all, you should know who those other two people with me are. The one with the little dagger is King Robion's closest aide. The man in the back with the short rifle and casual attitude—that's the Captain of the Royal Guard. How do you think Hiko Thalmew, Leader of the Council for the East, will react when he finds out how you've treated two members of Frontier royalty while in the middle of peace negotiations?"

A push from behind tumbled Zev forward. Rolling onto his back, he looked up to see all the bullying swagger drain from Chief Constable Drick. Axon must have noticed the change as well because she returned her Water Blade completely to its scabbard.

The confused murmur of his men brought back his strongman façade. He crossed his arms and widened his stance. He knew his men only saw him from behind, but Zev witnessed the tremor in his eyes.

"As much as I would love to see you all rot away in the dankest part of our jails," Drick said, bellowing each word as if he had the cuffs on them already, "our duty is to protect our citizenry. We don't have time to deal with miscreants like you when the daughter of our Leader is missing. Constable Kennet, have you secured the area?"

Snapping to attention, a fair-haired man said, "Yes, sir. We roped off the ruined komo, and I've chosen Hobart and Abram to stand guard."

Glowering at Zev, Drick said, "I don't think that will be necessary quite yet."

"Sir?"

"Have Hobart and Abram go down to the Fishen Street office. They can get some breakfast. They are to return here in one hour. I don't think anybody will be around before that. After last night's festivities, I suspect the majority of people will take the morning off. The rest of you are to come with me."

"Yes, sir," Constable Kennet said before issuing orders to the men.

As their weapons were put away and they broke off in different directions—most of the men congregating across the street, waiting for their chief—Zev rose to his feet and brushed off his clothes. Drick dug his meaty paw into Zev's shoulder. "One hour. If any of your people are still here when we get back, I'll arrest them. If you are here when I get back, I'll have you shot. I don't care about the consequences—I can come up with a pretty convincing story. Understand?"

Zev held the man's eyes in silence. Not out of bravery. Zev simply didn't trust his own voice.

Once Chief Constable Drick had joined his men and they tramped up the street, Zev faced the group. Axon, Pilot, and Bellemont circled around him. They were all smiling.

Pilot chuckled. "Is there really anything else here for us to look at?"

"I doubt it," Zev said. "But we can give the place one more quick inspection while we have the time. Bellemont, if any of those books or scrolls can be salvaged, take them. Perhaps we can find somebody to translate them for us."

"We can't. Not the translating, I mean taking them with us. I tried picking up three of them already, and they fell apart. Paper and fire don't mix well."

"Then we should probably get out of here. I don't think Drick's final threats were just bluster."

Bellemont said, "Would it be possible for us to inspect Ms. Thalmew's bedroom?"

"Absolutely. I would welcome having you there. A fresh set of eyes, especially ones that have worked with me before—you might find something I missed."

"That's a great idea," Pilot said. "After all, it appears you've lost every other lead you had."

"Encouraging as ever, I see."

As they motioned to go, Zev noticed Axon standing still. When he put out his hand to her, she said, "Go without me. I had not expected to be out all night, and I have a matter I need to attend to."

"More important than Mosol Thalmew?"

"Do you honestly think I don't know what's at stake?"

Zev painted on a smile, one he had used with Lady Jos many times before, and he immediately grew disgusted with himself. Axon must have seen something on his face because she said, "Don't worry. I'll be fine."

"Of course, you will," Pilot said. "Especially because I'll be by your side."

"What? No."

Pilot hopped closer to her. "Don't be silly. You told me these Vashon were targeting you, following you around, and now you're associated with these constables who burned down their church. It's not safe for any of us to be alone right now."

Not wanting to give Axon a chance to protest, Zev said, "Then it's settled. Bellemont and I will go back to the Thalmew apartment, the two of you will do whatever Axon needs to do. When you're done, go to the Thalmew building to meet us. If we're not there, we'll leave word where we're going."

Afraid to meet Axon's eyes, Zev put his arm out for Bellemont and escorted her up the street. Drick had been right about one thing—many people slept off the night's excesses. They would have no trouble finding a seat on the public autocart. But as he walked away, he could feel eyes staring into his back.

He hoped it was his imagination.

CHAPTER THREE

Axon

Walking through the main hall of Balison Temple, Axon barely noticed the beautiful tapestries or imposing statues. If not for Pilot's awed gasps, she would have forgotten how much she loved this place. Her thoughts had latched upon her current needs and refused to let go.

Pilot gazed up at the giant statues reaching three stories high. "I forgot how strange Easterners were. All these great works of art hidden away in buildings. I much prefer the Frontier's way—outdoor temples that shared their artistic feats with all who pass."

"Are you suddenly becoming religious?"

"Never. But I can appreciate a good sculpture as I ride by on horseback. Especially on a long ride. Breaks up the monotony of tree after tree, hill after hill."

Axon led the way into Shul Ranon's attached home. The rich-textured aroma of a full breakfast filled the hallway—morning pastries that dazzled the tongue, hot cerca that warmed the belly, and even sizzling meats that watered the mouth. Entering the kitchen, she found the Shul seated at his table, a small book propped up against a pile of books as his thick lips wrapped around a mouthful of breakfast. A young woman with

STUART JAFFE

straight hair down her back moved about the kitchen with the surety of a master.

Shul Ranon glanced up at with surprised joy. "Axon, you've come to join me. How wonderful. And you've brought a friend. Please, please, sit. Anera, will you please fix two more plates and join us?"

"Of course, Shul Ranon," the woman said, bowing slightly yet never missing a step in her food preparations.

As Axon and Pilot settled at the table, two plates heaped with the morning meal were set before them. Anera walked to the corner of the kitchen with her own plate and alighted on a stool.

The Shul tucked into his food again, shaking a knife at Anera. "I've told you over and again that it's okay for you to join me at the table."

"Yes, Shul."

"Yet you insist on sitting in the corner like a punished child."

"Yes, Shul."

"Yet even Ovlar would agree that you are no child anymore. He gave you up to the warm arms of Bieck at least a year ago."

"Yes, Shul."

"Then, please, come join us."

"No, Shul. I can't."

With a long sigh, the Shul tilted his head toward Axon. "Horses don't drink just because you're at a river. Hmm, I wonder if the next generation will even understand that saying. There are babies now that will only know autocarts. A horse will be an exotic animal to them."

Pilot scraped his plate clean. "Thank you for this food. We've been working all night and I was starving."

Shul Ranon laughed and waved his fork at Pilot. "I've never seen such an appetite. Doesn't that hurt your digestion, eating so quickly?"

"I suppose I've had a few stomachaches that might have been because of eating fast, but it never really bothered me."

Though the Shul never said a word, Anera rose from her stool and outfitted Pilot with another large plate of food. He thanked her, received a shy nod, and as he picked up a cottleberry handpie, Anera returned to her stool.

Axon nudged her food around her plate. She managed a few bites—she was hungry—but she hated the idea of disappointing this old man. And he would be disappointed. Best to get it over with.

"I'm sorry, Shul, but I cannot do what you asked of me."

Shul Ranon set his cutlery down with a soft clink. He glanced at Pilot. "Perhaps you and Anera should take your plates elsewhere."

"No," Axon said. "You can trust him."

The Shul gave the idea a breath of consideration. "Anera, thank you for this wonderful morning meal. I'm afraid I must ask you to leave for a short time. Tell your mother that I'm very pleased to have you taking care of me."

Anera set her plate on the counter, but she did not leave. She stared at all the dirty pots.

"It's okay," Shul Ranon said. "I can take care of the cleanup today."

"No, sir. If I let you do that—"

"Then I would be no better or worse than anybody else. That is the truth of the matter. Qareck is the god of everything, but he is no better or worse that Tiq or Bieck or any of the gods and goddesses. So it is with the Shuls. We are not above getting our hands wet to clean some kitchenware. Especially when these items were used to feed me with such wonderful fare. Now, go. I have private matters to discuss with our guests."

Though it visibly pained her, Anera offered another fast bow and scurried from the kitchen. Axon's stomach quivered as the Shul's attention turned back toward her. She wanted to join the little girl and escape.

"I'm sorry," she said. "I know this is not what you wanted to hear."

"You haven't given that matter enough time, enough thought. What's scared you?"

"I'm not scared. I don't scare that easily."

"That's what I thought. Part of why I brought the matter to you. Yet here you sit telling me you can't do what the Nine have asked of you. What happened? When you read over Byn's notes, did you find something? Something that's frightened you?"

She shuffled her food with more vigor. "I haven't had time to look at Byn's notes."

"What? I gave those to you so that—"

"I know." The harshness in her voice stopped Pilot from eating. "I told you about my friend, Zev. He and Pilot, myself and another, we're part of a group tasked with finding a missing girl. She's been kidnapped. We've been working on that for more than a day non-stop."

The Shul wiped his mouth even as he frowned. "I see. I brought you a problem of my missing assistant and a great treasure to be found, yet you do nothing. Your friend is brought a problem of some missing girl, and everything must stop. How do you think the Nine would feel about this? Does Qareck gaze upon you with pride or regret?"

Pilot said, "There's no need for that. I'm sure Axon feels plenty bad for your missing assistant, but the fate of the peace negotiations is at stake over this girl, and without peace, many others will die in the horror of war."

"Is that true?" the Shul asked Axon.

Pilot went on, "Of course, it's true. When the Leader of the Council's daughter is kidnapped, everything is at stake."

"Axon?" the Shul prodded.

"Yes, sir, it's true. But that doesn't change anything. Like you said, the Nine put your task in front of me. There are others to find Mosol Thalmew."

The Shul's entire face widened as he sat back, kissed his hand, and wiped it across his forehead. "Mosol? No. I can't—but of course, that is the way of the Nine. So it seems. Mosol is Mosol Thalmew?"

Axon stopped pushing around her food. "You know her?"

"I guess I do. That is, well, I didn't realize I knew her, but I do."

Speaking with his mouth full, Pilot said, "How do you not know that you know somebody?"

The Shul's bald head shined as he began to sweat. "You don't understand. What I mean is that it's nothing strange. Although, in a way, I suppose it is rather unusual."

Axon placed a firm hand on the Shul's arm. "Stop babbling."

"Yes, yes, of course. My apologies. The answer is that I have met Mosol on numerous occasions, but never once did I know that she was Leader Thalmew's daughter. I only knew her as..."

"As who?"

"As Byn's girlfriend."

Axon had to shake her head a moment. Sitting back as if struck, she said, "You're saying that your assistant, the one who you sent off searching for the Cistern of Qareck, the one who went missing—you're saying that he has been in a romantic relationship with the daughter of the Leader of the Council. Is that right?"

"Mosol and Byn have been seeing each other for almost a year now. They're charming together."

Pilot belched as he wiped his mouth. "Did you see her after this Byn fellow went missing? Did she even know?"

"She absolutely knew." Shul Ranon sounded insulted by the question. "I would never lie to her."

"Then you did see her after Byn disappeared?"

"Yes. I said that already."

Axon thought she understood where Pilot headed. "She knew all about the Cistern, then, didn't she?"

The Shul looked from Pilot to Axon before lowering his eyes. "She may have been more obsessed with it than we were."

"We've got to get back to Zev," she said and Pilot jumped to his feet.

"Wait, wait," the Shul said. "You can't leave. If Mosol has been kidnapped, it's connected to Byn's disappearance. These things wouldn't both happen by chance."

"That's why Zev needs to know. We've been assuming that the Vashon acted against Mr. Thalmew by taking his daughter. Perhaps in some manner trying to influence the peace negotiations. But that's not it at all. She's been taken because of Byn and you. Because of this search for the Cistern."

"And that is the proof you've been seeking. The Nine have given you a clear sign that they want you to pursue this."

"I am pursuing this. That's why I need to speak with Zev."

"If the Nine wanted this Zev to find Byn, Mosol, and the Cistern, they would have seen fit to guide him into this temple. But they guided you, instead."

Offering Axon a plaintive grin, Pilot said, "I can talk with Zev, if you need to stay here."

She raised one finger and Pilot did not move. "It was your idea that we shouldn't be alone out there with the Vashon targeting us."

"They're targeting you. Not me."

To the Shul, she said, "I apologize for my friend. He has a complicated relationship with religion."

"We all do," the Shul said. "Some more than others. But you have always been clear in your faith. Qareck has watched over you and led you to walk with all the divine. Don't stop now."

"Why does talking with Zev mean I've stopped? I want to find—"

"Your friends are searching for Mosol Thalmew. That's all. When they find her, their purpose is complete. They take her and return her to her family. That's wonderful. But what of Byn? What of the Cistern? Without those two, all your efforts are pointless."

"But if I explain all this to Zev, then he'll help me find Byn and the Cistern."

"Perhaps. Perhaps not. I only know what the Nine have brought before me, and they did not bring Zev into this temple."

Axon didn't like how her thoughts spun—especially when the Shul made a good argument. After all, what was the point of following the gods and goddesses if she would abandon her faith because she didn't like what the deities asked of her? A religion was nothing if its foundation could be altered to suit the follower instead of the other way around.

The Shul patted her hand. "The two of you should go look through Byn's room. See what he and Mosol have done in their search. Then, if you want to return to Zev, so be it. I have faith in you and in the Nine. Whatever decision you make will be right."

Axon might never have moved again if not for Pilot's loud drumming on the table. "That sounds like an excellent suggestion. Since Byn and Mosol were together, we might find something to help us find her—and him, of course." He walked around the table and nudged Axon's shoulder. "Come on. King Robion is counting on us."

"Okay," Axon said, but she did not sound so sure.

CHAPTER FOUR

The Shul led them upstairs. Apparently, he had set Byn up with a small bedroom as far from that lonely basement desk as possible. Guilt, perhaps.

After opening a wooden door that did not properly cover the doorway, the Shul stepped back and waited. He managed a short gesture toward the room. A lot of guilt, it seemed.

Axon understood. A good Shul felt responsible for the daily lives of his people. But here, this Shul actually sent Byn down the path that led to his disappearance. Here, the Shul was not merely responsible in the abstract but directly responsible.

With Pilot at her heels, she entered the room. The early-day sun cut through the room's single window, casting a bright rectangle on the wood floor. Byn kept his things neat, organized, and clean. His books had been lined carefully along a shelf, his clothes had been folded perfectly to fit the dresser, even his pillow had a crisp, spotless appearance.

"Was Byn once a soldier?" Pilot said as he meandered through the room.

From the hallway, the Shul said, "No. He's always worked for the temple."

Axon noticed a stack of papers by the bedside. Drawings. Cisterns of numerous types—some blocky, some smooth, some deep and plain, some shallow and ornate.

The Shul had positioned in the hall to see Axon. "Those are Mosol's. She has quite a talent. Byn would research all about the Cistern, anything he could find that referenced it, and he would read passages aloud so that Mosol could bring them to life in her drawings."

"Which one is the right one?" Axon asked.

He shrugged. With exaggerated surprise, he said, "Oh, I should not have left poor Anera with such a mess. It's one thing for her to clean up after me, but it's not right to leave her with the leftovers of three people. I said I'd clean up, so I will. I'll go get started now."

As the Shul's cane tapped a rapid-fire beat down the hall, Pilot chuckled. "I think he's starting to realize how much trouble he'll be in if Leader Thalmew ever learns about Mosol's connection to Byn."

"He's not that kind of man. Not so self-centered. He's upset because of the danger they're in, and he knows he's responsible in part."

"Responsible? Not really."

"If not for him, Byn would never have pursued this Cistern. If not for Byn, Mosol would never have known about any of it."

Pilot pulled out the desk chair and sat. "If you believe the Shul and your religion, then Qareck and the rest of your deities would have made this all happen anyway."

"It doesn't work like that. We're not puppets of the gods and goddesses. We don't put on a show for them."

"Good to hear. Because I loathe the idea of anything forcing us to live a certain way. Much rather think that Mosol got caught up in all of this out of love for Byn."

Axon lowered to the edge of the bed—she didn't want to disturb its near-flawless coverings—and continued to sift through the drawings. "Until moments ago, you didn't even know about Byn."

"Doesn't matter. Love is love. It's a better way to live than hate or faith —or the both combined."

With a piercing gaze and a half-grin, Axon said, "I think love is changing you."

"What, because of Bellemont?"

"You can't pretend she's just another conquest."

"Never. For one thing, no other woman in my life can cast a spell that'll remove my skeleton and keep the rest of me in a jar. Alive." Pilot hesitated before speaking again. "With Bellemont, I worry. We're getting closer and closer. I know all about her upbringing, I know what she remembers of living in the West before she was stolen, I know her fears and her passions and all of it."

"Isn't that what you're supposed to do? What's the problem?"

"There are fundamental differences with us. I've been a soldier for the East, a hired sword, I volunteered for you, and now I'm a soldier for the Frontier. She's a Dacci. Not by upbringing, but at her core. If she had never been taken from her home, she'd be an accomplished Dacci witch right now. She'd be the enemy. I'm not worried that she'll suddenly turn on me, but I do fear that our differences are too great. Will she wake up one morning and have the realization that I'll never be able to offer her anything close to the magnitude of a spellcasting world? I wish I had an answer. Makes me wonder—how do you do it?"

Axon's head clouded at the sudden turn. "Do what?"

"You and Zev. How do you maintain a good balance in your relationship when you're so different?"

"What relationship?"

Pilot winked. "Sure. Of course. There's no relationship between you two."

"I don't know how you came to such a wrong conclusion, but Zev and I are absolutely not together in any manner other than friendship. We're certainly not romantically involved. For one thing, he's already spoken for. He's with Lady Jos."

"This is the same Lady Jos that kicked him out of her house?"

"How do you know about that?"

"Because Zev blathered on and on while we waited for you at the constable headquarters. If you want the truth, I don't think he ever had any real interest in Lady Jos. He simply thought he couldn't be with you, so he settled."

"Stop it." Axon rose to her feet. "There is no relationship. We've never been together that way. We've never even talked about such a thing."

"I notice you haven't said you're not interested, though."

Axon uttered a few flummoxed noises before finally flapping her hand at him. "Why do you even care about this?"

"You're both my friends. And I think you'd be happy together. That's my point—love is love. You should not deny that joy simply because it's inconvenient. Look at me, I worry about Bellemont and our differences, yet I still pursue that relationship."

Axon turned her back to Pilot, afraid he might spot any hint of a blush. A folded piece of paper tucked in a book caught her eye. All the other books had been left neat and ordered—indeed, all other objects in the room had been left so—yet this one paper poked out the edges of the book as if placed without care or regard.

Approaching the book as she might a cackling trodog protecting its young, Axon's heart quickened. It was only a book. Why did she feel her battle instincts kicking in? All her talk with Pilot brought Zev to mind—did he feel similar when searching a room or questioning a criminal? Could there be more alike between a warrior and a master solver than she thought?

She pulled the paper loose, opened it, and her body flushed with the triumphant joy of defeating her enemies. In her hand, she held a hastily drawn map.

Barreling down the halls, Axon clutched the paper as if it were the head of a vanquished army's general. Pilot kept close behind. Bursting into the kitchen, Axon startled Shul Ranon. He sat at the table with another plateful of food and his chin quivering.

As he set a pastry back on the plate, he let loose an uncomfortable chuckling. "I am sorry. I should've stayed with you, helped in Byn's room, but you see, it's too upsetting. And, well, I was still hungry." Wiping his entire face as if he could clean away his embarrassment like makeup, he continued, "But I should not have said I went back here to clean up. There is no excuse for lies."

Axon slapped the map onto the table. "Then don't lie about this."

The Shul slid the paper closer and narrowed his eyes. One finger traced the curving lines as if following the track of a river. Axon swore she saw a touch of relief cross his brow. He eased back and laced his fingers in his lap.

"These are the caverns and tunnels," he said. "The ones that Byn thought led to the Cistern."

"Where?"

"I can't say for certain."

Reading the moment perfectly, Pilot pounded his fist against the wall. "Try."

"Under the city," the Shul spit out. "But this isn't the entire system of tunnels and old caverns. We know the Cistern has to be down there, somewhere, but mapping the entire area would take decades. Byn thought it better to focus on specific sections based on the stories we had about the Cistern. This must be a map he made because of that work."

"But he didn't draw this, did he?" Axon said. "The lines, the controlled hand behind them—that's Mosol."

The Shul agreed. "Byn preferred words over pictures. He may have described the caverns to her and asked her to draw this."

"These caverns," Pilot said, his curious tone pulling in Axon. "Have you been in them?"

"Not far. And only twice. I tried, but traipsing through the underside of a city is not the place for an old Shul like me. Especially since you start in the sewers."

"But you were in them. At least, twice."

"Yes. That's what I said."

"The dirt in these caverns—does it have blue streaks in it?"

"Have you been in there?"

"So it does?"

"Yes. It's caused by contaminants leaking in from above. At least, that's what Byn thought."

Pilot looked over at Axon, but she didn't need a word from him.

"How do we get into the caverns?" she asked.

The Shul said, "There are several entrances—they're caverns, after all. But I only know of the one, and I'm afraid you'll find that entrance difficult, if not impossible, to use."

"You're the one who wanted me to pursue all of this. Out with it."

With a shaking hand, the Shul picked up a glass of water and sipped at it. He placed it back on the table, looking no better, and said, "The Vashon komo. The entrance we used—we had to sneak in late at night—it was in the Vashon komo."

"Which komo?" Axon's stomach twisted, knowing the answer before it came.

"It's the one several blocks down from the constable headquarters."

As Axon and Pilot left the temple, she uttered a sharp curse. Pilot gave her a quick pat on the back. "You've got to stop taking everything so hard. On the good side of this, we know exactly where to go."

"Yeah, but I don't like how this is starting to look."

"Of course not. When does it ever look good for us? Which brings up something I doubt I want to know, but now that we're out of the Shul's hearing, I figure I better ask."

"Oh?"

"What's this Cistern all about?"

Axon stopped, looked at Pilot, and burst into laughter.

CHAPTER FIVE

Zev

Pain and disgust twisted across Thalmew's face as he watched Zev and Bellemont from the doorway of his daughter's bedroom. Zev tried to be understanding. Bad enough he had lost his daughter, but now he had to let a Dacci witch sift through her things. The nuances did not matter. Zev could have spent hours explaining that Bellemont was one of the Stolen, that she was more from the Frontier than from the West, that she had helped fight off the Dacci on numerous occasions, and that she was an essential part of this investigation, but Thalmew would only see that veil masking her mouth.

Shoving those disagreeable thoughts aside, Zev tried to focus on the bedroom. Under the strength of daylight, the entire room appeared different. Shadowed corners now became visible, piles of trash could be discerned from piles of clothes, and the colors brightened in his eyes.

"It's good to be doing this with you," Bellemont said.

"I've missed it, too. We've always made a good team."

"Maybe not always."

Zev thought back to that first experience—hired by Axon to find out who had murdered one of the team and pretending to be a member of their group while looking into each one. He snickered. "Okay, not always, but mostly. I'm simply saying that I consider you a great friend, and I miss you."

"You are sorely missed in the Frontier, too."

"Not by King Robion."

Thalmew's strained voice broke in, "Why are you chit-chatting? Find my daughter."

Zev closed a drawer. "Mr. Thalmew, you have to trust that we're working on it. That's why we're in this room, searching again. Perhaps you should go downstairs and let us—"

"No. I need to see this." Thalmew flicked his finger—get back to work.

With an understanding sigh, Zev leaned against the dresser and tried to take in the area as a whole. What looked off—besides the room being ransacked?

Bellemont knelt in front of the bed and sorted through several piles. "I think King Robion misses you more than he dares admit. And Pilot definitely wishes you were around."

"The two of you are happy?" Zev asked.

Her blush rose into her eyes. "We try to be. It's difficult being what I am. The world accepts me when it's useful, but people are not so accepting when I intrude into areas they don't want me in. I'm not a person to them. Not unless I can help them in some way."

Zev turned his head to the side and approached the closet door. On the floor, he spotted a small, leather pouch. It smelled awful. Holding it for Bellemont to see, he said, "Is this what I think?"

"A witch's pouch? Yes. But not Dacci. It's like somebody trying to make it look like a Dacci pouch, but I can see from here the stitching is all wrong."

On the floor, Zev noticed a dark splotch and a small bone—perhaps from a bird. "There's no doubt now. The Vashon have been dabbling in spells, and I think they used one to take Mosol without alerting the security in this building or Mr. Thalmew's staff."

"Quite likely." Bellemont leaned over the bed, and when she straightened, she held a small diary. "Did you read through this?"

"Where was that?" he asked.

"Under the mattress, on the wall side of the bed. I used to hide mine under the bottom corner, but the principle is the same."

Sniffling back tears, Thalmew stomped one foot against the doorjamb. "That's her private journal. You shouldn't go through that."

Zev moved to block Thalmew's violent glare. "I'm sorry, but we have to read it. Not the whole thing—probably—but any entries from the last week or so could be important. If she has a boyfriend, then perhaps—"

"She doesn't."

"Sir, please. I know this is difficult, but—"

"I would know if my daughter had a boyfriend. I would know if she was caught up in something nefarious. There's nothing in her life that could lead to this kidnapping without me knowing about it."

Bellemont held the diary open. "Who is Byn Forsean?"

Zev did not need to see Thalmew's face to know that icy fingers coursed over him. Sallow-eyed and swallowing hard, Thalmew said, "W-What? I don't know that name."

"It's all over this. She met up with him regularly."

Ushering Thalmew into the hallway, Zev said, "Go back downstairs. Please. Let us do our work. There's still time to find her, but we need to focus."

"Of course, of course. I'm, that is, I'm, well, I don't understand. Why wouldn't she tell me about a boy? I never judged her for that kind of thing."

"I'm not the best one to ask. I've never understood romantic matters well at all."

"Romantic?" Thalmew's eyes widened. "You don't think they—"

The butler approached, and Zev never thought he had seen such a welcome sight. "Pardon the intrusion," the man said, making a short bow. "You have a visitor."

"I told you Mrs. Thalmew and I were not accepting anyone."

"No, sir, not you. The visitor is for Mr. Asterling."

"Oh?" Zev said. "Who wants to see me?"

"The Lady Jos."

CHAPTER SIX

The butler led Zev downstairs to a private sitting room that rivaled most rooms in any of the finest family homes. Antique chairs, finely crafted trim, exquisite and tasteful paintings, and a massive clock worth more than an average worker's yearly pay decorated the room, pulling it all together to feel warm—even cozy. Lady Jos sat on one of two cushioned chairs positioned in front of a cold fireplace.

Zev pictured Mr. and Mrs. Thalmew chatting to the flicker of firelight on a frosty winter night. Mosol would be stretched on the floor, half-listening, half-leafing through a book. Perhaps their butler would bring a carafe of hot usup tea to settle everyone before bed.

A charming image, but one that did not belong to him. He remained standing as Lady Jos turned. She had lovely eyes. She knew it. And as she gazed up at him, she angled her head to accentuate such beauty.

Looking away, Zev said, "What are you doing here?"

"That's not a very nice way to begin a conversation with the woman you intend to marry."

"You threw me out. Made it clear we were done."

"I did no such thing."

Whirling on her, Zev said, "Excuse me?"

Flashing a guilty smile, she patted the chair next to her. "This is all a misunderstanding. Please, allow me the courtesy to explain how you got this all confused."

With the blaze cooling inside him, he sat. "I don't have a lot of time."

"When I refused to see you, it was because I was angry with you. But the next morning, you were supposed to come back. I would have let you in, we would have spent an hour in bed, maybe two, and everything would be fine now. That's how it works. I can see on your face you're still confused. After spending all that time in the Frontier, I guess you never learned the basic etiquette of a relationship. But it's okay." She put her hand on his knee. "I'll help you learn."

"Not interested in learning that."

"Nonsense."

"Upstairs, right now, the Leader of the Council, the most important man in all of the East, is relying on me to find his daughter. I'd forgotten how that felt. It's been missing from my life for a long time now."

"You want people to rely on you? That's all?"

Back on his feet, Zev said, "I want to use the skills I'm good at to help people. I know that sounds idealistic, but what's the point of having everything we have, if we're not going to do anything but sit around on a pile of money?"

Lady Jos flinched. "Is that what you think of me? Of us? That everything I do and plan is so we can sit around indulging our desires? You're such a fool."

"I've been told that before."

"Sit down. Please. I can't talk to you when you're prancing around like a caged animal."

Zev recoiled at the hurt in her voice. He eased into the chair, reached over, and clasped her hands. "I want you to know that I think you're wonderful."

"Stop. You are not going to end this relationship. I know you think you have found your purpose in life, but you're wrong. You need to be honest with yourself and look at the patterns of your behavior. You are an Asterling. That is your life—born into public service and successful business. Wealth comes with that. And you like it. You liked having your father plan out your future. Now, you will love having me do it. I know you hate to admit it, but it's true. Every now and then, you feel stifled by it all, so you run away. Where other men release their stress by whoring or drinking or gambling, you go off to the Frontier for some kind of adventure. Well, you're doing it again. You're scared—of me, of marriage—and I understand that. You're not used to a woman who can handle your life. So, you run off to the nearest adventure—this

116

problem for Thalmew which you believe that only you could possibly fix."

"It's not like that at all."

"It's exactly like that. You've always been this way. When we were in our youth, I watched you play out the same behavior. In school, you thrived when the teachers told you exactly what to do, what was expected, and how your success would be measured. But there always came a point when you would balk. You would act out, get yourself in trouble, and end up being punished by the school—and presumably, your father. I watched all of that from afar. The other girls always wondered why you did it. They wanted to understand you so that they could mold you into the perfect husband for them. Not me. I accept who you are. I only ask that you accept it, too."

"You're wrong. I do accept who I am—the Master Solver from the Frontier."

Lady Jos held his eyes for a moment, and he swore he saw pity. It angered him as much as it worried him. Could she be right?

She snapped open her small handbag and pulled out something wrapped in cloth. Staring at it as if it were a puzzle she had to solve, she pressed her hand atop it. "I know you feel like everything is clear to you. That's part of the pattern you follow. You think you're never going to need me or your father or the East ever again. Just like you did when you went to the Frontier. But when things fall apart, you come back. That's why I was at Ridnight Castle for that Taladoro celebration. I wanted you to remember the good things back East—like me. And that's why I want you to have this. When that day comes, when this missing girl is found and you are either cheered or blamed, I want you to know that I'm here. When you feel lost, allow this to guide you home."

She pulled back the cloth wrapping to reveal the pin with her family crest. Placing it in his hand, she added, "I won't give up on you. When you're ready, I'm here. I'll make you into the man you were meant to be."

Bellemont knocked on the edge of the door. "I apologize for interrupting, but I think I found something."

As if a spell had been cast, Lady Jos straightened her back and all emotion evaporated from her face. She closed Zev's hand around the pin. "Adventures are fun, but they always end. I think you deserve something better. Something stable and true."

She brushed her slim dress before walking out. She never once looked at Bellemont.

"I'm sorry," Bellemont said as she took Lady Jos's seat. "Should I go say something to her?"

"By all that is holy to the Dacci, to Axon, to you and Pilot, and to King Robion himself, please don't. Just tell me what you found."

She opened the diary and pointed to an entry. "All throughout the last months of this, she writes a lot about this gentleman, Byn. She's working on a project with him, but she's very evasive in saying too much about it. She's clearly afraid somebody might do what I'm doing—reading through her entries and trying to find whatever she was up to."

"Any mention of the Vashon?"

"Not directly, but she does talk about a cultish group that sounds a lot like them to me. She definitely didn't trust this group and was afraid her boyfriend might be getting in over his head."

"Recent events suggest she was right."

"Here's the important part. On this entry, she references withdrawing funds to help her boyfriend with his project. It happens twice early in this diary, but this is the last time, and it was a few days ago. It's the only thing which strikes me as suspicious, yet it's certainly nothing worth kidnapping her over."

"You're saying that she was kidnapped because of this project instead of being the daughter of Hiko Thalmew."

"I don't know for certain, but I think it's worth looking into. Especially if the Vashon are the group she's talking about. From my research before we left the Frontier, the Vashon have little interest in politics. I think if we find out where this money came from and where it went to, we might at least get an idea of what she was involved with."

Zev cracked his knuckles as he stood. "And that might tell us who is behind the kidnapping. Good work. Let's get going."

Bellemont paused. "I can look into this myself, if you have unfinished business." She glanced at the doorway.

"Lady Jos?" He felt the pin in his pocket—when had he put it in there? —and he thought about all she had said. He had failed in the past. But she did not understand the deeper truths—that success or failure did not drive him. Rather, he found purpose behind being a true master solver.

He walked to the door. "Are you coming?"

Bellemont hurried to catch up.

CHAPTER SEVEN

Axon

When her stomach rumbled, Axon wished she had partaken in some of the Shul's breakfast. By the time they had finished with Byn's room, sent a messenger to King Robion explaining that Pilot would be absent most of the day, stood at a transit stop, rode the public autocart through the city, and returned to the cordoned-off site of the burnt Vashon komo, lunch had come and gone yet Axon never found a moment to eat. Standing at the head of an alley half-a-block down, she watched the two constables guarding the charred rubble pile and considered grabbing food from a street vendor. She could still smell the hot rhy cakes they had walked by two blocks away.

Pilot took in the street, and Axon knew he saw the same thing as she did—people. After their late night of celebration, people had finally awoken, cleared their throbbing heads, and went about not wasting the entire day. Men in suits both fashionable and old, women in dresses and gemmed dots along their noses, autocarts public and private—the city had come alive with the day's bustle.

"I'm going to take a wild guess," Pilot said. "We shouldn't walk straight up to those constables and knock them unconscious."

Axon's brief laugh relieved some of her tension. "No, that would probably draw some attention. Though, with all honesty, notice how most people are crossing the street before they reach the komo. They don't want to get too close to the constables."

"Or the destroyed komo. Isn't there some superstition about that?"

"Oh? I don't know the Vashon beliefs."

"King Robion asked all of us that were assigned to this trip to research as much as we could about Eastern culture. I know plenty about the times I lived in the East, but I never lived in a city like this. Never knew the Vashon, either. And the Frontier's writings on the subject are rather thin."

Axon grew quiet as she thought. After a moment, she said, "The mounds of dirt and wood and everything are larger than this morning."

"Chief Constable Drick must have ordered his men to start the clean-up."

"More likely they allowed others to do the cleaning. Those mounds are big, though. Shul Ranon said the door to the cavern is in the floor near the back." She pulled out Byn's map and tried to orient it with where she expected the door might be. "This thing won't be useful until we're underground."

"You're thinking we could sneak around behind those piles and the guards would never see us."

"Only problem is I don't see how we get back there. The walls of the buildings on either side don't leave much room."

"What about the building behind the komo? We could drop through a back window, perhaps."

"Which would require somebody to let us into their apartment or storage space or whatever's there. If they don't like us or trust us, they might call the constables."

Pilot inclined his head to accentuate his mocking tone. "I think we can handle getting arrested."

"I'm not worried about that. But we'll only get one chance to find that door. If we get caught, either Drick will find the door and send his men down there, which will result in more destruction, or he'll have the area covered over. No door means no mistake had been made. He'll certainly prefer that over anybody finding proof that he could have saved Mosol Thalmew and failed."

Her stomach grumbled again. Pilot grinned. "Maybe we can lure them away. They've got to be hungry, too. Get them down here to the alley, crack them on the head, and we can stroll right into the komo site."

"That might work. But Drick keeps tight control over his men. They won't break from their duties for food. We'll need a much stronger lure." She gazed down the street that led back to the constable office headquarters and thought about her recent run to intercept Drick's posse. "I know the perfect thing."

CHAPTER EIGHT

Aprostitute?" Pilot's harsh whisper earned a few raised eyebrows from passersby. "Are you trying to get me killed?"

They stood across the street from the building with the garish colors. In daylight, the place looked rather childish like an inexperienced person's idea of class. But what it lacked in elegance, it made up for in savvy.

Axon remembered what the prostitute had said—that the charge would have been half-off for a constable. Coupling that statement with the fact that this brothel stood a block-and-a-half away from headquarters told Axon everything. This business had been allowed to continue operation because it serviced the law. Smart.

"We'll be fine," Axon said. "If there's one constant in the entire world, it's the stupid decisions a man will make when offered sex."

"I'm well aware. I spent much of my life based on that fact. But that was an older life. I now work for King Robion. I'm expected to help you and Zev find Thalmew's daughter. If we smack heads with the constables, that's okay. A lot can be forgiven in the name of peace. Even trespassing behind their guards won't cause a problem. But getting caught soliciting prostitutes is not going to look good no matter how we portray it."

Axon winked. "It's only a crime if we get caught. You taught me that."

"Using my words to justify any action is proof that it's a bad idea."

Though amused by Pilot's newfound respect for authority, Axon would not be deterred. She did, however, allow him to wait outside.

When she entered the brothel, the overpowering odor of too many flowers and too much perfume assaulted her nose. She guessed most preferred that to the smell of what occurred all night long in the various backrooms.

"I remember you," a woman with long red hair and a face far too old for her body said from behind a counter. "You went running by here last night."

"That's right. I'm surprised you're still working. They let you sleep?"

"Plenty of downtime on the day shift. I'll get to rest this afternoon so that I can work again tonight. Although, you've clearly changed your mind, so maybe I need to perk up a little bit for you."

"Not for me. But how would you like to make your full price with a couple constables?"

After explaining her plan to the prostitute, Vix, the details had to change. She did not like the idea of luring these men down an alley in order to double-cross them. Having them knocked unconscious would cause the brothel and the girls a lot of trouble. "We know these men. And they know us."

"You have a better idea?"

"There's no reason to be so violent. Let me bring a friend along, and I'll make sure both of those constables are well-cared for and plenty busy. You'll have all the time you need."

Less than an hour later, Axon and Pilot watched again from the alleyway as Vix and Lytta approached the constables on guard. Though Axon could not hear them, she expected they would follow the planned script—they would tell the constables that they had been sent by some concerned friends to make sure both men were properly warm while stuck guarding debris. The smile on the constables' faces was the answer. In moments, Vix and Lytta led the men away by the hand and headed toward a vacant building down the block.

As Axon hustled to the komo, Pilot said, "That worked frighteningly well."

"Let's hope those boys have some stamina. I don't want them interrupting us."

Despite his complaining, Pilot had not lost any of his bravery. When they reached the ropes acting as a barrier to the komo's remains, he stepped right over and entered the rubble-strewn area. If anybody paid attention to what they were doing, Axon and Pilot's certainty of motion would have dissuaded most curiosity. They acted as if they were authorized to enter the area, and that surety would calm the average person's concerns.

In the space of a few breaths, they hurried to the back. There, the search began.

Axon had prepared herself for a difficult time. However, she discovered that without the darkness caused by a roof or the confusion caused by walls and hallways, they easily picked out the spot on the floor. Everywhere else, the floor had been made of wood and showed the ravages of the fire. But the entrance to the caverns had been made of stone. It looked like a circular stopper meant to plug up a bottle of wine. When the building had stood, the wood floor must have been flush with the stone plug. But now, it poked above the dirt—only obscured by burnt debris. Metal rings on either side provided handholds.

It took only two tries to open. A rope and wood ladder connected to the rim and hung down into the dark.

Pilot said, "Any idea how we'll get that covering back over the hole?"

"We won't. When those guards return, they'll pick up their posts. They're not going to come exploring back here. If Drick or any other person comes to investigate the area, let them find the hole. By the time they catch up with us, we'll either have saved the girl, found her corpse, or discovered these caverns don't lead to anything. None of it is an arrestable offense—especially for a high-ranking member of the Frontier."

As they climbed down, Pilot muttered to himself.

CHAPTER NINE

Axon's boots squished into the muddy ground. An unwelcome stench of feces permeated the air. The tunnel reached off into the distance, flameless dotted the walls, wire stretched between them, as they lit the way.

"I thought these were caverns," Pilot said. "Smells more like a sewer system."

"Sewers don't end at ladders going up into temples. But Shul Ranon did say these caverns connected to the sewer system. A city as big as this must have some way of disposing all its waste."

"How do you—you know—go? I mean, have you used one of those new water seats? They have them in our quarters here. It's very strange, but it really reduces the stink."

Axon stopped. She turned back so that her face came close to Pilot's. "Do we really need to talk about this?"

"I think you've suffered enough. Lead on."

A short distance in and the flameless were replaced by torches with real flames. Axon guessed that given enough time there would be wires running through the entire cavern/sewer system and flameless lighting every filthy corner. Even with torches, though, she could see why the Vashon had dug beneath their komo and connected with these caverns— there was an entire city down here. Or there could be.

Perhaps the Vashon dreamed of populating these twisting tunnels until they had enough people to take control above. Perhaps they were content below. No. They were not content. They had kidnapped Mosol Thalmew. Could that act be the first blow in a battle for the city? Except the Vashon lacked the numbers to launch a coup. And the skill—if Chief Constable Drick's ten men could destroy the komo with such ease, the Vashon would never succeed.

"What are they trying to do down here?" she whispered.

"Live," Pilot said, his deep voice bouncing off the tunnel walls.

She could barely see him as his dark skin helped him blend in. "They can live aboveground."

"Not free. Why do you think I left the army and roamed the country-side until I teamed up with you? Why do you think I followed you around all those years?"

"To fight for good?"

"Sometimes. But always to live a free life. Down here, the Vashon have rules to follow but those they impose upon themselves. Down here, the world belongs to them."

"Unless they just use the tunnels to travel around unnoticed."

Pilot clicked his tongue. "There's that, too. But also—"

They both froze. Up ahead, the flicker of torchlight suggested a widening area, and in that orange hue, Axon thought she saw shadows of movement. She could hear a wet, slithering sound.

She pulled out the Water Blade, its blue glow bringing to life every nook and crag and crack. They moved forward with cautious steps and entered a junction between four tunnels. One tunnel matched the bumpy hole of rock and mud and stink they had emerged from. The other two had been finished with stone walls and wooden supports.

They held still and listened once more. Water dripped somewhere down those tunnels, the different notes echoing around them became a haphazard music. But Axon did not hear anything else.

Putting her Blade away, she said, "There must be all sorts of scav-engers living down here."

"As long as they're the small vermin kind, I'm fine with it."

She turned back. "You say that now, but I recall when we were in the town of Wabund and you—"

Pilot's brow dropped low as he shoved Axon aside. In that same motion, he pulled out his short rifle and squeezed the trigger.

Like a strike of lightning and a roar of thunder overlapping in a simul-taneous blast, Axon saw the flames flash out of the weapon as its explosive noise amplified against the stone walls. He held the short rifle steady. Axon's ears rang as her eyes readjusted to the shift back into dim torchlight.

But then she saw it.

A creature—the size and shape of a malnourished man, black-brown sludge for skin, in a constant state of dripping. It crawled out of the finished tunnel on the opposite wall. When it looked up at them, its three yellow eyes narrowed on Axon. It bared sharp teeth pitted with rot, and its angered hiss left a flatulent odor lingering in the air. With a sigh, it rolled to its back and died. Thick, green goo dribbled out of the fist-sized hole in its chest.

Pilot holstered his weapon. "That thing was much bigger than vermin."

Stepping over the sludgeman, Axon peered down the tunnel. "Guess we'll go this way."

"You want to find more of those things?"

She had been in plenty of caves and dark tunnels before, but this place crawled upon her nerves. Find more of those things? Hopefully, not. But she wanted to find Mosol and Byn so they could all return to the surface before the day ended.

"Look at that thing. I see a lot of human features—two legs, two arms, thin torso, regular head. Nothing like a creature, everything like a Vashon transformed into a creature."

"You really think they've figured out magic?"

"I saw it happen in the interrogation room. It wasn't like this, but it was just as much of mess. So, this tunnel will lead to the Vashon. I hope."

Pilot followed Axon into the next tunnel as he reloaded his short rifle. She pulled out the Water Blade and kept at the ready. There would be more creatures. She had no doubt.

CHAPTER TEN

Zev

Following Mosol's path proved difficult. The bank she withdrew money from refused to speak with Zev and Bellemont. The Thalmew family's finances would remain private unless they had an order from Hiko Thalmew. Though Zev knew Mr. Thalmew would provide the order, a lot of time would be wasted trudging back to the Thalmew Building, explaining everything, dealing with his frustration and his wife's distraught outbursts, and hiking down to the bank again.

Before they embarked on such a consuming approach, Zev stepped outside of the bank and chatted with the security guard—an off-duty constable. In short order, the constable saw the light of co-operation and how helping would also improve his position in the constable service. Especially because he recalled seeing Thalmew's daughter only a few days ago. She left the bank, crossed the street, and went inside the flameless candle shop.

Zev and Bellemont met up with the shop owner, Mr. Dewest, a stooped and wrinkled man with a constant need to lick his lips.

"Of course, I remember her," he said, sitting behind a long counter filled with flameless of various styles and sizes. "When the Leader's daughter enters your store, you don't forget."

"Did she purchase anything?" Bellemont asked.

The man looked at Zev. "You have any questions for me?"

Zev gestured to Bellemont. "Did you not hear her?"

Dewest wrinkled his nose. "I've got a busy day ahead of me, but I'm happy to help Mr. Thalmew in any possible way. Do you have any questions or not?"

"Yes, we have questions. She just asked you if Ms. Thalmew purchased anything?"

"Oh, I see." He opened a ledger. "Let me take a look."

Bellemont guided Zev aside. "I'll wait on the street," she said.

"What? Why?"

"You forget—they only see a Dacci witch when they look at me."

"The Nine can burn as far as I care about that. I'll make him answer your questions."

"That's kind of you, but no. We're not here to fight all the wrongs and ills of Eastern society. We have a woman to find. To save. I'll wait outside."

Zev's muscles tensed at the idea of letting these insults pass, but he had to admit that Bellemont was right. Finding Mosol remained their most pressing task.

"Ah, here we go," Dewest said, turning the ledger to face Zev. "You can see that Ms. Thalmew purchased two handhelds from me and that I gave her a discount. I asked why she needed handhelds, and she said she was going to explore in Grenit Park."

On the end of the counter, Zev saw a square handheld. "Is this the kind of thing she bought?"

"The exact model." He picked up the square and tapped a button on the side. The front of the handheld burst with light. "I mention the park business because it's strange. There's not really anywhere to explore for which you'd need something like this. I figured she might actually be sneaking in the park late at night for a little mischief, but I couldn't say. Young people, though, even those from prominent families, are prone to mischief."

"Thank you for your time." Zev pocketed the handheld.

"Hey, you have to pay for that."

"Oh, no problem. All of my money is held by my friend outside. Should I send her back in so you can answer her questions?"

Mr. Dewest scowled. "Get out of here. Don't ever come back."

CHAPTER ELEVEN

Grenit Park. The largest park in Balica City. As the afternoon crowd staked out their spots to enjoy a respite in the warm weather, Zev and Bellemont strolled along a wooded path, each watching either side with great care.

"I don't see any place that would require this handheld," Zev said.

"Perhaps the bigot was right and she intended to come back at night. The handheld might simply be for finding her way in the dark."

"Except her parents said that she was never observed leaving their home at night. She isn't some bratty kid who sneaks out of the house while Mommy and Daddy are asleep. This is the Leader's daughter. Even if she wanted to sneak out, there are guards patrolling the building non-stop."

Bellemont pointed to a park bench. Sitting, she said, "And if she managed to get out, at some point there would be bedcheck."

"Probably. I've often thought my family was a bit crazed when it came to protecting the Asterling reputation. I can't imagine how hard it would be for a Thalmew."

Pulling out Mosol's diary, Bellemont settled back and flipped through the pages. "Something I saw earlier—right here. Listen: *The project is getting harder to keep quiet. Byn is wonderful and brave but I worry.* She takes a page or so to gush out her feelings for this boy, but then over here, she says: *There must be more than one approach to the project. I've suggested this to*

Byn, and though his boss insists that their way is the only way, that doesn't make sense to me. And then, a few days later: *Byn has agreed to meet with me in the park. I think I know another path.* That's the last entry about the project. There's a few more pages of young love and then it's done."

Zev shut his eyes and leaned back. His mind felt weighed down by all the information untethered to answers. After a moment, he rubbed his face and sat forward. "Let's think this through—we now know this project isn't just between Byn and Mosol. Byn worked for somebody else."

"We know that Mosol tried to help Byn succeed, even when she worried about the dangers."

"A dangerous project."

"To me, the strange part is that this project can apparently have multiple ways to work on it but from different locations. And how does it tie to the Vashon?"

"The Vashon part is the real oddity in all of this. Why does a group of people who wants nothing to do with society suddenly rear their heads in such a visible way, the kind of way that's going to draw a lot of attention upon them?"

Bellemont perked up. She gazed around the trees, and Zev knew to stay quiet. Whatever she had discovered, she needed a moment for her mind to put it in place.

"We're focusing on the wrong things," she finally said. "It doesn't matter what the project is or why she came to the park. Our problem is figuring out where she went from here."

"I take it you've got an idea about that."

"No. But I know how to find the answer. I'll cast a spell."

Zev's excitement dropped like a curtain at the end of the final act. "You can't."

"I will."

"But I've seen you cast many spells—ones that cost more than a single tooth. How many more teeth do you have?"

Bellemont's eyes narrowed. "That is a rude question."

"I'm not trying to offend you. I'm your friend, and I worry that you want to waste a spell on a missing girl."

"Saving a life is a waste?"

"That's not what I mean, and I think you know it." Zev noticed the stiffness in her back, the tense arms clutching her legs as she faced forward, the way her eyes locked on a tree so she would not see him. As gentle as he could manage, he said, "Forgive me for being so clumsy. I was trying to express my concern as a friend. You have an important position with King Robion now, and this matter seems so minor compared to that. But friendship still has doors that should not be opened. I suppose even Pilot shouldn't open that door."

"Not if he ever wants to be a father."

"Let me say this, though—"

Bellemont snapped towards him, her eyes seething. "You should listen to your own words before saying more. The reason I choose to cast a spell is not over a minor matter of a kidnapped girl, but a matter of peace between warring countries. It is not for one life but the thousands that will die if fighting continues."

Zev shrunk before her. "I apologize. I don't know why I said any of that. I guess that for a moment, I only thought of you. I forgot about why Mosol is so important."

"My position to the King requires me to consider the larger scope of every decision I make. I don't have the luxury of thinking smaller."

A sad laugh escaped Zev's lips. "Sorry," he said.

"What did I say that's funny?"

"When I spoke with Lady Jos, we talked about how working on a problem as a master solver gives me purpose, but I've never felt the devotion to any role in life like I see you feel toward being King Robion's aide. Makes me think perhaps Lady Jos is a little right about me."

"Why is that funny?"

"It's not." He glanced around the bench. "If you're determined to go ahead, we should get off this walking path and find a place in the woods where nobody will see. A Dacci witch casting a spell in the open will terrify people. Plus, it's not the prettiest sight."

Without further comment, Bellemont walked into the thicker woods. As Zev followed, he scanned around for any snooping eyes, curious children, or wandering hikers. Nothing. They were alone. However, the voices of those lounging in the park, children laughing and playing, and the occasional rumble of an autocart in the distance reminded Zev that their privacy was limited.

"Is this a big spell? Will it take long?" he asked.

Bellemont settled on her knees and swept together a small mound of dirt and leaves. She produced a vial from her casting pouch and dumped its foul contents onto the pile. Not much of the slimy brown concoction came out.

She glanced up at Zev. "I didn't realize how empty this was. Do you need to urinate or defecate? Either will suffice."

Pointing at the pile, Zev said, "There?"

"If you'd prefer, I'll stick my finger down my throat. Vomit is a strong spell binder. Far stronger than needed for this."

"No," he said as he stepped over to the pile. "The things I do to solve a case." He unbuttoned his pants. "Do you mind looking away? I don't have a veil for this."

Without reaction—at least, without a reaction he could see—Belle-mont turned in the direction of the walking path. Zev stood at the pile of dirt, leaves, and drops of waste, and he waited. Nothing. He felt the need, but the situation blocked his ability.

"Done?" Bellemont asked.

"I'll let you know when. This isn't something I normally do on command."

Zev closed his eyes and took several calming breaths. When he finally began, his bladder released in full force. His body relaxed. After buttoning his pants, he stepped away and told Bellemont she could continue.

She knelt before the muddy pile and raised an eyebrow. "More than enough," she said.

Before he could retort, she brought out a metal tool that always chilled Zev's skin—her tooth extractor. With sure motions, she slipped the tool under her veil. In moments, she pulled it down with a tooth held in its jaws. Blood and spit clung to the tooth as a red line dribbled down her throat. Placing the tooth atop the pile, she closed her eyes.

Zev continued to watch the surroundings. But Bellemont did not take long. With every spell she cast, she became better at it, and this spell proved the point—Zev had barely settled in when she opened her eyes and stood.

He must have looked surprised because she said, "It was a simple spell."

A golden light snaked up from the mud. Long and thin, it wound through the air, unaffected by the breeze. About ten paces away, it stopped. Hovering, it waited. The tip of its form shined brighter.

"What's it doing?" Zev asked.

"Waiting for us to follow. This path of light will sense wherever Mosol has been. We can follow her steps through the park."

Feeling that surge that always came as he closed in on answers, he said, "You're incredible."

"Make sure to remind Pilot when we get back."

They walked ahead, and the flying snake of light slithered across the air. It went over the walking path and marked a route through the wooded area on the opposite side. They headed downhill. The faster Zev moved, the faster the snake moved—always staying ahead.

Until it stopped. Zev kept walking, but the snake circled in on itself. Looking back, Bellemont crouched over something. When he returned to the spot, he saw a metal grate for draining runoff.

"She went down there?" he said, looking at the snake as if it might answer.

"I would imagine a handheld light source would be very helpful in the dark sewers."

Zev bent over, stuck his fingers in the center grips and yanked the grate open. One side had hinges that whined as he swung the grate upward. "Not much resistance. As if it had been opened recently. I guess she really did come through here."

"You doubted my spell?"

"Hoped you were wrong. I'm not looking forward to slogging through the city's waste."

He flicked on the handheld and peered down the hole. Metal rungs formed a ladder built into the wall. They looked wet. And sticky.

With dark memories of plunging his head in an outhouse, Zev climbed down into the sewer.

CHAPTER TWELVE

Axon

The passages twisted like noodles, and Axon wondered how any mind could have conceived of such a convoluted system. But when they reached the third junction and she struggled to figure out which way wouldn't turn them back on themselves, Pilot took over the lead. He had no problems at all.

"Growing up in the East has its advantages," he said.

She allowed that perhaps the passages were not so convoluted and it only appeared that way to a Frontier mind. Give her endless fields or a thick forest and she would have no problems.

A scuffing noise brought them to a halt. They crouched next to a wooden post bracing the wall and peered ahead. The passageway ended at a T-junction, and an odd light bobbed along the branch to the right. Not torchlight. Far too bright to be a wall-mounted flameless, too.

As they watched, the light held still and the scuffing noises ceased. With cautious steps, they moved forward—both listening close, both ready to fight.

A man cried out. "No!" and the distinct sounds of a fight erupted.

From the other side of the junction, a sludge creature ran by. It looked like the first, except this one lacked a head. Instead, its broad shoulders spread into a sharp-toothed gap. Axon could not tell if it had eyes or how it could see. Flapping its arms like pennants on a windy day, the creature charged toward the sounds of fighting, leaving behind footprints of refuse.

"On your left," the man yelled.

Axon knew the voice. *Zev.*

She sprinted down the tunnel, Pilot right by her side, and whipped over the corner. With the Water Blade out, she planted her feet wide. Not too far down the tunnel, Zev and Bellemont dodged blow after blow by two creatures—the headless horror they had seen and another. This one wore a Vashon mask over its fecal-covered body.

A xon and Pilot bolted forward. Bellemont ducked a wild swing from the headless beast and pivoted behind Zev. He flashed a handheld into the face of the masked creature. It squawked and jumped backwards to avoid the harsh light.

With a shake of its head, it cleared its vision and spied the new threat. Axon raised the Blade. The masked creature arched its back and let loose three short, controlled croaks.

It never made a fourth.

Pilot blasted its head into pieces as he darted by. The massive noise and sudden flash from the short rifle startled the headless one. As Pilot secured one arm around Bellemont, the creature focused on Axon—the blue Blade as much a lure as a threat.

But then it appeared to realize that there were four enemies and no allies. It flapped its arms as if it had limited muscle control over its own body. Drool flowed from the gaping mouth. And it breathed hard—not in good shape to be fighting.

Axon strode close to the thing. When it attacked, its arms slapping through the air, she ducked low. As she rose, the Blade rose with her, slicing through the torso of her opponent. The Blade severed the creature's bones, barely meeting resistance. With a shocked grunt, its top half slithered to the ground and the bottom half collapsed like a string-puppet dropped by a child.

"Thank you," Zev said, clutching his arm—a shallow cut bled through his sleeve.

Bellemont kissed Pilot for a moment, their lips pressed with her veil between.

As the embrace continued, Axon cleared her throat. "Okay, you two, enough. I doubt these are the last of whatever they are that we'll find in here."

Releasing his love, Pilot reloaded his short rifle. "They don't seem too smart."

"They don't even seem in control of themselves."

"Wait," Zev said. "Before we go barreling down this tunnel, I need something clear—what are you two doing here?"

"Same as you—seeking out Mosol. And in our case, a man named Byn."

"Byn is down here, too?"

Pilot cocked an eyebrow. "You know about him and the Cistern?"

"What cistern?"

Bellemont snapped her fingers and pointed forward. "We can discuss how we all got here later. Mosol is down that way, and I have a dark idea that these creatures were created by spells. I don't want to see the same thing happen to her, and I very much don't want to be down here longer than necessary. So, let's get moving."

Without another word, they took up a diamond formation—as best as could be done in the confines of a sewer—and headed along the tunnel. Axon led. A deep satisfaction within filled her chest. This group belonged together. This felt right.

CHAPTER THIRTEEN

Zev

I
f he had to be creeping through a slime-covered, stench-riddled tunnel, Zev could think of no better team to do it with. The trust and familiarity built over time protected them in subtle ways that Zev thought they all understood. Not having to command every action, not having to explain every decision—these things allowed them to move and react as a single unit. They were like the individual parts of a performer, and together they created a powerful force.

After a lengthy hike, they entered a domed section of the sewers, and Zev knew they would need all the cohesion they could muster.

Along the far edges of the room, several large boxes similar to caskets had been set aside—each overflowing with dirt and rocks, each pile streaked with bits of blue. Much like the rest of the sewer, the walls had been carefully masoned stone, however, bits of blue speckled the mud and mortar between the stonework. Dominating the room in the center—a massive circular hole with a knee-high wall surrounding it. It looked like a giant well. Or a cistern.

The sewer foulness surrounded them, and this well appeared to be the main source. Zev glanced at the ceiling but saw no openings. He thought for certain that the well would be the dumping ground of several sewer paths, yet he saw no pipes or openings that led into it. In fact, besides the tunnel they came through, he spotted only one other exit—on the opposite side, off to the right a bit.

Gesturing towards the enclosed well, Pilot said, "Is that what we're looking for?"

Keeping her eyes on the exit, Axon said, "Not sure."

Protruding from the walls, Zev noted several rock formations. It appeared that the sewer's engineers worked around some of the cavern's natural terrain. Perhaps this massive hole in the ground was simply another natural occurrence.

Zev inched towards the stone wall bordering the hole. Each step hit him with another wave of wretched stink. About halfway to the edge, he could see that the well had been filled like an outhouse—a thick, soupy mix of excrement, urine, and whatever other wastes the city tossed this way. Continuing forward, he noticed sticks poking up from the surface— no, not sticks. Bones.

Things had died in there. More dead things had been thrown in, too.

Small bubbles of air rose to the surface and popped, releasing miniature explosive odors that caused Zev to heave. Covering his mouth, he hurried back to the group.

"You remember the Dacci village out west? The one with open pits that the entire village relieved themselves in?"

Axon nodded. "It's hard to forget."

Nodding his head toward the well, he said, "This is worse."

The rustle of clothes and the stomp of boots echoed into the chamber. With several sharp gestures, Axon maneuvered the group behind two short sections of rock and boxes of dirt. Keeping his head low, Zev peered through a gap between two boxes.

Four Vashon entered. Each one had a rifle slung over the shoulder. They turned left and formed a line in front of the pit as if soldiers preparing for inspection.

A woman entered next—tall and lithe. She wore a hooded, leather cloak that reached the floor. Over her chest, a chain mail shirt clinked, and her pants were comprised of studded leather. At first, Zev thought he looked upon a Vashon warrior. But when she pulled back her hood and lifted her head, his stomach threatened to empty upon the floor. She wore a veil across her mouth. If he held any doubt, hearing Bellemont's soft gasp confirmed it—this was a Dacci witch.

CHAPTER FOURTEEN

The presence of a Dacci witch explained how the Vashon acquired spells. But if the witch cast the spells, she would be using up her teeth. Zev could not fathom why a witch would be willing to use so many teeth on these zealots and this kidnapping.

Then again, perhaps Thalmew was right—perhaps this entire incident concerned the peace negotiation. If the East and the Frontier stopped fighting each other, they would be able to focus their attention on the West and the Dacci. Yet, that answer did not satisfy Zev's mind. He could understand how disrupting the peace negotiations might be a bonus to the original outcome sought, but not the outcome itself. Sneaking into Balica City, establishing a working relationship with the Vashon, using them to kidnap Mosol Thalmew—far too complicated a plan to succeed. The Dacci were smart. This did not seem like a smart way.

The manner in which this particular Dacci witch dressed also troubled Zev. Other than Bellemont, he had never seen a witch wear anything but the traditional garb of black shreds of cloth.

One broad step forward and the witch put out her hands. "It is time for another offering. It is time to grow stronger."

She turned to face the Vashon and pointed from one to the next. Like a child deciding who would get the first turn at a game, she tapped the air, going down the row of Vashon and back again. Finally, her finger stopped on one wearing a mask with vertical bars across the entire face. He stepped forward.

Though Zev could not see the man's features beneath the mask, he had learned to read Bellemont's expressions from behind her veil. He felt confident that this individual did not welcome being chosen.

The Vashon shrugged off his rifle and handed it to one of the others. With a gentle bow, he said, "May Nualla accept me."

Turning back to the well, the witch said, "May Nualla accept you as our offer, and may we all gain strength having you within our army."

She lowered to her knees and folded her hands in her lap. Without a word or gesture that Zev could catch, the Vashon stepped onto the low stone wall and jumped into the foul muck.

The other Vashon and the Dacci witch leaned forward to peer down. Zev's eyes stung from not blinking. His legs cramped from being stuck in a crouched position. But he, too, could not stop watching that well.

A hand covered in brown sludge shot out of the pit and gripped the stone wall on the far end. A second hand burst forth and latched onto the wall. Then a third and fourth hand did the same. A wet, painful moan bubbled up as the Vashon pulled itself out. It no longer looked entirely like a man. Its extra limbs dragged on the floor and its head lolled to the side as if it had been hit too many times. Its feet spread out on three wide toes connected by a mucous-covered webbing.

Twisting back towards the witch, the creature opened its mouth and cried like a tortured animal.

The anticipation in the witch drifted off, lowering her shoulders and her head. Without looking up, she gestured towards one of the other Vashon. This one wore a mask with painted flames of red that licked the tips of the eyeholes.

He strode across the room, preparing his rifle, moving without hesitation. When he reached the creature, he placed the barrel against the creature's head. "Thank you for your sacrifice." He squeezed the trigger and blasted the creature back into the well.

The splash of the body wafted a thick wave of stench across Zev and the team. It not only seeped with the foulness of human waste but also the unique odor of death. Pilot stuck his mouth into the crook of his arm but it wasn't enough to stop him from coughing.

The witch's head snapped up. She narrowed her eyes upon the rocks. If she issued an order, Zev missed it. But the result was clear—the Vashon

STUART JAFFE

gripped their rifles and approached. The click of the firing hammers being pulled into place rattled in Zev's ears.

142

CHAPTER FIFTEEN

Axon

The Vashon marched toward them, and Axon tightened her grip on the Water Blade. But already she knew they had lost. Crammed together behind a small outcropping of rock, they had no room to maneuver—not when facing three rifles. Even if these Vashon had no ability to shoot straight, it would be impossible for them to miss such a bunched-up group.

Not enough time for Bellemont to cast a spell, and Zev looked lost somewhere between fascination and nausea. Pilot must have recognized their predicament, too. Instead of taking aim, he set his short rifle on the ground.

The Dacci witch hung back a few paces but followed the line of Vashon, her curiosity glimmering in her eyes. Having seen Dacci in the West, Stolen like Bellemont, and the Lost on her journey to Taladoro, Axon understood that the witches came in many varieties. This leather-clad one, however, bothered her because it stood alone among the Vashon. Alone and underground, deep in the Eastern country.

The Vashon aimed their weapons. The Dacci said, "Time to come out. I'd rather we didn't kill you. After all, eventually we'll succeed, and then I'll need all the bodies I can get for my army."

Pilot raised his hands and stood. Good man. He knew, like Axon did, that they had no other valid choice. He also clearly knew that she would not be able to take that first step.

"Don't fire," he said.

Bellemont stood next, garnering an astonished gulp from the witch. "Now, this is something," the witch said. "I know who you are. There's only one of you to know. Bellemont the Stolen, now a witch for the Frontier. I should have guessed you would be accompanying the King."

"And you are?"

"Cova, sister of three, daughter of Nualla. Now who else is behind there?"

Bellemont nudged Zev, and he stood. Axon knew she had only a brief moment left. As much as her heart wanted to fight, her mind fully accepted no fight would happen. But she refused to let those Vashon or that witch touch the Water Blade.

Her eyes bounced about the small confines until she saw it—a crack in the stonework near the base. As Zev announced his name and traded a few comments with the witch, Axon stashed the Blade inside the wall and piled a few rocks in front to hide the crack.

Standing with her hands raised, she said, "I'm the last one."

A Vashon wearing a mask painted like dripping blood said, "Mistress, can't we at least throw one of them into the Pit? Won't that be better?"

"Be quiet," Cova said, and all the Vashon tightened. "Nualla always demands sacrifice. Murder is not sacrifice."

"But we tried with that constable."

"And I was not happy. The spell is specific to your kind. I won't convert strangers until I know that when they return from the Pit, they'll be our allies. Then I'll alter the spell."

Bellemont said, "We were right, then. You're here to disrupt the peace treaty. You want the war to go on."

"Not at all." Cova pushed between two Vashon. "We're going to end the war. We're going to bring peace to everyone. You'll see."

Under tight guard, the Vashon disarmed every member of the team—patting down Axon and Pilot, in particular. They confiscated his short rifle and a dagger. From her, they swiped two daggers. Bellemont gave up her spell pouch as well as a long knife. Even Zev carried a shortblade.

He's learned a lot, she thought.

Cova dismissed them, and the Vashon escorted the team through the tunnels until they reached a cube-shaped room with a wide drain at the bottom and intake pipes poking out of various sides near the top. With only one entrance that had an iron grill for a door, it made a serviceable holding cell. Axon made sure to enter last and saw the Vashon pull a lever that released the grill down with a rusty cry.

"Well, well," Pilot said, and Axon saw that his attention drew to the back corner. Two people stooped there as if they could avoid being seen. Grinning, he looked over at Axon. "I found Byn and Mosol."

CHAPTER SIXTEEN

I t didn't take long to gain the young couple's trust. Zev mentioned
that Mosol's father had sent them to find her, and Axon added that
Shul Ranon also had concerns about their well-being. She noticed
Zev's surprise but ignored him. He did not need any explanation
regarding the Shul or the Cistern in order to save Mosol. Those were
matters for followers of the Nine.

Upon hearing of Shul Ranon, Byn's boyish face seemed to drop a few
more years. "You're *the* Axon?"

Pilot said, "Not like that, kid. She's just Axon. She doesn't need a
bigger ego."

"Shul Ranon has spoken quite often about you." Though he wore the
traditional robes of a Shul-in-training, they were filthy at the edges and
his face needed a good washing, too. If not for the constant stink in the
air, she suspected he would be noticeably malodorous. He went on,
"When you joined our temple, he knew the Nine had sent you. That you
are here, now, proves he was right."

Axon gave the iron grill a shake. Sturdy. "I wouldn't be so sure. You
really think the Nine intended for me to be locked up like this? Waiting to
be executed?"

"They won't execute us," Mosol said. She had a small frame but a
strong voice.

As Bellemont pulled close to Pilot, Zev said, "What makes you sound certain?"

"Because you're here. That means people know I'm missing. And since she's Axon, it only makes sense that you're Zev, the Master Solver. Which means that woman is Bellemont—the only decent Dacci witch I've ever heard of." She turned her focus on Pilot. "And you're?"

"Not famous, apparently," he said.

Zev said, "Our fame—or lack of it—is not going to matter. And being a Thalmew might protect you for a bit, but it won't help all of us. Including Byn."

"But the fact that you found us, that you're here—it changes things."

"Why? Do you two know what's going on down here?"

"Please, sit. We'll tell you everything."

Axon looked at the wet stone floor. "I prefer to stand."

"I think we all do," Pilot said. "But don't let us stop you. If you like sitting in scummy waters, go right ahead."

Byn said, "Once you've been standing there for nearly a day, you'll find *scummy waters* not so distasteful. But we understand."

Leaning her head on his shoulder, Mosol added, "Go on. Tell them."

When Byn paused, Bellemont said, "You don't have to be skittish about it. We already know the two of you have been engaged in a secret romance, and that Mosol has been helping you on an equally secret project. She's even funded some of it."

"How could you know that?" Mosol's head lifted as the answer came. "You read my diary."

"We needed any help we could get to find you." She pulled the diary from her pocket and handed it over.

Byn gave Mosol's shoulder a squeeze. "I first met Mosol when she came to the temple looking for guidance. She did not like the political part of her life—it wasn't her choice to be involved in those things—and she needed to find a path to call her own."

Zev said, "There's no point in lying anymore."

"I'm not. She didn't want to be involved with Thalmew politics."

"Possibly, but if she sought religious guidance, there's no reason for her to have traveled across the city into the poorest sections to seek out a temple that's barely surviving. Not when she would have gone by several Cassun temples on the way, including one only blocks from her home."

Mosol stopped Byn with a hand. "It's true that I'm not interested in my father's line of work. My passion is for history, archaeology, understanding how we came to be what we are. I first saw Byn while I was at the library. I like to spend time there. It's quiet and filled with books and scrolls all about our past. He was doing research for his Shul, and I saw him conversing with the librarian, and it hit me. I was fascinated by him. I wanted to meet him."

"That sounds more honest," Zev said. "Did you follow him that day or did it take you time to find out which temple he worked at?"

Axon heard the shift in Zev. He had a person to question and a truth to learn. Her gut tingled as she watched him proceed with the confidence and experience that had earned him his title.

"I followed him," Mosol said. "When I met Shul Ranon, I knew I had found a second home. He's a warm, delightful man who truly lives by his beliefs. Most people I've met use religion as cover for their transgressions. But he uses it as it's meant to be used. As a guide."

"You asked him about Byn?"

"I didn't need to. When he learned of my interests, he suggested that I meet one of his pupils who worked on an important project. He took me into the basement and introduced us."

"What was this project you worked on together?"

Byn said, "Shul Ranon and I have been searching for the Cistern of Qareck. We've spent a long time on this and only recently realized it was somewhere down here."

Bellemont said, "That's when you fell in love."

"Yes. I did, at least. I think Mosol took a little longer."

Nudging his shoulder, Mosol looked away and grinned. Axon marveled at how the Nine wove lives together, even in this sewer—always seeking balance. Where Byn was earnest yet protective, Mosol was practical and loyal. Where Byn was emotionally surefooted, Mosol was cautious and wary. Even the simplicity of Mosol's dark skin against Byn's pale color—all in balance.

Zev scratched his jawline as he thought. "You started going into these tunnels searching for this Cistern. Mosol bought handhelds and even discovered alternate access points."

Byn gazed upon her with a smile. "She's been wonderful. The Shul and I had learned of an entrance through the Vashon komo, but it was dangerous to use. They didn't want us in their house of worship, and we didn't like breaking in."

"Why use that entrance at all? A sewer system as big as the one for

Balica City had to have numerous entrances. Mosol found one for you without much trouble."

"Despite all my research, I had been unable to find an accurate map of the sewers. Part of the problem is that the sewers were built to utilize caverns already in existence. Part of it was bad record keeping. What I did learn suggested the Vashon entrance would be closest to our goal."

"The two of you started exploring together."

They did. Mosol's hardheaded insistence brushed aside all of Byn's concerns and desires to protect her from such a filthy place. He also welcomed the company. Her company.

While searching through the tunnels, they stumbled upon the Vashon hauling dirt from the domed room. Under the rule of the Dacci, an excavation had been taking place—the Pit. Byn and Mosol hid nearby and watched, both fascinated. But their curiosity got them noticed.

"Actually," Byn continued, "it got me noticed. The Vashon caught me, but Mosol managed to escape."

"But not undetected. They saw you run off."

Mosol said, "I ran out of the sewer and grabbed an autocart home. I wanted to warn my father right away, but the welcome celebration for the Frontier had been going on and the peace negotiations were about to begin. He was so busy, he didn't have time to listen. It was late, and I figured I'd warn him in the morning."

"That's all you did? When the Vashon had Byn?"

"I didn't know what to do. I thought about going to the constables, but I had overheard enough of my father's meetings with the Chief Constable. They were spread thin at the moment. They would have had a hard time listening to me at all, let alone when they were focused on not screwing up the end of a war. I thought about my mother, too. But then I realized I was panicking. What I should have done from the start was go the temple and tell Shul Ranon. I cleaned up from being in the sewer and put together a bag of things I thought we would need."

Even before Zev spoke, Axon saw how this played out. Zev said, "You never got out of your home. The Vashon appeared in your room."

"That Dacci witch must have cast a spell because they just flashed into existence. I didn't even have time to scream."

"They used the same magic to whisk you back down here. But something changed. The witch. She realized who you are."

"She didn't have to figure it out. I told her. I thought my father's position might help Byn and I get free."

149

"Instead, the witch realized she had acquired a great asset to leverage."

Axon saw more, though. "Cova must have learned that the Vashon screwed up their job. It wasn't a clean kidnapping. They had been keeping an eye on me, perhaps because of my connection to the Shul. They worried Byn wasn't the only one the Shul sent searching, and in their exuberance, they had drawn too much attention. Even if she wanted to kill off the both of you, she couldn't. Not when the Leader was using every resource to find you."

Mosol spit to the side. "This is everything I didn't want. I'm being used for political sport. That's all it is to these people. War, peace, money, power—it's all sport to them. I just wanted to help a man I love, find an old relic, live quiet and content."

"Me, too," Zev said.

Axon wondered if he thought of his old farm in the Frontier or his new bed with Lady Jos. Whatever her brain tried to force her into thinking, she shoved it away and focused on Byn. "Can I speak with you in private?"

Byn took a moment to understand she had spoken to him. "Oh. Of course."

He stood, and they sloshed over to the opposite corner. Zev continued asking Mosol questions. While Pilot and Bellemont put on a brave face, they clutched each other for support. Axon saw it all. The longer they spent locked away, the worse they would become.

Lowering her head close to Byn, she spoke softly. "I didn't come here for Mosol. Her father didn't send me. Shul Ranon sent me."

Byn's body drooped. "Then you're not here to rescue me. You came for the Cistern."

"Looks like I'm here for both. With what that Dacci witch did to the Cistern, turning it into a cesspool, it seems to me that—"

"No, no. It's not that," Byn said, his face perking up. "That pit of rank filth and decay is not the Cistern at all."

Axon held still. "Then where is it?"

"It's close. I know that much. Mosol and I managed to follow several routes, all of which ended up with nothing. But there are only a few possibilities left. One, in particular, is the most likely."

"Unless it's not here at all."

"It is. You think Cova and the Vashon chose this section of the sewer by accident? Special energies flow through these walls. Under this ground. Shul Ranon knew it when he sent me here. He could probably feel it."

"I wouldn't believe that. Of all people, you should know that a Shul is just a man."

"When you're an apprentice, then yes. But upon lifting into being a Shul, the Nine connect with you. That's what gives the Shul the authority to represent the Nine to our followers."

In all her years of worship, she had never heard that before. The Frontier Shuls talked of balance and purpose and all of that, too. They always said they were the Nine's representatives in the Frontier. But they never claimed to have a direct connection, a greater ability, than that of any person. However, Axon had seen many differences between the temples in the East and those in the Frontier. Perhaps this belief in a divine touch was simply another local idea.

Her nerves wriggled. "Why haven't I ever heard of this before? I've been going to Balison Temple for nearly a year."

"I shouldn't have said anything."

"But you did."

He checked back to make sure nobody listened. "This is not something we share with our followers. The fact that we have a direct connection to the Nine is only revealed to us when we have apprenticed for two years. I must be exhausted. I'm not thinking clearly."

Axon wanted to ask more questions—how was this possible? why keep it a secret? was this what led to the godwalkers?—but three Vashon trudged down the tunnel. The iron grill screeched as it lowered in the floor.

A Vashon with a circle of circles around its mask said, "Back to the Pit. All of you."

CHAPTER SEVENTEEN

Zev

The Vashon guard marched the entire lot through the winding tunnels until they reached the Pit once more. Zev's stomach gurgled discomfort—from the reek in the air which infiltrated his senses despite becoming much like background noise, and from his depth of hunger which conjured savory images despite the mountain of vileness he had witnessed. Oddly, part of him wanted to be back in that cell. Not because he feared what would come—though he had no illusions that he would enjoy the near-future—but because he wanted to question Mosol further.

He believed her. Yet he also believed that she had not told the entire truth. The conviction in her words, however, suggested that she might not know the entire truth, either. In fact, he had come to the conclusion that he needed Byn back in the conversation when the Vashon arrived.

Axon, too.

She knew more than she had shared. More about Byn, at least. This project he worked on had something to do with Axon's temple and Shul Ranon. They looked for or needed a special cistern. In the sewer systems, Zev guessed there were quite a lot of cisterns collecting rain, run off, or filtering the used water.

He had tried to get the story from Mosol, but she protected her lover's secret. Or perhaps she didn't know. Perhaps that was the truth kept from her.

And perhaps it doesn't matter.

He had to trust Axon. She had earned that more times than he dared to count. If she thought he needed to know about Byn's project, she would have told him.

Still, his mind refused to let go. Not out of sheer stubbornness or his usual rabid curiosity, but rather, he knew his mind sought a distraction. *Might have something to do with the fact that I'm being marched off to my death.* A grin graced his lips only to be ripped away as they entered the domed area and he smelled the Pit.

The Vashon lined Zev and the others in front of the outcropping of rock they had hidden behind earlier. One Vashon remained at each end of the line while six others walked to take up positions where they had stood previously. Cova stood between the two groups, opposite the entrance, creating a head to this circular Pit.

Gesturing with a spear, the Vashon next to Zev indicated that they were to kneel. Though he wanted to resist, Zev did as commanded. Axon and Pilot had done so, and he knew enough to follow their lead. If an opportunity to act came, they would be the first to move. He simply had to be ready.

And if no opportunity came?

But then Zev noticed Cova's eyes—hurt, cowed, fearful. Her body lacked the brazen strength of a Dacci witch. She looked like a child caught in a lie, awaiting punishment, yet trying to hold a brave face.

Something had changed, and that gave Zev a tinge of hope.

The answer arrived with two people entering the room. Two people who dashed Zev's hope like swatting an insect. Like Cova, they dressed in armored robes, but the first wore all white and the second all red. They were Dacci witches, and from the way Cova knelt on one knee, bowed her head, and shivered, Zev did not want to know anything more.

The Red Dacci strolled by the Pit and glanced in like a chef checking on her soup. The White Dacci followed behind, her eyes in constant surveillance of the room. When they reached Cova, Red flicked a single finger indicating Cova should stand. She obeyed.

With a quiver, she said, "I'm pleased to see you arrived safely. If you had let me know you were coming early, I would have arranged to greet you."

"More likely," Red said, her voice like grating glass, "you would have covered up your transgressions."

"I have done nothing wrong to cover up."

Like a host presenting a great prize, Red swept her arm toward Zev and the others. "Their presence suggests otherwise."

"An unfortunate result of the Vashon's actions. I told you both that we shouldn't trust Easterners in this matter."

The White Dacci, speaking with a more feminine tone, shoved Cova's shoulder. "Is that why you've been killing them off? Oh, we know all about your hasty experiments."

With a confused frown, Cova said, "Are you suggesting that I shouldn't have tested the Pit before we commit to one of the most audacious spells ever?"

Zev had to give Cova credit. Though clearly nervous, her answers came out as natural as if she believed what she said. But even if he had not earned the title Master Solver, he knew she lied.

Red's derisive huff suggested she knew it, too. "Alone, you were never going to pull off a spell of transformation. You had to have known that."

"She did," White said. "But she's always thought she could be more than our servant."

"No matter now. We are here, and together, the three of us will change the world. The Dacci will never be forgotten to history for we will write the histories for centuries to come." Red regarded the group on their knees and addressed Bellemont. "I've heard of you, of course. I wonder, though, if you will side with your own people this time."

"My people? Yes," Bellemont said. "But you are not my people. The Dacci, the Easterners, and the Frontiersmen are all the same—they are all people who want to live in peace, raise their children, and find their joys in life. People like you want to have power over others. If we didn't have you in the world—"

"You've never met me. And I've never drawn attention like you. How can you presume to know what kind of person I am?"

"I only have to look at those you associate with."

Red shifted to indicate the Vashon. "We didn't think walking down the streets of this city would be an acceptable sight to the Easterners, and we don't have a king and his army to hide behind. But the Vashon—these people you show distaste for—they have been generous and welcoming."

"Because they think they'll share in whatever power you've promised them. But I've met those like you. I know that—"

"Please, stop with your speeches." She led White and Cova around the edge of the Pit. "I'll give you a final chance to join us, though I know your answer. I simply want it spoken aloud so that Nualla does not blame us for your failings. Well? Will you join us?"

"Never. Not even if—"

"Then you can stop talking."

Red stopped with the Pit between the witches and Zev's team. They knelt and lowered their heads, preparing their spell. Zev had seen group spells before, but in those instances, the witches each had a pile of waste in front of them. They were separate spells, each part of a larger whole. Yet this—this massive Pit appeared to be the entire offering.

White rose to her feet and pulled out her tooth extractor. "Nualla, creator of all, giver of life and devourer of death, we call upon you to bring peace to the world. Bring an end to those who wish to end us and allow our people to prosper. We offer great power and life to you."

She pointed to two of the Vashon. They hesitated, but Cova said, "Trust her. Trust me. With the strength of all three of us, you will emerge a great and fierce man."

The two men stepped onto the stone wall surrounding the Pit.

Red stood next. Brandishing her extractor, she said, "Great Nualla, you have provided endlessly for the Dacci. We provide in return."

Two more Vashon joined their brethren on the wall.

Zev looked at Axon and Pilot. Neither one appeared ready to make a big move. Even Bellemont watched in fascinated horror. "Are we going to let them do this?" he whispered.

With longing, Axon peeked back at the rocks they had hid behind. "We wait until we can do something that doesn't get us killed."

"But this spell looks like something really bad."

"Of course, it's bad," Bellemont said, her frustration biting the words.

"Quiet," the guard said, smacking his spear against Zev's back. "All of you."

On the end of their line, Byn and Mosol gazed back. They were not fighters, and the hopeless acceptance of a deadly fate painted their expressions.

Cova now stood, her extractor reflecting off the torchlight as if she had it cleaned for this special occasion and wanted all to know. "Nualla, accept us and all we have prepared for you. The time has come for the Dacci to rise with you. Send your emissary and allow us to welcome this world to you."

The last two Vashon moved into position on the wall.

"Now," Red said. "Together. As one."

All the Vashon walked forward, splashing into the Pit. But Red had not referred to the Vashon. Zev's heart froze as he saw all three witches pull out their teeth. All of them. One tooth after another, they wrenched free and tossed into the Pit. Blood streamed out of their mouths, drenching their armor, as they yanked tooth after tooth.

When they finished, they stood at the edge of the Pit, gasping for air, their veils torn aside, their mouths glistening crimson horrors. The ripples in the foul waters of the Pit settled. No Vashon emerged. Muted noises rumbled in that water like unseen workers crossing a floor below.

Zev wanted to think the spell had failed. He even glanced at Bellemont in hopes of a promising reaction. But her riveted focus darkened the chance for any such optimism. The witches, too, wore anticipation like an audience waiting for a show to start. This was not over.

The quake began in the walls. A slight tremor. Barely noticeable. But it built quickly, shaking into the ground, causing small stones to clatter loose from the ceiling.

In the space of half a heartbeat, the Pit drained like the ocean tide pulling all its water away from shore. In the next beat, it regurgitated the contents, splattering the domed ceiling, painting it brown and black. Clumps of waste plopped onto the ground with awful wet smacks. The witches stood in this rain of filth with their mouths open as if celebrating a summer shower.

Though far enough back to avoid most of this deluge, Zev and the others could not avoid the smell. Byn, Mosol, and Pilot doubled over, heaving on the floor. Zev covered his mouth and nose with his hand, breathing through this inadequate filter. Bellemont and Axon stood stoic.

A loud, low *clump* punched through the air and echoed off the walls. Zev dared snatch another glance at Axon—her eyes had widened. Another clump. Something was climbing out of the Pit. Something big.

The hand that rose had too many fingers that were far too large. Seven fingers. Each as big as person. When the hand clamped down on the Pit wall, the force cracked the stone. An ear-shattering cry came up from the depths of that hole and the fingers tightened their grip.

"Rise, Emissary," Cova said, spinning with arms out like a child dancing. "Rise and take your city, your new home." Without teeth, her words were barely decipherable.

With a lurch, the Emissary pulled itself upward. A thick trunk appeared covered in filth. It filled the Pit, scraping the edges of the stone wall, and slammed into the ceiling knocking loose some of the masoned stonework. As those hand-laid rocks tumbled to the floor, the Emissary smashed into the ceiling again like a living battering ram. A hole formed, and with the ease of a snake, it continued onward, troweling through the dirt and rock above. Arm after gigantic arm pulled it further along. This grotesque mass of limbs and muscles jutting out from all sides at odd angles like a misshapen, demonic tree, dripping in a gore of rot and waste, rose through the ceiling in an unending growth.

And mouths. Zev counted at least four, and those only because they opened to reveal row upon row of jagged, blackened teeth. Eyes randomly dotted its body—some even opened on the backs of some of its hands.

With his head arched back, Zev watched this monstrosity the size of building—so far—continue to rise into the ceiling, clawing its way to the surface. The witches laughed and shouted unintelligible phrases. The two Vashon guards stared at the ceiling, too. Zev could imagine that they never thought the witches would succeed to such a degree. Other Vashon gawked from the entrances.

One wearing a mask painted with a handprint, sauntered in, trying to get a better view. The witches congregated together and watched. Zev wanted to warn the Vashon, but he had no idea what to warn him about—other than it seemed foolish to get too close to an enormous creature created by Dacci spells.

One of the Emissary's endless hands bashed down upon this curious Vashon, but it did not flatten the hapless man. There was no cry of pain. No scream of a dying soul. Instead, a sludge-covered membrane encased the man like a cocoon.

All could see his figure spasm in the flickering silhouette from the torchlight. Even as the Emissary progressed further up, its one hand leaving the cocoon behind, everyone focused on this sole Vashon.

Accompanied by the ripping sound of wet fabric, four stick-like appendages broke through the sides of his prison. A warrior's roar followed, and two pincer hands cut apart the rest of the cocoon walls. What stood before them set the witches into further dances and cackles. Cova, in particular, marveled at the sight—the Vashon had metamorphosized into a thing of sheer repulsiveness. It maintained its mask-covered Vashon head and its torso, as well. But its body was supported on these oversized insect legs. Its two arms ended in the pincer claws, and its skin had become a hard carapace. Spiked ridges ran along its chest and back.

Unlike Cova's earlier failures, this thing looked viable, vibrant, and ready to harm.

From the corner of his eye, Zev noticed Axon missing. He turned his head to catch her leaping over the rocks behind them. *Now?* he thought. She bent down, and when she rose again, she wielded the Water Blade and a savage look in her eye.

An excited rush coursed through him. But then he heard that Emissary's multi-mouthed cry as it smashed its way further up. Dirt and rocks and masoned stone dropped around them.

Zev wanted to be optimistic. He had seen Axon do amazing feats. But this? It would take far more than the Water Blade to destroy this gargantuan beast. Far more than the spells in Bellemont's mouth. Far more than anything they had at hand. As the Dacci witches predicted, Zev saw now that this creature would indeed end the war. After it leveled the city, there wouldn't be many left to keep fighting.

PART III

CHAPTER ONE

Axon

F ury burned through Axon. Her muscles heated, her tendons taut,
her heart beating fire through her veins—she had dropped her
awe and replaced it with anger at what these witches had
wrought. An abomination.

Hurdling over the outcropping, Axon allowed the Water Blade to
funnel her rage. With swift motions, she sliced apart the Vashon guard
next to Zev. The guard at the other end locked his spear into a fighting
position, but Pilot launched into the man. Trusting Pilot could handle the
guard, Axon leapt toward the massive beast still climbing out of the Pit
and through the ceiling.

She shouted and brought down the Blade with all the speed she could
create. The Blade cut through the creature like curdled milk. And nothing. Before Axon had finished the attack, before the Blade sliced out of
the Emissary's side, the wound closed up. Axon stumbled back. It was as if
she had never attacked at all.

Behind, she heard a moan. Returning to the group, she discovered that
Pilot had already knocked the guard unconscious and commandeered the
spear and a short sword. She wondered why these guards had not been
outfitted with rifles, but the answer came faster than expected. Several
arms glistening with feces and mucous reached out from the Emissary

and grabbed the Vashon at the entrances. Mere breaths later, those Vashon were cocooned, gyrating, and breaking free, newly transformed into a twisted mind's plaything. One had five hands of teeth all off of a single arm. Another had two heads on long necks ending in a body of slate muscles. Yet another crawled upon the ground in an armored shell, eight clicking legs, and a tongue that snapped into the air every few seconds.

The remaining Vashon fled. Scurrying like the creatures they feared to become, they rushed away, and only their screams carried through the tunnels. The Red witch croaked a noise and the mutated Vashon skittered after their cowardly friends. Though the last of the Emissary emerged from the Pit—a lengthy, scaled tail with sharpened spikes on the end—Axon knew the fleeing Vashon would not escape their fate. A beast like that—one with soldiers like those creatures—it would hunt down the runners. Every last one.

Axon slid Mosol and Byn behind her. She felt Pilot on her left and Zev on her right. Bellemont hung back, probably getting her mind ready to cast a spell. With the Water Blade shimmering in front, Axon stood tall and watched the witches.

Red and White observed the hole in the ceiling as more rocks splashed down into the Pit. Cova pointed across the way at Axon and opened her bloody mouth to let loose a gurgling laugh. Axon made sure to keep an eye on both entrances as well as the Dacci. If any of those creatures returned, she needed to act.

Pointing upward, White smiled and Red clapped her hands like a debutante receiving a new ballgown. Axon saw what brought such glee—sunlight. The Emissary had broken through to the surface and sunlight cast down as if breaking through storm clouds.

Red turned to the other witches and garbled some toothless words. All three stepped onto the Pit wall. With barely enough time to form the thought—*what are they going to do now?*—each witch pulled out a steel dagger and slit her own throat. Dropping the weapons, they then walked forward, tumbling several feet into the refilling Pit.

Axon and the others rushed to the wall, gazing down into the muck below. They stared. They waited. Nobody dared speak a word.

Until Mosol finally uttered a simply question. "Why?"

Bellemont said, "They had served their purpose. They succeeded. If they had remained, they would have died at our hands. This way, they deny us any vengeance. More than all of that, though—a witch without her teeth is no witch at all."

Axon scrutinized those waters for any ripple or bubble, any sign that the witches would return. But the scum riding on top settled as the waves eased into a placid stillness. At least, this much of their problems had ended.

Dim sounds from the surface weaved their way down the hole in the ceiling and bounced about the domed room. Screams. Screams of pain and panic.

Pushing off the low wall, Zev rubbed his sternum as if he had eaten something too spicy. "We need to get up there. Help stop this thing."

"Yes," Axon said. "Of course."

But in a timid yet controlled voice, Byn said, "I'm sorry. We can't go. Not yet."

CHAPTER TWO

Without speaking another word, Axon knew why Byn wanted to stay. Everybody knew. But he spoke anyway. He needed to utter his thoughts, and the group let him.

"Trust me, please." He stopped, swallowed down the shake in his throat, and spoke again. "It is more important now for us to find the Cistern of Qareck. That vileness the witches conjured—well, you're right that we must go help stop it. That's why the Shul assigned this project to me. The Cistern is legendary. It must be found."

Zev set his jaw. "We did not come here for this. Any of it. The only reason we ended up down here was to find Mosol, to bring her back to her father. The rest of this—Dacci witches, mutated Vashon, and this, this Emissary—that's not our purpose. Let us finish our task first, let us meet with Thalmew and King Robion, and from there, we'll figure out how to deal with—" He whirled a finger towards the ceiling. "—that."

"You may all go, if you want, but I must stay."

Axon respected the young man's gumption, if not his sense. "Listen to Zev. There are still Vashon and those creatures they became. They're roaming the tunnels right now. That's a lot of danger to face for a relic that you may not find."

"But—" Byn halted. He stared into Axon's eyes with an intensity that made her want to look away. "Shul Ranon didn't tell you. You don't understand why you came here."

Rolling her shoulders to stand taller, she said, "The Shul tasked me with finding you. That was all I required."

Byn's head slowly turned as he observed each member of the group. "This Cistern is no mere relic of the past. This is not simply an artifact to be studied. It is of great power."

"The Shul told me as much."

"But he didn't tell the kind of power, did he? It's called waterfire, and if half the stories I've read can be trusted, it is a volcano of energy, a storage of immense force, the kind that fuels the Dacci's magic."

Bellemont said, "Nualla fuels the Dacci."

"Then Nualla gets his power from sources like the Cistern." As if he finally decoded a secret treasure map, he faced Axon. "All we have to do is focus the Cistern's energy upon this Emissary, and with Wiq's divine guidance, we'll see the end of that terrible monstrosity. We could save everybody."

Axon could feel a tear or two forming deep within her. She marveled at this, unsure why it had happened, until she lifted her head and saw Zev staring back. She read it on his face before the thought had completely formed in her own mind—she believed Byn. The Shul, the Nine, Byn— she had been sent here for this purpose.

"I will come with you," she said, and Byn cried out, dropping to his knees as if exhausted from an arduous fight.

It was Pilot who understood first. Axon appreciated that. She always felt more confident when they were in agreement. Almost as much as when she had Zev on her side.

"Are you insane?" Zev said, the words cutting to her bone.

"You weren't with her," Pilot said. "Her Shul said—it doesn't matter. She needs to help Byn finish what brought him here in the first place."

Zev's attention never left her. "We need you and your Blade now. Come back after we stop the destruction of half the city."

"Byn?" Mosol said, her eyes watering as she rushed over to him. "You can't seriously want to keep going. Zev is right. We should leave, regroup, and when this crisis is over, then come back. My father will provide us an entire staff to explore down here."

Byn kissed her hands. "You're only saying that because you worry."

"Of course, I worry. I couldn't live on without you in my life. I love you."

He paused as if she had never spoken the words before. Except she had —Axon had no doubt. She could tell by the expression on Byn's face. It wasn't that the words were new. Rather, Mosol had never said them with such vehemence before. Perhaps it hit Byn for the first time just how deep her love went.

Axon moved closer to Zev. "You have to trust me. Pilot and Bellemont will take care of you. If you even need them. You are far more capable than you believe. You can lead them all back. You must."

"Don't do this. You can't really believe this man."

"With all we have seen, why shouldn't I believe him?"

Zev opened his mouth but no words came out.

She sympathized. They had endured so much together that it was difficult to see each other facing such dangers again. She didn't want to consider what he would face without her, but they had to part ways here. "You said that creature might destroy half the city. If we don't find the Cistern of Qareck now, it could be lost forever. It's the reason I came down here. As for that creature—even with the Water Blade, what can one person do against a mountain? But the combined armies of the Frontier and the East, that might be enough." She opened her voice to the entire group. "That's why you must get Mosol back to her father. With this beast attacking the city and Mosol missing, Thalmew will be vulnerable. The other families and their companies will turn on him, on each other—some in panic, some seeking advantage. They may even blame King Robion and the Frontier. But if Mosol is returned by Zev, the one man who represents both Frontier and East, it might be the thing needed to pull everyone together against this Dacci nightmare. It is your job, your duty, like it is mine to help Byn find the Cistern. And if it truly contains this waterfire, then maybe we can help fight the Emissary, too."

"She's right," Pilot said to Zev. "She always is."

Zev moved closer to Axon. Something crossed his face. A desire to say...but she could not figure out what else he wrestled with.

"I'll be fine," she said. "I'm glad you're worried, but you forget that I'm a good fighter."

"I'd never forget that," he said.

Warmth flushed through her at the tremble in his voice. Did he have pride in her?

"Okay," Mosol said, rubbing her tears away with her palm. Axon had missed whatever Byn said to convince Mosol, but the woman looked toward Zev with stark determination. "Mr. Asterling, will you and your friends please escort me home?"

After a quick round of *goodbyes* and *good lucks*, the group departed leaving Axon and Byn behind. Axon strapped her scabbard on and set the Water Blade inside. She picked up a dagger and handed it to Byn.

"You better not fail me," she said.

"The Cistern is real. The waterfire is powerful. We'll find it."

"I'm trusting you and the Shul, but mostly I'm trusting that the Nine have guided me to this place."

"Then we're in the best possible hands."

Before his steps could falter, he walked toward the far pathway, making sure to avoid the puddles of blood and feces. Axon followed. But she couldn't stop herself from glancing back at the other tunnel, the one Zev and the rest had taken.

CHAPTER THREE

Zev

Through one shivering breath after another, Zev tramped back along the tunnels and into the unfinished caverns. If he made a wrong turn Bellemont and Mosol both recalled the proper way. But they course-corrected without a word. They must have felt like he did—unwilling to break the silence, as if his quiet could somehow stop the reality that Axon had stayed behind.

She had said that he could handle this. She believed in him, that he could lead, that in his hands Mosol would return to her father, but what had he done in the last year to warrant such confidence? If anything, he thought Lady Jos had it right. Now that he had found Mosol, solved the problem, he would slip back into his previous behavior. He could feel it crawling up his back, peering over his shoulder, whispering doubt into his ear.

He shook off those thoughts. Right or wrong—it didn't matter. He would only consider the job finished when he shook Thalmew's hand and presented Mosol.

They turned a corner and that possibility vanished. A mound of rock and dirt barred the way. Zev walked up to the collapsed tunnel and pushed on the cold rocks.

"When that creature, the Emissary, broke through the ceiling," Pilot said, "it must have sent tremors throughout the tunnels. We should expect more of this."

Zev shoved off the new wall. "Then we're in trouble."

"Why?" Bellemont said.

"Do you know another way out of here?"

"No. But she does." Bellemont pointed to Mosol.

With a huff, Mosol said, "I can't believe I have to lead my own rescue. Come on."

After being stymied by two more collapsed tunnels, she finally found a path to a metal-rung ladder similar to the one Zev and Bellemont had climbed down in the park. They hurried up, pushed open the old grate, and one by one they emerged onto a surface street.

Standing in the dimming light, nobody moved. Black-gray smoke poured into the air several blocks away, obscuring the full strength of the sun. The smell of burning wood warned Zev that his eyes did not deceive. All around them—chaos.

Mothers clutching children ran by, tears streaming, some screaming. Four autocarts had crashed into each other at an intersection further up the road. More autocarts jammed the cross streets as too many people attempted the same desperate escape. But not everyone looked to self-preservation. Zev saw too many taking advantage of the moment—smashing store windows to loot the displays, climbing in to steal the store's money, acting as if the tragedy only meant the constables would be too busy to enforce the law. These thieves must not have seen the Emissary. If they had, no amount of free wares could keep them from running.

Motioning for the others to give way, Zev walked toward the street corner. He needed to figure out where in the city they had popped out. But his team followed as he neared the end of the street. He couldn't blame them. Nobody wanted to stand still with menace on all sides.

Zev had witnessed several shocking sights in his short life. This topped them all. A swath of devastation cut through several city blocks as if a massive tree had fallen and crushed buildings in half, nipping the corners of others, and dragging bodies from the top floor to the ground, streaking blood and gore along the way.

But it was no tree.

The trail of festering sludge the Emissary left in its wake burned the air with its toxic fumes. Holes chunked out of walls told of where the creature had clawed its way through. The constant symphony of screams acted like a siren announcing the direction of the danger.

Pilot shaded his eyes with his hand. "There aren't enough curse words to begin describing how this makes me feel."

Zev checked on Bellemont—she appeared sturdy, though in as much shocked awe as Pilot. And Mosol held still as tears dribbled down her smudged cheeks. She made no sound. Peering through this mass of destruction, he saw the Thalmew Building in the distance.

"If we don't get started, we'll never get there," he said, and walked forward. His chest loosened when he heard Pilot follow, and soon the others, too.

CHAPTER FOUR

Only a block into their journey, Zev discovered they had more to contend with than simply the aftermath of a damaging force. Roving bands of brown-cloaked figures attacked the weak and helpless. These figures all wore red masks with unique designs in white. The Vashon.

Without needing a command, Pilot, Bellemont, and Mosol each grabbed a makeshift weapon. A brick, a stone, and a table leg with nails protruding from the top. Zev directed them behind an autocart that had run straight into a storefront. The driver of the autocart—a bald, hefty man—had tried to crawl to safety but died hanging half out the side door. In his cold hand, he gripped a short rifle. Pilot pried it free, checked over the weapon, and then felt about the dead man for extra ammunition. He found four shells.

When he settled back, Pilot noticed Zev and others staring at him. "Look around you. This is war."

Zev noticed his hand had steadied. His breathing had found a clear rhythm, too. Pilot was right. This was war, and Zev had been through enough battles that his body knew how to handle it. Not that he was comfortable with the idea, but rather, he knew panic would not increase his chances of survival.

"We've got to keep moving forward," he said, glancing into the autocart. No other rifles, but a couple daggers and a hunting knife. He distributed them to the group. "We'll take it slow and careful. Move from one shielded area to another. Behind a car, in a doorway, next to rubble—anything that will protect us. Pilot, you've got the ranged weapon now, so you're first. You scout out the next safe position and wave us forward. That way you can keep that rifle out to protect the rest of us as we move. Everybody clear?"

Nobody argued. Nobody said a word. Pilot and Bellemont were too focused to offer more than a quick nod. And Mosol—the fear pasted on her skin revealed more than enough.

With his rifle pointing forward, Pilot scurried across the street to another crashed autocart. Zev took the back position, placing Mosol between him and Bellemont. Then with a quick utterance—go—they ran across the street. When they reached Pilot, Mosol shuddered out a breath.

Pilot said, "Next time, you all come across one-by-one. All together like that is too big a target."

"Good idea," Zev said, cringing inside. He'd have to be smarter about all of this or risk getting Mosol killed.

The first few blocks progressed at a decent pace. Pilot would blitz towards a new position, and the others would follow at a fast trickle. One-by-one. But when they came upon a Vashon squad trading rifle fire with three men, they had to stop.

Pilot motioned for quiet and to keep low. Zev wriggled up next to him, peering over a broken wall that had once belonged to the third floor of a nearby building and now spread across the street. The Vashon were stationed on the left. The men fought back from an improvised barrier in the middle—surrounding themselves with two dressers, an autocart door, and a metal sheet that might have been part of a worktable.

"We should help them," Pilot said.

"I know. But we have to keep Mosol safe. That's got to be the priority."

"I won't leave these men to die."

"I'm not suggesting that. But we can't run in there blind, either. We've got to find a way to give them support that doesn't expose Mosol to unnecessary risk. There's more than enough necessary risk as it is."

Pilot covered his mouth with his hand as he observed the street. Pointing to a doorway missing the door, he said, "If I can get in there, I'll be protected and I'll have a different angle on the Vashon. Not quite a flank, but pretty close. The three of you can stay hidden back here until this skirmish is over."

Zev looked at the spot Pilot had indicated and waited for some brilliant warrior's insight to hit him. Nothing came. "I guess," he said. "I don't know. You're the one with training in all of this."

"But you're the one Axon put in charge, and I trust her. Completely. So, do I go for the doorway or not?"

Sounding defeated to his own ears, Zev said, "Yeah. We have to." If anything bad happened to Mosol, he hoped her father would understand.

Pilot started to rise, but Bellemont tugged him back. "Behind the Vashon," she said.

Zev had to shift further down to see what had caught her eye. He prepared for more Vashon or even part of the Emissary—could different parts of it fight on the different blocks it stretched across?— but what he saw dropped the world from beneath his feet. A Dacci witch strode down the sidewalk, her black-strips of clothing fluttering in the air.

Holding her fist above her head, she yelled, "For Nualla!" A ring of orange-gold light formed around her fist. Charged streaks of lightning arced from finger to finger. When she brought her fist down like a hammer, the ring sped through the air and tore apart the half-made barrier protecting the men.

"Here! Come here!" Pilot yelled.

Two of the men saw him, but their confusion prevented quick action. The witch lifted her other fist, formed another ring, and threw it into the men. A plume of fire tossed all three into the air. They were dead before they hit the ground.

If the witch had heard Pilot, she did not acknowledge the fact. Instead, she barked orders at the Vashon. They packed up their weapons and rushed behind her, heading west toward erupting sounds of screams and rifle fire.

"Why'd she let us go?" Mosol asked. "Is it all over?"

"No," Pilot said. "But that spell is. She probably only had the strength or knowledge to manage those two strikes."

Bellemont tapped her mouth through her veil. "If you could've looked under, she most likely has nearly a full set of teeth."

Stepping into the open, Zev said, "This whole thing wasn't just three rogue witches. This is a full-on Dacci invasion."

Bellemont lowered her head. "It's possible that the Dacci didn't know what Cova and the two others had done until the Emissary arrived. But even if that were true, once it was conjured, they all would have felt it. I did. I thought it was because I was so close to the event, but I was wrong.

No spell using that many teeth could occur without sending waves of energy throughout the world."

"What does that mean?" Mosol said, still unable to control the fear quivering through her actions and voice. "How many witches do we have to deal with?"

"Maybe all of them. Nualla is smart and so are the witches."

"What? Nualla is real?"

Pilot winked. "Did you see the Emissary? That didn't come out of nowhere."

"But there's only the Nine."

"When you live your whole life cloistered in a city, you miss what's really out there in the world. And there's a lot more than just Nualla. Trust me on that."

"Since Nualla granted the witches the Emissary they summoned," Bellemont said, "then he must have recognized the opportunity at hand."

Ushering Pilot to follow him, Zev said, "All the nearest Dacci are joining in the fight. I'm sure there are more casting spells in the West right now, either sending aid or transporting themselves here."

"It's a risky move. A lot of teeth will be used up."

"If they fail, they'll be weak. Vulnerable."

Pilot added, "Which means they'll throw everything at us to make sure they win."

Keeping low and watching for unseen attacks, they approached the center of the street where the men had died. Two of the three rifles had been shattered, but one still looked functional. Zev inspected it, pocketed some ammunition, and waved the others to join.

"Do you know how to shoot?" he asked Mosol.

She shook her head.

"It's okay. Next rifle we find is Bellemont's."

The sky cracked with a thunderous roar and the street shivered. The Emissary. The horrendous music of wood, brick, and glass showering the ground followed. Another building must have been destroyed.

"We need to keep moving," Zev said and jogged to the position the Vashon had held. From there, they returned to a more careful approach forward until Pilot reached the end of the block. He stood and called the others to join.

When Zev reached his side, he found they had arrived at a main thoroughfare—one that had been gutted as if an earthquake had pulled the street apart. A deep chasm replaced where the street had been.

Pilot leaned over to look left and right. "I don't know the city layout well enough, but I'm guessing we need to be on the other side of this."

"Yeah," Zev said, low and soft.

"And since the Emissary is the one who caused this, I'm guessing there won't be a bridge."

"Yeah."

"Then I'm guessing this is a big problem."

"Oh, yeah."

CHAPTER FIVE

Axon

Byn lit the way with a handheld as they descended further. The
echoes of violence grew softer as the destruction of the tunnels
lessened. Byn bounced ahead like an eager boy excited to get to
the town fair.

"It shouldn't be much further," he said.

"You already know where it is?"

"I've tried just about every path that made sense. If it's not this one,
there are only two others that I can suggest."

"And if those don't pan out?"

"It won't matter—the one ahead is going to be it."

The gentle slope of the ground took them into cooler air. Fresh, too.
Axon wondered if she simply no longer noticed the stench, but no—the
air was cleaner. She inhaled deeply. Satisfyingly.

"Is this why you think you're right? The change in the air? Does the
Cistern clean the surrounding area somehow?"

With a patronizing laugh, the kind of thing a Shul often did when
trying to teach a newcomer, Byn said, "I have no idea why the air quality
has improved. But I know that we are going to find the Cistern this time
because you are here. The Nine have orchestrated so much in your life to
bring you to this point in time and to this place. Who else but you would

176

Qareck send when facing that enormous demon of the Dacci witches? Axon Coponiv, a great and lauded warrior, a hero, and a devout believer. You are the right weapon at the right time. When you succeed at destroying that abomination, it will be proof to all that the Cassun religion is the correct one."

If he thought his words would fill her with pride, he was mistaken. "I'll do my best to help, but no act of mine will suddenly bring the whole world into believing in the Nine. I've traveled enough and met many people. Even if Qareck and all the other gods and goddesses descended upon us and declared themselves real and true—even then, there would be people who did not believe. No one person is going to galvanize a revolution."

"We shall see. I have my faith."

"I have great faith in the Nine, too, but I also understand the sad reality of people."

Byn snorted a laugh that echoed its way back through the tunnel. "You don't think a Shul studies human behavior? Of course, I understand the difficulty of getting people to change their beliefs. The mind will lie to itself in order to avoid change. Sometimes to the point of self-harm. But I also know that when faced with real miracles, undeniable truths, people can surprise you. Mosol was like that. She wasn't a believer."

"I don't mean to be offensive, but I suspect she's more interested in you than your religion."

"Perhaps, at first. But she soon realized that the Nine had brought her into my life to help find the Cistern. When I needed financing and a good mind to help, she suddenly appeared. We were attracted to each other, of course, but that attraction was provided by Sazieck as a way to further the Nines' desire for us to find the Cistern. Surely, your experiences with Zev have brought up similar moments which upon deeper reflection could be assigned to the guiding hand of the Nine."

"What does Zev have to do with any of this?"

Byn stuttered a few steps. "I thought the two of you, um, that is that when I saw the way you looked at each other, I assumed…"

"You assumed wrong."

"My apologies. Clearly I've misconstrued matters."

They walked on with only their footsteps making sound. The lack of Vashon or the creatures they had become bothered Axon. It suggested those things had escaped to the surface. Picturing Zev and the others forced to fight all those creatures without her to protect them sickened her stomach.

The passageway ended in a round section with smooth walls on all sides. About the size of her bedroom, the floor also had a finished look—smooth stone and unblemished.

"This isn't right," Byn said. He pressed his hands against the walls as if he could move them through sheer will. "There should be an opening and stairs leading down. I swear. I know this is the right tunnel. It should be here. It has to be."

Axon took Byn's handheld and inspected the walls closer. There were no markings to suggest a cave-in or blocked passageway from long ago. "Perhaps you're wrong."

"No. Somebody must have known about this place and closed up the access." Byn swiped the handheld back, dropped to his knees, and scooted along the edge, pressing his face close to the floor. "There has to be a way to open the door here somewhere."

"It's good that you have faith, but—"

"This isn't faith." He shined the light in Axon's eyes. "This is fact. I'm good at what I do. I've read every story, researched every possible avenue. I didn't come down here on a whim or by mistake. That Cistern is here. And it's behind these walls."

A laugh rolled down the passageway. The laugh of a mind half-mad. A laugh dripping with blood, mucus, and bile.

Axon turned to face the entrance, raising the Water Blade. Setting her feet into a comfortable and balanced fighting stance, she let the warrior side of her brain take over. Thoughts of the Cistern, Byn's convictions, Zev's well-being, the success of getting Mosol home—it washed away, letting her focus all of her attention on the entranceway. Whatever creature came, she was ready.

She startled anyway.

Dripping filth from the Pit, the Dacci witch dressed in white armor entered. Her once pristine clothing now looked as filthy as she smelled. With her toothless mouth wide open and her eyes bulging with insanity, she leaned forward and hissed. Then she uttered one word. Difficult to decipher, but Axon understood nonetheless.

Trapped.

CHAPTER SIX

Moving slowly so as not to provoke an attack yet, Axon slipped loose her dagger and tossed it behind. "Pick that up," she said to Byn. "Flank to the right. Be ready."

"I'm not a fighter," he said, remaining against the wall.

"You don't have a choice."

"The Nine brought you here, and I have faith this is part of your purpose. I will continue to search for the way through. Trust that Qareck and Wiq will look over you."

White hissed again and her sewage breath assaulted Axon's senses as bad as any weapon.

"Byn, pick up that dagger and help me. She's got no teeth. You don't have to worry about another spell."

White laughed. "Aw teep mean eby powapool."

Axon had to work on that one but only for a little. *All teeth mean very powerful.* As the heat rose within her, Axon lowered in her stance. "This is the famed Water Blade and I am its master. You are a toothless hag. That dagger on the ground would be enough to destroy you."

"Ga ma baids too." *Got my blades too.*

Bending over, White brought her arms in. Axon pressed her feet down, about to leap on the vulnerable witch, when White thrust back her arms and opened her chest as if greeting the sun on a bright morning. She howled. Blades—hundreds of them—snicked out of her skin.

179

Some curved around her arms. Others poked straight like jagged teeth covering her chest. Skinning knives and rippled daggers ringed her face. Spiral-bladed horns protruded from her skull and swords formed a skirt of sharpened death around her waist. Blood seeped like tears, and Axon noticed tiny needles ringing White's eyes.

"Byn," Axon said, using her full-throated commander's voice. "Grab that dagger now!"

"I have faith—"

"If the Nine sent me here, then follow my orders. They come from the Nine."

She didn't think Byn could offer much help in the battle, but he would be a distraction, and Axon wanted every advantage she could have. But Byn refused to move. Whether from cowardice or faith, she couldn't tell without taking her eyes off her opponent. Whatever the case, he remained behind her.

The witch clinked as she moved. Sparks snapped out where her blades scraped against each other. And she winced. Axon caught that and some of the horror dissipated.

Bellemont had taught Axon a lot about how spells worked. After forming the offering pile and sacrificing a tooth, the witch had to build an image in her mind of the result she wanted. The clearer the image, the more specific the details, the stronger the result.

But this—White had not thought it through. She had so many blades, she could barely move without causing herself injury. Axon had a possible advantage now. She simply had to figure out how to use it.

First, she had to keep her guard up. No matter what—this was still a fight with sharp-edged weapons. All the witch required was one opening and she could wiggle her bladed body into contact, causing a tremendous amount of harm.

White circled left and Axon kept her distance. When the witch closed in on Byn, Axon slashed with the Water Blade, forcing White to either engage or circle right. She chose to circle right.

Another key piece of information. White had cast a spell that turned herself into a weapon, but she had not given herself greater fighting skill or courage. Probably didn't want to use too many teeth on herself. They were all for the Emissary. If she had used any teeth at all. Like the Vashon, this witch could have been mutated by the Emissary—or the Pit. Yes, Axon thought the same spell which conjured the Emissary out of the Pit was at work here.

She needed no more. She saw the fight like a staged dance before her —her attack, White's response, her counter-attack, White's response, her victory. Not bothering to play it out again, Axon moved.

She swung the Water Blade in a wide arc from her right side. Though she put her muscle into the attack, she moved slower than normal—slow enough that even an amateur fighter would see it coming. White swung her own right arm across to block. As expected, she overcompensated the move. When she slammed her arm against the Blade, sending sparks into the air, her momentum carried her further over. Axon, however, allowed the block to spin her, bringing the Water Blade swinging around and bashing it into White's exposed side.

The Blade sheared off a section of White's weapons. As the metal clanged on the stone floor, White hissed and jabbed. Not part of what Axon had imagined, but she knew how to improvise. She parried the attack and countered with a swift slice at the neck.

It shouldn't have worked. Most fighters would have blocked the counter, backed away, and they would have reset for another faceoff. But White was far more a novice than Axon had expected.

The Water Blade cut through the witch's neck with ease and continued into the wall. There, the Blade stopped dead. A spark upon contact, and Axon felt as if she had struck a mountain. She had to yank hard to release the Blade from the wall.

When she turned to face her enemy once more, White's head wobbled, hit the floor, and rolled into the tunnel. A trail of blood mixed with excrement, bile, and ichor Axon could not name, led to where the head came to rest. As she gazed over the headless body of blades, Axon's muscles relaxed. The fight had not lasted long enough to cause much exertion, but her body reacted nonetheless.

"What's going on over there?" Byn said, pointing to the head in the tunnel.

He flashed his handheld on White's face. The witch's skin twitched hard enough to rock the head slightly. Axon had seen post-death spasms before. Nothing to be concerned about. But these spasms continued, growing stronger. The twitching muscles vibrated unnaturally—not that anything about a toothless witch with Pit filth running through her veins was natural.

With a soft pop, the head exploded. The tiny needles and knives sticking out of her skin shot off in all directions. They pinged against the ceiling and floor, and several flew through the entranceway, falling short of Axon's feet.

A jangling sound drew her attention to White's headless body. As the arms and legs convulsed, Byn pointed with a shaking hand.

"Get down," Axon said. "Cover yourself."

She rushed over to the body, reached down, but stopped. She couldn't see a way to grab hold without slicing up her hands. Except one.

Swallowing against the rise in her throat, she thrust her hand into the open neck. The severed spine worked as a handle. Axon dragged the dead weight into the tunnel, forcing her mind to focus on taking one step after another. Breathe through the mouth. Ignore the smell. Don't think about the hard surface biting against her hand. Don't think about the fluids sloshing against her skin.

When she reached the splotch that had been White's head, the torso jerked out of her hand. The constant clanging of metal against metal grew louder. Axon sprinted back into the room and cut to the left of the entranceway.

A strong thump and blades flew everywhere. Spinning bits of metal soared into the room as Axon pressed against the wall. Byn had curled into a ball, but he had not moved from being opposite the opening. Two small knives and part of a curved sword hit him in quick succession.

Axon jumped across the room. "Don't move," she said, pulling aside his clothes to inspect the wounds. The two knives had caused long but shallow slices. They would sting, but they would heal fine. The curved sword managed to remove a chunk off his lower back. Not life threatening, but she would have to tend to it or he would lose too much blood.

Ripping strips of cloth from the bottom of Byn's robe, Axon went about binding the wound. Not much more she could do. Even cleaning it wasn't possible in a dank sewer tunnel.

"Thank you," he said, sitting back against the wall after she finished.

In one swift motion, she unsheathed the Water Blade and pointed it at him. "You will never refuse an order from me again. You understand? You say the Nine sent me here to help you, then you do what I say, or you are defying the gods and goddesses you profess to have faith in."

He squirmed, pushing his feet out, trying to meld into the wall. Axon would have lowered the Blade, confident that her point had gotten through, but she had stopped paying attention to the frightened apprentice. Instead, her gaze fell upon the wall behind him.

She moved down to one knee and brought the blue glow of the Blade close to the cold stone. The sound of Byn's confusion turning into a stunned gasp confirmed that she did, in fact, see writing on the wall. Writing only revealed by the light of the Water Blade.

CHAPTER SEVEN

Zev

Keeping the chasm on the left, they searched for the narrowest gap—somewhere they could find a way to cross. But the destruction that had created the chasm left large hills of wreckage—dirt, stone, wood, brick, and bodies. Lots of bodies.

When possible, Pilot guided the group around these horror mounds, but often they had to climb over. Zev found that to be the worst. Stepping over the dead could be hard enough but having to step on them in order to climb an obstacle—that left Zev shaken and disgusted.

The smells were worse than in the sewer, too. The reek of death surrounded them—the bile, the innards, the foulness—but unlike below, here those putrid scents blended with normal, even enticing aromas—freshly baked bread, sun-warmed brick, the trees and flowers and grass. It twisted Zev's stomach.

From atop the latest grisly hill, Pilot called back, "I think we've got something."

Zev climbed faster. When he summitted the hill, about even with the third floor of the building to his right, he saw that the chasm pinched together. Not close enough to jump, though. They needed something tall enough—

"That beam," he said. The corner building had been blasted apart—

probably by one of the Emissary's endless fists. Most of the structure had fallen upon the connecting street creating another mound of destruction. But Zev had spotted two support beams that had managed to remain standing. One reached upward—two, maybe three floors high.

Pilot wrinkled his brow as he estimated. "It could work. We just need to cut it down."

"Make sure it falls toward the chasm. We don't want to have to haul the thing over."

"Not positive we could anyway. That beam must weigh as much as half a horse."

Bellemont headed downhill. "Chatting about it won't get the job done."

"Yes, my love," Pilot said with a wink.

Bellemont giggled—actually giggled—and as Mosol joined her on the climb down, Zev had to wonder at the mind's ability to handle such a dark day. He felt a smile creep on his lips, and the flash of pleasure it brought relieved him even as it revolted him. He shouldn't allow his thoughts to wander. Not until the job was finished. Axon counted on him to get Mosol home safely, and he had to be worthy of that trust. Simple as that.

He hurried down to the corner building and joined the others in inspecting the beam. It could work. But knocking it over wouldn't be easy. Perhaps.

"Everyone get behind and push," Pilot said.

Zev didn't have much faith in the idea, but they tried anyway. All four set their hands on the same side of the beam, and under Pilot's command, they strained their muscles, pushed with their legs, and achieved nothing. They tried again. No luck.

Breathing hard, they stepped back to think. Bellemont used her short sword to hack on the bottom. Zev thought she had the right idea but the wrong tool. When felling trees for timber in the Frontier, he had a strong ax and heavy saw. From all the shattered glass on the floor and the bitter smell of ale splashed about, the place had to have been a tavern. Not likely to find those tools waiting to be discovered.

But he did smell burning wood nearby. Following his nose, he came around a collapsed wall to find two small fires unable to expand against the brick. Zev grabbed a chair and slammed it on the ground. It broke into several pieces. Yanking the chair leg free, he set it on fire and hurried back to the beam.

"Here," he said. "Let me use this first." To Mosol, he added, "Find some water or something heavy you can pat down flames with. We don't want to set the whole beam on fire."

A moment later, she came back with two thick coats. Pilot took one, and everyone crowded around the beam. Zev put the burning leg against the base. Whenever the flames got too strong, Pilot and Mosol smothered them out. Then Bellemont hacked at it with her sword. They repeated the process five times before she managed to remove a sizeable chunk.

"Good enough," Pilot said. "Let's try it."

They all returned to their original positions, and once more pushed hard against the beam. It swayed.

"Again. More."

Zev moved in closer, pressing his shoulder into the wood. The beam groaned as it inched further out. Cracking like warmed ice sent them racing back and taking cover. The base burst, thick splinters shooting off, and the beam toppled over.

When Zev emerged from behind an overturned table, he peered through the dust and smoke swirling around. Mosol and Bellemont coughed as they joined him.

"Looks good," Pilot said from the street. He had one foot pressing on the beam, bouncing the wood that stretched across the chasm. "If we go one-at-a-time, I think it'll hold fine. I'm the heaviest, so either I go first to test it or I go last, just in case."

"You go first," Bellemont said. "And we secure you with a rope."

"You afraid I might die and find some other woman in the afterlife?"

"Death? You don't get out of our relationship that easy."

Zev said, "Do we have any rope?"

"We'll find some," Bellemont said.

A horrendous cry erupted down the street and the ground shook from a hard thump—the Emissary.

"Sorry, dear," Pilot said. "Don't think we have that much time."

Bellemont tried to protest, but Pilot had already hopped onto the beam and started walking across. Spreading both arms out for balance, he moved with speed and grace. Halfway across, the beam dipped under his weight, and Zev saw Bellemont's shoulders rise with tension. But no cracking, no snapping, no screams of a man plummeting to his death. Pilot continued on until he reached the other side. He stepped off, turned back, and bowed.

"I'm going to kill him," Bellemont said as she climbed onto the beam.

186

Using the same technique—arms out for balance, straight back and steady pace—she headed out. The ground thumped again. Bellemont held still for a moment before continuing. But Mosol pressed against Zev's arm, and he could feel her shivering breath on his skin.

"I can't do this," she said. "I thought I could. I want to. But I can't. I know it."

"It'll be fine," Zev said. "I'll help you across."

"I'll fall. I won't make it, and I'll take you down with me."

Clinching her hand, he said, "That beam is wider than you think."

"No, no, you don't understand. I'm terrible at things like this. My dance instructor, when I was a kid, she said I'd be better off slopping pigs because nobody would know when I fell from clumsiness. They'd all think I slipped in pig droppings."

Another thump reverberated through the street. Gripping her hand tighter, Zev pulled her towards the beam and the chasm edge. "If we stay here, that giant creature will stomp us flat. Maybe you're right and your coordination is so bad that we might fall while we're out there. We might die. But I guarantee that we *will* die if we don't try."

Mosol winced as she gazed down the street. "I—I'm scared," she whispered.

Zev hugged her. "I know. I am, too. But you've got to be brave. Don't you want to see Byn again? Only way to do that is to cross the beam."

"Yeah. I have to see Byn again. Just like you have to see Axon."

He didn't bother to correct her. As long as she kept mumbling positively, she could plot any tale she wanted of his life. When she finally placed a foot on the beam, he jumped up to lead the way.

"Keep your eyes on my back. Don't look down. Place one foot directly in front of the other and lock your focus on me. My back. Nothing else."

The ground thumped again. This time, when the Emissary roared, it sounded close. Far too close.

CHAPTER EIGHT

Axon

Time crawled around her. Each sluggish moment weighed her shoulders down, reminding her that far above her friends rushed through city streets, trying to avoid a monster as they hoped to reunite a father and daughter. And save two countries.

Yet here she stood, holding her famed Blade up to the wall of a tiny room, lighting up symbols and words that appeared to be hidden everywhere. Byn copied them into a small notebook while sitting on the floor trying not to wince each time he moved. Early on, he said he knew the language—an ancient derivative of the original Cassunite used in the Nine's first great scrolls given to the world. Shuls learned this language as part of their apprenticeship and were tested in it as part of their requirements to gain their title. Byn had hoped that someday he would travel to the Grand Temple and read the original texts themselves.

"Reading these walls would be a better use right now," Axon said when they reached the final handful of symbols near the bottom.

"I'm trying. This isn't easy. Give me a little time to work on it."

Axon lifted her gaze to the ceiling. "We don't have a lot of that."

While Byn studied the symbols he had copied, Axon meandered to the entranceway. She had the Water Blade at her side, but if she heard anything approaching, she could have it out and attacking long before whatever creature stumbled her way knew what happened.

Nothing came along. Nothing made a sound. The Dacci witch's remains cluttered the tunnel with gore, bone, and blade. Otherwise, Axon stood alone.

She pressed her head against the cool stone wall. A warrior's life never seemed at rest. As her new life had settled in Balica City with Zev's regular visits, her trips to the Temple, and the vibrant flowing city, she had started to believe that it could end—the violence that surrounded her. Even knowing a war raged along the borders, part of her thought she deserved to put away her sword and stop thinking about better ways to kill her enemies. She had dared to think about the things her mother dreamed of for her—romance, love, marriage, children.

But who would want to be with a woman drenched in so much blood? A woman who would keep looking at her closet, itching to dig that sword out and swing it into battle once again. She had seen people addicted to drink or gambling or any number of ill-chosen behaviors. Being a warrior had its own addictions.

The intensity of battle, the rush of the conflict, the high of success—nothing else compared. The way her body felt exhausted yet tingling with exuberance—nothing else could create that. Some claimed that sex would be the thing to top all other sensations, but that had not been her experience.

Perhaps she had yet to find the right partner. Perhaps a sexual relationship was akin to having the right weapon. From the moment she first held the Water Blade, it conformed to her hands and her hands conformed to it as if they had been designed for each other and none else. Maybe people were the same way.

"I think I understand this," Byn said, his voice too loud for such a small space.

Axon eased her grip off the Blade. "Don't shout like that again. I almost took a swing at you."

If Byn heard her, he gave no indication. Instead, he struggled to his feet and inspected the wall. "As I read this, it refers to the Nine's divine cycle of Life for all and everything. The part that confused me were these circular symbols that sporadically appear. They're not words and they're not letters. They don't belong to this dialect or even this language. Until I realized there were nine of them."

"One for each of the gods and goddesses."

"Exactly." He danced his fingers along the wall until he found one of these symbols. Blowing away the dust, it became clear that the line making the circle cut deeper than the other writing around it. Byn pushed against the circle and it slipped inward with a click.

Axon bounded forward. "Where are the others? Do we push them all in?"

The one Byn had depressed popped back out. "No," he said. "It's a lock. We have to push them in the correct order."

"Which is?"

"The Life Cycle, I assume. So, we start with Tiq, Goddess of Birth." He pushed one of the circles near the bottom. "Then Ovlar, God of Childhood."

"Here," Axon said, pushing the corresponding circle. "Next is Bieck, Goddess of Adolescence." That one had been placed near the top of the writings.

They proceeded to locate the remaining circles and Byn ticked them off one by one. "Sazieck, God of Adulthood. Orlar, Goddess of the Elder Years. Wiq, God of Death. And now, the Greater Deities—Tortu, God of Woman; Pralma, Goddess of Man; and finally, Qareck, Lord of All Existence." With a proud lifting of his chin, Byn pressed in the last circle.

A few clicking noises brightened his face, but all the circles returned to their original positions flush with the wall.

And nothing.

"What happened?" Axon said. "Why didn't it work? Or did it?"

Byn bent his head down, re-reading his notes. "It should've opened. It says clearly here that the door is the *Life of the universe, passage to purity, cycle of all*. Not the best poetry, but I'm sure I translated it right." Tapping his finger on the wall, he added, "I suppose I could have made a mistake. I'll check it over."

As he began translating again, Axon clenched her fists. They didn't have time for an academic's meticulous approach. Sometimes bashing a door down made more sense. Except she had already sliced into the wall when fighting White and nothing had happened. Looking at the wall now, she could not tell where that had occurred. Whatever spell hid this door, protected the walls as well.

She wished Zev were with them. He could have solved this before Byn managed to finishing translating. The moment he understood how each of the Nine had a button, he would work out the true meaning of *Life of the universe* and all the rest. After all, even she recognized that the Life

Cycle deities end with Wiq. The Greater Deities don't affect the cycle of a human life.

She froze. Could that be it? "We started at the wrong place."

"Maybe," Byn said. "Maybe we should reverse it. Life and Death are intertwined. Perhaps if we begin with Wiq—"

"No. The writing didn't say the *Life Cycle*, it spoke of the entire universe. Qareck, Pralma, and Tortu existed long before we were created. We must start with them first."

Byn's mouth tightened and twisted. Finally, he shrugged. "I don't see the harm."

But Axon had not waited for his judgment. By the time he had agreed, she already pressed in the circles for Qareck and Pralma. Together, they pressed in Tortu's circle and then followed the Life Cycle deities from Tiq to Wiq.

When Axon pushed in Wiq's circle, they heard a loud clang and a series of odd hisses like air being shoved through a small space. The unmistakable whine of gears at work followed. With a deep grinding, the wall cracked the outline of a circle.

Clutching his wounded side, Byn stumbled back as the round door became more defined. "I told you. I said it. The Nine sent you here."

The door rolled off to the right, sliding into the wall and revealing a dark passageway that curved downward.

CHAPTER NINE

Zev

D on't look down. Step. Don't look back. Step. Focus on Pilot waving like
a madman. Step. Focus on Bellemont by his side. Step. Give Mosol a
reassuring squeeze of the hand. Step. Don't look down.

The phrases bounced in Zev's head, a non-stop series of mantras that
kept him moving. Mosol's hand clamping on him shifted from nervous
shivers to terrified death-clenches and back again. The way her erratic
breathing mixed with whimpers had him expecting her to fall at any
moment. And if she fell, she would take him along.

Thump.

The beam shuddered as the Emissary slammed into a building or the
ground or something behind. But Zev would not look. He didn't dare
change the delicate balance that kept him and Mosol moving forward.

As they edged further and further along, he could feel the beam
dipping down. It had never been intended as a bridge—especially one
crossing such a wide gap. But it would hold. Zev had to believe it would
hold.

"We're almost there," he told Mosol. Not quite halfway, but she needed
all the encouragement he could offer.

Thump.

He needed some encouragement, too.

Instead, he saw Pilot standing straighter with an awed expression as he looked beyond Zev, gawking at a massive beast of muscle and limb. Snapping back, Pilot waved Zev forward with greater urgency.

Don't look down. Step. Don't look back. Step. Focus on Pilot waving like a madman. Step.

The mantra fought down the panic, yet part of him couldn't help but scream within. He noticed Bellemont kneeling next to Pilot. She had formed a mound of dirt and pulled a vial from her pouch.

"No," he said with as much force as he dared use—didn't want to startle Mosol into losing her balance. "We don't need a spell."

Pilot must have thought Zev spoke to him, but after his brief confusion cleared, he glanced down and saw Bellemont's intention. Her vial was empty, so she stuck a finger in her mouth until she gagged up what little was in her stomach.

Thump.

And that horrible creature shouted once more. The sound rattled windows. A woman who had attempted to hide gave up in fright. Bawling like a lost child seeking out Mommy, the woman dashed along the street. Beyond that, Zev could not tell by sound what happened, but the bawling cries ceased. He hoped she found another hiding spot and knew how to keep quiet. That was a story he could believe in. Except he noticed the Emissary no longer roared. If anything, Zev thought he heard munching.

Maybe they did need Bellemont's spell.

The beam bowed the most as they crossed the midpoint. Pilot climbed onto the end, but Zev doubted that would make much of a difference. Still, any bit would help. If it stalled the inevitable, he might have enough time to get across. As long as they kept moving.

Mosol stopped.

Her face pressed into Zev's back, sweat and tears soaking through, and her grip threatened to break the bones in his hand. "I can't."

"You're doing a great job."

"I can feel what's happening. This thing is going to break."

"All the more reason not to stop. Now, come on. Let's go. You want to make it home, don't you? You want to see Byn again."

He took a step. Then another. She did not move, and as he pulled away, he felt the tug on his shirt from her other hand.

"Bellemont," he called in a calm yet loud voice.

He didn't need to say anything more. She pulled out her extractor and got to work on a tooth.

Thump.

Mealtime had ended.

Thump.

The beam shook hard—almost a bounce—enough that Zev's arms flapped in sharp motions. Mosol screamed. Zev leaned to one side, trying not to overcompensate. As he felt balance returning, he eased into standing straight. Mosol had not moved. Her fear had frozen her in place and that had saved her. Pure luck. But Zev didn't think that kind of luck would last.

Thump.

The beam did bounce this time. As Zev realized what had happened, as his body failed to regain balance, his flailing yanked Mosol off the beam. Her shriek choked on her petrified gasp. Zev spun his body and reached for her—not that grabbing hold would save either of them, but instincts did what they did and he had no control. Behind her, back on the street, the Emissary clung to the demolished tavern like a mutated lizard. Brown-black sludge dripped down the battered wall as the creature climbed up to a neighboring roof.

And it jumped.

Bounding through the sky, this lizard of a hundred eyes, arms, and mouths flew across the chasm. Its noxious odor left a sickly wake in the air as festering bits of its body dripped off and splattered against the beam. When it crashed into a building on the other side and the walls crumbled beneath its weight, the ground shook, tossing away any chance Zev had of reclaiming his balance.

He thought it strange that this would be the last image he ever saw.

But as he and Mosol drifted over the edge, pieces of the city streets and rubble from the destroyed buildings flew through the air like a flock of talonjays. They swirled around each other and reassembled into a platform that widened off the beam—directly beneath Zev and Mosol. He hit the platform, air whooshing out of his lungs, and Mosol looked around confused. Not Zev. He knew exactly what had happened. He turned to see Bellemont deep in concentration as more scraps of the city chunked together to extend the platform into a bridge.

"Come on," he said, taking hold of Mosol.

He had to drag her for the first few steps until she finally believed they were not dropping to their demise. Her terrified sobs became joyful wailing as she rushed ahead of Zev, pushing him out of the way and nearly knocking him into the chasm. Breathing hard, he joined the others on solid ground. The instant his feet left the bridge, Bellemont exhaled and the disparate pieces fell apart, tumbling into the darkness below.

Pilot clapped Zev on the back. "I told you it would hold."

CHAPTER TEN

Axon

The tunnel descended in tight curves that lost all of their finished edges and became more and more like a cavern. Except for one thing—periodically, they walked by a framed painting nailed into the cave walls. There were nine paintings in total, each one a representation of the great works of life which the gods and goddesses took responsibility for.

Tiq's painting depicted a baby nestled with newborn animals, all surrounded by a field of blossoming flowers. And later, Orlar's painting showed the sun at dusk as those same animals rested at the feet of an elderly woman. The final painting honored Qareck by taking elements of the eight previous works and bringing them together in one masterful image.

"This was an old temple, wasn't it?" Axon said. "Why else would somebody hang these here?"

For an answer, Byn dropped to his knees and stared ahead. As Axon followed around, she saw it—a room, not a cave, but a room of brick and mortar, of gold and gems, of marble pillars and crystal statues. In the center, the Cistern.

A square marble pool collected water from four narrow troughs, each running from beneath the walls. In the middle, a pedestal rose on an island making a sculptured stand. Ornate with golden vines bearing gem-encrusted fruits, the pedestal held a wide bowl with a stone lip. Three rusting plates formed steps across the pool to the pedestal. Byn's hand-held cast pale light throughout the room, and when it hit the Cistern, dazzling flashes glittered on the walls like stars on a moonless night.

"I agree that it's beautiful," Axon said, "but we can't sit here admiring it all day. People need our help. Let's get this done." She nudged him with her knee. "In other words, what do we do?"

"Right. Of course." Byn jumped to his feet and nearly collapsed. Pressing his side, he groaned, and Axon helped steady him.

Together they entered the room. Squish. The handheld revealed a thin layer of water covering the entire floor. Disturbed for the first time in ages, the flat surface now rippled from their movements and the eerie sounds of the water drops sang off the walls.

They stepped out of the water and onto the marble base outlining the pool. With cautious motions, they reached the metal stepping stones and then the pedestal. Peering inside the wide bowl of the Cistern, Axon saw shimmering amber light like fire. Byn reached over and placed his hand in the water.

A sound like metal planks banging onto a hard surface crashed around them. Byn's hair spiked outward as his body blasted across the room. He slammed into a pillar, cried out, and clutched his side as he crumpled to his knees. Axon rushed over to help him back up.

"I'm fine. I'm fine," he said, his teeth gritting each word.

One pillar over, Axon noticed a shred of Byn's robe. She took a step closer, leaned down, and swiped it—similar material but darker than Byn's. She glanced back. Byn's robe looked fine.

"It's you," Byn said.

"What?" She shoved the fabric into her pocket.

"Why else would Shul Ranon have insisted on sending you here? He saw what the Nine wanted. He understood what the Cistern needed. The touch of a true hero. You."

"But I'm not—"

"There's no need for modesty. We are the only two down here, and the Cistern has obviously rejected my touch. Please. Try."

Shaking her head, Axon approached the Cistern. This was foolish. Hero or not, she had no special power over a spell—and in her opinion, the water in this thing had definitely been spelled. If Bellemont were with them, she would know right away what to do. She could probably rip out

197

a tooth or two and solve the matter. Or Zev—he would search the room and find some sliver of information that would clear everything up and make their way forward undeniable. Even Pilot would be better suited. He'd toss out a few jokes before saying words that cut right to the bone of the problem.

She could hear him—*The problem is that you still doubt yourself.*

That simplified it too much to her ears. Because she didn't doubt everything. She was a superior fighter, she knew that. She was loyal and smart and faithful. But the label *Hero* did not sit right. Not after Taladoro. Not after she lied to King Robion. She could argue that her actions had been to protect peace and the Frontier, and she knew that was the truth, but it didn't change the other truth—a hero would have been honest. A hero would have faced the situation head on.

Byn flicked his fingers as if spraying holy mist upon her. "It's okay to doubt."

"I don't," she said, the words echoing in the room, amplifying the lie.

"Trust the Nine. Have faith that they sent you here for this purpose, this moment. Have faith."

That much she could do. She crossed the Cistern to the pedestal. Gazing into the bowl, she saw the swirling firelight in the water so clear she could practically smell the burning. Passing her hand across her forehead, she closed her eyes and thought of the Nine.

"Qareck, watch over me," she said, and reached into the water.

The jolt up her arm vibrated her bones and flashed through the rest of her skeleton. A hard surface bashed her back and she slid into the water on the floor. Byn stood over her.

"You okay?" he asked, helping her stand. "That thing threw you twice as far as me."

Rubbing her backside, she glowered at the Cistern. "Guess I'm not worthy, either. Now what?"

Byn laced his fingers behind his neck. "We think. There has to be an answer that we're not seeing. I'll look through my notes."

An odd clicking noise sounded in the distance. Axon glanced at Byn as she pulled out the Water Blade. "You better think quick. We're not going to be alone for long."

CHAPTER ELEVEN

Zev

Hurrying through the streets, they dodged more and more fighting. The Vashon packed in greater numbers, and more often a bone-armored Dacci witch led them. As they crossed an old square hosting a statue of famed pioneer Jerda Makor standing proud with her eyes cast toward a future far different from this moment, Zev noticed blood on the stonework. More and more, block after block, they encountered greater amounts of destruction and blood—spatters, splotches, pools, and streaks. Whereas before, people were startled by the appearance of the Emissary and sought to escape, enough time had passed now for the streets to empty and a serious defense to be mounted. That brought yet more blood.

Twice they skirted around fighting between Vashon and squads of constables. Rifle fire clapped off in the distance. At one point, they darted by a dead Dacci witch. All of her teeth had been knocked out of her mouth. While Zev understood the fear that death might not stop a witch and therefore, they needed to remove her teeth to be certain, he also saw the violent release in the way the constables had abused her mouth. All of their fears and frustrations mirrored in the scattered teeth. Zev hoped the witch was truly dead before they got to work on her.

At last the Thalmew Building drew near.

Pilot kept low as he approached yet another corner. They needed to turn north, but every block they attempted had a problem. Vashon, Dacci, and for the last three blocks, a wall of bile dripping sludge—part of the Emissary.

As it devoured buildings, autocarts, and people, it continued to grow. Some of its sharp muscles bulged in odd places with no apparent purpose. It sprouted arms and eyes as necessary—or maybe at a whim. If something blocked its way, an eye would open to see the obstacle and an arm would grow to fix the problem. Twice, Zev caught sight of the thing's skin splitting into a mouth so it could chomp down on whatever it had acquired—one time it had been a young man.

"This way. Hurry," Pilot said, and the rest of them rushed for the corner.

At first, Zev didn't understand why Pilot chose this block. Part of the Emissary could be seen at the far end. It had three massive fists pounding down upon a ten-man constable unit defending from behind a barricade of overturned autocarts, salvaged brick, and the wooden skeletons of former buildings. But then Zev noticed two things that must have changed Pilot's perspective—first, Chief Constable Drick stood at the back, fists on hips, commanding through his thick mustache; second, they not only fought the Emissary, but a Vashon unit and a Dacci witch as well.

"We have to help them," Pilot said.

"Are you crazy?" Mosol said, her voice cracking an octave. "We go up there, all that's going to happen is that we'll die alongside them."

A series of loud rifle shots forced all of them to drop lower. The Emissary roared—a lot of anger and a little pain.

"Not if we're smart."

"That thing—we can't stop it. You all know that, right?" Mosol's desperate tears hit Zev's arm as she whipped from one of them to the other. "Look at it. There's no way adding the four of us in there is going to take down that beast. Right? You see that, right? You must."

But Pilot's eyes did not fall on the Emissary. "We don't need to kill it. Not yet, anyway. We go up there, along the left side of the street, and we can drop a few Vashon before they know what's happening. That should give Drick and his men some relief. Once we join them, we'll be providing enough extra rifle-fire that the entire squad can retreat without being slaughtered."

Drick bellowed several orders and the men volleyed with the Vashon before ducking under the barrage of foul fists slamming around them.

Zev gazed up the left side, trying to picture what Pilot had imagined. "It might work."

"*Might?*" Mosol's voice rose so high it nearly disappeared. "You can't. Not on a *might*. You want to think about *might*, you should think about this—you're supposed to take me to my father. Detouring into this *might* get me killed."

The witch squatted over a pile of dirt. Though her clacking bone armor covered the details, Zev knew that she defecated on the pile. The beginning of an offering. The beginning of a spell.

Bellemont saw it, too. "They'll all die, if we do nothing."

"We'll all die, if we do," Mosol said.

Zev reloaded his rifle. "Getting you home safe is pointless if all those who can fight are dead. We help Drick and his men retreat, they can meet up with other constables, form a stronger line of defense—gives you a better chance of getting home without the Vashon and the Dacci killing us from behind."

That caught her. As she weighed the idea of fighting now so as not to fight later, Zev nodded to Pilot. Looking to the left, he said, "What's your plan?"

"Oh, nothing special beyond what I said. Work our way up the left side and shoot at the enemy. I doubt our little rifles will do anything to that giant, but the Vashon and the Dacci—we know how to deal with them."

The witch had finished fouling her dirt and knelt before the new mud. From her pouch, she pulled out several small bones and arranged them onto the pile.

"We need to move fast," Zev said to the entire group. "The further up we go, the better. If the Vashon spot us, that's where we'll most likely end up fighting from. If we're lucky, we'll get close enough to the constables that we can dash for that barricade. Everybody clear? Then let's go."

Holding their rifles at their sides, they scuttled along the side of the street. Chief Constable Drick must have seen them because he shouted, "All men on the Vashon!" Those of the squad firing at the Emissary shifted their weapons to face the Vashon and the witch, providing Zev and his team an excellent diversion so they could push further up.

Rifles cracked out their shots, back and forth while the witch brandished her tooth extractor. "We've got to stop her," Zev said.

Pilot had already lowered to one knee and aimed his rifle. Flames leapt from the muzzle and the deafening blast reminded Zev that the little snaps of rifle fire in the distance were only quiet because of that distance.

Pilot's shot hit the witch in the shoulder. Not enough to kill her, but enough to disrupt her spell. Also, enough to get noticed.

Four Vashon turned their masked faces toward Zev and his team. They surrounded the witch to protect her and then returned fire. Zev dove behind an overturned street vendor's stand. He couldn't tell what happened to Bellemont and Mosol but the lack of crying worried him. Pilot ducked around the side of an autocart and set up another shot.

"Give up, you Vashon bastards," Drick said, cupping his mouth. "The army is coming to clean you off these streets. Give up now, and you'll be treated far better than you deserve."

A volley from the barricade struck two Vashon—one in the head, one in the gut. Only the four protecting the Dacci remained. Pilot fired two rounds before dropping down to reload. Zev thought he spotted movement near a couple of trashcans. Possibly Mosol and Bellemont.

Getting his legs underneath him, he eased onto his knees and aimed his rifle with care. He targeted a Vashon wearing a mask painted to extend the mouth to the ears. Ticking off all the steps of a good shot— sturdy base, hands in the proper positions, easing breath, squeeze the trigger at the bottom of an exhalation—Zev cracked a shot right through the Vashon's neck. He had aimed for the forehead, but it had been a while since he had practiced shooting.

The constables started shouting. Zev glanced up the street—seven fists of the Emissary rained down on the barricade like a line of bakers taking turns beating dough. Blood exploded from behind the barricade, splashing the sludge-covered fists, as the shouting turned to cries turned to silence.

One large man remained standing. Chief Constable Drick. He held a handgun and pointed it at the beast. "You bastard! You won't get to take me down," he barked. And as the Emissary's fist rushed down, Drick turned his weapon toward his own head.

But he wasn't fast enough. And he wasn't lucky enough.

The fist did not squish Drick like a child popping little kly-bugs. Instead, it altered shape to wrap around and cocoon the man.

As more shots flashed around Zev, he stared at the crimson mess of the barricade and the oozing waste of the cocoon. Bits of wood flew across his vision, but he could not look away. Only a small part of the Emissary was visible, three of its eyes flicking back and forth trying to spot any nearby threats. Perhaps trying to see if it could make a meal from the mash it had created.

The cocoon undulated. Once. Then its muddy walls hardened.

A death cry rattled off to Zev's side. One of the Vashon? Maybe even the witch. He needed to help his friends, but all he could do was stare at what had been Chief Constable Drick.

The Emissary lifted its arm away, leaving behind the cocoon beading with moisture. When the base of the cocoon wriggled, Zev raised his rifle. When the middle of the cocoon jerked hard enough to form a long tear, he nestled the rifle in place and peered down the sight. And when the top of the cocoon peeled back, he squeezed the trigger.

A hole appeared near the bottom. The top pulled down more, and Drick stretched his arms like a newborn. Long hairs thick as eels hung from his arms and ears and jaw. His face had melted into odd folds and his skin hung loose off all of his limbs. He stepped out of the cocoon, dripping in waste, and blood streamed from below his knee where Zev's bullet had grazed him.

More bullets winged around Zev. Another cry announced the death of more Vashon. But Zev simply reset his rifle and aimed. He knew little of Drick, but the little he knew suggested the man would rather die than be this malformed evil.

Taking more care with the steps of a good shot, Zev aimed for the Drick-creature's chest. The thing made a noise somewhere between Drick's commanding tone and a boy embarrassed that he wet his pants. It approached, arms reaching forward. Zev couldn't tell whether it wanted to attack him or wanted his mercy.

He went with the latter.

Before the bullet even left the rifle, Zev knew the shot had been true. Drick stumbled back at the hit and a blood-bile shower burst out of his back. He dropped to the ground, still alive, crawling, but unable or unwilling to fight. At length, he settled his head into the street and sighed. Zev lowered his weapon.

Bellemont stepped over. "It's done," she said. "You need to sit down."

He looked at her, let her kind eyes bring him back, and when he gazed up at the barricade again, the Emissary was gone. He could hear it rumbling through another street, tearing down another building, but it no longer threatened their lives. Not for now, at least.

Bellemont took his hand and led him toward the others. He moved like an old man—slow and bent crooked. The Vashon and the witch on the other side of the street were all dead. But they had not been pulverized and that seemed unfair—unbalanced.

"Is he okay?" Mosol asked.

She hunched over Pilot, her hands pressing hard against the right side of his chest. Blood seeped between her fingers.

"Just a little shocked," Bellemont said. "He's seen some horrible things before, but I'm guessing he witnessed the attack that killed all those constables."

Pilot groaned. "Would've been better if he had been paying attention to shooting our enemies."

"Sorry," Zev said, his brain pulling him back to the moment. He rushed to Pilot's side and checked for an exit wound.

"Don't bother," Pilot said. "I can feel it stuck near my ribs."

"Can you breathe okay?"

"I'm not dead, so I guess so."

He looked pale, even with his dark skin. Zev scanned the empty and bloody street. "We have to get him medical help."

Mosol said, "We should keep going to my home. My father will get him the best doctors around. At least, those that are still alive."

"He won't last." Though Bellemont spoke clear and firm, Zev heard the truth simmering beneath. "We have to get him stable, first. Then we can take him to the Thalmew Building."

Behind the dead Vashon, Zev noticed the building had no door, smashed windows, but otherwise, solid walls. Crouching close to Pilot, he said, "Put your arm around me. We're going to shelter in that building across the street. We'll do our best to get you in shape for the last run to the Thalmew Building."

"We can't stop now," Mosol said.

"We have to. We need to regroup and figure out the safest, fastest way through all this."

"But what if they come back? What if that thing comes back?"

"Don't worry about that. The battle's moved on."

Pilot yelled several curse words as they hoisted him to his feet. Hobbling toward the building, he rested his head against Zev. "This battle is all over the place," he said, soft and strained. "Eventually, they're going to go after Thalmew. Which means they'll be following the same path we're going to take. Which means there's a good chance they'll be back."

As sweat broke across Zev's chest, he kept his eyes on the building ahead. "I know."

CHAPTER TWELVE

Axon

The answer was like a storybook princess removing her disguise to reveal that she was actually the peasant girl. It had been in front of everyone the entire time. For Axon, the revelation came not from a clever disguise but from her shimmering blue sword.

Byn continued to search through his notes, getting more frantic as time drifted by without an answer. But the answer was simple. Byn had been the one saying it all along—the Nine had guided Axon to the Cistern for a reason.

She simply had to accept it.

From the very beginning, their divine hands had been in play. She never recognized it, of course. She thought that the decisions had been hers entirely. But the fact that there were decisions to be made at all—that had been brought to her by the Nine.

When she had a traitor who murdered one of her team, the Nine saw that her suspicions rose when they were in the town of Fernbund. The same town that Zev lived in. She could have ignored her suspicions. She could have stayed in town with Pilot and Bellemont instead of going out to Zev's farm. But she didn't.

That decision set her on a course to not only gaining the Water Blade but to discovering her strength against Nualla. Those experiences led her to becoming valuable in the eyes of King Robion. That sent her to the north after the Shield of Taladoro. And once again, the Nine presented her with a challenging dilemma. She chose country over leader. She had great admiration for King Robion, but her country meant more. Leaders would come and go, but to betray the core values of her country meant destroying all that it represented.

So, she lied to King Robion. She knew he would see it as a betrayal, but she had to do what was right.

That decision led to her leaving Ridnight Castle and the Frontier. It led her to join Zev on his journey east to Balica City. It led her to a place where her faith would be what kept her sane.

Just as Shul Ranon had suggested, the Nine guided her to his temple. That led to yet another crucial decision—take on the request of the Shul or ignore it all. She could have simply been one of the faithful who prayed regularly, showed up for services, and did little more. But he saw the shine in her. He knew the Nine had something special planned. Why else would they have sent a woman who held the Water Blade straight to him?

"It doesn't make any sense," Byn said, jumping to his feet. He splashed around the room, looking at the designs on the walls, seeking any clue that would give him the answer.

Perhaps he was right. All of her thoughts required her to believe that the Nine focused incredible effort upon her life. Why would they? She had never seen any evidence of direct meddling in the world before from the Nine. Bad crops led to starvation. Wars led to deaths. Many crimes went unpunished. They let it all occur. She believed in them—her faith was strong—but that didn't mean she had to accept the fairytale thinking that they involved themselves in all the business of everyday life. If she were to jump off a bridge, she expected to fall and die. No matter how faithful, no matter how devout, the Nine would not reach down and pluck her out of the sky. That's not how gods and goddesses worked.

"Yet here I am," she said.

"What?" Byn sprang over to her, kicking up water against her pants. "Do you have something?"

Stepping up to the Cistern's pedestal, she said, "I guess so."

The fiery, golden water in the bowl rippled as if it anticipated her touch. Not hers—the Blade's. But she remembered the pain when she touched it previously. She would never forget that.

Would she feel anything this time? If only the Blade touched those waters, would it affect her at all? She had become so comfortable with this weapon that it resonated within like her lungs or heart or stomach. It was part of her.

As with the idea of using the Blade, she knew the answer to this as well. She would feel everything. Even if she had Byn set the Blade in the Cistern, even if she ran all the way back to the Pit or the temple or the surface or even her apartment—no matter how much distance she put between herself and the Blade, she would feel it. Every painful jolt.

If not, then anybody could have brought the Blade here. But as Shul Ranon never stopped saying, the Nine chose her.

"What are you doing?" Byn asked.

Though her thoughts had been far from traditional, she knew the answer to this question, too. "Praying."

She lifted the Water Blade overhead, her fingers laced around the hilt, the tip pointing down toward the center of the bowl. The need to speak to the gods and goddesses, the need to call upon them with a loud voice that would fill the chamber, rushed within her. But she kept silent. She had seen too many leaders, soldiers, and witches call out to their deities as if in doing so their actions, no matter how despicable, would be anointed by divine praise. No. Not her.

Before Byn could ask another question, she plunged the Blade down into the Cistern's waters.

The pain came at once. Different than before but every bit as intense. She kept expecting to be thrown across the room, but instead, her laced fingers locked tight around the hilt. Tighter than she intended. She tried to release her grip, but her fingers would not obey.

With a high-pitched squeak in his voice, Byn said, "Do you hear that?"

She heard. She heard everything. Every dribble of water hitting the surface of the floor, every churn within the Cistern, every breath filling Byn's lungs, even the scratching of a spider's legs as it doled out new webbing. The air vibrated around her, swirling from her body down her arms, serpentining along the Blade and into the Cistern. Yes, she heard it. Coming down the halls. Two multi-legged creatures that had once been Vashon. Vile, malformed brutes of the Pit.

"Stop them," Axon said.

"That's your job," Byn said. "You're the fighter."

She glared at him, and the light shining from her eyes reflected on the water and brightened his face. Byn shivered but managed to nod. He stepped toward the entrance, shaking as he pulled out his dagger.

CHAPTER THIRTEEN

Zev

O n the second floor of the pummeled building, Zev found a torn mattress. Ignoring the dark stains on the corner and the dead man on the floor, he lugged the mattress down to where the group huddled against an empty fireplace. Mosol cleared an area, and after Zev set it down, they managed to get Pilot situated and comfortable. Or at least, not in excruciating pain.

Bellemont pressed her hand on his forehead. "You'll be okay. We'll get out of this."

"You got that right," Pilot said, forcing a wink that turned to a wince.

Zev rushed back up to the bedroom with the dead man. The corpse wore a white shirt, part of which still looked clean—most of the blood was located on the right side near the hip. Zev ripped several strips off the shirt and raced them back to Pilot.

"Thank you," Bellemont said, taking the strips. Her fingers shook.

"He'll be okay."

"I'm not so sure."

"Hey," Pilot said. "I'm right here. And it's just my shoulder. I'll be fine."

It was more than that. The shoulder wound looked bad and would require months to heal properly, but the pain must have been worse than

Pilot let on because he never acknowledged his ribs. Zev kept waiting for the big man to gingerly touch the small bone poking out his side, but Pilot only focused on the shoulder. However, Zev knew that eventually they would have to look at that bone, and when they did, Pilot would become acutely aware of the additional damage.

As a kid, Zev once fell down a flight of stairs. He had been wrestling with Marcel, and they had not paid attention to where they were. They rolled over the edge and tumbled the full flight. Marcel broke an arm while Zev snapped two ribs. It didn't hurt at first. He felt discomfort but assumed every part of him ached from the fall. His brother wailed while cradling the broken arm. Only when Father pointed out that Zev had blood on his side, only when he touched the broken ribs, only then did he feel anything. It suddenly burned like an inferno. Enough that he passed out. Zev assumed the rush of fighting for his life kept Pilot numb to the full pain in his body because the fire of a bullet hole in the shoulder would not compare.

"This won't work," Mosol said. She stomped over to the window and peeked at the street. "We can't carry him all the way."

"We don't leave people behind," Zev said.

"I'm not trying to be cruel, but it's the truth. If we build a stretcher or if he can only walk with assistance, how are we going to make it block after block with everything going on out there? How?"

"She's got a point," Pilot said, his forehead beading with perspiration. "We should split up. You take Mosol, get her back to the Thalmew Building. I'll stay here with Bellemont. She'll protect me, and maybe I can persuade her to give up a tooth to heal me."

"You can do that?" Mosol asked, staring at Bellemont. "What are you waiting for? Heal him and let's go."

Bellemont's hesitation told Zev all he needed to know. "She can't," he said. "Healing is difficult without medical knowledge. But it's more than that, isn't it?"

She nodded, and Pilot held her hand.

"I hate to be so rude," Zev said, pausing to summon his courage, "But we need to know the full truth of our situation. How many teeth do you have left? How many spells can you actually perform?"

Though she cringed, she said, "Not many. Some small spells or maybe one last big one."

"You hide it well. I never noticed a change in your speech."

"I've been strategic in which teeth I used, and all the modern witches never stop working on their diction. We learned long ago that hiding our mouths wasn't enough." She brought Pilot's hand under her veil and pressed his fingers to her lips. "I'm sorry, my love. I'm so sorry, but I don't have what I need to heal you."

"So what?" Pilot said. "I'll still heal. Just in normal time."

"Um..." The fright in Mosol's voice pulled all attention her way. "I think we're too late."

Zev peered out the other side of the window. A battery of Vashon marched down the street. Two Dacci witches headed up two clear groups —one group of normal Vashon; one group mutated. At the front of them all, another witch led. One that chilled Zev's skin. The Red witch. The Pit had twisted her face into a savage horror. Worse—she had no arms. Only long strands of sinew that reached back like leashes tied around two young Dacci.

"How bad does it look?" Pilot asked.

Zev returned to his side. "Oh, you know, dire and hopeless."

"Ah. The usual."

"That red witch that killed herself—she's back with an army of friends."

Bellemont glanced at the window but made no motion to check for herself. She kissed Pilot's hand again.

"No," Pilot said. "You can't."

With a sharp sniffle, she said, "They're my teeth. I decide what to do with them."

"But you said it yourself—it won't work. You can't heal me."

"I can give you the strength to push through for a few days until King Robion's medical staff can take real care of you."

Mosol said, "They've stopped. They know we're in here."

"See, love? No point in healing me. We can't get out."

"There's got to be a backdoor, right?" Mosol headed toward the opposite side of the building, but Zev blocked her way.

"There isn't. I checked. All the walls are shared by the other buildings around us. And in this case, the walls haven't been torn down yet. Solid brick and stone. Only way out is through the front."

Bellemont rubbed her eyes. "It'll be okay. I'll take care of it all." To Zev, she added, "Promise me that you'll make sure Pilot is safe. Promise me that you'll get this girl home and make everything worth it."

"No!" Pilot tried to sit up but the pain pulled him back. "Don't do this."

"Zev. Promise me."

Zev pulled Bellemont into his arms. He held her in silence for a moment, not trusting his voice to hold steady. But at length, he knew what she needed. Holding her tight against his chest so that he could focus on the wall behind her, he said, "I promise." He tried to say it again, but the words choked him.

When they finally separated, she said, "I need some privacy with Pilot."

"Of course. Mosol, come with me."

He climbed the stairs and crawled over to the second story window. Mosol followed.

Red stood in the middle of the street with her two Dacci witches at either side. The masked Vashon formed a half-circle behind her, standing at attention, awaiting orders. Behind them, the mutated Vashon writhed and wriggled, crawled and clawed, pushing against each other, over each other, like a mass of insects trapped in a box. But nothing held them back. They could have spread across the street and into the building. Nothing but Red.

Zev noted the way all the creatures—the Vashon and the Dacci, too— watched Red for any sign of what she wanted them to do. It was more than soldiers looking to their leader. It was servants looking to their queen.

"Why aren't they attacking?" Mosol asked.

"Not sure."

Perhaps Red waited for orders just like her Vashon. He had seen her die in the Pit—he'd thought so, at least. When the Emissary resurrected her, maybe it created some kind of mind link. Or maybe she just wanted to torture everybody inside by making them wait.

"Sorry for downstairs," Mosol said. "I'm not a heartless person."

"I don't think Pilot was offended. We know you're scared. And scared people—life or death scared—well, it can make you say some awful things."

"I would never leave him behind. I want you to know that. Not like this. If we had to split up like we did with Byn—" She shook quiet and lowered her head.

Zev rested his hand on her back. "You didn't betray him. You didn't do anything wrong leaving him back there. He wanted to stay. He had to stay. You know that. Besides, we left him with Axon. I don't know anybody who is a better fighter or has a greater heart."

"I should've stayed with him."

"I'm sure he's happy to know that you're on your way home."

She chuckled. "Byn would say that happiness is an illusion. A fleeting moment of pleasure that can't be sustained."

Peeking out the window again, Zev finally understood why Red had yet to attack. Nothing so fanciful as speaking with the Emissary's mind—though, Zev did not discount that possibility as still existing. But in this case, the two witches Red had brought along now knelt as they created spells. "On the good side of things, that red witch is scared of us. Well, Bellemont—she's scared of Bellemont. She's got at least twenty soldiers down there but won't storm the building because she has no idea what sort of spells Bellemont has cast to protect the place."

"And the bad side of things?"

"It won't be long before those witches cast their spells. Then they all attack."

Mosol nudged Zev's rifle. "Shoot the witches."

"Bad idea. I'll only be able to get off one shot, so even if I hit perfect and kill one of the witches, the other will go right on with her spell. But the moment I open fire, Red won't hesitate. She'll send those Vashon in and suffer the losses."

"You don't know that. She might behave differently."

"I've dealt with a lot of Dacci in the past. Not to mention—Red is wrong. We don't have any spells protecting us, so if we instigate anything, we're done for."

"Sitting here doing nothing isn't any better."

Pilot howled his pain. Zev and Mosol raced down to help. But they found Pilot unconscious on the mattress.

"What happened?" Mosol asked.

Tears stained Bellemont's mouth veil as she gazed upon Pilot's sweat-soaked head. She pulled a vial away from his wound—blood and bile swirled inside. She dumped what remained in her vials onto the floor. The acrid odor assaulted them, but nobody moved. Bellemont shook her pouch over this small mound of waste and two bird bones dropped out.

"Will that be enough?" Zev asked.

Bellemont placed one hand on Pilot's leg. "He's very brave and even more generous." In her other hand, she held Pilot's rib that had been sticking out of his side. Setting it atop the mound with respectful care, she then leaned over Pilot and kissed him gently. "He asked me to marry him. I said yes." She pressed her mouth to his ear.

Zev could not hear her whispered words, but he knew what she said anyway. Variations of those words had been said between lovers for ages.

When she finished, she pulled out her tooth extractor and caressed it like an old pet. "One last time," she said. And she started to cast her spell.

CHAPTER FOURTEEN

Axon

In her life, Axon had experienced several surges of magical energy that eclipsed her normal sensations and transported her to another plane of understanding—perhaps even existence. Those unique moments did not prepare her for holding the Water Blade in the Cistern.

At the physical level, she endured jolt after jolt of bone-rattling pain. Her muscles would contract all at once as if they sought to pull into themselves. When she reached the point of thinking they would never release, everything within her loosened. Except her hands. They would not let go.

Beyond that, however, she travelled away from her body, from the Cistern, from the sewers, from the city. She rose into the sky, a cloud controlled by the wind, able to look upon the world and witness its glory as well as its pain. She wondered if the Nine lived here, if they saw the world as she did at that moment. The people were too small to matter. They moved about like the flow of mud after a heavy rain. And she could divert that flow, make it go where she wanted with nothing more than the swish of a finger.

Her body jolted again, and she returned to the sewers and the Cistern.

Byn backed away from the entrance, the dagger in his hand shaking so badly he threatened to harm himself as much as the Vashon creatures that entered the room. Two of them. The first was a big brute with mottled skin, discolored purple and black as if the creature had drowned and risen from the dead. Its stringy hair hung over its face—at least, Axon assumed a face existed under that mop.

"Please, I don't want to hurt you," Byn said. Probably had no clue what words came out of his mouth.

The second Vashon crawled along the walls. It had fingers that stretched out on extra knuckles and ended with round cups that sucked to the stone. Gray-skinned and smooth like a water-lizard, the creature sniffed the air through nostrils flat on its face. No nose. No eyes, either.

"I'm warning you," Byn said. "The Nine will prevail. They'll destroy you."

He did not move as the brute circled around him. The gray one flitted up onto the ceiling. Axon wanted to yell at him, warn him to be quiet, that these creatures had no eyes and silence would only help him go unnoticed. But her jaw locked as another blast of energy ignited her muscles. It was far too late for Byn anyway. Not only had the creatures heard him, they could smell his fear. They had to smell it—because Axon could, too.

She closed her eyes, pouring her thoughts into releasing the Blade. Clamped to its hilt, she could not help Byn, and he was helpless on his own. But more shots of power ripped through her. Flashes of light dappled behind her eyes.

When she looked again, the brute had lowered its head directly in front of Byn. It inhaled his scent. Stab—that's all Byn had to do. He had the knife in hand. Just shove upward and cause the creature pain. It would roar and cry out and it might even swat Byn to the side, but mostly, it would shy away. Probably. Better than standing there waiting for it to attack.

The gray one had crossed the ceiling until it hung directly above Byn. Ah. Axon saw now that the creatures were working together. Brute distracted the victim while Gray did the dirty work.

Gray stretched downward, opened its toothy maw, and hocked a white glob of mucous. It hit Byn's head with a wet thwap. Byn looked up and another glob dropped onto his face.

He never had time to panic. The toxins in the creature's attack acted fast. Axon watched the dagger fall from Byn's open hands. A breath and Byn followed the dagger to the floor. His legs no longer worked properly. His bowels let loose as his body spasmed in the water.

Brute grabbed a fistful of Byn's hair and dragged the young Shul apprentice from the room. Axon screamed her frustration. She heard it ringing her ears but felt nothing in her throat. The sound never escaped her body. Gray, however, noticed something. Instead of joining its partner, it skittered to the wall, onto the floor, and up to the base of the pedestal.

It cocked its head toward Axon and listened.

She tried to hold still. She tried not to breathe. But the Cistern kept shocking her system, forcing her body to jitter, creating small noises as her feet shifted on the wet marble and as the Blade pressed against the Cistern bowl.

Brute grunted from the tunnel, and Gray scampered out of the room.

Axon arched her head back and thundered all her anguish at the ceiling. Not a sound left her lips. Tears streamed back into her hair mixing with the sweat that dampened her skin. She heard Brute and Gray dragging, dragging, dragging Byn further away from her, and still, she could not let go of the Blade.

Until the jolts ceased.

The pain dissipated.

And in the lonely quiet, the Cistern released her.

She fell to the floor, splashing water outward from her impact. It felt cool against her burning skin. Her fingers ached. She turned over and sipped the water. The filthiest water she ever drank, but the raw pain scratching her throat demanded it.

After a moment's rest, she pushed back to her feet and approached the Blade. It stood straight in the Cistern. The shimmering blue had flecks of gold flowing through it. Axon reached out but held back. No. She couldn't be afraid. She'd end up standing there forever.

With a short growl, she snatched the Blade by the hilt and yanked it free.

CHAPTER FIFTEEN

Zev

The spell Bellemont cast formed a green mist that snaked off the waste pile and wrapped around Pilot. Zev stood at the window to keep an eye on Red and her witches, but he snatched enough glances to see Pilot healing—at least, to the point that he soon sat up. But when he tried to stand, he flopped back. The mist had yet to finish with him.

While he rested his head down and Mosol patted his forehead with the arm of her shirt, Zev noticed the witches starting to glow. Bright like sunlight. The mutated Vashon ceased their constant moving and joined the other Vashon, staring in awe and fright. Red stepped a little closer, her greedy eyes blazing at the front door. Zev guessed that she debated simply bursting in, taking whatever punishment Bellemont had waiting, and getting to the business of killing.

The fact that she checked herself bothered him more than the thought that he remained safe as long as she stood still. It suggested that she had enough mindfulness to know such rash actions would be counter-productive—to the immediate moment, and more importantly, to the Emissary's overall goal. Which also suggested there was a clear goal and not simply wanton destruction.

"How much longer until we go?" Mosol asked.

But Bellemont did not answer. Instead, she spit blood on the waste pile. Picking up the tooth extractor, she proceeded to remove seven more teeth. Zev knew—just *knew*—she had no more to give.

Outside, the two witches stood. The brightness no longer glowed off their bodies. Instead, it had become a sphere floating between them. With their hands held as if they carried the sphere without touching it, they walked toward the door. Red grinned and followed. With a snapping motion, the strands of sinew released the witches and slithered back into Red's body. Her Vashon army brought up the rear.

"This is it," Zev said, hurrying over to Pilot. "We'll get you upstairs. When they breach the house, we'll wait until most of them are inside. Then we try our luck dropping out the window."

"That's your best idea?" Mosol said.

Pilot reached out toward Bellemont. "I'm not leaving her."

But Bellemont raised a flat hand to stop them all. She kept her eyes closed and the rest of her concentration on her spell. Zev wanted to rush them all as far from Red as possible, but like the others, he remained still, watching Bellemont, waiting to see what she had planned.

Light from the bright sphere leaked around the edges of the door. Red shouted a garbled command, and the witches cackled with glee. At that same moment, Bellemont turned her outstretched hand toward the front.

"Now!" Red's words penetrated the building with clear authority.

The light flashed in a burst. The door rattled on its hinges. Zev crouched, turning his back toward the light, expecting to hear an explosion of energy. Instead, the door held. He saw Bellemont's strained hand and the door held. But that wouldn't be enough. She had to know.

As if reading his mind, she opened her eyes and winked at him.

When the next burst of light came, the door did not budge. And the light—it bent around the door, shot through the room in slivers, and funneled right into Bellemont's hand. That same light traveled up her arm and converged on her spine. When the last of it pooled together, it blasted out like a sheet of metal and tore a hole in the back wall.

As dust plumed around them, Bellemont stood. Keeping her eyes on the front door, she said, "Go. All of you."

Through the wall, Zev saw an intact room with a sofa, reading chairs, and a large rug. A normal room in a normal home. He heard frightened cries and caught sight of feet racing up the stairs. He wanted to chase after the occupants, warn them to leave their home, but there wasn't a truly safe place for them to go.

Mosol helped Pilot to his feet—he moved as if only a little banged up instead of seriously wounded. He shrugged off her hand and turned to Bellemont. "My dear, listen to me."

Bellemont whipped her head toward him. Her face had turned stone white, her eyes flaring with energy. When she spoke, her voice no longer sounded like her own. It was as if several voices within her all chimed in unison. "Go," she said, and said no more.

Pilot reached out for her but Zev and Mosol took him by the arms. Normally, they would have been no match for his size and strength. But with a bullet hole in his shoulder and his body healed only superficially by Bellemont's spell, Pilot could not break free of their grip. They pulled him through the hole in the wall.

"Wait, wait," he said, struggling against them.

"Don't do this," Zev said.

"I can't leave her."

"Don't waste the time she's making for us."

"But she's to be my bride, my wife, my life."

"And she's giving you that life now."

Though Pilot pushed hard, though tears trailed his cheeks, his head drooped. He nodded. Turning toward Mosol who checked their exit, the front door behind them exploded. Bits of shattered wood knocked about the floor, but none hit Bellemont—any that could have hurt her ricocheted off the air around her.

Red entered alone. Whatever spells her witches had cast, Zev suspected that magic was being funneled into her. The pulsing light that outlined her twisted form confirmed it.

Opening her mouth, blood and bile dribbled down Red's chin. She thrust back her head. Like spitting a heavy ball, she heaved the bright light across the room. It slammed into the air before Bellemont, spreading out as it continued to press forward.

Bellemont leaned her shoulder into the attack, holding both hands up while wincing at the blinding light. Zev and Pilot tried to watch while squinting and walking backwards toward Mosol.

"Please," Bellemont said. "Go. I don't want you to see this."

Her back split open along her spine. Red spit another blast and Bellemont slid several steps. Something inside Bellemont's back wriggled.

"We better go," Zev said.

Pilot had the sense to turn away. Not *sense*, Zev corrected himself. *Respect.*

But before Zev could turn, he caught sight of chiseled alabaster arms breaking out from her spine. First one, then another. And another. And more. Ten oversized limbs spidered out, each one glowing with the energy she had absorbed.

Snarling like a ferocious animal, Bellemont charged Red, her ten fists pummeling anything in her way. Zev could feel the same freeze creep up his legs that he had experienced when the Emissary's fists destroyed the constables. But Pilot pulled him away.

They blundered out of the building, crossed the street, and turned around. All three of them. Zev wanted to say that they should keep moving, but they all needed to see.

Bellemont moved like a tornado—spinning fast, her fists whipping around, destroying everything in her path. Vashon after Vashon lunged into the room only to be cut down by Bellemont's merciless strikes. Red attacked again, and the two locked together, the glowing energy cycling across Bellemont's body, then transferring to run through Red's body. Back and forth, faster and faster. Until they could no longer contain it.

The entire building collapsed, the sound of the energy blast coming seconds delayed, and a wave of burning air knocked Zev to the ground. Stone and wood clashed as it piled atop itself. When he got back up, he found Pilot staring at the mound of building, watching it as if he could will Bellemont to rise. Mosol hopped one foot to the other, desperate to speak but smart enough to stay quiet.

Zev watched the rubble, too. If any of the Vashon army escaped, that could become a problem. He checked his rifle, reloaded it, and noticed he had only two bullets left in his pocket. Gazing across the street, he saw nothing—not a living thing moved.

Pilot turned toward Mosol. His face wiped away all but a stoic chill. He looked her up and down, and Zev knew what went through his mind —appraising the value of this girl's life over that of Bellemont. Mosol must have understood, too, because she stepped behind Zev.

At length, Pilot headed down the street. In a cold voice that tremored beneath the surface, he said, "Let's get her home."

PART IV

CHAPTER ONE

Axon

Walking back through the cavern tunnels and into the constructed sewers, Axon could feel everything and nothing simultaneously. She moved as if she had been punched in the head too many times—wobbling and numb. But she also sensed each minuscule vibration coming off the Water Blade. Even through the parts of the scabbard not resting on her side—she felt those as if they dug under her skin. Losing Byn had awoken the full warrior within her, the stoic fighter who could bury all her emotions until the current crisis had ended. But she also tingled with each minor shift in the air. If an insect flew behind her, she could feel the infinitesimal currents its wings created. The world had become thriving and dead, endless and pinpoint.

When she returned to the Pit to find Brute and Gray huddled over Byn's body, eating him raw like ravenous animals, she wanted to scream the horror. But she also shut down. She walked forward, slow and calm, slid out the Water Blade, and thought more than felt that these creatures needed to die.

Gray noticed her first. It raised its head as if sniffing the air, tensed, and whirled on her. Sliding her right leg back for proper balance, Axon swished the Water Blade into a fine attack position. Gray leaped back and avoided the vicious assault. But drops of gold-flecked, glowing-blue water sprayed off the Blade. When a few of those drops landed upon Gray, the slick creature disintegrated. It transformed into burning ash and crumpled into a pile on the stone floor. Gray only had time to register shock. Couldn't even cry out.

Brute sprang to its feet, a long strand of skin hanging from its mouth, and flexed its muscular arms. Axon switched sides—putting her left foot in back and swinging the Blade to her opposite side. A few more drops of glittering water flew off, and those that touched Brute spread their deadly burn through him.

Axon held still with her feet holding her firm and the Blade ready to strike. But she did not scan the room for more attackers. She did not think about the Pit—now empty—or the rank odor emanating from it. She saw only those piles of ash that had been the two Vashon creatures.

At length, she lowered the Water Blade and stared at its swirling golds and blues. She had a powerful weapon, of course. But holding a jacksnake against her enemies would also be a powerful weapon unless she lost her grip. Then she might end up the one bitten and curled in a ball as her blood slowly turned into poison. She had to make sure the Water Blade didn't turn against her. With great care, she eased it back in the scabbard.

Once it was safely returned, she turned toward what remained of Byn. The creatures had devoured much of his torso, but she would take the best care of him with the rest. He deserved whatever she could offer.

She considered using the Water Blade to dig a grave into the stone floor but held back. It wasn't a pickaxe or a shovel. The power in that weapon, the way it annihilated those two Vashon creatures, the way it felt in her hand—warm and friendly—the entire experience left her excited and confused, thrilled and fearful. Focusing on collecting rocks did nothing to stop her mind from recalling every single moment of wielding the Blade. It repeated in her head as if tempting her to find another Vashon and use it against.

When she finished outlining Byn's body with stones, she did her best to wrap his corpse in his robe. Though the old garment had been stained in blood, it covered most of his gaping wounds. She had not intended to search his body, but her hand bumped against the notebook he kept in one of the robe's pockets. She set it aside and used the remaining rocks to cover him. Then she bowed her head. Hopefully, the Nine would not take offense at her bare head—she didn't have a prayer cloth to cover with.

"Wiq, god of death, watch over young Byn. He gave his life in service to the Nine. He gave his life so that I could serve the Nine as well." She paused, stretching her mind for something more to say. Finally, she lowered her head to the floor. "Amen."

Sitting back, she granted herself a few moments of silence—partly to honor Byn, partly to absorb all that had happened. At length, she picked up Byn's notes. Most of it dealt with historical references to the Cistern and attempts to uncover what it might look like. Stuck in the back, Axon found a folded paper, yellowed and brittle. Handling it with gentle care, she opened up a map of the caverns. Far more detailed than the scrap she had been working with. There were notes in the margins—some dated over twenty years ago. All of it written in another hand. She had seen that writing before. Shul Ranon. Off the center of the map, she spotted the Cistern room. The Cistern itself had been circled and one word had been underlined next to it. That word resonated for Axon. It gave voice to what she had experienced so far—*Waterfire*.

CHAPTER TWO

Zev

While Bellemont had healed Pilot some, he still could not move quickly through the city streets. Zev had to take point, running up to the corners and scouting which directions were safest to travel. They heard a lot more violence than they saw, and for that, Zev was grateful.

They did have a few skirmishes with Vashon travelling in pairs, perhaps separated from their squads. At one point, while Zev stared at an autocart hanging halfway out of a building's fourth floor, a mutated Vashon managed to sneak up on them. It had sharp bones protruding from every joint—even the fingers and the toes—and its body clicked as it moved. One of the team should have heard the thing approaching, but they all failed that time. Zev fired his rifle—two shots, both missed. He had yet to figure out where the weapon needed adjustment. It seemed to shoot lower than his aim, but when he compensated, it suddenly seemed to veer left or right. Mosol saved them that time. While the creature worried over Zev, she came up behind and slashed its back open.

After that, things settled down. They crossed four blocks without incident. Only the periodic roars of the Emissary and the repeated shaking of the ground reminded them that no matter what they went through, something worse was still out there.

With his back sliding along a brick wall, Zev approached another corner. He squatted low in case anybody happened to be looking in his direction, and he peeked around. It took his brain a few moments to register what he saw.

Soldiers. Eastern soldiers as well as members of the Frontier's Royal Guard. They had erected barricades and had sentries on duty. Mounted on either side of the street were two of the East's repeating guns—big, spinning barrels that shot off numerous rifles in sequence, one after the other. And behind it all—an awning with the words *Thalmew Building* painted on the side.

M osol bolted into her father's arms. The two stood near the front of a wide room on the third floor—the Battle Room. The walls were lined with soldiers busy at work on large tables. They shuffled papers, murmured information, and rushed to other tables to hand over more papers and information. Near the ends of these tables, young soldiers were handed sealed papers which they pocketed before darting out of the room. Others darted into the room to start the process all over again. And in the middle of this machine, an enormous table had been set up with a map of the city and numerous wood-carved miniatures denoting troops and enemies—as well as one braided strand of yarn for the Emissary.

Pilot slumped into a chair near the lifter while two medical staff attended to him. They wanted to take him to the second floor where they had all their equipment and medicine, but Pilot refused. "Not until this is over," he said.

Zev understood. Returning Mosol to her father, seeing her collapse into his embrace, hearing her deep cries while tears flowed—Zev should have felt relief and possibly pride at succeeding. But Axon and Byn were still out there. And out there was still out there—the Vashon, the Dacci, and the Emissary. They didn't have time to celebrate a small victory.

It was more than that for Pilot, of course. Zev saw the long stare in his eye, the restrained shudder of his shoulder, the grim line of his mouth. Pilot must have been replaying those last images of Bellemont over and over like a performance that never altered. He would mourn her deeply, perhaps forever, but at that moment, Zev watched his friend force down the sadness and convert what remained into rage.

The lifter door opened and King Robion entered. He strode over to Thalmew and stroked the back of Mosol's head. After a word or two, he headed straight to Zev. "Good work. Thank you," he said before moving to Pilot. He would soon learn of Bellemont's death, but Zev suspected the King would hide any feelings behind a role of leadership.

Keeping an arm around his daughter, Thalmew approached. "My deepest respect and endless thanks to you. I must admit that I saw you as a last effort—a prayer to the Nine, perhaps—but you proved my doubts wrong." He kissed the top of Mosol's head. "Dear, you should go upstairs to Mother. She needs to see you, and I'm sure you'd like to bathe."

Sniffling and laughing, Mosol said, "I'm sure you'd like me to bathe, too."

"Excuse me," a heavy voice said as a balding man with gray wisps curling out the side tapped over on a cane. "Where's Byn? Is he okay?"

"You bastard," Mosol said, slashing her hand at the man.

Thalmew pulled her back. "Calm down. That's the Shul from Byn's temple."

"I know exactly who he is."

The Shul leaned hard on his cane, the extra fold around his neck bunching up as he gazed down. "I'm truly sorry that you got caught up in our search."

"What about Byn? You should be sorry for ever starting him after that stupid Cistern. The only reason he was down in those sewers was for you."

"He may have told you that, but it's not true. He loves this pursuit. Now, please, stop berating me and tell me what's happened to him."

"How should we know?" Folding her arms, she glowered at the man but made no further attempts at assault. "Your star apprentice refused to come back with us just so he and Axon could keep searching."

"Axon made it, then. Excellent. He'll be quite safe with her by his side. The Nine will see to that."

"Please, my sweet," Thalmew said, ushering her aside. "We still have to deal with the attack on our city. Go see Mother. Don't worry about the Shul. He's only been trying to help."

"Help? It's his meddling with ancient relics that's got us in this mess. The Vashon would never have gone exploring those sewers, if not for him."

"Then it's my fault, too." Thalmew held his daughter at the shoulders. "My company funded Shul Ranon's research."

"What? Why would you do that?"

"I had hoped finding proof that the Nine are the true deities of the world would end so much of the fighting. Maybe even bring real peace to our time."

"But you don't believe in the Nine."

"I'll believe in whatever helps our people. But it was foolish of me—especially seeing how it brought harm to you. Nothing is more important to me and your mother than you. If you want me to cut the funding, I will."

Zev did not hear the answer because a door near the back opened and Marcel entered the room, his limp more pronounced. Zev rushed towards him along with two soldiers carrying several papers. He waited for Marcel to read the communications and send the soldiers off in different directions.

"I'm glad you're alive," Marcel said. No embrace, no smile, not even a handshake.

"Are you in charge here?"

"You sound surprised. But no, I'm here as the Asterling rep. We fund nearly a third of the standing army, so I'm here to coordinate with Leader Thalmew and your King Robion's soldiers. We've got to make sure all our forces are working together."

"I'm sure you're doing a great job."

Marcel eyed Zev as if he couldn't tell whether he had been complimented or criticized.

Zev asked, "What about Father? Is he safe?"

"Upstairs in Thalmew's place." Marcel smirked. "He's being a nuisance because we won't let him down here to be a part of all this. But he'd only be in the way with constant criticism and little in the way of productive ideas. Mrs. Thalmew seems to be able to handle him, though."

"That's got to be a sight."

"Go up and see him. I've got a lot to do right now." Marcel pushed toward the big map in the center of the room. "Oh, and Lady Jos is up there, too."

CHAPTER THREE

A thunderous *BOOM* rolled across the city. Climbing upstairs, Zev thought how odd that a simple noise, not much different from the thunder accompanying a rainstorm, signified death and destruction. Somewhere on the streets of Balica City, people hid in their homes or sought shelter to avoid the threats around them. And somewhere below those streets, Axon and Byn fought in an effort to find the Cistern and create the peace that Thalmew wanted.

Peace. That sounded good to Zev's ears. When he entered the Thalmew residence, his father sat with Mrs. Thalmew. Neither looked too pleased to be with the other, but everyone had to make sacrifices during a crisis.

At least Zev could bring a little joy to Mrs. Thalmew. "Your daughter's safe. She's downstairs with Mr. Thalmew."

Mrs. Thalmew burst into tears. Father sat still—uncomfortable as he watched the outpouring display.

"She's on her way up," Zev said.

"Oh, I look horrible." Mrs. Thalmew rushed down the hall. "I have to clean up."

Father stared at Zev, too weak to stand, too bitter to speak. No matter. Zev had not come to make peace with him. Not this time.

As if answering these thoughts, Lady Jos stepped out of a door when Mrs. Thalmew ran by. Zev strode toward her, and as she returned to the room—one of many studies in the apartment—he spied her scowl. After facing the streets of Balica City, he surprised himself with a touch of nervousness.

"I'm pleased you've survived," she said, sitting prim in an oversized reading chair. "But I don't see why you'd bother coming here to visit me."

Zev's stomach clenched. He stood in front of her and tried to ignore the fact that she would not meet his eyes. "I thought you'd be happy. Back from my adventure, ready to settle down with you—all that stuff you said."

"Is that why you're here? You've had your fun and now want something stable, less chaotic, so you come to Lady Jos because she's always waiting for you."

"Isn't that what you said when I left? Isn't that what you've been doing since we were in school together? If I misunderstood, I apologize. As you pointed out the last time we talked—I don't know the basics of relationships very well. Please, help me out here. You seem cross."

With a huff, she looked up at him. Though her brow knitted down in a hard-V and her mouth locked into a tight line, tears ran down her cheeks. "You've ruined it all."

"What did I do?"

"Are you making a joke?" She stomped over to the window and gestured to the burning city.

"You think it's my fault that the Dacci are attacking the city?"

"I think you'll be blamed in part, and that might as well be the same thing. Some failures you can't crawl back from." She rushed over to him, buried her tears in his chest and heaved a sob. "It's not fair. Not to us. We were going to be the best couple in all of the East. You had a path to becoming Leader that would have been easier than most, and I was going to guide you with a loving hand, and it would have worked out fine. I should have known better than to let you go off on this job for Thalmew. He probably knew all along what would happen. He sent you to sabotage our chances."

Patting small circles on her back, Zev said, "I doubt he had his daughter kidnapped just to—"

"And that's why you needed me. You would never have succeeded on your own thinking so highly of people. In politics, everyone is a criminal capable of horrible things in order to attain power."

"Then you should be happy that we won't be a part of it."

"Don't be stupid. We wanted to be a part of it. We wouldn't be like the others. We wouldn't become corrupted. That's the good we could have accomplished. We could have—but it doesn't matter anymore."

Holding her closer, he said, "That's right. It doesn't matter. I came back here. I wanted to see you. That's what matters."

Even as he said the words, he didn't believe them. They simply slipped from his mouth, hoping to console this woman. Except he wondered if she needed consoling at all. Her tears, her anguish, came not from a loss like Pilot suffered over Bellemont. She mourned a future she never had.

"I'm sorry," she said, pushing away from him. "I hope you know that I am crying for you. I do wish we could have made this work."

"You're breaking it off with me—again? Am I supposed to show up tomorrow or is this a real breakup?"

Brushing her tears, she said, "I can't teach you everything. You'll have to figure it out." She added a patronizing smile. "You should go back downstairs. I'm sure Mr. Thalmew has more jobs for you. And wash up. You smell atrocious."

With the battle for Balica City still raging on, Thalmew did need every capable soul. Zev wondered if Lady Jos hoped he would stay, make her cry more before he pledged undying love or something like that. But Bellemont never played such games with Pilot—not that Zev ever saw—and they were the closest couple he had known. If Lady Jos acted more like Bellemont, Zev thought he might have a chance at reacting in the proper way. But why was there a proper way at all? Why couldn't he be allowed to feel the way he felt?

Lady Jos dropped back into her chair, resting her head on her arm. Her body quivered with more tears. Zev stood there, waiting for some clue to what he should do, until at length, he decided to do as she had asked. He headed back to the Battle Room.

CHAPTER FOUR

Axon

Walking through the demolished streets of Balica City, Axon felt as if she strolled across a scene designed to emulate a torn city rather than the actual thing. The pieces looked real enough—after all, they were real—but she had become something different, something removed from it all.

At first, she behaved like the warrior she had been trained to be. Keeping low, moving from covered position to covered position. But when a pair of masked Vashon stepped out of a tavern with stolen mugs of ale, she slashed the air in front of them and droplets of waterfire left nothing behind. One dropped his mug in shock and it cracked into tiny shards soaked in ale. The other one clung to his mug, and the waterfire scorched him into ash—mug and ale, too.

After that, Axon no longer bothered to take cover. She moved down the center of the street with the Water Blade at the ready. Her eyes still scanned ahead and to the sides. She still regularly checked behind her. The Blade caused instant death to her enemies, but it did not stop bullets from killing her or an ambush from beating her down before she could react.

She came upon a deep chasm cutting the city in two. Following it for a long time, she eventually discovered where industrious folks had constructed a makeshift bridge by toppling a corner beam of a nearby building. Crossing required her attention at maintaining balance while still keeping aware of any possible threats. When she set her boots on the other side, she let out a held breath and continued on toward the Thalmew Building.

Several blocks down, she came upon a creature that must have been two Vashon melded into one, covered in feces, and blended with numerous worms. It had been slurping on the corpse of a young family. When it noticed Axon, it reared on its hind legs, towering in an intimidating display—intimidating to anybody else. Axon ambled toward the creature. When she was in range, she whipped the Blade in a large arc, sending a drizzle of waterfire upon it. Walking onward, she listened to the sizzle and the scream.

The closer she came toward the Thalmew Building, the more evidence she saw that an organized defense had been formed. Squads of Eastern soldiers, fully armed and armored, rushed across junctions, heading toward the sounds of violence. Autocarts with mounted repeating rifles navigated the rubble-strewn streets to lend support. She even spotted mounted Royal Guard from the Frontier clearing out the straggler Vashon.

She wanted to followed the soldiers. Join the battle. And she would. But first she had to return to Thalmew. Make sure Zev had arrived safely with Mosol. Make sure Pilot and Bellemont were ready to go back out and fight for the Frontier. And she had to let Mosol know that Byn was dead.

At the street corner, she stopped and gazed off toward the battle. Fire plumed into the air, adding to the skies darkening with smoke. She could do a lot of good with her waterfire.

But she was not a soldier anymore. Running around like a rogue vigilante—no matter how effective—would only cause problems for those in charge. Problems like that could get young soldiers killed.

Better that she finish the job she had been asked to do. Mr. Thalmew would be able to direct her to the most effective location for her waterfire. And if he didn't see the value, she had no doubt King Robion would. He might not like having to deal with her once again, but he never let his personal problems interfere with the right decision.

She had to close her eyes in order to turn away. The lure of the battle tugged at her, but at length, she got moving again, heading toward the Thalmew Building.

Two blocks on, she stopped in the middle of the street. Ahead of her, a Dacci witch knelt before a pile of excrement and bone. The Dacci witch that started all of this—Cova.

"Lep one chus or yoo," Cova said.

Axon only deciphered the words when Cova held up a single tooth —*Left one just for you.*

Cova set the tooth on the pile and giggled as she cast her spell. Axon lifted the Water Blade up high so as to spray the most waterfire when she slashed downward. Then she charged forward.

CHAPTER FIVE

Nothing.

Axon had timed her movements with perfection, bringing down the Blade with the right pressure to create an arc of deadly liquid. But when the waterfire reached Cova, nothing happened.

Nothing.

Cova laughed—a rhythmic, hissing sound.

Uttering her war cry, Axon hauled the Water Blade back upward, flicking more droplets across Cova. Again, nothing. But this time Axon noticed the waterfire puffing into bits of smoke before it touched her.

"A shield," Axon said. "You cast a protection barrier."

"My sisters have always treated me like I was the lesser of them. They produced spells that shine in the eyes of the other witches. But Ellik, my sister in white, she never thinks through the consequences of her spells. She once gave herself skin made of iron but forgot to make herself strong enough to move its huge weight."

Axon thought of the numerous blades that cut the witch as much as they posed a threat. "She's dead now."

"My other sister, Tulra, always overestimates the fear she causes in others. Rather than move with a decisive attack, she'll put on a display meant to cower you until you're no longer a real threat. I suppose you've killed her, too."

"Haven't seen her. But I'll happily kill her when I get the chance."

"I'm more careful with my spells. I cast practical, useful spells."

Axon frowned. "I can understand you clearly." Her blood chilled. "Did you hold back more teeth?"

Opening her mouth wide, Cova's lips sucked inward—no teeth at all. But with all the clarity of a full set, she said, "Just a little benefit of my spell. You see? Practical. Useful."

A rapid succession of pops in the distance erupted followed by a deep blast. More weapons engaged in the assault. Sporadic bursts of rifle fire followed by heavier return fire—the soldiers must have been fighting Vashon. Until the unmistakable roar of the Emissary drowned all other sounds of battle. As that noise dimmed, a cascade of screams followed.

Cova's hissing laugh returned. "You'd best run. The Emissary will destroy your army, and eventually, you as well. Anybody who stays in this city will die except the witches."

"And you plan to sit there under your protection spell until it's all over?"

"Once this day is over, the war is over. Only the Dacci will remain, and I will be perfectly situated for a powerful, ranking position. Practical and useful."

Axon didn't have time for this. The longer it took her to get to the Thalmew Building, the longer it would take her to be assigned a task in the battle, and the longer it would be before she could aid those already in the fray. Dealing with Cova felt like a stupid waste.

But Axon could not live with herself if this witch went on to cause more pain and more death. And she would. Axon had no doubt.

She swung the Blade again, and as before, she only saw puffs of smoke hovering in the air where the waterfire touched the spell.

"That won't work, and I can hold this shield for days."

Axon sneered as if she could destroy the witch's spell with merely a look. Perhaps she should be more like Zev. He never worried about the expectations of others. He only followed rules when they made sense to him. At least, it seemed that way. Did she really need to go back to the Thalmew Building? She had one of the most powerful weapons in her hand. Surely when she arrived on the battlefield, those in charge would welcome her addition. After all, a good army had to adapt to changing circumstances—the battlefield changed all the time.

But this debate did not matter—not yet. As long as Cova remained alive, Axon had no room to choose between the Thalmew Building or the battlefield. She glowered at Cova.

Hissing more laughter, the old witch rocked from side to side. Axon spotted something. Little marks hovering in the air. She would never have noticed them if not for the witch's shifting motion.

Those marks were at the same points Axon had struck with waterfire. She looked closer at Cova—inspected every twitch of her mouth, every narrowed gaze, every flared nostril. The witch looked worried—perhaps even scared.

"I don't think you can hold that spell as long as you claim."

Cova put her arms out as if bracing the air around her. No witty comeback. No hissing laughter.

Not bothering to stand back, Axon brought the Water Blade in a wheeling arc that clashed down upon the spelled air. She pulled back the Blade, pausing to inspect the damage done—a long, smoking gash glowed where contact had been made. Axon noticed Cova staring at the gash as well. As the witch's eyes widened, Axon's narrowed.

She hacked down with the Water Blade. Once, twice, again, again. White smoke clouded the air around them. The smell of unnatural burning filled Axon's airways. When she next brought the Blade down, the burning marks caused by the waterfire jumped.

Not the marks—the shield. It no longer held firm to the ground. Axon grinned, letting the triumphant warrior have a moment of release.

She resumed attacking, using the Blade like an axe. *Whack. Whack. Whack.* Over and over. Waterfire pooled in the deepening crevice. More strikes splashed the liquid into the air, and as it fell down upon the shield, it burned new holes, bigger holes.

"Wait, wait," Cova said, the pleading in her voice fueling Axon to hit harder. "Please, have mercy."

Axon raised the Blade once more and pointed it straight downward. She plunged it into the shield. Pushing, pushing, the Blade sank deeper. It punctured the shield, slowly moving towards Cova. The witch shrank from the Blade but had nowhere to go. As she screamed, Axon roared.

Waterfire dripped down the Blade and formed a large drop on the end. It glistened like a teardrop catching the summer sun. Warrior and witch watched this drop descend through the air. Wobbling and rippling as it fell, its taste of death drew closer. When it landed in Cova's lap, she shrieked. Her spell dissolved, and Axon tumbled forward, plunging the Blade through Cova's chest.

It drove through her back and dug into the ground. Axon's momentum knocked her forward and off balance. Cova turned to ash as

Axon rolled through and back onto her feet. Whirling around, her eyes darted from point-to-point, seeking any potential ambush.

Confident no other threats were present, she stood straight and glanced down at the ash pile. A soft breeze blew over her, and she felt the cold of her soaked clothes press against her skin. She was drenched. In waterfire.

Yet she lived.

With her head bowed, she gazed over herself, amazed that this powerful weapon could discern her foes. She had to be careful, though. She had no proof it singled out anyone but herself. Okay—she could experiment later. For now, she had to assume that she was the only one immune.

A trickle of waterfire ran down her cheek and into the corner of her mouth. Without thinking, she licked her lips.

The instant the waterfire touched her tongue, a glorious sensation swelled through her body. She gasped as if plunged into a cold lake on a blazing hot day. Her bones started to ache even as delightful warmth caressed her muscles. Something was changing.

Like the receding tide, the moisture left her mouth. Her tongue craved that sensation again and her eyes drifted to the Water Blade. With all the desire of a starving person seeing perfectly cooked meat, she brought the Blade towards her mouth. She hesitated.

Pilot would do it. Bellemont might. Zev would protest, urging for caution, but in the end, if things looked dire, he would do it, too.

Glancing down the long avenue, knowing that in the distance, a monstrous creature devoured the city, she said, "Couldn't get much more dire."

She brought the Blade closer and began to drink.

CHAPTER SIX

Zev

Once the commotion caused by Mosol's reunion with her family had ended, the Battle Room returned to its steady hum of activity. Zev stood at the large map in the center with Mr. Thalmew and King Robion. Nobody objected to his presence, but Zev guessed that level of courtesy would not last long. For the moment, he was the hero who had saved the Leader's daughter. Later, he would simply be in the way.

Reports came in at a regular pace, following the path through the room's many hands until they finally reached Marcel. He then marched to the map and adjusted the figures to represent the current state of the battle. Others had a similar job creating a staccato motion on the map.

Thalmew twisted his bottom lip as he focused on the moving pieces. Zev thought the man looked frazzled—not to the point of recklessness, but rather near the point of being unable to make a decision. This was not political maneuvering nor the machinery of a company. This was war. This was death. And now that his daughter was safe, his mind could no longer be distracted by his worry for her. Zev cringed. That was the answer. Thalmew only now looked upon this map with his mind fully engaged in the situation.

King Robion, on the other hand, observed the map with the clarity of someone who understood battle. Like most kings, he had been trained to think in militaristic terms. Like most good kings, he had learned to think beyond that. Even if Zev had not observed King Robion directly on several occasions, he would see now that the man should be the one in charge.

But, of course, this was not the King's city. This was not his country. That didn't stop him from doing what he could.

"During his time in the Frontier, Zev became widely known as a great Master-Solver." King Robion passed his hand over the map. "Tell us, Master-Solver, what do you think is the answer to all of this?"

Thalmew looked upon Zev with more than hope. He had a desperation in his eyes betraying a fantastical wish for a miracle solution. Zev imagined the man thought something akin to *If he saved my daughter and returned her safely through all of this, then surely, he can save us all.*

Axon or Pilot were better suited to this, but Axon was off in the sewers and Pilot had been escorted by force to another room for medical care. The map didn't look too bad, so perhaps he could see something the others did not. Certainly, King Robion thought so, and if the King wanted to give Zev a chance, no point in wasting it.

The basic layout of troops appeared simple enough. About twelve blocks away, a rough line had been formed where soldiers fought Vashon and witches. About half that distance back, more forces gathered in five large groups, each spread several blocks apart from the other. The Royal Guard filled in wherever needed. Sporadic figures were added and removed throughout the city as reports of small clashes arrived. Beyond it all, the braided yarn representing the Emissary moved toward the main battle.

Off toward the coast, Zev noticed a red line had been drawn as well as a second line near the southern border. Thalmew answered, "Any civilians we find on the streets or hiding in their homes or wherever are being relocated behind those lines. I've sent requests to our neighboring cities, and with any luck, there will be boats arriving soon to get our citizens safe. The ones in the south are scattering into the countryside, but I'm expecting our southern cities to send public autocarts—the big ones—to transport as many people out of here as possible."

It sounded good. Even hopeful. But taking in the size of the city, Zev understood that these rescue efforts would barely help one percent of the population.

"Are there any other forces coming?" he asked. "These other cities are providing boats and autocarts, what about soldiers?"

Marcel brushed Zev aside so he could remove several soldiers and two Vashon from the map. When Thalmew did not answer, Marcel said, "They won't sacrifice their own people. Not until they're sure the threat has hurt Leader Thalmew as much as possible."

Zev kept his eyes on the map for fear of looking at Thalmew with disdain. "Politics. They're going to let their political ambitions allow the death of Balica City. But they're Easterners, too."

"That only goes so far," Thalmew finally said. "For now, they see opportunity. If we die here, if this creature rampages towards them, then they'll band together."

Zev turned to King Robion. "The peace treaty? How could you make peace with the East if they're this divided?"

"We have to start somewhere," King Robion said.

Marcel said, "Perhaps, brother, you should focus on helping the current problems instead of on the past. That defensive line won't hold, and these troop gatherings are no stronger. The moment that monster decides to stop smashing buildings and start helping the Vashon, we've lost."

"What other weapons do you have?" Zev asked. "I've heard about the East's constant innovation. If you have some experimental weapons, now would be the time to try them out."

Thalmew shook his head. "The monster has already destroyed what prototypes we had. What is on this map is all that's left."

"You see?" Marcel said. "No amount of your brain power is going to solve anything. We need to evacuate ourselves and get those behind the red lines to safety."

"And the rest of the city?" Zev asked.

"They're already dead. Whether they know it or not."

"That's disgusting. We don't give up on our people."

"It's practical. Realistic. And they are not *your* people. You left us to go play farmer in the Frontier."

"You can't just discard all those lives. You can't be that callous."

Thalmew said, "Nobody would do such a thing lightly. But your brother has a point."

"Thank you," Marcel said. "The Asterling family, those of us who have stayed around, have learned a hard lesson of business. Knowing when to cut your losses is key."

Zev smacked the table. "These aren't products that fail to sell or a bad advertising campaign. These are people."

"Then give me the number of how many are worth killing so that you can save one? Because that's what you're asking. If we go now, those that live will be able to reorganize, analyze what has happened here today, and develop a strategy that will destroy our enemies—saving everybody else. Including you and those of the Frontier. How many of those people are worth sacrificing so that we might get out another block of the city's citizens?"

"Those aren't the right questions."

"Those are exactly the questions we face. Right or not, that's what we're dealing with. You want to know why Father never once seriously considered you to run the company—it's right here. You're not willing to make the hard decisions. You want to let your emotions rule."

"If you're going to be a heartless bastard at least be an honest one. You are acting out of emotion just as much as me. The only difference is my emotion is that of caring for others. You're simply acting out of fear."

"You should remember that you're only allowed in this room out of respect for saving Mosol. Keep talking like this, and we'll have you thrown out."

King Robion's hand came firmly down on Zev's shoulder. "There is no good that will come fighting each other. Especially brothers. Mr. Thalmew, my Royal Guard is still at your disposal. While we should make plans for a safe retreat that will preserve as many as we can, let us keep seeking a better solution."

"Agreed," Thalmew said. "Marcel, your input is appreciated. But I think you need to step back and calm down." Before Marcel could respond, he added, "That's an order."

As Marcel stormed off, King Robion said, "Zev, come with me."

CHAPTER SEVEN

They rode the lifter up, and King Robion chuckled. "Allow a friend to offer a little advice—stay out of politics. It's not for you."

Zev could not hold back a snicker. "I suppose not. Although Lady Jos seems to think that I could lead this whole country."

King Robion burst into hearty laughter. Zev joined in, and for a brief moment, the past disappeared and the present floated away. For a few precious seconds, they were two men, two friends, and nothing more.

But then the lifter stopped. King Robion's wide smile dropped and his eyes looked away as cold reality chilled the compartment.

He opened the door and stepped out onto the roof. The pungent burning hit hard this high in the air and the temperature chilled their skin. King Robion walked out to the edge, and Zev followed.

"Look," the King said. "See for yourself what it is we are facing."

Stretching out before him, Zev's eyes took in a huge swath of the city. The battle was no longer a single city block filled with rubble and roving bands of Vashon. It was no longer empty streets with citizens cowering behind closed doors. It was no longer Dacci spells sprinkled between sporadic bursts of rifle fire. This was something far different. Far more horrifying.

Just as the Emissary had carved a chasm down a wide avenue, the destruction it left behind created a winding path through the city. Entire blocks were gone. Simply gone. What debris remained had been flattened. Fires blazed along the western section of the city—not in small little glowing patches, but an inferno engulfing the equivalent of a small town. The distinct flash of spells flickered throughout the dark streets like heat lightning on a summer night. But it wasn't night. The sun would still shine for hours more, but the smoke of destruction crowded out the daylight. In the distance, lording over it all, the Emissary clutched the side of building as it ripped apart walls and smashed through floors.

"This is why your brother seeks to retreat and regroup."

"Sounds like you agree. But why didn't you say so? Why did you suggest we should still look for an answer?"

"Because we should. Retreat is not an option until there is no other option. From the way you and your brother spoke, I thought perhaps you did not grasp the full situation from the map alone. Now, I think you do."

W hen they returned to the Battle Room, Thalmew studied the city and Marcel stood nearby like a scolded child. Zev noticed a new tension hanging in the air. The soldiers still bustled about performing their tasks, but they kept part of their attention on Thalmew. He looked different, too.

He still twisted his lip, but the worry had gone from his eyes. No. Zev had to look harder but the concerns were still there. A layer of fierce concentration, of calculation, had covered over the fears.

"You've got an idea how to win this," Zev said.

Thalmew brought his finger away from his mouth and tapped at locations on the map. Each time, he left a wet circle behind. "We are not dealing with an enemy that organizes in any logical manner. At least, not logical to us. Whether the Dacci or the Vashon or a combination of both, whoever is in charge does not think like you or I. And that monster has shown every sign that it thinks like an animal. What we've seen throughout these smaller skirmishes, especially here and here and here, is that even when we win, we lose soldiers. Little by little, they are whittling away at us. If we are going to strike hard and decisively, we must do so now. Forget about these smaller conflicts and let our trickles of soldiers combine into a massive river that will wash away our enemy."

King Robion looked closer at the map. "A final push to wipe away the Vashon and the Dacci."

"The monster will be another matter. But if we can use a large force to destroy everything else, we'll have a chance."

Marcel stepped forward and faced Zev. "Do you understand that abandoning the smaller fights means adding to the death toll of our citizens."

Zev said, "Allowing our enemies to reign free in the city will be worse."

"An assault like this will mean the loss of many soldiers. If we fail, we might not have anything left to stop the Dacci and Vashon from taking the city."

King Robion said, "And the longer we wait to act, the more attrition we will suffer. Mr. Thalmew, I suggest using my Royal Guard to spread the word. With the roads in such shambles, they'll move faster on horseback than your men can in an autocart."

Thalmew snapped a finger at one soldier. "We begin."

The room burst into a flurry of activity far beyond what had been. Orders that had been prepared and waiting now flew between people, notes being recorded, the map being updated, and soldiers running in and out of the room. It would take time for the various gatherings to move together as one large force, but it would happen. They simply had to wait.

King Robion sent one of his own attendants to summon Pilot. Provided his injuries were taken care of, as Captain of the Royal Guard, Pilot needed to be part of this.

But a short while later, the attendant returned with an odd look on her face. "Forgive me, sir, but Captain Pilot cannot be found."

"What?" King Robion said. "How could you lose an injured, high-ranking officer? Send out every available person. Check every floor. The roof, too."

"Already done, sir. He's not here."

Zev's stomach sank. "He went back. He went to fight."

"That's insanity," King Robion said. "Why would he—oh. Bellemont. He wants vengeance."

"Or worse."

"Suicide? Perhaps a combination. Kill as many of the enemy as he can until they destroy him. Then he can join his love in whatever is after."

Zev headed toward the lifter. "I'll bring him back."

"No. We can't afford to lose you, too. The Royal Guard can spare a few to find their captain."

"Sorry, King, but I don't answer to you."

"Then Mr. Thalmew will order you."

"Don't answer to him, either. I'm a man without a country. Or perhaps I belong to them all. Right now, I'm a man with a friend in trouble."

Thalmew showed no signs of interfering. His attention remained on the map, and Zev doubted he had heard a word of this. King Robion must have noticed as well because he waved Zev off.

"Don't fail," he said.

When Zev reached the main floor, he stepped outside and approached the outfitter—several tables put together where soldiers could get equipment. He needed a rifle, extra rounds, and some armor would be a good idea, too. The soldier in charge refused.

"I don't give nothing out unless you got an order. And you don't even look like you're in this army."

"If I go back up there, I'll be returning with an order personally signed by Leader Thalmew—as well as a demotion for you."

"Good friends with the Leader, huh?" The soldier grinned. "You and everybody else. In fact, I hear his daughter's back. Maybe you're going to marry her and call the leader *Pops*. Is that it?"

"Look here—"

"You want these supplies, then you go ahead and get that order. I'd like to see it happen."

Zev's fist curled, but a voice called out his name. He looked back to find Marcel standing near the building entrance. His brother wore a heavy hunting coat that looked as if it had never been used before. And he carried two rifles. The first had belonged to Marcel, and though Zev thought his brother had only fired it twice in his life, he held it with comfort. The second rifle belonged to Zev. Marcel had sent it as a gift years ago.

Zev rushed over and snatched up the familiar weapon. "Thank you. I know how to shoot true with this darling."

"I thought you might appreciate it. Perhaps you can give me a few tips on our way to your friend."

Zev stared at Marcel, unable to find words that made sense to him.

"Is it that odd for me to care about you?" Marcel said. "You are my brother, after all. You're a sore on my ass, but you're still family. Besides, Father would never forgive me if I let you go out there alone without orders. If Thalmew had simply demanded it of you, then I wouldn't have to help. But as it were, oh, stop gaping at me. I'm babbling out of nerves, not because I don't care. Now close your mouth, load your rifle, and let's get going."

"Thank you," Zev said again for nothing else seemed appropriate.

"Yes, yes. Just don't tell Mercy. If I die out there, she'll kill me."

CHAPTER EIGHT

Axon

T he world brightened. Despite the waning hours, despite the smoke-choked sky, despite dust and grit clogging the air. Even amongst the wretched screams, the foul smells, the unending death—the world brightened.

Axon had never experienced such detail before. All her senses fired off, tingling her mind with clarity. She saw a strand of hair clinging to a broken window two blocks away. She heard the heartbeat of a soldier facing down a Dacci witch. She smelled the endless list of ingredients making up the air around her—burning wood, a rotten apple, soup that somebody had been preparing before the chaos, a gentle perfume, a heavy sweat, the rot of the sewers, crushed leaves, and fresh blood.

The assault of information overloaded her mind, and she struggled to make sense of it. But that passed. Each breath filling her lungs, each pulse of blood through her system, pulled her out of the dissonance. She could not explain how she learned to control the sensory flow. Instinct controlled the moment. She just knew.

Leaning back, she peered through the dark billows and the gray clouds and found the stars. Even with the sun still shining, she could see the stars. In fact, wherever she looked, she could pass through anything that obstructed her view and see what she wanted. Or needed.

Needed? Yes. She felt a need, an urgency.

The world had shifted askew. It was all wrong.

She wondered if the Nine felt like this. When the Shul told her that the Nine had guided her path so that she would find the Cistern, was this what those gods and goddesses experienced? Did they see the world with this ultra-clarity? She thought so. Because she also thought that, perhaps, given enough time, she could learn to see the consequences of moving any single speck of dirt, how they would bloom into changing entire lives.

Opening her eyes—she didn't recall when she had closed them—she discovered that she sat cross-legged and only her fingertips brushed the ground. The rest of her hovered. Nothing held her up. She floated over the ground.

"Am I a goddess?"

CHAPTER NINE

Zev

Long before they reached the battle, Zev and Marcel grew cautious at the growing sounds of conflict. For all his courage in accompanying Zev through the streets, the constant drumroll of weapons, the shouts and screams, the Emissary's multiple-mouthed shrieks all filled Marcel with visible apprehension. Zev wanted to tell his brother that it was okay to be nervous, that even after being in numerous battles both large and small his own nerves still fired up as well, but he stayed silent. Better for Marcel to put on a brave face. At least, it had been Zev's experience that faking bravery often led to feeling it. Or, at least, helping survive and breaking down later.

Hustling down the next block—Marcel moving well despite his limp— the violence grew louder and the smoke thicker. Wounded men hobbled along the sidewalk, heading back to medical stations set up on off-streets. On the opposite sidewalk, dead soldiers from earlier in the day had been lined up shoulder-to-shoulder.

Zev peeked at his brother. Marcel moved like a horse with blinders— eyes ahead, facing the task ahead, everything ahead. No wounded, no dead, nothing around him.

Not a bad coping strategy. For the moment. But Zev knew that should they live through this, Marcel would suffer greatly. He could pretend not to see the horrors around him, but it was only pretend. His mind would revisit these sights for years. Zev thought he should say something but stayed silent again.

When they hit the next block, all opportunity to impart some battle-field wisdom vanished. They were *on* the battlefield.

Eastern soldiers had taken two positions on either side of the street while a wall of Vashon blocked the end. Behind them, barely visible, a Dacci witch sat on her knees working a spell. In the space between these two forces, dead Vashon and dead Easterners bloodied the ground.

Zev pulled Marcel down. "Stay low," he shouted over the constant barrage of weapons. "Follow me."

Marcel, pale as moonlight, nodded hard.

They scurried toward the right. Zev had spotted a man who appeared to be in charge—at least, the man gave orders that were being followed. As they approached, soldiers on the left shouted, "Ten on the run!"

Ten of the mutated Vashon sprinted forward. The other Vashon opened with covering fire. Zev grabbed Marcel's shoulder to stop his brother from running and directed him behind the remnants of a large wardrobe on its side and the brick wall it had been thrown through. When he heard the Eastern soldiers return fire, he peeked over the top of the wardrobe.

Several of the creatures had thick-shelled skin, one bore only the bottom half of a head, and another looked more shaggy beast than man. All lay in pools of blood. What a waste.

Pointing Marcel onward, Zev wondered why the Vashon thought such a charge might work. Perhaps he could get answers up ahead. They reached the soldiers on the right, and Zev went to the man in charge.

"Who are you?" the man said.

"Zev and Marcel Asterling. You?"

"Epit Conwell," he said, barking for his men to hold steady and keep the enemy pinned down. Zev thought he recognized the family name—the Conwells were rather new to the business world, and he imagined very new to war. Epit glanced beyond Zev. "You're all I'm getting for rein-forcements?"

"We're not reinforcements, but we'll help where we can."

"Then what are you doing here?"

Bullets spit across the building to their right. Marcel flattened to the ground while Zev and Epit continued to talk.

"We're looking for the Captain of the Royal Guard."

"Royal Guard? Like from the Frontier?"

"Right. He's injured and roaming around here somewhere. We have orders to—"

"Sorry. Haven't seen him."

Epit froze. Following his gaze, Zev watched as the Dacci witch sprouted giant claws, massive muscles, and a thick hide as she towered over the Vashon. Now he understood the previous attack. They were sacrificing their own fighters to locate the safest path forward for their witch.

"Concentrate fire on that thing!" Epit pointed to the Dacci beast, but nobody needed to be told. Rifles already cracked bullets at the altered witch.

Slobbered drool swung from its jaws. Round after round shot holes through its body, but it persisted onward. The Vashon continued to fight back with volleys of their own.

"Why are we staying?" Marcel said. "Pilot's not here."

"You want to leave these men to die?"

"Better than dying with them."

Zev set his rifle in place, aimed, and took a shot. "We're here to help as well. Start shooting."

Snarling, the altered witch bounded forth, lowered its head, and rammed the barricade on the left side. The soldiers scattered. All but one that got caught between the barricade and a wall. Blood streamed beneath. He wouldn't last long.

The entire contingent on the right, including Zev and Marcel, swung their rifles and let loose a barrage of firepower. They put two dozen holes into the witch until she finally fell to the ground. She kept breathing but showed no more fight.

The other soldiers regrouped. Buoyed by the death of the witch, they charged the Vashon. Zev thought such a reckless attack would fail, but the Vashon retreated. Ran like frightened kids.

"Now can we go?" Marcel said.

"I think so. We should check with—"

A massive mucous-covered limb slapped down across the junction, flattened three soldiers into a mush of blood and waste. All eyes turned upward as the Emissary stomped across several blocks. It did not appear to noticed the killing of these soldiers. They were merely bugs under its hand—unnoticed as the enormous creature plowed through building after building. The Emissary moved on, leaving the dead stuck to the street.

Marcel sat with his rifle cradled to his chest. "That-that-that thing is huge."

"Yeah," Zev said, trying to pull Marcel to his feet. "It smells really bad, too."

"This is insane. Throwing our entire army against that thing is going to fail." He grabbed Zev's arms. "We've got to go back to the Thalmew Building. Make them understand this is hopeless. Call a full retreat."

"Too late for that."

"B-But you were the one concerned about saving lives. What's the point of forcing every soldier we have to commit suicide against that thing? W-We have to face reality. We've lost."

Zev shrugged off his brother's grip. Then he slapped Marcel's cheek hard enough to leave a red mark. "I didn't ask you to come along, but you are not running out now." A better approach flashed in his mind. "These soldiers have seen you and word will spread that the Asterlings are actually fighting. We're not hiding away with the other rich families. We're doing our part. Think how that will look when this is over. You'll have raised the family name higher than it's ever been."

The conflict within Marcel played out on his brow, but he managed a slow nod of understanding. Zev would take it.

Conwell waved Zev over as a runner took off with a message for another part of the battle. "Got a report that a single member of the Royal Guard is fighting off a bunch of Vashon two blocks west over by Genfort Square. Might be your man."

"Thank you."

"Better hurry. Those Vashon we scared off are heading in that direction. I'd offer help, but we've got to keep pressing forward so that pile of crud doesn't turn back on us."

Zev put out a hand. "Good luck."

"You, too." Conwell shook Zev's hand before issuing orders to his men.

To Marcel, Zev said, "Come on. We've got to go."

"Go? You don't know if that's Pilot. We should stay with these soldiers until we know. At least, we're not alone here."

"A single Royal Guard taking on every Vashon in the area? That's Pilot. Now move."

CHAPTER TEN

T he last time Zev visited Genfort Square, he must have been around ten. Marcel was with him then, too, and it was possible that his brother had also not returned in all these years. He remembered the trip well. The Square was a vibrant, open area surrounded by four tall, perfectly square buildings. Instead of a road circle for the horses (and now, the autocarts) like in most open areas throughout the city, the Square had the roads removed. Only people had access. The entire area had been paved with brick and an impressive statue of a soldier on horseback dominated the center.

On most days, the Square acted as an open market, but once a week, it transformed into a place filled with amusements for children. Puppet shows, skill competitions, music, dancing, fresh sweets both hot and cold, a tent of oddities found from around the world, artists who would paint a funny picture for a coin—an amazing assortment of adventures for two young boys to spend the afternoon enjoying.

Peering over the lip of a glassless windowpane, crouched against a wall in what remained of the bottom floor of one of those perfectly square buildings, Zev saw nothing enjoyable at all. Most of the Square had been emptied out. The fine brickwork on the ground now looked like an uneven, pocked mess of chipped bricks, mud, and blood. A small fire of market stands burned in one corner and the statue in the center had lost its top half—it lay in several pieces scattered across the bricks.

Eleven masked Vashon were spread throughout the back of the Square, taking cover behind the statue, a few stands, and a wall made from two autocarts turned on their sides. Beyond this line of armed men, fifteen dead Vashon bloodied an open area leading to the building on the far end. At odd intervals, a rifle would shoot from one window or another on the third floor.

Pilot. By shifting from window to window, and by killing so many of their men, he left the Vashon unsure of how many soldiers they faced. Nobody appeared too eager to attempt to cross in order to find out. But Pilot would not have unlimited ammunition. They were waiting him out, taking the occasional shot in hopes of a lucky hit, and trying to figure out a way to end this faster.

No witch. That much was good. Possibly, Pilot had help inside that building, but Zev doubted it. Even if they were being conservative with every shot, there should have been a few times where they fired close to simultaneously or from different floors or in some other way that took advantage of having more than one rifleman.

Well, he had more than one now. Turning to Marcel, Zev said, "We're in a good flanking position from here. When we open fire, we want to kill with both our shots. After that, they'll have to engage with us, and it'll get rough. You understand?"

Marcel nodded, his eyes unblinking as he watched the Square.

"Can you make a shot like that from here? Marcel?" Zev shoved his brother's shoulder.

"Yes, yes," Marcel said. "I'm sure a better shot than you. I actually practice."

Zev dug out all the rounds from his pockets and placed them on the ground within easy reach. He motioned for Marcel to do the same. As they prepped for the fight, he said, "I'm sorry that you came along. I mean, no, I didn't mean it like that. I meant that I'm sorry that I've put you in a position where you felt it necessary to come along. I know when I left for the Frontier—I assume anyway—that Father was not kind to you."

"That's an understatement."

"I knew he would take out his anger on you, but I also thought that you wanted to be where you are now." Zev snickered. "Not actually right now, but in broader terms—you wanted to be the family representative and you want further political positions. That hasn't changed, has it?"

"Doesn't matter what I want. This is where I am. I'm well-suited for it, too. You? I'm glad you left. You would have ruined this family if you had stayed. All your soft-heartedness. You'd never be able to make the cold decisions. Like now. I'm right. We shouldn't be here. We should be organizing the retreat. I know I'm right about that. I know it." Marcel kept repeating those last words as they drifted into a mumbling mantra.

Zev wanted to say something else, find some way to let his brother know that he still cared, that their bond meant something to him, but fear occupied too much of Marcel's mind. The man would never hear Zev. The best he could do was set his rifle on the windowsill, look over at his brother, and say, "For the Asterling family."

Marcel did his best to nod with courage. "For the Asterling family."

They opened fire.

CHAPTER ELEVEN

Both rifles unloaded. Four rounds between them. Three Vashon dropped. A far better result than Zev had hoped for.

When the return fire came, Zev and Marcel kissed the floorboards as bullets flew overhead. But it didn't last long. Pilot took advantage and popped off two more rounds, killing another Vashon.

And as simple as that, the battle had shifted. The Vashon panicked, waving their rifles from one threat to the other, unable to figure out how many soldiers they faced. Zev and Marcel reloaded fast, and this time, when they brought out their rifles, Zev held back as Marcel shot. The moment Marcel dropped to reload, Zev opened fire. He took his time, aiming with care, and knowing that when he finished, Marcel would be ready to fire again. Add in Pilot's unpredictable shots and they had the Vashon confused and careless.

One wearing a mask covered in screaming faces sat a bit too tall. Zev zeroed in on that mask. But before he squeezed the trigger, blood burst out the side of the Vashon's head. The crack of Pilot's rifle came a second later.

Searching for the next good target, Zev noticed the Vashon had ceased firing back. In fact, they had flattened to the ground. Trying to piece together what sort of tactic this would be, the Vashon jumped to their feet and bolted away.

"Ha! Run, you bastards, run! Ha!" Marcel's triumphant shouting tinged with laughter bordering on hysterics.

Zev did not join in. While they had succeeded in knocking down the enemies' numbers, a retreat seemed odd. The Vashon still had the advantage. Perhaps they sought to regroup with more and return. Perhaps they had used more ammunition than Zev had realized. Whatever the case, he figured the best thing now was to gather Pilot and get out of there before the Vashon reconsidered their actions.

Thump.

The sound struck Zev in the chest.

Thump.

Marcel stopped shouting.

Thump.

The broken glass danced on the floorboards, and Zev's lined-up bullets toppled over.

With shaking hands, Zev scooped up his ammunition and shoved it in his pocket. "We've got to run. We've got to get to Pilot's building."

"I'm not going out there. That's crazy."

"We run across, get Pilot, and leave."

"Then he should run to us. We go get him, we've got to turn back to here again."

"We're not coming back this way. The Emissary is somewhere behind us. Near that way, I think. We get Pilot and keep going."

Marcel looked over his shoulder as if he could see through the walls. The next *Thump* made the floor jump beneath them. "Okay, let's go. Now. Go. Come on. Go, go."

They scurried to their feet and sprinted into the open.

The world shrunk. Nothing existed but the distance between buildings. Nothing made a sound but Zev's breathing and the crunch of his boots against the debris-strewn bricks. This emptiness surrounded him like a protective bubble conjured by Bellemont. But thinking of her broke the illusion. As did the eruption of weapons a few blocks over.

Marcel raced ahead, his uneven gait not encumbering his pace, but Zev stuttered to a halt. He turned his head, gazing over his shoulder and up into the air. Four spots moved through the smoke-filled sky. They grew larger.

At first, Zev thought the Emissary had thrown pieces of wall or entire autocarts into the Square. An aerial attack of sorts. He even inhaled to yell for Marcel to take cover.

But then the four spots took shape. They had limbs. They were screaming. With damp thuds of finality, each solider bashed into the Square. No rolling, no bouncing. Just hit flat and stopped like a mud patty.

"Keep running!" The voice came from above—Pilot.

Despite the difficulty of looking away from those horrible dead, Zev managed to get his feet moving. But only a few steps. The Emissary arrived, and Zev froze.

It stood on its hind legs—hands, actually—like a rejected creation of Axon's gods and goddesses. Arms and hands poked out like misshapen tree limbs. Mouths opened with no sense of order. Only the constant smell of burning in the air saved Zev from the foulness of the Emissary's stink. Well, muted it a bit, at least.

"You bastard!" Pilot opened fire from the third-floor window. Spewing a mouthful of vengeance and hate, he screamed as he fired again.

If the bullets found their target, and Zev could not imagine missing such a massive target, they did not appear to do any harm. Probably felt like bug bites. And while receiving hundreds of bug bites would not feel good, they would not kill a thing, either.

The Emissary moved further into the Square, each footfall trembling the ground. A high-pitched noise rang in Zev's ear—Marcel. His brother stared at this incomprehensible beast and did all that his mind could manage. He screamed.

That got Zev moving. He sprinted toward Marcel, grabbed his wrist, and yanked him into motion. Pilot squeezed off two more rounds as Zev led his brother toward the building.

Uttering croaked, scratchy cries from several of its mouths, the Emissary punched holes in the walls to its left. From all Zev had seen that day, and more from that moment, the Emissary did not discern between soldiers and property. It had one simple purpose—destroy the city. Everything.

Which meant that as long as they didn't draw the monster's attention, they could slip away, unseen like mere skittering bugs. Except that Pilot acted like the biting kind.

"Stop shooting," Zev yelled as he ran. No way would Pilot hear that. Not over his rifle fire. Not over the Emissary's ear-shattering roars.

The top of the building the Emissary worked on tore away. When it crashed below, dust billowed out to fill the entire Square. Zev dropped to the ground, taking Marcel with him. Thin shards of brick and tiny daggers of glass peppered them. Large chunks of wall rained down and endless pebbles rattled the ground. One long section of floorboard smacked across Zev's legs and bounced away end over end.

The instant the noise of falling debris settled, Zev heaved back on his feet. Coughing, he helped Marcel up, and the brothers half-ran, half-stumbled forward. Zev hoped the thinning dust cloud would obscure them enough to get to Pilot safely, but he heard Pilot yelling obscenities at the Emissary and firing once again.

Spitting dust, the Emissary stomped on the ground—Pilot's little needles had finally bothered the creature. Zev tried to keep moving, but the shaking street knocked him down. Even crawling proved difficult. His mind judged where to place his hand or knee, but then the ground moved.

Blocking the entranceway, a marble dining table stood on end, partially buried in the brick ground. They would have to climb over to get inside. Not that Zev wanted to be inside any building near the Emissary, but they had to get Pilot out of there. Stumbling to his feet, he coughed and peered at the window he last saw Pilot. Maybe if he could get the man's attention, he could wave him down instead.

But Marcel changed matters. Painted in dust, he wobbled toward the Emissary, his eyes locked open wide, his mouth agape. He held his rifle across one shoulder as he shouted. "You want to kill us? Then kill us already. We're right here. Stop toying around and get on with it."

"Lay down," Zev said.

"Why? Look at it. There's no stopping that. It's pointless." Marcel gazed back at the Emissary, tears turning the dust on his cheeks to mud. "I'm not afraid of you. See that? No reason to be afraid when you know it's all over."

Zev bolted towards his brother but not fast enough. Marcel swung his rifle down toward his hip and shot. He laughed and shot again. The Emissary swept one hand as if discarding an annoyance. Marcel reloaded and shot a third time.

Reaching out, Zev's fingers brushed Marcel's arm, but the Emissary stomped the ground. Zev fell over. Not Marcel, though. He saw it coming and had the presence to use his rifle for support. Then he ran toward the Emissary, rambling madness, his voice so high-pitched and cracking that Zev couldn't understand any of the words.

At closer range, Marcel managed a fourth shot. Zev watched, helpless to stop the moments playing out before him. The Emissary's hand that brushed the ground flicked out fast and smacked Marcel into the air. With an accepting grin on his face, Marcel soared backward and crashed into a pile of rubble that had once been several market stands.

Zev dashed to his brother. Cut and bruised, Marcel lay in a nest of splintered wood, some old cloth, and plenty of rocks. Giddy laughter escaped his mouth.

"I think I broke my leg," he said.

Zev had seen this kind of thing before—usually with drunks. Marcel had accepted his death as inevitable, so when he flew across the Square, his body relaxed. Like a drunk, his limbs flopped and flowed when he hit the rubble instead of resisting and breaking. Well, all but his leg apparently.

"Take cover," Pilot yelled.

Zev saw his old friend jumping down from the marble table and bolting away from the building. Standing over him, the Emissary pounded the walls with some of its numerous fists. No time to move Marcel. Zev covered his head and draped over his brother.

"Why'd you come here?" Pilot said as he approached through the fresh dust plumes.

The refuse of destroyed buildings hit the ground like hail. When it slowed, Zev pushed off his brother. "I couldn't let you get yourself killed."

"You think I tried to kill myself? I'm angry, heartbroken—not stupid. I wanted to kill as many of those bastards as possible." Pilot peeked back at the Emissary as it shoveled the contents of an entire floor toward one of its gaping mouths. "I didn't expect that thing to bother with me."

"Good. Help me with my brother, and we'll leave."

"That'll be a problem. Before I ran out the building, I saw them coming up the street."

Zev's gut squeezed. "Who?"

From the northern end of the Square, three autocarts with mounted repeating rifles drove in followed by a sea of soldiers, Royal Guard on horseback, and more autocarts with weapons Zev had never seen before. More soldiers entered from the same street Zev and Marcel had approached earlier. The only open exit required Zev and Pilot to carry Marcel across the Square in front of all the army and the Emissary. Yet even as Zev contemplated how they could possibly engineer such a feat, that route filled with Vashon and Dacci.

Nobody waited. The mounted weapons on the autocarts blasted over the Square. Huge streams of smoke trailed behind projectiles that exploded when they hit the Emissary. The noise promised to deafen anybody that survived. Rifles cracked through the air and bullets drummed the walls, the ground, and many, many bodies. Soldiers dropped. Vashon dropped. Dacci dropped.

A javelin of green energy soared from the middle of the Vashon—they must have been protecting a witch while she cast her spell. The energy slammed into one of the autocarts, erupting in a blaze of emerald flames. As the soldiers shouted, the autocart blasted into a fiery ball. Pieces of metal burst out in all directions, taking down several more men.

Zev and Pilot bracketed Marcel, each taking turns to shoot. Zev aimed with care—he only had four shots left. Pilot shared a few rounds after that, but he had little to begin with.

Marcel swung his hands like an orchestra conductor. He sang, *"Here's our death, here's our death. You will die. And you."* He pointed at different parts of the battle as lives were lost.

Though the Emissary had shown little interest in Zev or Pilot's rifle shots, it took greater interest in an entire army blasting in and around it. Turning from the building, it roared with all of its mouths. The sound vibrated glass as it drowned out the cacophony of the war. The creature stormed across the Square, stomping soldier and Vashon—anyone in its way. The Vashon emerged from beneath its sludge steps as mutated creatures. The soldiers never moved again.

"We'll all die, and that's okay with me," Marcel sang on. *"I only hate to die while I still have to pee."* He barked laughter and continued conducting the battle.

"He's not wrong," Pilot said, his words barely audible.

Zev fired his last round at a bone-clad Dacci warrior. He missed.

Setting his rifle down, he watched two Royal Guard surrounded by mutated Vashon fall. The creatures tore into the men. Only one of the horses made it out. The Emissary whipped its spiked tail back and forth while its mouths opened to chomp on anything caught in its path. As the enemy lines thinned, Zev spotted several witches busily working at spells.

Pilot crawled over and put out his hand. "I've felt truly honored to have known you and fought by your side."

"We can't give up."

"Oh, I'll keep fighting. Maybe take a few more with me. But your crazy brother ain't so crazy. Even if we destroy the Vashon and the Dacci, there's no stopping the Emissary. Now, shake my hand and let's get back to our final battle."

Dazed by Pilot's words, Zev shook the man's hand. How could it simply be over? Even when they fought on? He wanted to cry. Not for his own life, though. That surprised him. He only thought of the world itself. For once the battle ended, the Emissary would destroy everyone else. King Robion, Lady Jos, Mosol and Mr. Thalmew, every citizen of Balica City, then the East. And as it ripped through the countryside, the Dacci would regroup. Nualla would order his followers to attack the Frontier from the West and the East. It would not take long. Not when the Royal Guard also fell this day. That was it. Zev gazed over the battle and saw the end of civilization, the rise of Nualla and the Dacci. And the Vashon? No. They were tools to the Dacci. Maybe they would become slaves, if they were lucky. If not, the Dacci would eradicate them, too.

Marcel's hoarse voice improvised another equally horrible tune. *"The smell of this war is as bad as the sound. Dacci and Vashon are all around. A spell and a shot and a big, noisy boom. Death comes for us all. As does our doom."*

"Hey," Pilot said. "We've had a great bunch of years. But you can't always win."

"If Bellemont were still alive, you'd feel different." Zev had not meant to sound so harsh.

Pilot winked. "Probably. But she's—"

A bullet put a hole in his leg. Zev caught him as he fell. Sitting Pilot behind the pile Marcel rested upon, Zev searched for medical help as three bursts of energy destroyed another autocart. In the smoking ruins of the army, he saw only death. And pain.

Zev pressed hard on the wound to stop the bleeding. He looked at Pilot's face to see if the man's dark skin paled or if death riddled his eyes. Instead, he saw a smile.

And he eased back. "Okay," Zev said. "You're right. Strange."

"Come on, I've been right before."

"Strange that it ends this way. I feel oddly calm."

"Yeah, I'm the same. Well, except for the pain in my leg."

Zev laughed. It boiled up from deep within. A rich, full-throated laugh. He dropped onto his back, held his belly, and laughed.

And as he wiped the tears away, as he gazed up through the smoke and dust and haze, he saw a huge, shimmering blue light floating in the air. A shimmering blue sword held by a giant woman with golden flames burning over every part of her. "Is that—"

"Axon?" Pilot said.

CHAPTER TWELVE

Axon

The world had become both infinite and minuscule. Each detail magnified while the vastness of time and space engulfed her. She heard the emotions of millions, felt their thoughts, tasted their heartbeats.

Clarity came slowly. She had to concentrate. Hard. With unending sensations rolling over her, she had to rely on her warrior instincts to focus her thoughts. It took time. More than she had. But eventually, she started to see again, to think, to learn control.

While part of her wanted to marvel at the idea of floating in the air, the rest of her sensed the deadly battle raging, the urgency to help those she loved. After several attempts, she gained control of her body's new ability—not too difficult, mostly balance and intention, like walking—and she rose higher.

And higher.

When she floated above the rooftops, when she saw the wide swaths of city leveled like a child's blocks strewn on the floor, her pulse quickened, her eyes narrowed, and she ground her teeth. Scanning the destruction, she spotted the Emissary as it tossed several soldiers through the air. At this distance, they looked no more than odd-shaped rocks, yet Axon also saw them with perfect lucidity as if she tumbled through the air with them, terrified, disoriented, and in one case, knowing that he would not survive the coming impact.

She headed toward them, the same direction as the Emissary. But she did not move fast. Though she crossed over buildings with the wind and smoke in her hair, she could only move at a walking pace. Her legs held still. Intuition suggested she should be able to move faster, though she had yet to understand how.

If only she were bigger. Like the Emissary itself. Then she could step over everything and reach her enemy before more buildings fell, before more lives were lost.

The tingling in her skin continued. It never stopped. In a snap, a wretched pain shot through her bones. They didn't fracture nor did they break, but each bone in her body sent shockwaves throughout her system.

As fast as it began, it ended. Gasping for breath, she hovered over the avenue where some brave individuals poked their heads out from hiding and gazed up at her. Their shocked eyes, their pointing fingers, reminded her of being at the center of several parades after saving the Frontier.

But these faces were different. Pulling her attention down to the street level, able to witness each person's expression to the elemental detail, she did not see the awe of hope, the release of salvation, the knowledge that rescue had arrived. Rather, she saw the thrall of fear. The twitches and tremors of people trying to process a catastrophe epic in scale and tragic in depth.

It made no sense to her. Until she saw her reflection in the glistening eyes of one lady. Bringing her view back to her hovering body, she saw that she had grown. Significantly. That burst of pain had launched her body in all directions, leaving her at least half the size of the Emissary. Maybe bigger than that.

Of course the public was afraid. That did not change the truth. She was not here to harm. Well, not harm the public. The Emissary was a different matter.

Turning towards that creature once again, her body shot off, leaping over buildings and city blocks with the greater strength her new body brought. The waterfire flowing through her blood shined on her skin. She pulled out the Water Blade—it, too, had grown—and she held it out, ready to fight.

At Genfort Square, she took in the scene with the ease of inhaling a breath. The dead littering the ground, the demolished buildings which the Emissary fed upon, the weaponry and spell work, the horses and autocarts, the soldiers and the Vashon and the witches—she could see how it all had arrived at this point.

Her focus locked on the Emissary. Destroy that abomination, and the enemy would fall.

Axon wanted to swing the Blade and let the waterfire shower the Emissary, but to do so meant that some drops would sprinkle down on the soldiers below. She could not use that method unless she managed to maneuver the Emissary into an empty block. But she could still use her Blade as a blade.

Stabbing forward and up, she sheared one of the Emissary's arms clean off. As the arm smashed to the ground, sluicing fetid scum in all directions, the Emissary howled. The sizzling of its body spread out, and Axon dared to marvel at how easy the fight went. But the wound closed over and a new arm started forming above. The dying skin flaked off, and new sludge grew in its place.

Watching in amazement, Axon never saw the counterattack. A column of the Emissary's fists clobbered into her side—striking from her head down her arms, her ribs, her hip, her thigh, and even one brutal punch to the knee. The blows drove her body through the remains of a brick wall.

Pain registered up and down her side, but so did the constant tingling of power that came with waterfire. Shaking off the bricks, she reset into a classic fighting stance—even though her sense of balance did not depend upon standing on the ground. Her muscle memory knew what it knew— she was a warrior, and this fight was something she understood.

Lunging forward, leading with the Water Blade, Axon skewered the Emissary through one of its mouths. As she sliced upward, cutting through the creature's filth and muck, she heard the gratifying burn of the waterfire destroying its insides. The beast made a sorrowful squeal.

But even as the Blade broke free through the top of the Emissary, Axon could peer into the details of its torn flesh and see the sewage of its innards pooling together, reforming, weaving tighter and stronger connections. The bottom arms of the Emissary jabbed forward while Axon's arms were raised with the Blade. She doubled over, giving it the opportunity to ram her head with three other fists. That sent her tumbling through one of the untouched buildings around the Square.

Soaring out of the rubble, she rose through the air, letting her distance from the Emissary provide a few moments to catch her breath and rethink her strategy. Part of her attention dropped down to the surface where she saw the Eastern army re-engaging with the Vashon. A small squad had broken away from the main army, and they took sporadic shots at a group of Dacci witches. Looking closer, Axon spotted Pilot and Marcel—both injured—and holding the squad together, she saw Zev.

The witches had created two balls of energy—one swirling red, the other a noxious green. The balls fluctuated in size as they grew stronger. While Zev managed to disrupt their concentration with the occasional rifle shot, Marcel had broken several bones and given up in his mind. Pilot tried to help but was losing blood fast. The Vashon kept coming at the army, pinning them down with unending fire power. And while the Easterners had most of their soldiers surrounding the Square, Axon could see high above the city as well—and the Vashon had more on the way. Far more than anybody had realized.

She needed to do something. She could feel the power within her, shaking her muscles and reverberating her chest. The waterfire. Its pressure growled and prodded. But she did not know how to utilize it. She did not want to be a toddler waving a dagger—liable to injure herself as much as those she cared about, doubtful to injure those she intended to harm.

But to do nothing, to only fight the Emissary, meant failure. The Emissary would continue to regrow any damage she inflicted, and eventually, the Eastern army would fall.

The next heartbeat, she saw only Zev's face. She saw the struggle as he aimed carefully with his final round. She saw the disappointment in his eyes, the knowledge that they had lost, they had failed, they would die. For half an instant, not even time enough for another pulse of blood through her veins, she watched as Zev gazed up at her. She saw his heart at that moment—the things he cared about, the people he cared for, the pain of knowing it all would cease—and it matched her own heart. Her own pain.

"No," she said. She thought she had spoken quietly to herself, but every warrior on the battlefield paused to gaze up at the thundering noise above them. Even the Emissary paused.

From the depths within her, the waterfire rushed forward. Her head snapped back, her mouth locked wide open, and the burning liquid gushed into the sky like lava from an erupting volcano. But instead of dropping back upon the soldiers in a rain of burning fire, the waterfire split apart and snaked off in different directions.

Each tendril twisted and curved as if alive. Axon could see through each one. The thickest tendril goose-necked over and blasted down into the Emissary. Seven smaller snakes of waterfire found their way into seven of the Emissary's mouths. More poured out of Axon. So many more.

Hundreds of slivers of waterfire tore out her mouth. They shot down upon the Vashon and the Dacci like liquid spikes from the sky. Each strike disintegrated the enemies in an instant.

The tendrils reached further out, blocks and blocks away, and Axon guided them as if she had eyes watching from each tendril's head. They ripped through the streets, seeking out targets, finding their enemies like a predator sensing its prey. Soon, Axon did not need to guide the water-fire at all. It saw the pattern of targets and it took over.

Axon turned all of her attention into the Emissary.

CHAPTER THIRTEEN

While the Vashon ran from the waterfire winding through the city streets, while the Dacci disintegrated one after the other, Axon closed her mouth, cutting off more waterfire from seeking out targets. She lowered her head and lunged for the Emissary. Years of training provided her with the edge. She locked onto two of its arms and yanked it in close.

The Emissary wriggled and jerked its body. Its eyes sought freedom in every direction. If it could break loose, Axon had no doubt that it would skitter away on all those hands like a thousand-legged insect.

But it could not break loose.

Ignoring the horrendous stench and the slimy skin, Axon wrapped one leg around its thick torso. This freed up one hand which she used to wrench open the nearest mouth of the Emissary. Its jagged teeth dug into her palm, but she refused to let go. And when she opened her mouth, when she leaned close like a lover ready for a deep kiss, she felt every muscle in the Emissary's body contract.

Waterfire flowed out of her mouth and into the Emissary's. It lasted seconds. With a final, desperate snap of its body the Emissary dislodged from Axon's grip. It jumped across the Square, landing near the central statue. Its feet cratered the ground, and it whirled back, uttering a loud, vibrant roar.

Only the sound trailed off at the end, turning into the creak of an old chair on an old porch. It stumbled. Three mouths vomited blood, and seven of its eyes melted away, oozing their gore down its side.

The Emissary flopped onto its back—or front, Axon could not tell one side from the other—and it cramped, released, and cramped again. Over and over as the smoke of its dissolving innards slipped out between its teeth.

Its body tried to repair itself. Axon could see individual fibers knitting together. But not fast enough. Pulling back her view, she watched as it suffered longer because it could not stop trying to heal.

But eventually, a soft hiss. A muted cry. And the Emissary's eyes all closed for good.

I t would take half a day for the waterfire to completely remove the Emissary from existence, but it would happen. Far sooner, Axon returned to normal size and the power surging through her vanished. She had used it—all of it—to destroy the enemies of the city. Now, she only wanted one thing—sleep.

PART V

CHAPTER ONE

Zev

After. After the raging violence. After the barked orders and the panicked screams. After the shivers and the sweats, the bloodied shirts and the pissed pants, the taste of death and the pain of living. After all of it drifted away like the smoke clearing the Square, Zev leaned back against the uneven bricks of a wall no bigger than a stump, and he closed his eyes.

The gentle sounds of people mulling about. Some trying to organize. Some starting the monumental task of cleaning up. Some offering medical aid.

To Zev's left, Marcel had passed out. To his right, Axon slept with her head against his shoulder. Pilot sat across, and Zev knew that if he opened his eyes, he would see an empty man in front of him. A man lost in his loss.

The smoke had cleared enough for dusk to be spotted. The moon still provided light enough to work by, and in those area where they needed more, some smart soul had erected flameless candles on tall poles.

At some point, several soldiers helped Zev and the others load into an autocart headed back to the Thalmew Building. They drove slowly—partially to avoid jostling Marcel and Axon, partially because the roads were covered with debris that had to be negotiated with care.

Zev watched the homes and stores pass his view. On each street, he found people crowding the sides, helping one another clear the damage, put things back right, start to heal. It would take a long time. Years. For some, even among those who did not suffer a scratch, there would be no healing ever.

But others did suffer. A man sat with his legs in a puddle of bloody water, his arms wrapped around a small child. Zev could not tell if the child lived. A woman with a gash in her cheek and a blood-soaked bandage around her head wandered along the sidewalk with a lost glaze in her eyes. Further up, several men placed corpses in neat rows while still more survivors stood by with rifles in hand, their eyes roving for the next attack. Zev wanted to tell them that Axon had destroyed the Vashon, the Dacci, and the Emissary, but part of him couldn't be entirely sure. There might be Vashon or Dacci that escaped her wrath.

"I'm going to be okay," Pilot said. His empty gaze ahead suggested otherwise.

"Then at least one of us will be."

"I know you're worried. I see you looking at me. But I'm telling you, I'll be fine. Not anytime soon, but when the mourning is over, when we've found her and buried her, I'll keep going. Might take a while. I'll have to ask King Robion to relieve me of my duties, but I'll get through this."

"Of course," Zev said, though he thought Pilot spoke more to himself than anybody else.

"We wasted too much time. I knew I had fallen for her long before I admitted it to myself and even longer before I dared to reach out to her. I was a fool. But don't worry about me. That's what I want you to understand. I'm sad, devastated, but I'll carry on."

He said nothing more, and Zev did not press further.

A few blocks before they reached the Thalmew Building, Axon roused and sat up. She smiled at Pilot and squeezed Zev's shoulder. She said nothing, and neither man pressed her.

The night crept along, promising Zev that the exhaustion he felt would only get worse before he could enjoy sleep. Thinking of Pilot's empty eyes, Zev wondered how well he would sleep even when the chance arrived. The way people stared at them as they rode the lifter to the eager faces in the Battle Room, Zev figured they all looked as dead-eyed.

The first few hours were a bizarre mixture of emotions. Eruptions of excitement and celebration rolled through as people realized that they had not only lived through the battle but had won, too. Zev and Axon accounted for what they knew while other soldiers—those with battle-field promotions that put them in charge—did their best to sound professional with their own reports. Thalmew's genuine relief relaxed the room. He wore an astonished grin as he heard each tale of the battle. Until Axon told of the death of Byn Forsean. Mosol broke into a wailing cry, and Mrs. Thalmew rushed to her daughter's side. They left the Battle Room, presumably to mourn upstairs in their home. Zev wondered where Pilot had gone off to, but he had no doubt that Pilot mourned as well.

Before the night had ended, King Robion and Hiko Thalmew breezed through negotiations and signed a peace treaty. A bigger ceremony would be planned and an enormous celebration would follow—the city deserved a party. This wasn't simply the end of the battle nor the end of hostilities between the East and the Frontier. With the peace treaty in place, with waterfire a threat to any creature conjured for Nualla, the Dacci would have no choice but to give up the fight.

The war was essentially over.

CHAPTER TWO

Axon

She felt good. Whether from her short rest or from some effect of the waterfire, she simply felt good. In fact, the satisfaction within her made it easy to ignore the offhand glances from people as she walked through the Battle Room. These were not the looks of people stunned at seeing the woman who saved their lives, who should be remembered for as long as the Frontier and the East existed. These were cautious, even frightened looks. They loved that she had saved their lives, but they feared the power she wielded.

Only she didn't have the power anymore. She didn't think so, at least.

When King Robion spotted her, he rushed across the room. She braced herself for any number of reactions but the one she received. The King bowed. "You have my sincerest and deepest apologies. I was wrong to have dismissed you. Clearly, you've proven that today. Your loyalty to the Frontier will never be questioned again. I hope that you can forgive me and know that should you ever wish to return to the Frontier and to my service, you will forever be welcome."

Mr. Thalmew shook her hand and promised a medal for her service. Others wanted to get some private time to discuss business opportunities. Axon tried to be polite, but she never had the skills of a politician.

"Please, everyone," Zev said, emerging from the crowd of onlookers.

"There will be plenty of time for you all to meet with Axon. For now, let her recover from this arduous day."

The words sounded pleasant enough, but an undertone flowed through which tasted like a threat. Yes. Axon thought that was the perfect way to think of Zev's words—that she could taste them. Perhaps she retained some of the waterfire after all.

As people cleared away from her and returned to their stations, Zev said, "Are you okay?"

"Fine."

"Want to get out of here? I know how to access the roof."

He moved closer as if he might take her by the hand. She stepped back. "I think I've had enough rooftop views for one day."

He chuckled. "Of course. But I would like to talk with you. We all went through a lot these last few days, and I've had a lot of thoughts that clued me into some important matters—matters about you. And me."

But Axon missed the last of what he said. Her mind hyper-focused on the word *clued*. Something about that word. The answer plowed into her. She headed for the lifter.

"Axon?"

"We can talk, but later. I—well, I have to be a master-solver right now. I'll be back."

When she arrived at Balison Temple, her heart sank. A massive hole had been punched through the front architecture. Chunks of marble and glass littered the steps leading into the once immaculate place of worship. If only that were the limit of the destruction. But Axon knew the truth now, and the Shul's damage far exceeded the Emissary's.

She walked through the halls and reached the main room where the stone slab of a blacksmith—the cause of the damage—had crashed into the ground. The head of Pralma, goddess of man, had been cracked in half, the remains of the fine artistry nothing but more rubble.

"Shul Ranon?" Axon called out.

No answer.

She climbed over the damage and found her way into the Shul's private residence. The kitchen table had been turned on its side and the windows shattered. No sign of the Shul or his helper.

Working her way back through the temple, she checked every room she could get access to—the Shul's office, the small library, a dressing room, a storage room. No Shul. At least, the further in the temple she went, the less damage she found.

When she reached the back, she discovered a door that led to an area that reminded her of the open-air temples she knew from the Frontier— from home. A single statue representing Qareck stood near the center, his arms outstretched in welcome. At his feet, a marble slab had been placed with a stone bowl in its center. A ring of stones encircled the area and several marble benches had been placed outside the circle.

Shul Ranon sat on one with his head bowed. When he gazed up, he smiled at her. Not with friendship or relief or satisfaction. Rather, it was the grim grin of inevitability. As she approached him, she thought that he must know she figured it all out.

"When this temple was constructed," he said as if they were in the middle of a long discussion, "the Shuls had to fight for this outdoor section to be included. They insisted that we not lose our connection to the past ways, the traditional ways we were taught to honor and pray to the Nine. Not just to have the circle and the statue, but even the *yewla* bowl which symbolized the life cycle. I doubt many of the Frontier temples include it anymore. They wanted a space that reflected the true essence of the Nine."

"Clearly, those Shuls won."

"They did. But in order to get the politicians to allow the construction, they had to make certain concessions. Deals were negotiated that were unsavory but necessary. If the public had ever found out what the Shuls agreed to do, their faith in the Nine would have vanished."

Axon sat on the edge of the bench. "What was the deal?"

"It doesn't matter now. That past is long dead. Even if it came to light, those involved were buried decades ago. Nobody would care."

"But that's not the same with you. You're still alive."

Shul Ranon crossed his arms over his belly and nodded. "That I am."

"You're not going to make this easy, are you?" She shook her head. "There's no point in holding back. I've had the clues in front of me. I was a bit busy, though, so I never put them together."

"But you have now?"

"You've been supporting both sides of this all along."

"I would never—"

"Don't. We've known each other for long enough now. Don't lie anymore."

She waited until he bowed his head again. "You knew where the Cistern was all along. I found a ripped piece of robe in the Cistern room, and I have no doubt that it will match the rips I've seen in your robes. The map I found on Byn was not the half-drawn, barely useable thing you gave me. His had all the details I needed. You gave him that map before his last journey underground —probably provided some story about finding it in a forgotten book."

"A scroll. Byn always believed the old scrolls held the answers we needed. He didn't question it at all."

"It wasn't the Nine guiding me to those sewers. It was you. You knew all along that only the unique properties of the Water Blade mixed with those of the Cistern could create waterfire. From the moment you learned that I had taken control of the Blade, you hoped for some way of contacting me. You must have been ecstatic when you heard that I was in Balica City."

The Shul wagged a finger but did not look up. "That was the Nine influencing the world, guiding you to me. I needed you, and you were provided."

"But you didn't wait for the Nine. Not with the Cistern. Not with Byn. You sent him on his search when you already knew where the Cistern was. That confused me. Until I realized that the Vashon have not been around nearly as long as you have. When they took ownership of the building you had been using to access the sewers, when they turned it into their newest komo, everything changed. Was that when you decided to deal with the Dacci?"

"The Dacci? No. They didn't come until later. I approached the Vashon but they refused to speak with me. They wanted nothing to do with anybody."

"That's why you got Byn involved."

"Not at first. At the time, you were still in the Frontier and I had no reason to think you would come here. I feared the Vashon would explore the sewers and find the Cistern."

Axon frowned. "You walled off the entrance?"

"I'm not that capable. No, the entrance had been there and open for decades. I closed it, let the locks engage. But then you appeared. I tried to find the Cistern myself, but I only knew my way from the Vashon komo. I attempted twice from two different access points, but each time I got lost. I think, perhaps, the Nine did not want me to return."

"I don't think the Nine had a hand in any of this. They certainly wouldn't want you setting a young Shul apprentice on a path that led to his death."

Shul Ranon covered his face. His wide back shuddered. "That poor boy."

"You sent him in hopes that he would find the Cistern room. He dug into the research better than you had prayed for. But then what? Why did you get involved with the Dacci?"

Clearing his throat, he said, "You arrived. That's what changed everything. Until you walked into this temple, I only wanted to find the Cistern again so that I would be ready, should the day ever come. But then suddenly the day was here. You stood in the temple—the one who wielded the Water Blade. I had to find the Cistern."

Axon gripped the edge of the bench. "Are you trying to blame me for all this?"

"No, but surely you can see that the Nine are involved. How else to explain events? Those three Dacci witches—they were the ones who approached me. Only a few days after I met you. It was as if they knew you and I were going to succeed, that you'd gain the power of waterfire, and that if they didn't stop you, they would lose the war."

"After all the battles I've been involved in the West, I doubt it has anything to do with the Nine. Those Dacci were sent by Nualla. They were watching my movements—they even hired the Vashon to keep an eye on me while in the city. They knew the day I stepped into the Temple, and they knew what that would mean. But I still don't see why you didn't tell me the truth. Why did you choose to deal with the Dacci and Vashon instead?"

He turned his tear-stained face toward her. "Please, believe me, I never wanted any of this to happen the way it did. When the Dacci told me that they planned to dig a hole in the sewers, I swear I thought it was the Nine offering more help to my cause. I saw the path so clearly."

"I think I do, too. In order to help the Dacci, you would tell them they had to deal with the Vashon, and that meant you suddenly had access to the sewers via the Vashon's komo once again."

"Exactly. What did I care if the Dacci wanted to dig holes in the ground? It seemed harmless to me. All those caskets of dirt that the Vashon removed only made them look crazier to the public."

"Which you wanted because should any of this become known, all the dirt, the Dacci, the sewer access was through the Vashon. Nobody would believe that you had any involvement. The Vashon were your cover."

"But then it all went awry. The constant digging led to cave-ins deeper in the ground. The paths to the Cistern, the ones I knew of, were lost. All except one."

"And you couldn't simply go there directly. That would betray the truth to Byn—that you knew all along."

Dabbing at his eyes, he said, "I couldn't show you the direct path on a map because of the same. I thought about sneaking down there with you, taking you myself, but if the Dacci found out what I wanted, they might have killed you or destroyed the Cistern."

"No, no. Stay honest."

"I feared they might kill me."

"You felt trapped. The Dacci's intentions and their growing ties with the Vashon probably scared you, too."

"Terrified me."

"You had a choice. Admit the truth to me and the public or ride it out. You prayed and bargained and pleaded with the Nine to save you. If Byn could find the Cistern or if I found it, you could suddenly discover how it all worked, we'd create the waterfire and end the war before anybody got hurt." Axon watched the weak man's head bobbing guilty acceptance and a darker thought struck her. "By helping the Dacci, you figured that should I fail, should the Dacci win the war and we all were to live under their rule, you would be spared."

"It was more than that. I admit I cared about my own survival, but the way I did things, regardless of the outcome, I would be there to help our people. Under the Dacci or under our government, the people would need—they *do* need—a guide back to the old and sacred ways. I will provide that guidance. Just like the old Shuls who knew that we needed to stay connected to the roots of the Nine and fought for those beliefs. They understood that moral compromises sometimes had to be made for the greater good."

With a bitter snicker, Axon said, "A master-solver once told me that the guilty could twist the truth to squirm through any hole that allowed them to live with themselves."

After a cold silence, Shul Ranon said, "I suppose so. Your master-solver should be proud. Solved this one yourself. He'll be out of a job soon."

"Not really a job for him. And even if it was, I would never take it. A master-solver only finds the guilty. He lets the authorities take it from there." Axon shoved down her disgust with all her anger. "Not me. Not this time."

She walked into the ring of stones and approached the marble slab. A swift maneuver and she pulled out the Water Blade. Holding it over the stone *yewla* bowl, she waited as four drops of waterfire fell.

"Out of respect for our faith," she said, "I leave you the choice."

Shul Ranon stared at the bowl. "You can't mean this."

"What you've done must be answered for. One way is for the truth to be revealed publicly."

"But that would undo all of it. People would lose faith in the Shuls and eventually the Nine. Surely, you wouldn't punish our entire religion over my poor decisions."

"I'm not doing that at all. The choice is yours entirely."

She watched him staring at the bowl, paralyzed by the decision, and she turned away. The answer would be obvious soon enough. No need to make it worse by glaring at him the whole time.

She walked to the door into the Temple. Tomorrow—she would return tomorrow and the evidence of his decision would be clear. Part of her thought it possible that he would still be sitting on that bench, unable to choose. But when she reached for the door, she heard the rustle of his robes, a stark cry as he jabbed his hand in the bowl, and a familiar sizzle as the waterfire ended the entire matter.

Glancing back, she saw ash floating in the air.

CHAPTER THREE

Zev

The next several weeks whisked by in a barrage of interviews, meetings, parades, and parties. Everybody wanted a piece of those responsible for saving the Leader's daughter—which they determined to be Zev and Pilot—and more than a piece of the woman responsible for ending the war—namely, Axon. Thalmew made a point of offering Zev a political post at least twice a day, and each time Zev politely declined. He caught Thalmew doing the same to Pilot, but that ended with a terse word about the glory of the Frontier.

Zev worried about Pilot. The man knew how to put on a smile during the parades, how to let the public get what they needed from him, but the moment people turned away, Zev would see the pain in Pilot's heart. The man needed time to mourn. Thankfully, that would be happening soon enough.

Word from Ridnight suggested that while the Dacci had backed off the borders in the west, and as far as Frontier scouts could tell, they seemed to recognize they had lost the war, small flareups of fighting still occurred. King Robion, perhaps recognizing the distress of his Captain, assigned Pilot to take a few squads comprised of Royal Guards and godwalkers and patrol the western border. Now that the East and the Frontier had a signed peace treaty, they simply had to make their power officially known to the Dacci. Unofficially, of course, they already knew. Nualla would have seen to that.

Before Pilot rode out of the city, Zev made sure to visit one last time. Though Pilot smiled and winked, his deep sadness read clearly through the lines on his face. Still, he gave Zev a strong smack on the back and said, "I don't care where your life takes you, no matter what happens, you promise to come back to Ridnight and visit me."

"I promise," Zev said with a somber grin.

"I mean it. We have to cherish the short time we have. Friends like you are a rarity. Besides, I'm sure Axon would want to see you, too. Maybe even the King." Pilot laughed, mounted his horse, and trotted away.

As busy as things had become, Zev looked forward to the final party that night. Afterwards, the world had to continue on. There would be an annual celebration, and for the next several years, he would be expected to make an appearance, but for now, after this last gala event, he could rest.

The music had already started and plenty of revelers filled Tannlier Hall, one of the few enormous ballrooms not destroyed by the Emissary. Wonderful aromas of food and drink slipped through the air. Zev had started to feel sluggish with all the food he had eaten lately, but one more night wouldn't hurt. Before he could get to work crunching into a fried furtail wing, however, he had one last duty to perform.

One of the private offices in Tannlier Hall had been kindly set aside for his use, and when Zev entered, he found Marcel already waiting. Alone. No sign of Mercy. Good. Without her around, this meeting had a chance to go much easier.

The moment Zev had closed the office door, Marcel said, "I want to say that I appreciate your discretion regarding my behavior during the battle. I would have thanked you sooner, but it's been rather busy rebuilding the city, and you've had your schedule full of praise."

Since his brother dispensed with any formality, Zev figured he'd launch straight to the point, as well. "I'm leaving after tonight."

"Oh?"

"For good. I won't be coming back."

"I believe we've heard this before."

"Those were the words of a naïve and rebellious young man. This time, I'm not running away from you or Father. This time I'm choosing to go because I know I have a better life waiting elsewhere."

"What about your duty to this city? To our family?"

"That's for you to do. You're the Asterling family. You're the one that carries our name forward the way Father intends it to be."

"True. But I'm not the one being offered all the prime positions."

"You will. I've recently spoken with Leader Thalmew and explained how integral you were to our success. The public knows you were in the battle, and now they'll know of your heroic efforts that helped to save my life and Pilot's."

Marcel puffed a little, even as he had the decency to redden. "I'm only going to offer thanks so much. We both know that if the truth of my—failings—on the battlefield were to become public, support for the Asterling name would decrease. Especially once they see that you've left the city."

"Which is why Thalmew will offer you a top role in the new government."

"How has Father taken this news?"

"Don't know. I haven't told him."

"I see. In that case, I wish you safe travels wherever you plan to go. I will stay and pick up the pieces that you've left scattered behind."

Biting back the urge to snap, Zev said, "Father doesn't need to hear from me. You're the one he trusts, the one he wants to lead the family. I'm an embarrassment to him."

"Not after all your success. Besides, the man won't last much longer."

"I've found peace with our lack of a relationship. He's had ample time to make it better between us, and I've reached towards him more often than I can remember. I wish you could find that peace, too. If he can't figure out how to love his sons, that's his problem. Not ours."

Scratching his arm and sighing, Marcel said, "You said you wouldn't be coming back. Ever?"

"I'll return for a visit. But never again to live here."

"And what are you going to attempt this time? Start a fishery? Perhaps you'll buy a rifle factory?"

"Nothing."

"Excuse me?"

Zev grinned. "I'm not going off to start another business, not going to seek some success that will earn Father's approval, none of that. I'm simply going to travel the world and be content with what it brings me. After all, I've learned one thing for sure—there's always a need for a master-solver somewhere."

Marcel thought it over and extended his hand. "I wish you the best.

May the Nine watch over you. I think that's how it's said, I've never been much for religion."

————◦◦◦————

By the time Zev returned to the gala, crowds packed the main hall. He smiled and nodded while standing at the side nursing a drink. His meeting with Marcel replayed in his head several times over. In particular, he thought about his future plans. After laying it all out to Marcel, Zev realized he had made it all up on the spot. Yet he felt he had been honest.

Except for one omission—he did not want to go alone.

Scanning the crowd, he searched for her. Surely, she would be at this party. The last big event.

Lady Jos emerged from the mass of people and sauntered towards him. Her lips curved into her unique smile—the one he found both pleasing and seductive.

"You are a difficult man to get time with," she said.

"I've been busy lately."

"I suppose being a hero is a bit consuming."

"For a while. This will all die down soon. People get back to their lives —work, family, meals, sleep."

"And making more family. My favorite part."

Zev laughed, listening to the slow music and keeping his eyes on the crowd. "I'm surprised you wanted to see me at all."

"Because of our last talk?"

"I don't recall things ending well."

Shaking her head like an exasperated parent, she said, "You still haven't learned. A woman like me doesn't always mean what she says— except when it comes to love. I always mean what I say then."

"Love, is it?"

"Don't tease me. We've been through a lot together. In such a short time, our future has fallen and risen again with such speed, it makes a lady have to catch her breath. Yet, if you paid attention, you'd see that whether you are sitting in the back, using your brain to solve matters, or if you're boldly running down the street with rifle in hand, in the end, I'm always standing here, ready to be by your side. Oh, I admit that it's taken me time to figure out how to handle you, but I'm getting there. I know what you need in a wife, and I'm prepared to be those things for you."

"I don't think the gala is best for this conversation." Zev glanced at those nearby. Thankfully, nobody appeared to hear her.

"I know, dear, but this is the only time I've been able to see you, and you know me well enough now to know that I won't be deterred when it's important." She pressed in closer. "What could be more important than the love growing between us?"

Then Zev saw her. Really saw her. She hadn't simply come to the gala. She had come for him. As she entered the party, all eyes seemed to gravitate toward her, but he caught a glance his way. Her stunning beauty warmed him as much as the glint in her eye.

Looking down at Lady Jos as if only now noticing her, he clasped her hand between his. "Thank you. But I'm sorry." He slipped her family pin back into her hand and walked away.

The crowd parted for him as he approached Axon. She stood near the dancing area where couples moved to the slow rhythms, and he marveled at her beauty once more. Whatever bruising she had suffered, now healed. Her dark skin looked flawless, and her silken, yellow gown brightened her eyes. She always made him forget that she was a woman with a wealthy upbringing, made him see her as a warrior battling through the mud and blood, but then she would appear like this and stop his heart.

He put out his hand, and when she slipped her fingers between his, his skin prickled. It was everything.

"So," she said.

"So." He looked around at all the expectant eyes following them. He paused, wondering what would happen should they walk right out and start exploring the world. But there would be years ahead for that. Giving her hand a gentle squeeze, he said, "Would you like to dance?"

She smiled, and it blasted right through him. "I'd love to."

THE END

ACKNOWLEDGEMENTS

And here we are at the end of this long road. A few years ago, when I sat down with John Hartness to discuss writing a trilogy for Falstaff Books, I had no idea it would be this. I mean, who in their right mind would allow me to create a magic system based on feces and other bodily waste? Who would let my story shape into a strange mixture of classic fantasy and classic mystery while also being a bit pulpy and modern all at the same time? If you've ever met John, you might say that he was the only choice. And I think that's one reason why Falstaff Books is such a great publisher. They allow writers to do what we do best. So, while there are many people at Falstaff to thank, none deserves more credit than John. Thanks, man.

I also want to give special thanks to Darin Kennedy. If you've read any of my other work, especially the Nathan K series, you've seen Darin's name mentioned before. Besides being a wonderful writer and friend, Darin is a doctor. He has always been generous with his time in answering my seemingly ceaseless questions about how the human body reacts to various trauma, what's the best way to kill a person under certain circumstances, and the like. My books would be far less interesting without him. And should I ever disappear under mysterious circumstances, he's the one with all the knowledge. Just sayin'.

I also want to thank my wife and son. More than other books of mine, this trilogy owes a lot to their input. And finally, I want to thank you, my reader. All of the fine folks who helped make these books a reality, all the work we put into this, means nothing if there is nobody on the other end to read it all. Without you, I'm just a lone tuna wondering where the school went. And nobody wants to be a lone tuna. So, thank you.

ABOUT THE AUTHOR

Stuart Jaffe is the madman behind *The Max Porter Paranormal Mysteries*, *The Malja Chronicles*, *The Bluesman*, *Founders*, *Real Magic*, and much more. He trained in martial arts for over a decade until a knee injury ended that practice. Now, he plays lead guitar in a local blues band, *The Bootleggers*, and enjoys life on a small farm in rural North Carolina. For those who continue to keep count, the animal list is as follows: one dog, two cats, three aquatic turtles, and a bunch of chickens. As best as he's been able to manage, Stuart sees that the chickens do not live in the house.

ALSO BY STUART JAFFE

The Ridnight Mysteries
The Water Blade

The Waters of Taladora

Waterfire

Max Porter Paranormal Mysteries
Southern Bound

Southern Charm

Southern Belle

Southern Gothic

Southern Haunts

Southern Curses

Southern Rites

Southern Craft

Southern Spirit

Southern Flames

Southern Fury

Southern Souls

Southern Blood

Southern Graves

The Malja Chronicles
The Way of the Black Beast

The Way of the Sword and Gun

The Way of the Brother Gods

The Way of the Blade

The Way of the Power

The Way of the Soul

Nathan K Thrillers

Immortal Killers

Killing Machine

The Cardinal

Yukon Massacre

The First Battle

Immortal Darkness

A Spy for Eternity

Prisoner

Desert Takedown

Lone Star Standoff

The Parallel Society

The Infinity Caverns

Book on the Isle

Rift Angel

Lost Time

Short Story Collections

The Marshall Drummond Case Files: Cabinet 1

The Marshall Drummond Case Files: Cabinet 2

For more from Stuart Jaffe, visit him
on his website — www.stuartjaffe.com

FRIENDS OF FALSTAFF

Thank You to All our Falstaff Books Patrons, who get extra digital content each month! To be featured here and see what other great rewards we offer, go to www.patreon.com/falstaffbooks.

PATRONS

Dino Hicks
John Hooks
John Kilgallon
Larissa Lichty
Travis & Casey Schilling
Staci-Leigh Santore
Sheryl R. Hayes
Scott Norris
Samuel Montgomery-Blinn
Junkle

Made in the USA
Columbia, SC
25 August 2021